THE
CASE
OF THE
MURDERED
MUCKRAKER

Books by Rob Osler

THE CASE OF THE MISSING MAID

THE CASE OF THE MURDERED MUCKRAKER

Published by Kensington Publishing Corp.

THE
CASE
OF THE
MURDERED
MUCKRAKER

ROB OSLER

KENSINGTON
PUBLISHING CORP.

kensingtonbooks.com

KENSINGTON BOOKS are published by

Kensington Publishing Corp.
900 Third Avenue
New York, NY 10022

All Kensington titles, imprints, and distributed lines are available at special quantity discounts for bulk purchases for sales promotion, premiums, fund-raising, educational, or institutional use. Special book excerpts or customized printings can also be created to fit specific needs. For details, write or phone the office of the Kensington Special Sales Manager: Attn. Special Sales Department, Kensington Publishing Corp., 900 Third Avenue, New York, NY 10022. Phone: 1-800-221-2647.

Library of Congress Control Number: 2025945762

KENSINGTON and the K with book logo Reg. US Pat. & TM. Off.

ISBN: 978-1-4967-4951-2

First Kensington Hardcover Edition: February 2026

ISBN: 978-1-4967-4953-6 (ebook)

10 9 8 7 6 5 4 3 2 1

Printed in the United States of America

The authorized representative in the EU for product safety and compliance is eucomply OU, Parnu mnt 139b-14, Apt 123
Tallinn, Berlin 11317, hello@eucompliancepartner.com

"Chicago ain't no sissy town!"
—Michael "Hinky Dink" Kenna, Chicago First Ward
Alderman, 1897 to 1923 and 1939 to 1943

"Workingmen of America, learn the manufacture and use of dynamite. It will be your most powerful weapon; a weapon of the weak against the strong. . . . Then use it unstintingly, unsparingly."
—The *Alarm*, Chicago-based newspaper at the turn of the nineteenth century, affiliated with the anarchist International Working People's Association

THE
CASE
OF THE
MURDERED
MUCKRAKER

Chapter 1

Harriet Morrow's morning bicycle ride to the Prescott Agency had left her overheated and agitated—and she ran hot as it was. Shedding her black suit jacket and bowler hat, she dabbed her nape with a handkerchief, wishing she could loosen her bow tie and unbutton the collar of her men's dress shirt. Feeling the damp fabric clinging to her back, she wondered if ironing her wardrobe before each workday would be time wasted now that Chicago had finally emerged from another frigid winter—her twenty-first, and by recollection, the most severe. As for her undercarriage, she was grateful that her trousers, also men's, were no warmer than conventional attire, although she'd be first to admit a petticoat and long skirt provided superior air circulation, especially when pedaling her Victoria bicycle at high speed. Desperate for a cooling breeze, Harriet plucked a letter opener from her desk drawer and stabbed at the dried paint holding the window sash firmly in place. Apparently, the office's previous occupant, another junior field operative, had never desired the relief of outdoor air.

"I say, Miss Morrow, Lizzie Borden might admire your approach to subduing that window."

Recognizing the voice, Harriet spun around, wearing a

wry smile. "I'll have you know, the case against Miss Borden lacked sufficient evidence, whereas I've been caught red-handed and readily admit my murderous intention." She waggled the letter opener before her colleague. "I might as well be trying to carve a Christmas ham with a spoon. You don't happen to keep a crowbar in your office by chance?"

Matthew returned a grin. "As would any reputable operative, I keep mine in a locked cabinet nestled between a blowtorch and sticks of dynamite."

"Jest, if you like, but I'll be looking no better than those"—she nodded toward a vase of wilted roses on the edge of her desk—"if I don't get this window open right quick." Grimacing at his long wool coat, she added, "You must be half reptile to withstand wearing that heavy thing indoors."

"My office may be next door, but it's freezing." He pointed to a vent high in the wall. "The heat from the boiler blows directly into your office, bypassing mine altogether. It's like that throughout the agency. Half the staff are threatened by heat stroke and the others hypothermia."

"Before it comes to that, perhaps I could have your assistance in prying open this dadgum window."

"We both know I'm no stronger than you are," he said matter-of-factly. "Perhaps if we both put our muscle to it . . ." After much tugging and whispered curses, he snapped his fingers. "There might be a useful tool in the janitor's closet. I'll be right back."

Harriet watched Matthew depart, knowing the swoony effect his lean physique and meticulously oiled red hair, with a touch of curl, had on the other women in the office. That he did nothing to stir her desire simplified their friendship. Moreover, the feeling was mutual. As decisively as Harriet Morrow was attracted only to women, Matthew McCabe would forever disappoint any woman who lingered in his office doorway hoping for a luncheon invitation. Although they were both junior field operatives,

Matthew had worked at the Prescott Agency for two years, whereas Theodore Prescott had hired Harriet only three weeks earlier as his agency's first-ever female detective. Matthew had not only helped her solve her first case, involving a missing maid, but he'd also become her trusted—and only—true friend at the agency.

Harriet swept the dried rose petals from her desk and into the rubbish bin. Although the flowers were a week past their prime, she hadn't been able to bring herself to discard them. Even in their lifeless condition, they reminded her of their sender, Barbara Wozniak. Thoughts of the woman reliably added a tinge of pink to her apple cheeks.

Sensing someone's presence, Harriet turned to see Madelaine, Mr. Prescott's private secretary, standing in the doorway. "He wants a word," she announced, radiating the charm of a prison matron.

Before Harriet could respond, Madelaine added a curt "Now" and marched off, her heavy footfalls rattling the frosted panes of the office doors lining the corridor. Knowing her boss was not to be kept waiting, Harriet snatched her suit jacket from the stand and pulled it on as she hurried after the secretary. She caught up to Madelaine at her desk, where she sat like a sentry before the double doors leading to the principal's inner sanctum.

"He's expecting you. No need to knock." Madelaine's words, although perfunctory, marked a change. Most of the women in the office had yet to warm to the notion of a female detective and remained standoffish. That Madelaine offered any remark at all was a sign, however modest, of progress. Standing at the threshold of Prescott's office, Harriet took a deep breath and set her shoulders. In three short weeks of employment, she'd learned her boss valued confidence as much as brevity in conversation—unless he was doing the talking, which was usually the case.

She opened the door.

Theodore Prescott sat behind an enormous desk befitting a man of his position but nearly eclipsing a man of his diminutive stature. Always nattily attired, the agency principal wore an immaculately tailored charcoal suit and white shirt, no doubt made in Paris or New York and purchased from Mandel Brothers at State and Madison. Although they were hidden from view, she also knew his silk-stockinged feet would be perfectly fitted into a pair of finely made shoes, not even the laces of which she could afford. Prescott's plush surroundings always struck Harriet as more suitable for someone of the aristocracy than a detective, even considering this particular detective's chief rivals were Robert and William Pinkerton, sons of founder Allan, who jointly ruled an agency tenfold the size of Prescott's just a few blocks away.

"You wanted to see me, sir?" Harriet stepped farther into the room, squinting against the sunlight pouring in through the tall windows behind Prescott's desk.

"This is Miss Morrow," Prescott said, looking past her. "The operative I was telling you about."

"So it would appear." The voice, pinched and affected, came from behind her.

She turned as a man emerged from the back of the office. Wearing a pince-nez, he struck her as the type of man to make grand gestures, ensuring his diamond cufflinks never went unnoticed. He exuded an air of importance or wealth—which was more or less the same thing. She wouldn't be surprised to find him among the dozens of well-dressed, bearded men gripping golf clubs or tumblers of brandy captured in photographs on Prescott's office wall.

"I need not inspect her, Theodore," he declared. "If this girl is your choice, you have my agreement." The man stepped closer still, appraising Harriet from head to toe; his gaze lingered on her trousers before settling on her men's shoes. "Provided she makes the appropriate modifications, of course."

Prescott introduced the man as Gerald Cole, a leader of

the Municipal Voters' League, an organization in the long tradition of the Citizens' Association. Harriet was familiar with the latter, having heard of it from her late father, a lawyer who had fought on the side of labor. Founded by George Pullman and Marshall Field, the Citizens' Association sought a more businesslike administration of municipal affairs and wished to protect citizens against the evils of bad government. Cole explained that he had formed the like-minded Municipal Voters' League with the express purpose of ridding Chicago of corrupt politicians by working to elect candidates who were vetted as honest.

Cole went on to say that earlier that morning, he was sent a substantial amount of money along with a letter from an anonymous supporter regarding the recent murder of a muckraker found stabbed to death in the hallway of a tenement building south of downtown. The letter's author claimed the victim, one Eugene Eldridge, had confided to him that he had obtained incontrovertible proof of a powerful local politician's corruption. That evidence should have been in Eldridge's possession when his body was found, but it wasn't. Furthermore, the letter instructed Cole to use the money to hire a professional detective agency to find the missing proof of corruption and see that justice was done.

While Cole spoke, Harriet occasionally glanced at Prescott, curious that he refrained from interrupting with questions, as was his habit. It then occurred to her that he had already heard Cole's story.

"Given the information's profound sensitivity," Cole continued, "and that one man has already been killed because of it, once recovered, this proof, whatever it may be, must be handled with extreme care."

The comment drew Prescott's remark. "Naturally, Gerald, we would handle it no other way, but precisely what *would* you have me do with it?"

"That, Theodore, is not as simple an answer as you might think, considering the corruption that pervades every pocket of government. But the letter instructs that the re-covered material be turned over to John Scanlon in the prosecutor's office."

"Scanlon?" Prescott repeated. "I know the men in the prosecutor's office but not him."

"I believe he is new. Which I take as a good sign. Over time, those holding the position lessen their resistance to corruption and its financial rewards. When so pervasive, a person looks around them and thinks, 'Why should I be the only honest person? Why should I be the only one not benefitting from the system as it's set up? I can't win, so why continue trying?' "

Cole held the letter out to Harriet, then hesitated, ap-pearing to have a second thought. Receiving Prescott's ap-proving nod, he handed it over. Harriet fought the urge to scrutinize every sentence, unusual word choice, or distinc-tive lettering for hidden clues about the sender, knowing it would test Prescott's patience. As her eyes fell upon the final line, "*With appreciation and humble respect, a most enthusiastic supporter of your work*," Cole reached out, asking for the letter's return.

"I don't understand," Harriet said. "Why the subter-fuge? Why didn't the letter's author simply hire an agency directly?"

Cole was quick to reply, apparently familiar with the question. "Some wealthy citizens who support our organi-zation's progressive reforms prefer discretion. If their ef-forts appear too forceful, they might be misconstrued as reflecting radical beliefs and alienating those in one's so-cial and business circles."

Prescott summarized. "When you've got yourself a golden goose, you're reluctant to ruffle feathers."

Harriet shook her head, uncertain of her boss's meaning.

He explained, "Being rich and championing social jus-tice risks undermining your own standing."

Harriet scoffed at such equivocating, as would her parents were they alive, but she knew better than to argue with her boss in front of his important new client.

Cole further explained that given the victim's occupation, unpopular among many government officials and persons of power, not to mention the place of the crime, the police had been eager to solve the murder with minimal effort. They simply arrested the woman who found the body, a Mrs. Lucy Fara, mother of four young children. Cole asserted—and Prescott's silence suggested he agreed—that the police had concocted a story of convenience: Mrs. Fara, nearly destitute from her husband's abandonment, had taken up with Eldridge. When Eldridge threatened to leave her, she stabbed him in a fit of madness. The crime and arrest would have usually received little attention were it not for the letter sent—*and money.*

The discussion continued with Cole's description of the living conditions common to tenement buildings, such as the one near the Union Stock Yards where Eldridge was killed, five miles southwest of downtown. On each floor, four to six families—some as large as a dozen—lived crammed in a few dim, poorly ventilated rooms. Household members as young as ten worked as many hours as possible at nearby factories, leaving a woman, usually the mother of each house, to do the backbreaking chores of raising the younger children, shopping, cooking, cleaning, and hauling water from a backyard spigot and coal from the basement up flights of narrow stairs in the dark. Eugene Eldridge was killed in one of those hallways in the middle of the day. The adults in the building at the time were likely to have all been women.

"If anyone can shed light on the crime or what might have happened to the evidence," Cole asserted, "it is one of them. However, immigrants tend to fear talking to the police or anyone else outside their small, tight-knit communities."

Seemingly satisfied that Cole had said his piece, Prescott

fastened his gaze on Harriet. At long last, she sensed the conversation was getting around to why she had been summoned.

"You do recall why I hired you, Miss Morrow?"

Harriet's mind raced. Prescott's intonation made clear there was an obvious answer, but she was unsure. Although reticent, she said the only thing that came to mind. "You mentioned something about my stout ankles, sir."

Cole's brows jumped at hearing the scandalous remark.

Prescott frowned. Glancing at Cole, he explained, "That was an observation, hardly my reason."

Thankfully, she recalled something else. "I said that because I am a woman others won't suspect me of being a detective. And because of that, I will be more successful in gaining people's confidence."

Prescott offered as much praise as he ever did by nodding abruptly. "Quite right. And now you shall have the opportunity to prove yourself correct. As this agency's lone female operative, you *will* get the women at the tenement to tell you what they saw and if anyone knows anything about this supposed evidence that should have been in the possession of the muckraker, Eldridge."

Cole stepped forward. "Presuming the claims in the letter are true, and there's no reason yet to doubt them, whomever the evidence incriminates will be desperate to recover it."

Prescott lifted himself from his high-back leather chair. "This Eldridge fellow was murdered in a tenement building. We must ask ourselves, why?"

Harriet didn't know Theodore Prescott well but had observed on several occasions that he could not stay seated when particularly captivated by a topic. "Was the muckraker on the job or the make? Had he been pursuing a story or a strumpet? Or had he been drawn there for some other reason? What was the man after? It could be connected to the evidence. Or it might not. Still, it's a place to start."

The scheme Prescott described was simple. Harriet would pose as a settlement house representative and infiltrate the tenement's immigrant community. "We must consider the possibility that the place of the crime is connected to the missing evidence. That being the case, the guilty party could well be a resident or keeping watch of the tenement. A woman doing the work of a nearby settlement house should draw little interest."

Harriet admired Prescott's clever thinking. Settlement houses provided local immigrant communities with essential services including English language instruction and job training. Associating herself with one would provide an ideal cover for her investigation.

Cole returned the letter to his case. "So then, I take it we're agreed, Theodore? You'll take the case? For the fee provided by the letter's sender?"

"The terms are agreed. I'll find your missing evidence," Prescott replied confidently. "And I suspect the murderer along with it."

The men shook hands. Cole tipped his hat, acknowledged Harriet with a sharp nod, and left.

The moment the door closed, Prescott sat back and grumbled, "Politics, Miss Morrow. The only thing that drives men to take up arms against one another more than religion is politics. Unlike Pinkerton, which grew by leaps and bounds by providing muscle to industry and beating the daylights out of labor, I have tried very hard to steer this agency clear of such thuggery. We are gentlemen detectives, not an army of roustabouts masquerading as honorable law enforcement. Pinkerton's involvement in the strikes at McCormick Harvester and Homestead are just two examples of why I've turned down many a good-paying case that takes a side between business and labor. That includes many opportunities brought to my attention by the *Progressive Age* and *Chicago Tribune*, as well as that mouthpiece of big business and nationalism, the *Inter Ocean*. But Gerald Cole is an old friend, an honorable gentleman, and well-connected. I can't turn him down. Nor do I want to. And so it happens that the reputation of this agency, *my agency*, depends on you successfully retrieving the evidence in question—with dispatch."

Harriet's stomach twisted. When she'd been assigned the case of the missing maid, Prescott had considered it nothing more than a favor to his neighbor and was at first unconvinced the woman was really missing. Although the search for the maid had become perilous, a murder investigation was something altogether different. What's more, the victim claimed to have had evidence of a powerful politician's corruption. She liked to believe she had what it took to be a good detective but also acknowledged her inexperience. Did Prescott actually think she was prepared to solve such a case on her own? Or, with no other woman operative to assign, was she his choice by default?

"Are you familiar with the University of Chicago Settlement near the stockyards?"

Stuck in worry, she heard only the tail end of his question. "A settlement? I've only a general knowledge of them. I do recall reading about the Hull House, however."

"Precisely. Hull House has its Jane Addams and Ellen Gates Starr. My wife is a booster of Mary McDowell, head resident of the university's settlement. As it happens, it's not far from the tenement where the muckraker was murdered. I'll arrange for your visit to the settlement as soon as this afternoon. We won't reveal your true purpose. That will be kept strictly between you and me. The less anyone knows about an investigation, the better. I shall say you are my visiting niece who is interested in learning about Chicago's settlement houses. Advocacy is as much Mary McDowell's work as is providing services. The woman can talk the stockings off an auctioneer. Speaking with as many people as possible about her mission is to her benefit. You're to listen and learn as quickly as you can. Don't dillydally. We're already playing catch-up. Every hour that passes after the moment of a crime is an opportunity lost. Evidence disappears. Memories fade. Alliances are formed. Lies constructed. You need only learn enough to speak convincingly about the settlement's offerings to the women living in the tenement. That's how you will disarm their distrust of outsiders. Get them to talk, Miss Morrow. And while their chins are wagging and their guard down, slip in a few questions about the recent murder. It's a delicate balance. Be measured. Be deft. You can't waltz into a home—even the most squalid imaginable—and start interviewing its residents. When you feel the time is right, don't ask straightaway about the murder. Instead, inquire whether the woman feels safe in the neighborhood. Don't ask if anyone in the building is known to consort with corrupt ward bosses or is involved in politics, but do raise the issue of tenement conditions and whether the household believes their local representative is advocating for their best interests. You get my point, Miss Morrow? Sleuth. Don't interrogate. Your task is straightforward: discover whether Eugene Eldridge did, in fact, possess incriminating evidence on someone of importance and, if so, retrieve it. It's more likely than not that your success in either endeavor will first require that you discover the muckraker's true killer."

Harriet listened intently for another thirty minutes as her boss relayed additional instructions and advice, concluding with, "Any questions?"

"Just one, sir. What did Mr. Cole mean by his remark about me making 'appropriate modifications.' "

"Ah, *that*." Prescott's expression softened. "While office whispers of your men's clothing interest me no more than what flavor jam you spread on your morning's toast, the investigation requires that you present yourself as an *unremarkable* young lady representing a reputable local settlement house. There is also a legal matter. Am I correct that you are unfamiliar with Chicago Ordinance 1297, pertaining to indecent exposure?" With Harriet's blank expression providing her answer, Prescott continued. "Let me illuminate you. No person shall appear in a public place in a state of dress not belonging to his or her sex. The fine shall be no less than twenty dollars, not to exceed one hundred dollars."

He paused a moment to allow his remark to sink in. "Your dollar trousers could cost you twentyfold—or more. Do I make myself clear?"

Harriet nodded, hiding her dismay at hearing about the preposterous law. Worse was her disappointment about returning to skirts and shirtwaists only a week after making the bold move to start wearing a full suit of men's clothing. Surely, a city as large as Chicago had more pressing problems than criminalizing a woman for preferring trousers. And the fine! One hundred dollars was the equivalent of three months' salary.

"Never forget, Miss Morrow, a man was savagely murdered in that tenement hallway. While there's no reason for you to be suspected of being anyone other than who you claim to be, you must tread carefully and never presume safety—not for one second. I trust you carry your pistol at all times?"

Harriet nodded. "I keep it in my handbag, sir."

"Loaded?"

"Not always, no."

Prescott held her gaze for a long moment. "From this moment forward, I insist that you do."

Chapter 2

Returning to her office, Harriet found Matthew McCabe with a hammer and screwdriver, chiseling free the stuck window. She explained her absence by recounting her meeting with Mr. Prescott, the agency's new client, and the particulars of what was to be her second case at the Prescott Detective Agency. Matthew appeared undecided whether to be impressed or concerned that she'd been assigned a murder investigation so soon.

Sensing his mixed emotions, she added, "As it happens, I stand alone among Mr. Prescott's operatives in possessing the one essential qualification for the job."

"Hmm." Matthew tapped his chin. "Let me guess. Courage? Resilience? No?" He slapped his forehead. "Of course! It's your sharpshooting!"

"Ha! As my tutor on the gun range, whatever skill I do or don't possess is as much your doing as mine." Turning serious, she glanced at her handbag, where she kept her .41-caliber derringer pistol. "Speaking of such matters, Mr. Prescott insists I keep my gun loaded from now on. I'm not so brave that his request isn't worrisome."

"But you've proven yourself competent with the weapon," he said, referencing a life-threatening encounter during her previous case.

"I wouldn't go that far. Pulling the trigger under sudden duress is instinctive. It's quite another thing to operate with a cool head when the threat of danger is persistent. I wouldn't say my upbringing was sheltered, but I have only ever passed by the tenements. I'm not without trepidation in entering one."

Still at work on the stuck window, Matthew looked over his shoulder. "You do realize, Harriet, that crime knows no geographic boundaries. Given the right—or wrong—circumstances and proper incentives, anyone is capable of nearly any crime. In my few short years as an operative, I've worked the case of a rich old granny using a hatchet to murder a too-noisy neighbor and a priest poisoning the sacramental wine to kill a parishioner after he'd been discovered canoodling the man's wife in the organ loft. The only difference between those living in a tenement and supposedly upstanding citizens is that tenement residents, immigrants mostly, are desperately poor."

He set down the tools and gripped the window sash. With one easy push, it opened. "Voila!"

"My knight in shining armor!" Harriet moved closer to the incoming breeze. "Thank you, Matthew. To be both handsome and handy"—she lowered her voice to a whisper—"you're sure to be *the* catch at the Black Rabbit."

Her reference to the secretive queer club he frequented and she'd once attended startled him. "You must speak with more discretion, Harriet."

Although it was impossible for anyone to overhear, she wilted; her remark *was* inappropriate for the office. This was all new to her. The job, of course, but also having Matthew as a confidante. She had found in him someone who understood, as no one else did, her struggles to prove herself as a professional detective while yearning for a romantic life that society deemed anathema. As much as their camaraderie delighted her, she couldn't blur the lines. Here, he was her colleague.

Before she could apologize, Matthew lightened the mood

by posing on the sill as if sitting for a portrait. "I'll forgive you this once, but only because what you say is true." He flashed his winning smile. "But one can never be too careful, Harriet. Not unlike being a detective, the wrong slip of the tongue could invite grave danger."

Reflecting on Prescott's caution about wearing men's clothing in public, Harriet asked, "Are you familiar with Ordinance 1297?"

"You sound as though you are not."

"It's only recently been brought to my attention."

"Ordinances 1297 and 1298 are used to arrest and fine people like us. I forget the precise language and which is which, but one covers dressing as the opposite sex and the second relates to committing 'lewd or filthy acts' anywhere in the city. The police don't go out of their way to enforce either, but if they do catch someone doing something they consider a violation, they're not likely to look the other way. I know of three men who, after a neighbor complained about music, were arrested and fined ten dollars each. Although found together in a private home, one fellow had been wearing a dress and his face was powdered. That's all it took for the police to throw them in jail for the night and haul them in front of a judge the next morning."

Matthew was right; she must exercise caution. Still, she couldn't change who she was. Nor could she imagine not pursuing her burgeoning relationship with Barbara. Was she prepared to risk arrest by returning to wearing men's clothing when her new case was resolved? Although Prescott wasn't bothered personally, would he continue to allow one of his operatives to flagrantly flout the law?

Today was the start of her third week as a detective. Her prior success may have extended her employment, but hardly was she indispensable. As with finding the missing maid, she would have to prove herself again, starting at the settlement house. But not before she returned home to iron a shirtwaist and skirt.

Chapter 3

Pushing her Victoria into the apartment she shared with her younger brother had been a mindless routine before Harriet adopted Susan. Now, the tiny tortoise-shell kitten was constantly underfoot.

"Susan, careful! Susan! If I roll over your paw, don't say I didn't warn you. Susan!"

Harriet scooped up the wriggling kitten, who was demanding attention, playtime, or a second breakfast. Although in a hurry, Harriet couldn't deny her. Before she left the apartment, she would spare ten minutes to give the cat all three.

Before leaving the office, Harriet had been informed by Madelaine that Mr. Prescott had arranged her visit to the University of Chicago Settlement House. Upon arriving, she was to ask for head resident Mary McDowell. The instruction had come with a reminder that she was to present herself not as an operative with the agency but as Prescott's niece.

Deciding among three skirts laid across the foot of her bed, she wondered what style of clothing a relation of Theodore Prescott would wear. Her superior hadn't offered guidance, but surely she should be well-dressed, well-spoken, and come across as educated. With the passing of her parents and assuming financial responsibilities for her brother and herself, Harriet hadn't been able to attend college, but she had been a good high school student, achieving the highest marks in her graduating class. Her wardrobe, however, was neither high-quality nor fashionable. Eschewing puffed shoulders, frilly shirt fronts, and a too-vibrant hue, she preferred simple styling, black, and a discounted price. Although she'd been directed to appear as an "unremarkable young woman," the instruction had not explicitly mentioned footwear or a hat. She chose to read that ambiguity as allowing for her bowler and men's shoes. Determined as she was to succeed as a detective and mindful of the legal risk, there were some sacrifices she was unwilling to make—donning a broad-brimmed hat festooned with fake flowers and pedaling a bicycle in women's shoes were two of them.

Remembering a box beneath the bed where a few pieces of her mother's wardrobe were saved, she dropped onto her knees. Holding up a pale green dress in the mirror, Harriet frowned at the excessive pleats and exaggerated shoulders. Fortunately, Mayre Morrow had been amply framed like her daughter and matched her height: five foot six. Although worn at the cuffs and hem, the dress should fit well enough.

At the kitchen table, Harriet reviewed the few typed pages describing the settlement house that Madelaine had placed within the case folder. The address, 4638 Ashland Avenue, was near the Union Stock Yards, an area southwest of downtown and connected to the city's main railroad lines by miles upon miles of tracks. It seemed everyone knew someone who worked at "the Yards," the sprawling marshland that was said to employ more than twenty-five thousand workers. Articles in the *Progressive Age*, the liberal-leaning newspaper that had been her parents' favorite, claimed that ten million animals—mostly cattle, hogs, and sheep—were butchered there each year, producing more than 80 percent of America's supply of domestic meat. As much as Harriet enjoyed bacon and a good chop, she wasn't eager to see—and smell—the actual cost of her appetites.

Turning the page, she continued reading about the settlement house. She would soon learn much with her own eyes but didn't want to arrive without basic knowledge of its history and services. Established four years ago, in 1894, by University of Chicago faculty members, the settlement was formed to provide neighboring poor immigrant families with teachings and training to integrate into society and make a livable wage. Harriet had surprisingly mixed emotions—her parents would be proud of her representing the settlement house's programs, but is that really what she would be doing? Her true purpose—Prescott's scheme—was to use talk of its offerings as a means for her to infiltrate the tenement and gain the women's trust. Although her motive was dishonest, could she still provide a benefit by spreading the word about the settlement house's noble work?

Nearing the noon hour, Harriet made a meager ham sandwich with what little remained in the ice box after she'd made her brother's lunch that morning. Aubrey, sixteen, was growing at an alarming rate and seemed to require a fuller plate at every meal. Her nine-dollar-a-week salary was 50 percent more than what she'd made as a bookkeeper at the grain elevator, but at the pace Aubrey was outgrowing his clothing and depleting the cupboards, she might have to find a place to scrimp—not easy to do when the essentials already consumed her pay. One thing she refused to consider eliminating was the sole luxury she allowed herself: a single scoop of chocolate ice cream each evening. As her mother, from whom she'd adopted the habit, had preached, "Whatever unpleasantness might befall your day, you can always end it with a bit of sweetness."

The journey to the University of Chicago Settlement House by bicycle took Harriet nearly two hours. It wasn't that the distance was terribly far, about ten miles, but the roads were in a frightful condition. As she neared her destination, streets that had been paved with timber had deteriorated, creating precarious splits and gaps that threatened to snag her tires. Compounding the challenge, she couldn't travel for even a minute in a straight path without swerving to avoid heaps of rubbish, buggies, hansom cabs, teams of horses pulling large wagons, crowds of pedestrians, and, occasionally, other bicyclists.

The neighborhood's appearance was that of a frontier town like those she'd seen in magazines, though she imagined there would be more space between the dwellings out West. Constructed primarily of wood, the buildings surrounding the Yards were one and two stories tall and crammed side by side and front to back on what looked to be every possible square foot of space. The smell of manure and other odious garbage was overwhelming. As much as she wanted to cover her nose, she dared not remove a hand from the handlebars and risk taking a spill.

Relieved to finally arrive, she coasted to a stop before a spacious playground flanked by buildings. The settlement comprised a two-floor tenement, a small cottage, and what appeared to be a small shop. She dismounted and wheeled her bicycle inside the unlocked gate.

Prescott's instruction was explicit: she was to learn as much as she could as fast as possible and then begin her investigation at the tenement building. It had already been more than twenty-four hours since the muckraker's murder, and Prescott had stressed that the memories of tenement residents would fade, clues would evaporate, and fears would take firm root in witnesses.

After locking her Victoria to a fence post, Harriet strode toward the largest building in search of Mary McDowell. Upon entering the settlement house, she asked the first person she saw if they might know the whereabouts of the head resident. An older girl with long red pigtails and wearing a too-large gingham dress pointed toward the end of the hallway. As Harriet neared the room, an imposing woman, big-boned with dark hair and small round spectacles that accentuated her seriousness, emerged. Seeing Harriet, she gestured toward a small stack of books sitting on a chair. "Bring those and come with me." Her tone, which might have come across as demanding in another situation, conveyed confidence in purpose.

Before Harriet could introduce herself, the woman, presumably Mary McDowell, was already marching in the opposite direction. Harriet hurriedly gathered the books and followed the head resident, who was already halfway up the staircase to the second floor. The woman entered a large sun-filled room that was alive with the chatter of dozens of children, most of them speaking languages other than English.

"There, please." Mary McDowell glanced back at Harriet before tilting her head toward a bookshelf painted a cheerful yellow. Shelving the books, Harriet noted a particularly whimsical cover: *The Wallypug of Why* by G. E. Farrow.

"Fine choice. The children adore that one," Mary McDowell said. "It owes much to Carroll's *Alice's Adventures in Wonderland*. Both are fantastical and great fun. Limit your reading to a quarter hour, then take out the mats for naps. Pay no mind to the children's protests. They'll do as they're told."

Seeing the woman turn to leave, Harriet said, "I think you've confused me for someone else. My name is Harriet Morrow. I'm Theodore Prescott's niece. I've come—"

"To help, yes? I spoke with Mr. Prescott earlier today. Your visit is most fortunate as it happens. Miss Newberry has come down with a bad cold, and Miss La Croix is delayed"—she scowled—"*again*. I'll check in on you later, dear."

The sound of Mary McDowell's footsteps quickly receded down the staircase. This was not at all what Harriet had planned, but appraising the roomful of children, she realized her objection would have to wait. Like puppies eager for a meal, they gathered around her ankles, looking up expectantly. She lowered herself onto a tiny stool before them, opened the book, and began to read.

> *Chapter One. The Way to Why. It was a very warm afternoon, and Girlie was sitting by the playroom window watching the goldfish idly swimming about in her little aquarium. She was feeling very 'sigh' as she called it, that is, not very happy, for all her brothers were all away from home, and she had no one to talk to.*

Glancing up as she turned each page, Harriet took in the many small faces. Although she couldn't tell from physical features alone, she guessed many were Irish while others had parents who had immigrated from Germany, Italy, or Bohemia. Without exception, their slender frames, cloaked in worn and, in many cases, ill-fitting clothing, spoke to their poverty.

> *Oh, you dear old thing!" cried Girlie, jumping up excitedly, and catching Dumpsey Deazil up in her arms. "I always knew that you could talk if you only would, and now at last you are going to do so, just as dolls always do in fairy tale books.*

Enrapt, every set of eyes fixed on Harriet. When she paused for breath, the room was so quiet that the wall clock's ticking could be heard. Her initial bother at being asked to read to the children had evaporated, replaced by delight in providing them such easy entertainment. She read with gusto, adopting distinct voices for Girlie, Boy, the Wallypug's doctor-in-law, and the story's other silly characters. At the end of chapter three, she consulted her wristwatch and closed the book. The children complained with groans and objections needing no translation. Whether they had understood her reading in English, they didn't want story time to end.

"It's nap time." Harriet glanced around the room. "Apparently, there are mats about."

The remark triggered a half dozen children to dash to a large wardrobe and swing open its doors, revealing a pile of blanket squares. Harriet distributed a mat to each child. She wasn't wrong in presuming they understood the routine. In less than a minute, they had all positioned their blankets around the room and laid down. The discipline on display was nothing short of a marvel. While the ailing Miss Newberry might be responsible, Harriet had a strong feeling that this was Mary McDowell's influence. Given what she'd observed so far, the University Settlement was orderly and well-run. Although impressed, she was eager to be relieved from duty as a kindergarten minder and learn about the other services. The primary focus of her investigation was but a few blocks away, and she'd hoped to make an initial visit before having to navigate the neighborhood's treacherous roads by bicycle with only spotty gas streetlamps to light her way.

She was grateful when a middle-aged woman, thin as a willow branch, appeared and, introducing herself as Miss La Croix, said that Mary McDowell was awaiting Harriet in her office downstairs. Quietly stepping toward the door, Harriet weaved through the sleeping children. *Perhaps I shall return someday and finish reading about the Wallypug's adventures to the children*, she thought. As she was not destined to marry, having a child was out of the question. Besides, she barely made ends meet as it was, and the demands of motherhood were incompatible with full employment, especially with a detective's irregular hours. Still, there was no denying a maternal feeling about which she was ambivalent.

Downstairs, Harriet found Mary McDowell sitting before a cluttered rolltop desk in a high-ceilinged room of unadorned white plastered walls.

"Ah, Miss . . ." Mary McDowell raised her gaze from a pile of paperwork and examined Harriet over her small spectacles.

"Morrow," Harriet offered, clutching her handbag and stepping inside the office.

Mary McDowell nodded as if Harriet had answered an exam question correctly. "Quite right. Now then, your uncle tells me you're in town a short while and would like to learn about what we do here at the settlement. That's all well and good. But I trust the time I spend educating you about our work here will translate into action at home. Come to think of it, I don't recall him saying where you're from."

Another test? Prescott hadn't covered this detail of her fictional persona. What if he'd been asked the same question and improvised? Giving herself better odds of matching his answer, she said "the East."

Mary McDowell frowned, dissatisfied with the ambiguity.

Guessing a city where Prescott might have family, Harriet replied, "Boston."

"Boston? Mr. Prescott should have said. There are few cities I know better than Boston. You'll surely be acquainted with the Sinclairs and the Abbotts. Tell me, how is dear Maude these days?"

Thoughts racing, Harriet struggled to hold her nerve. She'd been foolish to arrive at the settlement house unprepared. Hers was an amateur's error. But what was Prescott's excuse? He must have known she would require a basic backstory about which they'd previously agreed.

Mary McDowell shifted her weight, causing her chair to squeak. She stared at Harriet, awaiting an answer.

"Oh, you know Maude," Harriet said, adding a casual shrug. "One can never be too sure."

"*Pfft*. Maude Abbott never tires of providing any listener with a comprehensive inventory of her maladies. But listen to me. I'm being unkind. Please give her my regards, won't you?"

Desperate for a change of subject, Harriet said, "I am so looking forward to a tour of the settlement and hearing about your services. I don't suppose we could begin straightaway."

Mary McDowell looked at the grandfather clock in the corner and pursed her thin lips. "I suppose I could manage that. Mr. Prescott didn't mention you might desire a tour. But his wife is a tremendous supporter of our work. Out of respect to her benevolence, I will make the accommodation. Still, we must be quick about it. I have a meeting in the next hour with an alderman about the appallingly unsanitary state of the neighborhood's water. Though I'm not so naïve as to expect much action. Politicians like Alderman Powers hold office for only one reason, and it has nothing to do with serving others."

Before Harriet could offer a well-meaning remark, Mary McDowell was bustling down the hallway. Apparently, the tour had begun.

After being shown parts of the main building she'd yet to see, primarily dedicated to flats for recent arrivals to the city, Harriet followed the head resident across the playground to an auditorium. "We use this large room for all manner of meetings," Mary McDowell said. "One of the impediments to workers organizing is having a large enough meeting space. Before we acquired this building, there was no place of sufficient size. The men used to gather above a local saloon." She lowered her chin and peered over her spectacles. "There're no fewer than two dozen of them within a few blocks' walk in any direction. Men meeting above a saloon is one thing, but a group of seamstresses once attended a meeting there. Their families got wind of it, and the furor nearly upended the call to organize. Vice, Miss Morrow, in any forum or format, is and forever will be the devil's hobby. As head resident of this settlement house, I won't have it. Those we help must commit to bettering themselves by all means, not just through education and training. The straight and narrow path is the only path." She stopped abruptly, turning back to Harriet. "I presume you agree?"

Harriet sputtered, unsure of a good reply. Presuming all that Mary McDowell implied by a "straight and narrow" path, she wouldn't tolerate a sexual invert—or *queer* person, a term slowly making its way into the public consciousness. From the file that Madelaine had prepared, Harriet knew that the settlement's leader was a devout Methodist and that her motivation to help the impoverished and downtrodden was founded on her Christian beliefs. Although not religious, Harriet didn't care if a person read the Bible, the Torah, or the Katzenjammer Kids. But she didn't like someone judging her heart when they didn't know the first thing about her. Deciding on an honest yet agreeable reply, Harriet said, "I believe that everyone has the capacity to better themselves."

After a long moment, Mary McDowell nodded decisively, accepting the answer, and led Harriet to the last building, a small shop comprising a smaller meeting room and playroom where immigrant families took classes in English and citizenship. The space also accommodated weekly gatherings of a women's club and youth groups.

"As you doubtless observed on your journey here, Miss Morrow, there are no well-paved streets in this area. There are few sewer connections. The many surrounding ditches are fouled with scum from standing water. Garbage abounds everywhere one sets their gaze. An essential part of this settlement's work is improving the neighborhood beyond our gate. A pleasant place to live should not be a luxury afforded only to denizens of the city's wealthier wards. A clean and safe environment is crucial to a person's mental outlook, ambition, and physical health. Poverty must not be society's excuse that allows someone to live among mountains of rubbish, putrid creeks, and dizzying odors."

Harriet understood why the university leaders and Hull House's Jane Addams had selected Mary McDowell to lead the settlement. Her passionate advocacy and accomplishments were inspiring. Although uncomfortable with the woman's religious moralizing, Harriet couldn't help but admire her commitment to helping the tens of thousands of Chicagoans living in squalor. Moreover, she was relieved she would not have to feign enthusiasm when singing the service's praises to the women at the tenement.

With the tour concluded, Mary McDowell escorted Harriet to her bicycle. A hansom cab halted at the entrance. The door opened and out stepped a disheveled-looking man. He waved amiably in their direction, apparently recognizing the head resident. In reply, Mary McDowell grumbled but pasted on a smile. Harriet wasn't sure what to make of the man. He was of average height but alarmingly slender. His brown suit, although appearing to be of high-quality material, hung loosely on his frame, and the too-short pants showed his red socks, which ascended from expensive but badly scuffed shoes. Most unusual, he wore no hat, a choice made more curious by his having only a few remaining strands of brown hair that he'd let grow long, oiled, and combed back.

Approaching, he extended a hand, showcasing rings on each finger. Harriet was no jeweler and didn't wear any adornments herself, yet she guessed, by their size alone, that the gems set into the rings were of high value. Mary McDowell hesitated, then received his hand, and introduced Harriet as a visitor to Chicago and the niece of a benefactor.

Stepping close—too close—he lifted Harriet's hand and planted a wet kiss on her fingers. "Welcome to our fair city, lovely maiden. I am Alderman Michael Powers. This is my ward. I trust your stay will be agreeable."

When he didn't release her hand, she yanked it away, fighting the urge to wipe the moisture lingering on her fingers on her skirt.

Mary McDowell grimaced. "Alderman Powers *represents* the area."

Harriet had never met an alderman, but the man hardly matched her expectations. He looked more like a once-wealthy carnival barker than an important elected official. Harriet's parents had opened her eyes to the world; she knew men like Michael Powers were influenced by money and power, and she didn't envy Mary McDowell having to deal with him. Still, she didn't doubt the head resident's resolve to do whatever she could to persuade him to act on behalf of his constituents.

Mary McDowell wished Harriet a pleasant stay with her aunt and uncle before leading the politician into the building. With the sun soon to set, Harriet's visit to the tenement would have to wait until the morning. She couldn't deny feeling relief. The muckraker had been murdered in the middle of the day. She didn't relish discovering how dangerous the building might turn after dark.

Chapter 4

Harriet was already in a morning frenzy when she again discovered that Aubrey had used all the hot water in the bath. As siblings, occasional bickering and minor disputes were natural, but she had become head of the household when coming of age and inheriting the family's apartment four years after their parents had succumbed to pneumonia. At sixteen, Aubrey was no child, yet half the time he acted with the self-centeredness of a six-year-old. Harriet's struggle to balance authority with compromise and to project calm when overwhelmed by exasperation was a daily challenge. Fighting the urge to speak her mind, she focused on her investigation, knowing a quarrel with her brother wouldn't be a helpful start to either of their days. What would set things right was toast with raspberry jam and two scrambled eggs.

"Why are you wearing Mother's old dress?" Aubrey asked, buttoning his shirt as he lumbered into the kitchen.

"I've been given a new case that requires me to wear one."

"Why not wear one of your own?"

"You know my tastes. Today, I need something more—"

"Like a normal lady would wear?"

As recently as a month ago, the remark might have ignited indignation. But Aubrey had supported her recent switch to wearing men's clothing, saying she looked more like herself. Besides that, his "normal lady" comment had merit. Her skirts and shirtwaists, masculine in cut and color, were commonly met with frowns. "Unremarkable" had been the word Mr. Prescott used to describe how she was to present herself at the tenement—and so she would try.

Aubrey's interest in breakfast replaced his curiosity in his sister's clothing. "Are you making me eggs?"

Harriet shot him a stern look. "I think you can do better than that."

He groaned as if he'd been the one to find ice-cold water when turning the tub's tap. "Can I *please* have some eggs?"

"Since you asked politely, yes." She waved a wooden spoon cheerfully in the air. "Sunny-side up, coming right up." She stopped short of cracking an egg into the hot skillet.

"Nooo, Harriet. I hate runny eggs. I want them scrambled." As a second thought, he added a drawn-out "*Please.*"

"I know, I know. I'm only jesting."

The banter soothed her jangled nerves. Their mother had performed the same back-and-forth with Aubrey countless times, always sparking his panicked reaction. Reprising the routine familiar to only them reminded her of their bond and why she put up with his dirty clothes on the floor, cereal bowl left sitting on the counter, and selfish use of the bathroom that threatened to make her late for work on a daily basis.

After the morning meal, with the dishes cleared, Susan fed, and her sandbox cleaned, Harriet wheeled her Victoria out to the street. She was giving herself an extra hour to make the journey to the tenement building. Starting from home instead of the agency's offices was a farther distance, and the roads would surely be busier in the morning.

Gerald Cole had provided the address of the tenement, and Madelaine included the information in the case folder.

Although unfamiliar with Robey Street, Harriet had a general sense of its location relative to the University Settlement House. Plus, its proximity to the sprawling Union Stock Yards provided a monumental—and grim—landmark.

After pedaling south on Halstead for several miles, she turned west on Forty-Seventh and found her destination. Occupying nearly every inch of the property, the two-story structure built of rough-hewed timber signaled dubious construction. Given the city's history of cataclysmic fires, Harriet couldn't shake the thought that the building resembled a massive funeral pyre. If not a match, a strong gust of wind might also precipitate the tenement's collapse. She didn't want to assume the neighborhood was prone to thievery but was wary about leaving her bicycle on the street, lock notwithstanding. She wheeled it inside the front door.

As dilapidated as the building's exterior was, it hadn't prepared her for the bleak conditions awaiting her inside. With no light, she could barely make out the narrow hallway and staircase ahead. Thick, dusty air made breathing difficult. Worse yet was the smell of perspiration and rotten food. Harriet was hardly wealthy, but her modest home resembled her friend Pearl Bartlett's mansion more than it did this forbidding place.

Fast-approaching footsteps caught her attention. Pasting on a smile, she readied the introduction she'd rehearsed while riding there. The next instant, a hard-charging body emerged from the darkness, knocking her backward.

"Girl, get da way from da door!" the man bellowed, his accent attacking each consonant like a hammer.

"I'm sorry, sir. You see—"

"Stupid girl." He pushed past her and continued out.

The collision hadn't injured her, but it was unsettling. She gripped her handbag, straightened her hat, and rapped on the nearest door. Almost immediately, it opened. Despite the dim lighting, she could see there was no one there. Had her knock alone pushed the door open? Sensing movement, she looked down and saw a small boy. The moment their eyes met, he dashed back into the home.

"Hello?" she called out. "Might I have a word with the woman of the house?" Hearing no reply, she took a tentative step into the apartment. Scant light from a window dirtied with soot illuminated the room. A coal stove and lime-stained sink sat against one wall. A rickety wooden table stood in the room's center. Someone had pinned the underwear of men and women, girls and boys, to a makeshift clothesline strung from the window to a nail in the opposite wall. Harriet took in the surroundings. The home had two other rooms, both small and windowless. Despite their size, each held two narrow beds covered with threadbare blankets. She turned back to the boy, now sitting, cross-legged and hunched over, before the window. He appeared to be playing with a tiny toy.

"Where is your mother?" Harriet's voice disrupted the silence that added to the home's gloominess. If the boy hadn't responded to her knock on the door, she might have thought him deaf. He neither replied nor looked up. So as not to frighten him, she moved slowly to where he sat. "My name is Harriet. What's your name?" Her breath caught. The child's toy was a half-dead cockroach.

Again, the boy said nothing nor even acknowledged her presence. Perhaps he didn't understand English? A strange woman in his home couldn't be so common that he gave no notice. But then, what did she know about what he encountered on a typical day? Still, a five-year-old—her guess—shouldn't be left alone. Harriet faced a dilemma: leave him or stay and wait for an adult to arrive. Just yesterday, she'd found herself reading to kindergarteners. Now this. Although the boy appeared unbothered by being at home alone, she could no more leave him in the apartment than abandon him on a street corner. Resigned to the setback, she carefully lowered herself onto a creaky chair, testing its sturdiness to hold her weight. She checked her wristwatch—it was already eleven o'clock.

Nearly an hour later, Harriet was rethinking her decision to remain in the apartment when the boy sprang to his feet and spoke for the first time. Despite the foreign language, she understood him perfectly. He tugged at the front of his pants, and his twisted expression conveyed urgency. After a hurried search of the room revealed no chamber pot, she realized the front door stood open. He was gone. She raced into the hallway in time to glimpse light at the back of the building.

Outside, she was amazed to find not the privies but another tenement of the same height squeezed onto the rear of the property. Built less than ten feet from the front building, sunlight would find its few windows for no more than an hour each day. That wasn't the worst of it. The ground level was dedicated to stables. The odor of horse manure was overwhelming. Harriet hadn't imagined there could be worse living conditions than the apartments in the front tenement. She'd been wrong.

After navigating a single passageway to an alleyway, she found three privies standing among piles of garbage and roaming cats. One of the privy doors was closed. The boy emerged several minutes later, tugging up his britches. Wordlessly, he walked past her toward home. He needed no supervision. Harriet could do nothing for him that he couldn't do for himself. However, when given the chance, she would tell the boy's mother about the University Settlement's kindergarten. Could anyone argue that he wouldn't be better off spending the day among other children in a clean, light-filled room instead of cooped up alone in a dismal apartment playing with an insect?

Returned to the front building, Harriet tried knocking on the door of another first-floor apartment. A haggard-looking woman not much older than herself, a baby resting on her hip, answered. Harriet counted six more children in the room beyond. The encounter was short-lived. The woman spoke only German or perhaps another language common among Bohemians. Whatever she said was decidedly unwelcoming.

Farther down the hallway, Harriet tried another door. Commotion within preceded the door opening to reveal a middle-aged woman with magnificently long black hair. The woman greeted Harriet with genuine pleasure, introducing herself as Mrs. Horak and ushering Harriet inside. Counting three children and five beds, Harriet marveled that so many family members could share a space half the size of Theodore Prescott's office. It took less than a minute for Harriet to understand the reason for Mrs. Horak's warm reception; she misunderstood the purpose of Harriet's visit as a settlement house representative, thinking she was there to help with household chores. Mrs. Horak handed her an empty pail. "Coal is in the basement. Don't fill it all the way. It's too heavy to carry. Better you make two trips."

Harriet started to set the woman straight but held her tongue. Mrs. Horak spoke English. How many other residents would? Wasn't her objective to work her way into these women's homes, earn their trust, and get them talking? She didn't like the idea of hauling coal, but what if this woman could tell her everything she needed to know? She might even know the whereabouts of the muckraker's lost evidence. Imagine how impressed Mr. Prescott would be to learn his newest and only female operative had solved a murder case in less than two days. With thoughts of success, she took the pail.

The door to the basement wasn't easy to find, primarily because it wasn't a door as much as a hatch alongside the building. After lifting a rotted wooden cover, she descended the half dozen steps into the darkness. The smell of cat feces and mold struck her nostrils like a punch. She covered her mouth and nose and blinked, allowing her eyes to adjust. At least the coal bin was easy to spot; a shovel was planted upright in the middle of the pile. She recalled how, when she was a child, before her family's home had been converted from coal to gas, the impossible to eliminate dust had driven her mother batty. Now, with each shovelful clouding the air and coating her hands and shirt cuffs in a grimy film, she imagined emerging from the basement looking like a street urchin who hadn't visited the public baths for weeks.

Harriet was soon joined by another woman carrying a metal bucket. So similar was her appearance to Mrs. Horak's that Harriet wondered if she might be her younger sister. If the woman was surprised to see Harriet, a stranger in her building's basement, she didn't show it. Instead, she nodded a wordless greeting and sat on a short stool, awaiting her turn with the shovel.

"Hello, I'm Harriet."

"Antonia. You are new, yes?" She shook her head and frowned. "So quick to replace."

Harriet continued shoveling, using the time to think. *Replace?* Could Antonia be referring to anyone other than Lucy Fara, the woman arrested for reporting the dead body to the police? Harriet had anticipated needing to cautiously raise the subject of the murder, but Antonia had just done the job for her.

Seizing the opportunity, Harriet momentarily abandoned her persona as a settlement house representative in exchange for that of a new resident. "I don't know who lived here before me," Harriet said. "Did you know the family? Were they good people?" To avoid appearing overeager, she returned to her work.

"The children were well-behaved. But the woman . . . her I didn't like. Always talking. And her husband"— Antonia sniffed—"no good."

With the pail halfway full, Harriet tested its weight but

kept filling, using the chore as an excuse to extend the conversation. "Why did the family move away?"

Antonia seemed to give the question undue consideration. "Mind you, I wouldn't gossip if they still lived here, but I suppose it hardly matters now. The husband drank too much. He got fired from the Yards, then up and left. The woman has four children and no money. I worried how they'd live,"—another sniff—"as if that was the worst of their problems."

The pail could hold only one more shovelful, and the woman's constant shifting conveyed her increasing impatience. Harriet needed to move the conversation along.

"Why did she move away? Where did she take the children?"

Antonia stood and reached for the shovel, signaling it was her turn. "The police took them. The woman to prison. The children to an orphanage."

"That's horrid. Why? What happened?"

"A man was killed." Antonia glanced up at the ceiling. "On the second floor." She shrugged. "Someone must be guilty. I'm lucky I didn't find the body. They'd have arrested me instead."

As Antonia filled her bucket, Harriet slipped in more questions, but the woman had lost interest in the topic, answering "Who is to say?" or "What do I know of such things?"

Emerging from the basement, Harriet appreciated Mrs. Horak's advice to not completely fill the pail. The pail proved nearly impossible to lift even with two hands, and its steel handle pressed painfully into her fingers. She was grateful the woman lived on the first floor. How on earth did women manage who lived on the third?

Considering the dirty, physical chore, Harriet might have expected more gratitude than a passing nod from Mrs. Horak, who had pinned up her long hair and changed out of her housedress while Harriet had been in the basement.

Harriet set the coal next to the stove before sitting to rest at the table. The woman clucked and pointed to the chamber pot. Harriet was too appalled to speak. Thirty minutes ago, the idea of ingratiating herself to residents by performing household duties seemed like a good idea, but Harriet wasn't about to empty human wastewater without information to make it worth her while—and it had better be good.

Ignoring the chamber pot, Harriet said, "I'm curious, Mrs. Horak. I hear that one of your neighbors, a Mrs. Lucy Fara, had some trouble with the police. Did you know Mrs. Fara? Is it common for residents to find themselves on the wrong side of the law?"

"Where did you hear that?" Mrs. Horak snapped. "It's best not to speak of such things." She gestured again to the chamber pot. "The privies are out back in the alley."

Purposefully, Harriet hadn't mentioned the nature of the crime, leaving it to Mrs. Horak to make the assumption. Moreover, she thought the manner of veiled speaking might appeal to the woman, encouraging her to reveal information without doing so plainly.

Harriet continued, "But if Mrs. Fara is innocent, surely you'd want to help. If the police can arrest just anyone regardless of guilt, who might be next? If neighbors don't look out for one another, who will? Perhaps you or another resident saw someone or something that might point the authorities to the real culprit. It must be terribly upsetting to know that an innocent woman has been blamed for something she didn't do."

"You seem to know plenty as it is. There's nothing for me to add. One should keep to their own business."

Keep going, Harriet urged herself, sensing that despite Mrs. Horak's claim, she knew more than she was letting on. Hoping to touch a nerve, she asked, "How old are the

Fara children? I don't suppose they are the same ages as yours? To be separated from your children . . . why, I can't fathom it. Just imagine Mrs. Fara's distress. Though, as a mother yourself, I suppose you can imagine."

With her chin raised, Mrs. Horak appeared taller, projecting defiance. "The police care nothing for any of our children. Lucy's two older boys, Chester and Grover, are ten and eleven. They were taken first. The younger two, a four-year-old boy and a girl, three, stayed here with me until later that afternoon when other officers came for them. The poor little dears screamed and cried. It was awful. I thought about letting them stay, but look around." She gestured to the tiny, cramped apartment. "We haven't an inch to spare and can barely feed ourselves. Besides, it wouldn't have made any difference. People like us have no say in such matters. The police were set on taking them, and so they did."

"And the woman who was killed? Was she a relation of Mrs. Fara's? Is that why the police arrested her?" Presuming her host knew the basics of the crime, Harriet sought to draw her into revealing more, knowing she couldn't resist making the correction.

"*She?*" Mrs. Horak looked insulted. "They say it was a man. Lucy had no family to speak of, so he was no relative. I didn't see him myself. Those that did say they had never seen him before. Who he was and what he was doing here is not my concern." She paused. "No one cares. Not really. The police have someone to blame. Someone to hang. That's all they need."

Harriet took a long, steadying breath, quelling her excitement. "So others observed the body? Can you describe what they saw?"

Mrs. Horak's expression suddenly changed. "I've said too much. I'm sorry, I must ask you to leave."

The woman's willingness to forego free help spoke to

her discomfort with discussing the murder further. Harriet smiled, satisfied with what she'd learned and happy to avoid an argument over emptying the chamber pot.

"I understand, Mrs. Horak. I'm sure you have much yet to accomplish in your day. Please do consider availing yourself of the settlement house's many services. Perhaps I shall see you there one day soon?"

"I'm much too busy here," Mrs. Horak said, showing her the door.

Standing in the hallway, Harriet was irked that the woman never thanked her for hauling coal. Was the chore so routine that it hardly counted as a favor? Or did Mrs. Horak's lack of appreciation stem from how inconsequential the act was, given the unsurmountable drudgery of her daily life?

Harriet visited another six homes, navigating the tenement's dark, narrow hallways. Other than the third-floor apartment belonging to Antonia, the woman from the basement, none of the apartments had residents who spoke or understood English. Rapping her knuckles on the last door, Harriet was greeted by a young Bohemian woman who reminded her of Barbara Wozniak. Both women were tall, possessed prodigious noses, and had waistlines suggesting a penchant for sweet desserts. Also like Barbara, this woman, named Edita, spoke English well, although heavily accented.

Edita's second-floor, street-facing apartment was light filled and tidy, not wholly depressing like the others Harriet had visited. Edita invited Harriet to sit before settling her infant twins in a makeshift crib made from a trunk on two chairs. By the time Harriet had finished describing the services offered by the University of Chicago Settlement House, the twins had finally fallen asleep, and she turned the conversation to the "unfortunate event that resulted in a man's death outside her door." Immediately, Edita became frightened and refused to discuss the matter. Harriet had encountered only three women conversant in English in the tenement. Desperate to learn something useful from Edita, Harriet changed the subject, asking about the neighbors in the four apartments whose doors had gone unanswered that afternoon. Whether divulging information because she considered it harmless or relieved to avoid any discussion of the murder, Edita told Harriet the apartment down the hall had belonged to the Faras and awaited new tenants. The one on the third floor was home to the building's newest residents. Edita had never met any of them but heard from others that they were a quiet and reserved immigrant family, recently arrived from Germany. The two apartments at street level, where no one had been home, housed large Italian families, all gone for the day, working stockyard jobs.

With as much accomplished as possible at the tenement and eager to reach the Prescott Agency before dusk, Harriet wheeled her bicycle to the street. Pedaling against a strong southern wind, she recounted the highlights of her first day at the tenement. Antonia had said "a man was killed" and seemed to doubt Lucy Fara was the killer—though she offered no reason why. Mrs. Horak had inadvertently revealed that others had seen the victim before abruptly ending the conversation. Whatever Edita might know would take more time and a different approach to discover.

When first hearing about the case of the murdered muckraker from Mr. Prescott and Gerald Cole, Harriet was told that Lucy Fara, a single mother of four, had been accused of the murder. To hear that in the wake of her arrest the children had been split up compounded the injustice. Harriet knew the wrenching loss of parents. The Fara children were sure to be terrified and confused. And Lucy Fara? How dreadful was her plight! Left penniless by a drunkard of a husband, she'd been falsely accused of a capital crime and her family had been scattered. As important as it was to solve the case and prove herself to Mr. Prescott, Harriet realized an even greater mission. If she could recover the missing evidence and discover Eugene Eldridge's real killer, she could win Lucy Fara's freedom and reunite her family. With the added weight of the Fara family's fate in her hands, she would need to work faster than the authorities, who seemed intent on sending an innocent mother to the gallows.

Chapter 5

At nearly five o'clock, Harriet stepped off the elevator onto the sixth floor and entered the Prescott Agency's lobby. The petite blond receptionist was typical of women who worked in downtown offices. Harriet wouldn't deny the woman was pretty but found her type of conventional beauty—an unspoken requisite for such jobs—uninspiring. Moreover, it bothered Harriet that a woman might be refused a secretarial or reception job because she was too heavy, old, or plain looking, as if such attributes had anything to do with one's ability to file paperwork or type fifty words a minute. The injustice was compounded by men such as Prescott's senior operative Charles Bonner. His monumental girth made him long odds in a footrace with a toddler when agility and strength *were* essential to the job. Harriet's full frame, mannish features, and unstylish wardrobe would be three obstacles to her landing a "proper young lady's job," but it was her unfeminine deportment that had assured Prescott she could handle the physical rigors of detective work. Her strength was uncommon, but it was her foot speed and agility that never failed to amaze.

Entering her office felt like opening the door to an icebox. Earlier in the day, she'd left the window open, but the wind had kicked up, and the temperature had turned chilly. She lowered the sash and rolled a sheet of paper into her typewriter. The male operatives were each assigned a secretary to perform typing and other administrative duties. That she hadn't been given the same support was dispiriting but also a relief; she avoided the awkwardness of another woman performing a task she would think Harriet should do herself. Mindful of the skepticism surrounding her role as the agency's first female detective, she sensed several of her colleagues anticipated "Prescott's experiment" to inevitably fail. Such ruminations, she knew, were not helpful. Only one person's opinion mattered, and his name was printed on every operative's calling card. Moreover, the agency's principal claimed his opinion was shaped only by "the efficiency with which my men solve their case." Harriet's job was, in part, to force a one-word amendment to his oft-mentioned measure.

With her day's report completed and delivered to Prescott by way of Madelaine, Harriet stuffed her wiry auburn hair into the crown of her bowler and tugged on her coat. Before leaving for the day, she poked her head inside Matthew McCabe's office. "May I assume you have spent your day successfully righting all the wrongs in our fair city?"

Matthew chuckled. "If that is my responsibility, I must have a word with my boss about a pay increase."

Seeing Harriet's expression, his grin dissolved. Discussing salaries, even in jest, was too personal a topic. If Matthew suspected Prescott had started her at a wage lower than normal because she was a woman, he would be right. Eager to change topics, he asked, "How was your day at the tenement? Did you learn anything useful?"

Halfway through her lengthy recounting, she removed her coat. By the time she'd finished, she was sitting.

"At least one of the women at the tenement must know something about the murder," Matthew agreed.

"It's imperative that you return and discover what that something is."

"Yes, but how?" Harriet said. "I may be welcomed back to haul coal and empty chamber pots, but on the matter of Eugene Eldridge, everyone is decidedly tight-lipped."

Matthew stood and started pacing, which in the small room amounted to walking in a tight circle. "You say the woman, Mrs. Horak, was quick to correct your mistake in saying the victim was a woman. Yes?"

"That's right."

"Tell me, Harriet. How old are you?"

She frowned. "I fail to see—"

"My sister is your age. I'm quite sure of it. She just celebrated her thirtieth birthday."

Offended, Harriet gasped. "Come now, Matthew. You know I'm not that old. I'll be twenty-two next month."

He stood before her, spreading his hands wide.

"Ah," she said. "Clever. Quite clever, indeed."

"You stumbled upon the method yourself. You just didn't appreciate its broader application. Direct questions cause a person to stop and think. Should I answer truthfully? Make up a lie? Leave something out to satisfy my self-interest? Or should I give any answer at all? Conversely, hiding questions in conversation is usually more effective. A good detective approaches an interview as a dance, not a tug-of-war."

"That's a fine theory, Matthew, but what I need is practical advice. I've already asked the women about the crime. How do you suggest I further engage them in conversation about a topic they refuse to discuss?"

"Think expansively. Take Mrs. Horak, for example. She raised her defenses when you asked about the murder but lowered them just as quickly when you smartly mentioned Mrs. Fara's children. Instinctively, you shifted topics to one you sensed she *would* discuss. Don't all the women have children? As mothers, the plight of Mrs. Fara hits closer to home than a stranger's death. The woman you first met in the basement, Antonia, was it?" Harriet nodded. "Okay, so Antonia said it was lucky she didn't find the body. Otherwise, the police would have arrested her instead. Correct?" Another nod. "So there you have it. Mrs. Fara's neighbors' self-interest inclines them to be far more concerned about the injustice done to a woman like themselves than the justice served by finding the killer of a man they claimed not to know." He grinned. "Is that practical enough for you?"

"Thank you, Matthew. I should think my return to the tenement stands a good chance of bearing fruit. But first, I shall pay a visit to Mrs. Fara. Where would the police be holding her?"

"The County Jail at Dearborn Street and Illinois Street. Fortunately for her, it's a tremendous improvement over the former police prisons. Built a few years ago, the new jail has separate facilities for women and juveniles."

Harriet gasped. "You can't tell me that women and children were housed with the men before?"

"As I say, your Mrs. Fara is fortunate."

"I shall go first thing in the morning." She put on her coat. "You're staying late?"

Matthew explained that he planned to work another hour. Harriet suspected that instead of leaving the office for the northside apartment he shared with a roommate, he might visit a particular Levee District saloon to meet a companion. For her part, she had planned a simple stew with ingredients she'd stocked the previous weekend.

As it was a Tuesday, Barbara would attend a meeting of the Polish Women's Alliance, an organization that helped women become financially secure through education and better employment. She would extend the time away from her family's home in Polish Downtown by joining Harriet and Aubrey for supper. Barbara had never mentioned whether her family suspected she had a romantic interest in women, but knowing the Wozniaks' Catholic faith, Harriet presumed the family avoided the issue. Had Harriet's parents been alive, would she confide her secret to them? As much as they loved her and were progressively minded, she wouldn't deny that not having to broach the issue was a relief. Her brother, however, was a conundrum. He seemed to think Barbara was Harriet's new friend and nothing more. That she and Barbara had never gone beyond briefly holding hands and trading sisterly kisses on the cheek did nothing to betray their deeper desire. With a lifetime ahead of her, Harriet knew a day would come when her brother would need to be told or figure it out on his own. But with the pressure of her new job and managing a household, albeit just the two of them and the kitten, she was happy that the revelation of her true self could be put off. But for how long?

Harriet was just beginning to learn how women like herself navigated the world. Her education started two weeks ago. While investigating the case of the missing maid, Harriet met Barbara, the servant's older sister. Following a clue, Barbara took Harriet to the Black Rabbit, a private club where men were free to rouge their cheeks and dance arm in arm, and trouser-wearing women flirted over flutes of champagne—in truth, a cheap concoction approximating the real thing's color and fizz. It was there that Harriet spied Matthew McCabe dressed as Mattie, unmasking their common secret. The experience at the Black Rabbit had been thrilling. Harriet had never imagined such a glorious place might exist. As eager as she was to return, she required an invitation from Barbara. Harriet didn't think she was wrong in sensing mutual interest, but how could she be certain? The bouquet of red roses would seem an unambiguous signal were it not for Harriet having saved her sister's life. Roses or not, they could have been a gesture of gratitude. Though Harriet hadn't made her growing affection clear either. Perhaps that evening, something would happen to remove all doubt.

A surprising smell greeted her as she entered the apartment. For an instant, her mother was alive and wrapped in her familiar floral apron before a sizzling skillet in the kitchen. Were it not for the wistful memory, Harriet would have been only delighted to see Aubrey cooking the beef for the evening's stew. On the counter, peeled potatoes and carrots sat on the cutting board alongside crushed cloves of garlic. She had good reason for finding no immediate words for the occasion: Aubrey had never made a meal in his life.

Harriet sat quietly at the table. Susan circled her legs. Noting Harriet's smile, Aubrey said, "What? Am I doing something wrong?"

"Not at all. It smells wonderful." She took a moment to mull his reaction. He often complained she was overly critical. She knew it to be true. But wouldn't anyone admonish him for leaving muddy footprints across the floorboards or leaving breadcrumbs on the counter to attract mice? Stirring the pot, he bit his lower lip—a sign of nerves. Deciding the moment called for encouragement, she said, "You appear to have things well in hand here. Shall I set the table?"

Aubrey's furrowed brow and refusal to risk a glance her way confirmed his uncertainty. Knowing he hated being under observation, she left him with a "Shout if I can be of help."

Susan padded after her into the next room. Harriet retrieved placemats and napkins from the sideboard that had been her grandmother's. Rumored to have been brought over from England by ancestors, the mahogany piece with oval side panels and tapered legs stood out like a top hat on a janitor as the home's most handsome and highest-quality furniture. The sideboard also stored her most valuable possession: a set of silver cutlery that had been a wedding present to her parents from her mother's wealthy uncle—a man she'd never met and whose name she couldn't recall. Harriet and Aubrey rarely opened the crimson, satin-lined case, but Barbara constituted company, and she imagined her mother lecturing, "Nice things are to enjoy, not sit in a box."

A knock on the door startled Susan and sent her scampering beneath the sofa. A moment later, Barbara handed Harriet a bundle of violet bearded irises.

"They're beautiful," Harriet said. "But truly, you needn't have brought a gift."

"No?" Barbara lowered her voice, not knowing Aubrey's whereabouts. "Would you rather I *not* do everything I can to woo you?"

A rush of heat flashed through Harriet, warming her ears and cheeks. Overwhelmed, she stammered, "We're having stew."

The non sequitur hovered between them, broken seconds later by Barbara's throaty laugh. "And so it seems you know the way to *my* heart."

"Harriet!" Aubrey shouted from the kitchen.

"Our chef calls," Harriet whispered. "Please. Sit." She gestured toward the living room.

Aubrey started speaking the moment Harriet appeared in the doorway. "It looks dry."

"Just a bit more broth will do the trick," she said, feeling strange about dispensing advice for a role she had never felt comfortable in. At that moment, she realized there were two types of learning. Intentional study, as she was applying to her work at the Prescott Agency and Aubrey to his high school studies, and routine observation, which explained how they both knew the basics of making a stew without ever being instructed or following a recipe. Like the dress she was wearing, the stew was also a hand-me-down from her mother.

Aside from adding too much salt, Aubrey did an admirable job with supper. The mood around the table was warm and pleasant, and Harriet allowed herself to envision the three of them living together contentedly. The notion, while wildly improbable, would have been absurd to contemplate just weeks ago. But Barbara's arrival into Harriet's world had shifted the boundaries of possibility. But would a life with a woman ever be practicable? As much as the idea thrilled her, the realities of how it might work and the risks involved were terrifying. Not wanting to spoil the evening's happy mood, she shoved the subject from her mind.

She wanted to ask Barbara for advice about how to engage the immigrant women at the tenement but hesitated; turning the conversation to her work was self-serving. Aubrey, however, had no such reservations. Unwittingly, he did her a favor by asking, "Did you find out who killed the journalist?"

Harriet was circumspect when sharing details of an investigation with her brother, confident that an exaggerated version would soon circulate across the schoolyard. Despite his promises, she knew tales involving real-life criminals and detectives would prove too much for a sixteen-year-old boy not to boast to his friends. In this case, by focusing on the women—Antonia, Mrs. Horak, and Edita—Harriet figured her brother would lose interest while Barbara would be rapt.

"It's about trust," Barbara said after hearing about the residents' reluctance to speak about the murder. "Or rather, lack of trust. Women come to this country with practically nothing. Often brought here by a father or husband, they probably don't know the language or customs. But it doesn't take long before they understand being a poor immigrant in America is often no better than the life they just traded away. My family is lucky. My uncle came here years before the rest of us and established a good business. When we arrived, he found us a place to live and gave my father and brothers jobs at his banner and badge shop. Most are not so fortunate. The women you met in the tenement fear a government they see as corrupt. They are not wrong. After all, from what you say, the police accused the Fara woman despite having no evidence. The other women would be foolish to get involved."

Harriet knew all that but appreciated that Barbara's remarks supported Matthew's belief that the injustice done to Mrs. Fara would be of greater interest to the women at the tenement than the crime done to Eugene Eldridge, a man who was a stranger to them.

With Susan in tow, Aubrey wandered off to his bedroom to finish his homework. Barbara insisted on helping Harriet clear the table and wash the dishes. They fell into an efficient rhythm while discussing various topics of the day, from the city's settlement houses to Barbara's saving for a bicycle to Susan's fast growth and obsession with chewing holes in Aubrey's socks. When it came time for Barbara to leave, Harriet walked her to the sidewalk. Barbara retrieved a nickel from her change purse, explaining with a smile, "I don't like to flash my fortune in a crowd." The number 104 streetcar would take her, if not with speed, safely with others to Polish Downtown, where she lived with her large family.

"Thank you for a lovely evening, Harriet Morrow. Please relay my thanks to our cook." Barbara leaned in and kissed Harriet's cheek. "Promise me you'll take care tomorrow. The jail is sure to be an unpleasant place."

"However frightful the environs, unlike poor Lucy Fara, I will be free to leave whenever I choose."

Harriet felt a pang in her chest as she lost sight of Barbara in the distance. Why hadn't she been able to return the kiss? How could she wish for more from Barbara when she couldn't reply to the affection shown to her? Compounding her unease, the past few days had emphasized the suddenness with which people came and went from each other's lives. Lucy Fara's children had lost their mother nearly as suddenly as she and Aubrey had lost their parents. For the first time, she considered Eugene Eldridge in that same light. To her, he was a victim. But surely, he had meant more to others, starting with being someone's son. Had he also been a brother? A husband and father? Had he any friends? Even working independently as a journalist, as Gerald Cole had said he did, he must have had other writers or publishers with whom he did business.

Harriet realized she had been dull-witted to limit her investigation to the moments immediately preceding and following the murder. What had transpired in the days or weeks leading up to the muckraker's final minutes? As Prescott had wondered aloud when assigning her to the case, why was Eugene Eldridge in the tenement that day? Who was he there to visit?

Chapter 6

Could just anyone visit a prisoner? Harriet should have considered the question before that morning. Although her initial plan was to meet with Lucy Fara straightaway, prudence dictated that she first consult with Mr. Prescott or Matthew McCabe about how to present herself at the city jail. When she arrived at the agency, Madelaine informed her that Mr. Prescott was away. Fortunately, her colleague was in his office.

"I've only visited the new jail once," Matthew said, "but I don't imagine the rules have changed much in a year. First, your presumption is correct—not just anyone can walk in off the street and ask to visit a prisoner. Were it otherwise, victims, enemies, accomplices, or simply the curious would be lining up at the cell door. I've heard from other operatives that, aside from an accused's lawyer, visitation rights are limited to immediate family members. However, there might be stricter rules for visiting your Mrs. Fara, who awaits trial for a capital crime."

Discouraged, Harriet slumped onto the guest chair by his desk. "So it's hopeless."

Matthew frowned, giving her a long look. "Good grief, Harriet. You act as though one little obstacle is tantamount to being tied to railroad tracks. I didn't take you for a damsel in distress. Instead of giving up so easily, you might ask how *I* managed to interview a jail inmate the very day I realized I needed to speak with him."

Harriet bolted upright. "How?"

"The inmate's brother presented me to jail staff as a third brother. I rode in on his coattails, as it were."

"But surely, the guards reviewed your identification. How did you explain having a different surname?"

"Obstacles, Harriet . . ."

". . . are to be overcome. Yes, I understand, but still—"

"She is Bohemian? Your Mrs. Fara?"

Harriet nodded.

"Given your fair complexion, I don't imagine you'd be convincing as her sister. A cousin, perhaps. But then you'd not be immediate family. I'm not sure that would work."

Springing to her feet, she said, "I have an idea."

"That's more like it. Care to share?"

She grabbed her coat. "I shall spare no detail . . . provided it works."

The jail's location at Dearborn Street and Illinois Street was between the agency and Harriet's apartment. She occasionally rode past it when taking a two-block diversion to her favorite bicycle shop for a new tire tube, oil for the gears, or a look at the latest Overman models. She imagined the jail's architect's intent was to intimidate visitors with monumental height and copious use of stone and brick. Adding to the building's imposing street presence, a half dozen policemen, clad in brass-buttoned long coats and tall, bowler-shaped hats, stood with nightsticks hanging from their belts before the broad arched entrance.

Once inside, Harriet followed the signs to the women's jail. Were it not for a cacophony of loud conversations and all manner of sounds from all directions, she might have heard her footsteps echo in the cavernous space of cold, hard surfaces and matching expressions. When a matron asked her if she was a relative of Lucy Fara, she smoothly replied "sister-in-law" and was handed a form to complete.

An hour later, Harriet shifted uncomfortably on the wooden bench she shared with three women of as many generations, who, judging by their interactions, were family. Harriet couldn't help but overhear the women's conversation about someone named "Lenny" and how he had got himself "in hot water this time." At first, Harriet wondered if she had misheard the male name. But after observing the comings and goings of other visitors, she realized the area was shared by those waiting to see a prisoner in the women's or the adolescents' jail—two sections separate from the men's jail that were a first for the city. Harriet also discerned that Lenny had turned a fight with a neighborhood boy into something more serious when he drew a knife and plunged it into his enemy's thigh. Despite facts accepted by Lenny's sister and mother, his grandmother was incredulous. "Lenny would never do such a thing. He'd never hurt anyone. He's a good boy." The eye rolls traded by mother and daughter said they didn't share the grandmother's convictions.

Harriet guessed that Lenny was roughly the same age as Aubrey. Over the years, her brother had had his share of schoolyard scuffles. Most recently, his eye had been blackened by a bully who was jealous that a particular girl was sweet on Aubrey instead of him. Thank heavens the other boy hadn't had a knife. As for Aubrey, he owned no weapon, and even if he had, she couldn't imagine him stabbing someone. Then again, could she be so sure? Was it possible that, like Lenny's grandmother, she held an idea of a loved one that had become outdated at some unmarked moment in the past? Aubrey would reach his age of majority in five years. That was a long time to rely on him to make only good choices and avoid situations that would put him where Lenny was at that moment. The thought made her anxious. Her brother ought to have a male role model in his life. But with no beau in her future, who? Not for the first time did she wonder if Matthew McCabe might not play that role in some small but still affecting way.

"Harriet Morrow!" the matron announced loudly.

Jumping to her feet, Harriet hurried to where the woman stood before a closed door. Despite having inspected Harriet's credentials an hour earlier, she barked, "You Morrow?"

"Yes. Harriet Morrow. I'm here to see my sister-in-law, Mrs. Lucy Fara."

Harriet dug into her handbag to prove her identity, but apparently satisfied, the matron flicked her head in the direction Harriet was to follow her. They traveled down a long corridor to still another guard and a gate of iron bars. Using a key from a ring fastened to her belt, the second guard unlocked the door. En route, Harriet was instructed to sit where she was told, keep her hands off the table, not raise her voice, and alert the guard inside if she wished to leave before her fifteen minutes were up. Under no circumstance was she to move from her chair unless accompanied by a matron. Harriet was already apprehensive, so the *clang* of the disengaged lock gave her a start. A third guard stationed inside the room escorted her to one of four small tables, each positioned at a maximum distance from the others and the walls.

Lucy Fara sat slumped in a chair. Seeing her, Harriet realized she had formed an expectation about Lucy's appearance based on the other women she'd met at the tenement. Her idea of a dark-haired, strong-framed woman in her twenties was wrong. Lucy was older, late thirties, and couldn't have weighed more than one hundred pounds in heavy shoes. But what stood out most was her thicket of curly reddish-brown hair. Harriet lowered herself onto the chair opposite as the guard returned to standing by the barred gate.

"Thank you for seeing me, Mrs. Fara," Harriet said, her voice lowered.

"I have no sister-in-law"—Lucy added a disparaging sniff—"only a sister in Prague. She'd never come even if she could."

Harriet knew she must first explain her position and purpose with dispatch, presuming that once Lucy understood her intention, she'd willingly, if not eagerly, divulge everything she knew about the body she'd found in the hallway. Again, Harriet's preconception of Lucy Fara was wrong.

"I know nothing about that," Lucy said wearily. "I can't help you. You've wasted your time."

"Perhaps you misunderstand, Mrs. Fara. By finding the journalist's true killer, I will prove your innocence. You'll be freed." Registering Lucy's continued disinterest, Harriet tried another approach, "I confess, I don't know all of the official procedures involved in returning one's children in such cases, but, mark my words, I shall do whatever I can to help reunite you with your young ones as soon as possible."

Lucy scoffed, "Freed? Trading one cell for another? At least this one promises a way out of my misery."

Harriet examined the woman across from her, too stunned to speak. She never thought a person's life could feel so hopeless that she'd prefer its end over another option.

"But your children, surely—"

"They are better off," Lucy sighed. "What can I offer them? I have nothing. Nothing."

A long moment passed. Every second was precious, but Harriet needed to think. This was likely to be her one chance to speak with Lucy, who had probably granted the visit out of curiosity—that wouldn't work a second time. Harriet was no psychologist, but it was clear the woman had sunk low into despair. Convincing her that she had reason to be hopeful didn't seem possible—not in the short time remaining. Again, a different approach was needed.

"I don't imagine the food at the orphanage to be much good, but you're correct that the children's bowls will at least be filled each day. And they'll be kept safe from trouble, too busy working and, when not, too exhausted for anything other than sleep."

Lucy's eyes flashed with alarm. "Work? They're only children."

"There's no reason to worry, I'm sure. The authorities know what's best. Children are nothing if not adaptable. I've no doubt yours have already become used to living apart from you and now from one another at different orphanages." In truth, Mrs. Horak had told Harriett that the children had been taken in pairs. Still, the description of the situation was close enough to the sad reality. "As for you, Mrs. Fara, I commend your loyalty. By refusing to speak about the crime, you are surely saving the life of a neighbor who would otherwise be accused—falsely or not. However, I must say, it's unfortunate that the other women aren't as grateful for your loyalty. Listening to them talk, I was nearly convinced you *did* kill that man."

While Harriet spoke, Lucy's face grew red. "Who?" she said, the word sounding like a curse. "Who said I killed him?"

Harriet brushed a hand casually through the air. "That hardly matters. But if you must know, Antonia, Edita, Mrs. Horak . . . everyone, I suppose." She didn't relish lying, but if that's what it took to employ Lucy's help in saving her own skin, she would.

"Liars!" Lucy seethed in anger. "That man was a stranger. I'd never seen him before in my life."

Steady . . . Like coaxing Susan out from under the bed, an abrupt move could threaten to halt progress. Harriet said, "But you *were* with him when he died."

Lucy pounded a fist on the table. Harriet jumped at the outburst.

"Hey, there!" the guard shouted. "Keep it down over there, or I'll haul you out."

"*With* him?" Lucy hissed under her breath. "I'd never laid eyes on that man before. I heard shouts in the building. People running down the staircase. There was a fight in the hallway. I was frightened. I listened, my ear to the door." Lucy paused in reflection, dropping her head. "Such horrible sounds. Then silence. The silence was worse than the shouting. When I was sure they'd gone, I opened the door. The hallway was dark, but with light from my apartment, I could see a man was on the floor. He wasn't moving. Still, I dared not go near him. I asked if he needed help. If he was all right. But I knew he wouldn't answer. He couldn't. There was too much blood. I told the children to stay inside and not open the door no matter what. I grabbed my coat and locked the door. It took some doing to get around him and not step in the blood. I ran to the police station and told them what had happened. Two policemen followed me back. The next thing I knew, they accused me of killing him and brought me here."

"Five minutes!" the guard called out.

Harriet turned toward the gate and received the end of a pointed finger. The ticking clock demanded she come straight out and ask, "I don't suppose you noticed an object, say a book or case or bag, a bundle of papers, perhaps? Anything lying near the body or observable on his person?"

"No, not that I recall. But again, it was dark. And the blood. I can't be certain. It all happened so fast."

"And you didn't"—Harriet knew her next question would agitate Lucy, but she asked it nonetheless—"examine his coat pockets or wallet?"

In an instant, Lucy's anger returned. "You take me for a thief, now? Have you listened to a word I've said? I told you. I didn't touch him."

"Yes, I understand, Mrs. Fara. My apologies. You also said you had never seen the man before, but do you have any idea, even a guess, about who he had been there to see? He didn't just wander in off the street. There was a reason he was there that day."

"I don't know."

"The shouting you first heard. Think back. Could you tell which part of the building it came from? Was it downstairs, on your floor, or above on the third?" Harriet presumed it must have been above or below; otherwise, Lucy's account of footsteps on the staircase would not make sense. But knowing which floor would winnow the list of apartments Eugene Eldridge might have been there to visit.

"The third." Lucy punctuated her answer with a sharp nod, her confidence negating the need for Harriet to ask if she was sure.

How much time remained? A minute? Two at most? Harriet speeded the pace of questioning. "Your neighbors upstairs—is there anyone in particular who seemed unusual or suspicious?"

"What do you mean?"

"Did you suspect anyone of criminal activity?"

"You think because we are poor, we are thieves and killers?"

Footsteps approached.

Harriet stared hard into Lucy's eyes as if the strength of her gaze could unlock a final vital recollection in the woman's mind. "Is there anything? Anything more you can remember?"

"Time's up," the guard said, tapping Harriet's shoulder. "Let's go, miss."

Standing, Harriet resumed her fictitious role, offering a comforting smile to her sister-in-law. "Do try to keep up your spirits, dear Lucy."

Harriet was halfway to the door when Lucy said, "My children." Harriet turned back. "Please see they are taken care of."

"That's enough," the guard scolded. "Visit's over."

Harriet was shoved from the room before she could answer. She was grateful. For as much as she wanted to promise the woman that all would turn out all right, she couldn't. It remained the case that the Fara children's only chance to be returned to their mother was for Harriet to find Eugene Eldridge's real killer. Given what little she had accomplished so far, she wasn't sure she would.

Chapter 7

Harriet could think of no better place for a next step than the *Progressive Age*. The newspaper was the unofficial voice of Chicago's progressive movement. If Eugene Eldridge had indeed been intent on proving a powerful alderman's corruption, the *Progressive Age* was the type of publication that would have supported his journalistic efforts. Perhaps the paper's editor had commissioned the story that got him killed or at least worked with him in the past. Either way, he could refer her to like-minded publications that might have employed Eldridge.

The *Progressive Age* offices were on the second floor of a squat brick building west of downtown and alongside the river, near her former bookkeeping job at the Rock Island Grain Elevator. No receptionist or secretary sat stationed at the entrance. Instead, a large room was filled with a dozen desks at odd angles and occupied by men scribbling in notebooks, clacking away at typewriters, or reading from stacks of documents piled so high she could make out only the tops of their heads. Standing in the doorway, looking uncertain, she caught the eye of a man at the back of the room. He immediately began zigzagging his way toward her with a stride so smooth she imagined he could balance a book on his head without its falling.

Uncommonly tall, he had his white shirtsleeves rolled to his elbows, revealing long forearms no thicker than a rolling pin. He was bald and wore a long beard and monocle.

"Can I help you, miss?"

Harriet introduced herself as an operative with the Prescott Detective Agency and explained that she was looking into the recent death of an independent journalist named Eugene Eldridge. The name drew a visible reaction.

"Wait here." He crossed the room, plucked a hat and coat from a stand, and rejoined her at the doorway. "Please. Follow me," he said, before descending the staircase.

Wary of leaving with him, she was reassured by the weight of her derringer inside her handbag. Mr. Prescott had instructed her to keep it loaded, and it was. But should danger befall her, asking an assailant to kindly pause his attack while she retrieved her pistol from her purse would never do. She made a mental note to look into a concealable holster that would enable quick access to her gun. She grumbled quietly, appreciating the disadvantage of a woman's jacket compared to the looser—and more preferable—fit of a man's suit coat.

Once outside, the tall man turned back abruptly. Harriet shrieked. He raised his hands, showing he meant no harm. "I didn't mean to startle you, miss. My name is Alexi Scholtz. I am the newspaper's editor. I apologize for the precaution, but since Eugene's murder, we are all on tenterhooks. As much as I trust every one of my reporters, I can no longer be certain. And before you point out that both statements cannot be true, I'll acknowledge as much. Such are the times we live in. Nothing but discord. Opposing forces of right and wrong. Still, I'm proud that this paper's moral clarity has not been blurred despite the efforts of those wielding power in this city. The few that rule will stop at nothing to hold on to power. Nothing. Eugene's murder is only the latest proof."

"So you knew him," Harriet blurted excitedly. "You knew Eugene Eldridge?"

"As a journalist, yes. Eugene was one of our more regular contributors, writing a story or two each month."

A thought struck. "So you and he had occasion to correspond by mail? Would you have his home address?"

Alexi Scholtz recited an address on Wells Street, shockingly, in a building on the same block where Harriet lived with her brother. He tapped the side of his head. "Facts and figures I remember. It's part of the business." Returning to the subject of Eugene's work, he said, "For the past three months, Eugene had been working exclusively on a piece he promised would 'shake the foundation of City Hall.' I expressed interest, of course. With such a claim, what editor wouldn't? I made him promise I'd have the first right to consider running the story when he'd finished. He said he was 'dangerously close'—his very words. That was just last week."

"And you've no idea, none at all, about who or what he was looking into?"

"Chicago being Chicago, I've no shortage of guesses but nothing definitive. The two First Ward aldermen might top the list. One of them is Irish Dan, otherwise known as Daniel Walsh. If I had to bet, I'd put my money on the other, Mike Powers. He's known to everyone as Saloon Micky. They're both as corrupt as the day is long. If you are wondering how Powers got his name, 'Saloon' refers to his stake in dozens of bars and taverns in the Levee District. Whether he owns them, has a share, or extorts the owners has proven hard to learn. But make no mistake, he takes a large share of the profits. His business dealings, if they can be called that, aren't limited to liquor sales. He's also known to have a hand in many of the area's brothels and burlesque clubs. No one dares challenge him. Those who do are made an example of. A few months back, couldn't have been more than two or three, his purported bookkeeper, a fellow who went by the name Bat, was discovered savagely murdered."

Registering Harriet's curiosity, he explained, "Nicknames go with the territory, miss. You see, Bat was rumored to work only at night. I imagine the name's implied menace appealed to the bully. It was said the difference between Bat and a bulldog is that a bulldog has a bit of charm and two ears. Bat lost one of his to a meat cleaver in a bar fight when coming up the ranks. All that remained on his right side was a twisted mound of pink flesh. If you tried speaking to him from that side, he'd take it as an insult and backhand you to next Tuesday. Still, Bat's tough-guy reputation didn't protect him from someone slitting his throat from ear to . . . well, you get my meaning. His body was stuffed into a burlap bag and tossed in the river. Make no mistake, it was a warning. Otherwise, his body would never have been found. Trust me, in Chicago, dozens go missing every year without a trace. Word on the street is that Bat crossed his boss, Saloon Micky. That's not something you do if you want to see the next sunrise."

"And you think Eugene Eldridge was looking into the matter?"

"Eugene was a good reporter. Excellent, in fact. And shrewd. Now, this is mere rumor, I have no way to verify this, but as Saloon Micky's bookkeeper, Bat would have had access to a trove of damning information about his boss. My guess is that Eugene was in pursuit of that information. If that were the case, it would have been a race against time."

Registering Harriet's questioning look, he explained, "Once Saloon Micky got wind that Bat was betraying him, Bat's days—if he had any left—would have been numbered. But Bat had some insurance as protection—the financial information, presumably illegal payments, and various other records of criminal activity. You see, Bat must have known that his only way to survive was if his boss was stopped first, either arrested or killed. Trying to eliminate Powers would be perilous. However, if my newspaper or any other published hard evidence of Saloon Micky's crimes, the authorities would have been forced to act, and Bat might have stood a chance at surviving."

"But that didn't happen," Harriet observed.

"Before Eldridge had secured the alleged proof, Bat was murdered. But Eldridge believed the evidence was still out there. If he could find it, not only would Saloon Micky be charged with extortion but perhaps also Bat's murder."

"And you didn't attempt to get answers from Eldridge."

"Of course I did, but he refused to share all that he knew . . . or suspected. The secrecy surrounding his investigation was all a part of stirring my interest and ultimately driving up the price. Depending on its scope, I might have ended up bidding against the *Tribune*."

"Perhaps another of your reporters, then?"

He shook his head, confused. "Another of them, what?"

"Is it possible Mr. Eldridge shared more information about his investigation with another of your reporters?"

Alexi Scholtz considered the question for longer than it seemed to warrant. "It's possible. However, I very much doubt it for all the reasons I've already mentioned. A man like Eugene would protect a story with his life." Catching the irony of his remark, he added, "I suppose he did just that, didn't he? But no, Eugene would have feared another reporter would steal the byline."

"You said, 'It's possible.' Who were you thinking of?"

Before he could say otherwise, his expression confirmed he did have someone in mind.

"Please, Mr. Scholtz, whoever murdered Eugene Eldridge can't be allowed to get away scot-free. As long as the killer remains at large, he poses a threat to others—journalists in particular."

Whether concerned for his or his men's safety, perhaps both, Alexi Scholtz led Harriet back inside the office and pointed to a nearby desk where a younger man sat absorbed in work, his fingertips working the keyboard of a hulking black typewriter. The man hadn't noticed Harriet when she'd first arrived, but sensing he was the focus of his boss's attention, he looked up. Alexi Scholtz introduced the man as Steven Bliss and left them to talk.

Harriet wrinkled her nose before considering the message the gesture sent. Steven Bliss smelled like sweaty socks and garlic, and his appearance reminded her of an unmade bed. After she'd explained the reason for her visit, the young reporter convinced her that he knew nothing about the big story that Eugene Eldridge had purportedly been working on. If anything, Steven appeared vexed to have not heard about it before.

When Harriet mentioned Saloon Micky and Irish Dan, the corrupt First Ward aldermen, Steven scowled. "Eugene loathed the Gray Wolves, but even a man of his conviction would be foolish to go up against one of them."

"The Gray Wolves?"

"You say you live in the city?"

"All my life," she replied proudly.

"I suppose it's possible a person like yourself hasn't heard of them. But every newspaperman or business owner in the Levee District can't avoid them. No matter how hard they may try. The Gray Wolves have their grubby fingers in every pie. Saloon Micky and Irish Dan aren't the only ones, but they're purported to be the most powerful. They're also rivals, as you might guess. Irish Dan is . . . well, Irish. Saloon Micky's real name is Mike *Powers*." Steven Bliss scoffed and raised his hands upward. "Seems he was destined for greatness. I take it you've never seen the man?"

Harriet demurred. Although she had briefly met Alderman Powers when he had arrived at the University Settlement, she didn't want to influence what Steve Bliss might say about him.

Steven scoffed again. "Suspecting you will one day, I'll let you make your own judgment. Suffice it to say, he thinks he is quite the ladies' man. Ladies, I'm sure, will beg to differ."

Harriet sidestepped the intriguing comment in pursuit of the information she'd come for. "And Eugene Eldridge? You were colleagues. Were you on good terms?"

Steven told her that he and Eugene had occasionally shared a drink at a local tavern after work. Hearing the word "tavern" raised Harriet's hopes. Nothing lubricated lips like a strong pint. When asked about Eugene's personal life, Steven disappointed her with the news that Eugene never spoke of any family, but then he contradicted himself by saying that Eugene had been engaged to marry.

"Jorinda, it was. Jorinda Grimm." Steven said. "When Eugene first told me, I nearly fell off my chair. Eugene wasn't a particularly handsome fellow, but that's not why I was so surprised to hear his news. Eugene was a solitary sort. Quiet and reserved to an unusual degree. When you got him alone, he could be amiable enough, but in the company of other people, he'd say nary a word. Poor fellow had a stutter, you see. I always thought it was one of the reasons he turned to art and writing—ways to communicate without having to speak. But then, he never said. Which goes to my point."

Steven went on to say Eugene grew up in Philadelphia, had a passion for art, and spent countless hours roaming the halls of the Art Institute. Although he dreamed of becoming a painter, filing stories as a muckraker proved to be a more pragmatic way to pay his rent. Otherwise, Steven claimed to know nothing more about Eugene's private life—except for one final recollection he offered as an afterthought. Eugene Eldridge met his fiancée at a meeting of socialist radicals. For a moment, Harriet couldn't decide if she was more shocked by the news or the fact that Steven had almost failed to mention it. Her eyes grew wider still upon learning that the radicals called themselves the People's Cause.

Harriet prodded, asking, "Mr. Eldridge's mention of such

a nefarious-sounding group must have stirred your interest. Am I to believe you didn't inquire further? If anyone would, I should think it would be a reporter."

"I did!" Steven shot back defensively. "Of that, you can be sure. But Eugene was on his third or fourth pint by then. Even sober, the man would work himself into a lather about City Hall corruption and the Gray Wolves feeding from the public trough, giving away sweetheart deals to utility contractors for kickbacks and extorting every business in their ward by demanding protection money. Hearing that Eugene attended a People's Cause meeting was hardly surprising. Like him, they loathe the current government. The difference between them is what they were willing to do about it. Eugene's purpose was to publish and expose criminal activities to the public. The People's Cause, on the other hand, believes that corruption is so entrenched that nothing short of revolution will root out the crooks. Opposition to dirty politicians is understandable, but the radicals' beliefs go much deeper than that. To them, any form of hierarchical government is anathema to human beings' nature. I assume Eugene was infiltrating the People's Cause as part of some story he was working on at the time. One thing you should know about Eugene is that he was very thorough, working every angle and considering contrasting viewpoints."

"And how did your conversation with him end?" Harriet asked.

"Eugene got so angry talking about the subject that he abruptly got up and stormed off." Turning somber, Steven added, "That was the last time I saw him."

"And when was that?"

Steven's reply took no thought. "Three weeks ago to the day."

"You seem sure?"

Steven sniffed. "I remember all right. Eugene left me with the bill."

* * *

Harriet reveled in pedaling her Victoria at top speed. Swerving around pedestrians and buggies and passing streetcars, she drew angry looks from conductors whose consternation was compounded by their passengers' shouted encouragement. Traveling to the apartment building near her own, she wondered if she might have seen Eugene Eldridge on past occasions. If he had lived in the neighborhood for long, the odds were good that she had. After all, aside from the several years between her parents' deaths and inheriting the family apartment, she had always lived on that same block of Wells Street. Fortunately, she was friendly with several residents in Eldridge's building. Learning which apartment was his should be easy enough. But first, she'd need to find a way inside.

After returning her bicycle to her own apartment, she walked up the street. The entrance was unlocked, and a directory on the vestibule wall listed Eugene Eldridge as occupying number 4A. She frowned at seeing no elevator and hiked to the fourth floor, grateful the staircase was wide and well-lighted. Apartment 4A was in the back, next to a large, cracked window leading to a fire escape. Fortunately, no one was around to observe a nonresident hovering outside the apartment of a recently murdered man. She had never picked a lock but saw no risk in trying as long as the hallway remained empty. She removed her bowler and plucked a pin from her hair. After straightening the bit of wire, she slipped the pin into the lock and, with her other hand, twisted the handle. The door creaked open with a loud and unnerving squeak. Not only was the apartment unlocked, but whoever came out last also hadn't properly closed the door. She glanced behind her. With the corridor still empty, she snuck inside and closed the door tightly behind her.

It took all of a half second for Harriet to register that Eugene's home had been ransacked. Papers were strewn about the floor, sofa cushions were overturned, drawers hung open, and pictures had been yanked from the walls.

She nearly tripped over an appointment ledger from which pages had been ripped. Should she take it? Dare she? It had been days since Eldridge's murder. Whoever had been here before couldn't have been the police. Had the authorities even bothered to search his home? Were they doing anything to find Eldridge's killer? Had the ledger been larger, she might not have taken it, but since it fit easily in her handbag, she made her decision.

She moved to the other rooms—the kitchen, bedroom, and bathroom—observing a similar chaotic state. Would her own search amount to anything? She doubted it. Whoever preceded her had done a thorough job. And unlike her, they presumably knew what they were looking for.

Back in the sitting room, an easel holding a canvas caught her attention as one of the few items left undisturbed. Eugene had been painting a nude female figure, though the woman's sideways pose and the manner in which her long, dark hair fell across her body masked her private areas. A table next to the easel that had held a supply of charcoals, brushes, and paints had been overturned, leaving a frenzy of color on the floorboards that reminded Harriet of the splatter-barrel pictures she and her brother enjoyed making at the annual Cook County Fair.

Harriet wasn't a student of art, though she did enjoy many of the illustrations in *Harper's Weekly*. And yet something told her Eugene Eldridge had possessed talent. That he would never finish the portrait—doubtless now destined for the rubbish bin in the alley—overwhelmed her with sadness.

Ten minutes later, Harriet was greeted by Susan as she entered her apartment. The kitten reliably brightened her mood. Susan followed her into the bedroom and curiously watched as Harriet cleared items from the top of her bureau. She would properly hang the canvas frame later. For now, the sketch of the nude woman would sit on her bureau, leaning against the wall.

She thumbed through Eldridge's ledger. Someone had

haphazardly ripped most of the pages for the past few weeks from the binding. However, several remaining partial pages indicated a few of Eldridge's appointments in the weeks preceding his death. Among them were the barbershop, the People's Cause, Chicago property records, and the *Progressive Age*. Most curious was the inclusion of addresses for immigration records departments in Boston, New York, Boston, Baltimore, Philadelphia, and New Orleans—the primary points of entry for newcomers— along with a notation of a letter received from one city just days before his murder. The portions of the pages that might have contained additional information were missing. If there were valuable clues in what she was seeing, they were not obvious. Still, the recent chronicling of Eugene Eldridge's interests suggested he was looking for something—or, perhaps, *someone*.

Chapter 8

"The People's Cause." Theodore Prescott said the name slowly, appearing to savor its intriguing sound as he might a sip of scotch. "And they are radicals, you say?"

"Socialist radicals or radical socialists," Harriet replied. "Either way, Eugene Eldridge attended at least one of their meetings. He met a woman named Jorinda Grimm there. That must have been some time ago as they were to be wed. Naturally, I am eager to speak with this Jorinda, but finding one woman in a city of more than a million and a half people will take some doing. If I can learn more about the People's Cause, specifically where and when they meet, I might get lucky and find her there. At least someone in attendance might know her or her whereabouts."

Prescott sat taller, though the top of his head still didn't exceed the height of his chair's back. Harriet recognized his increased interest. It seemed Theodore Prescott had three settings, each of which was calibrated to his level of engagement with a subject: sitting comfortably, spine straight as a broom handle, and too excited to stay seated.

He leaned forward. "The woman's beliefs place her on the fringes of political thought. To counter the isolation of her rabble-rousing notions, she will seek the company of those with a like mind. However, to catch your bird, you must first locate the flock. I've not heard of the People's Cause. There must be dozens of organizations agitating for better wages, an eight-hour workday, cleaner water, safer working conditions, lower taxes . . . The list is endless. Fortunately, our country has a time-honored mechanism to effect change." He raised a finger as if declaring a personal triumph. "The ballot box."

"I see." Harriet's eyes twinkled with mischief. "So you're a supporter of suffrage then?"

The moment's silence signaled either Prescott's quiet consideration or impending admonishment. She squeezed her handbag in preparation for the latter, as if a firm grip would help her to withstand the blowback.

"Point taken, Miss Morrow. If I didn't know better, I'd think you were in cahoots with Mrs. Prescott."

Although Harriet had never met her boss's wife, in that instant, she had another reason to like her. The first was the kindness shown to her seventy-two-year-old next-door neighbor, Pearl Bartlett. Harriet had befriended Pearl when searching for the woman's missing maid—Harriet's first case was a begrudging favor from Mr. Prescott to his wife. It was because of Pearl that Harriet owned several fine pieces of men's clothing, all hand-me-downs from the late Mr. Bartlett. Although she'd been married for most of her adult life, Pearl confided in Harriet that it had been a union of mutual convenience—the couple had never shared a bed or had children. Pearl further stunned Harriet by sharing that she had loved a woman early in life. The revelation was both encouraging and cautionary: Harriet shouldn't allow societal conventions to dictate who she could and couldn't love. Had it not been for Pearl, Harriet was quite sure she'd not have the courage to entertain a romance with Barbara.

Harriet continued her report, informing Prescott that the men at the *Progressive* Age newspaper had mentioned Aldermen Daniel Walsh and Mike Powers and shared their suspicions that one of them might have been the subject of Eugene Eldridge's investigation.

"Don't know much about Irish Dan, but Saloon Micky is a scoundrel. He is nothing but a two-bit gangster masquerading as an upstanding politician. Without unassailable proof of Saloon Micky's crimes, making an accusation against him would be as foolish as a mouse taunting an alley cat. If he is indeed involved, the precaution of the anonymous note sent to Gerald Cole is understandable. A person would be wise to exercise care and not gain his attention. He's one of several aldermen, along with Irish Dan, known as the Gray Wolves. Your expression tells me you've heard of them."

"Yes, but only recently. From the young reporter Steven Bliss at the *Progressive Age*."

"The Gray Wolves are blackguards." Prescott practically spat the words. "How Chicago has managed to become one of the world's great cities despite so many of our civic leaders being nothing more than grandiose pickpockets is a marvel. Imagine the heights we could achieve with men like Carnegie and Morgan in charge."

Harriet doubted that ousting corrupt men only to replace them with society's richest would be much of an improvement. In particular, Carnegie's muted response to the violent melee instigated by his CEO, Henry Clay Frick, at his Homestead steel plant was reason enough to prove him unsuitable for public office. But arguing the point with an admirer of the industrialists would gain her nothing. She remained silent on the matter, grateful her boss was at least on the side of men like Gerald Cole and his colleagues at the Municipal Voters' League.

Before leaving Prescott's office, Harriet was handed the name of a well-known socialist organization, the Socialist Labor Party, which had spawned the short-lived International Working People's Association, implicated in the 1886 Haymarket Square bombing. Prescott's most senior and rotund operative, Charles Bonner, was the agency's resident authority on socialist activities. Harriet had never spoken with Mr. Bonner, but his reputation for orneriness preceded him. Having worked at the agency for three weeks, she'd already witnessed him berate a clerk for a single misspelling in a voluminous case file, reducing the young man to tears. Harriet wasn't afraid of Bonner, but she did fear her own tongue if he spoke to her as he did the secretaries, which amounted to barking orders with a disparaging "And do it right this time" or "Damnit to hell, don't take all day, woman!"

With her hand raised to his office door's frosted pane, she hesitated. At moments like this, memories of her father's words provided encouragement: "Wading into chilly water will only prolong your discomfort, Harriet. Better to jump and get it over with."

She rapped her knuckles on the spot where SENIOR OPERATIVE was stenciled onto the glass.

"I'm busy!" growled the voice from within.

Unpleasantness, she could manage, but she wouldn't accept being refused a moment of his time. Besides, given a detective's frenetic schedule, it could be hours, even days, before she found him again at his desk. She was fortunate to find him present on her first attempt. Calling to mind Prescott's instruction, "Don't dillydally, Miss Morrow," she took a deep breath and opened the door.

Hearing someone enter, Bonner jerked in surprise. Harriet's eyes immediately fell on the playing cards neatly arranged on his desk in a pattern she recognized as the solitaire game.

"Tarnation, woman! Have you wool in your ears? I said I was busy."

Harriet's low opinion of the man, formed by his poor treatment of everyone except Theodore Prescott, to whom he kowtowed in a most obsequious manner, sank to a new depth upon seeing him loafing on the job. Ignoring his rebuke, she coolly replied, "Mr. Prescott suggested I consult with you. Unless you'd prefer that I report back to him that you are"—she swept her gaze across the neat columns of cards—"otherwise engaged, I will appreciate your help."

Bonner cursed under his breath, but not so low that Harriet didn't hear his foul language. With a single swipe, he dumped the cards into an open desk drawer and slammed it shut. "Whatever it is. Make it quick."

Harriet couldn't abide a man like Charles Bonner thinking he was in a position to give orders. He was senior to her, but that was all. If there was to be any respect between them, it must go both ways. She pulled out a chair and sat.

Countering his obvious annoyance, she straightened her spine. "My current investigation requires that I find a certain individual who is likely a member of the People's Cause. Presuming you, like everyone else I've spoken with, know nothing about the organization, I plan to begin my inquiries at the Socialist Labor Party with the hope that someone there has knowledge of the other organization. As Mr. Prescott considers you our resident expert on the socialist movement, I would appreciate it if you would kindly point me in the right direction."

"*Our* expert on the subject?" He sniggered. "As if *you* are one of *us*?" As stinging as the remark was, he wasn't finished. "I'll have you know, the Prescott Detective Agency has been in operation for over sixteen years. I have been Mr. Prescott's senior-most operative for fifteen of them. In all that time, we have never had a woman detective. Moreover, the daft notion has never come up. And for a good reason. It's high time, young lady, that someone tells you plainly that this job—"

Harriet raised a hand, cutting him short. "This *job* is *my* job. Frankly, Mr. Bonner, whether or not you would have hired me is irrelevant. It also holds no interest for me. As you are keenly aware, this is the Prescott Agency, not the Bonner Agency. If you have an issue with my employment, you are free to take it up with your superior—who, to be clear, is the same as mine. Now, I don't doubt you are eager to return to your important work"—another glance at his desktop—"so, I'll ask again. The Socialist Labor Party. What can you tell me about them? How might you suggest I infiltrate their ranks?"

Bonner's dark expression didn't brighten, but at some point during her speech, he silently calculated that telling her what she wanted to know would be less onerous than a subsequent visit from Prescott.

"These days, the SLP wields little influence. Police cracked down on them after the Haymarket bombing. They used to meet every month or so. Their gatherings are not well publicized, but neither are they a secret. Anyone can attend. However, fewer and fewer see the point. Regarding the other group . . . The People's Cause, you say?"

Harriet nodded.

"Never heard of them."

Disappointed, she tried, "The SLP, where and when is their next meeting?"

"As I'm not a member, I can't say." He glanced at his desk drawer, signaling impatience with the prolonged conversation.

"Then perhaps as the agency's most senior detective, you'll do me the favor of making the inquiries necessary to find out."

Whatever collegial assistance was traded among operatives was yet to include her—with the notable exception of Matthew McCabe. She wasn't so prideful that she'd not ask for help when needed, but she would never grovel, loathe to confirm any man's wrongheaded belief that only by riding his coattails could she succeed at the job. Bonner's and the other men's skepticism would be refuted by one thing: her solving cases on her own.

The senior detective stared back at her, half leering, half smirking, and exuding disdain as clearly as if strong-arming her out to the sidewalk. *How tiresome,* she thought. As much as Bonner enjoyed games, he was wasting her time. "As a junior operative, it is hardly my place to issue you a command, Mr. Bonner. That is the purview of Mr. Prescott alone." Holding her forced smile, she waited for a beat before adding, "To whom I shall speak forthwith." She stood and turned toward the door.

"Wait!"

A minute later, Harriet was in the hallway, hurrying toward her office. She had until the next morning, when Bonner had told her to return. He felt confident that by then he could find out when and where the Socialist Labor Party would next meet. As it was late in the afternoon, she would finish the day typing a report for Mr. Prescott. She had never questioned the value of chronicling her activities for the boss; it was a requirement of every operative. But the routine delivered a secondary benefit she had come to appreciate. Summarizing her progress in succinct, factual statements, as Prescott demanded, crystallized a case in her mind. Her scattered thoughts were forced into a coherent narrative. It was a sobering exercise. Gaps in her understanding became more pronounced. What story was Eugene Eldridge working on? Who was the subject of his exposé? Why was he visiting the tenement the day he was killed? If he had indeed possessed proof of a politician's corruption, what happened to it?

Harriet unrolled the paper from the typewriter, reread the text for spelling errors, and, satisfied, reached for her bowler on the coat stand. Matthew's door was closed, and there was no light from within. His absence confirmed her idea to pay Pearl Bartlett a visit before it became too late. Harriet hadn't seen Pearl for a week and missed her motherly reassurance—especially on matters of romance.

Chicago had several neighborhoods and prominent streets featuring resplendent mansions. The most prestigious was Prairie Avenue, south of downtown, just blocks from the lake. Harriet knew the best route to travel by bicycle.

She'd made the journey numerous times in the preceding weeks. This time, however, she would arrive not as a detective but as a friend.

"Harry!" Pearl wrapped her arms around Harriet, pulling her into a tight hug. The woman's bony arms belied her strength. Her unkempt white hair smelled of cinnamon. Toby, Pearl's large white cat, circled their legs. As sudden as was the embrace, Pearl held Harriet at arm's length and said, "I see you've returned to wearing dresses. That's a story I very much want to hear. But not without dessert and a glass of milk."

Harriet followed Pearl and Toby into the mansion's kitchen.

"Where's Abigail?" Harriet asked, referring to Pearl's new maid.

"Girl wasn't a scrubber. Dragging a broom across the middle of the floor isn't my idea of thorough cleaning. On top of that, she burned the bacon three mornings in a row."

Knowing how bitterly Pearl complained when her former maid went missing, Harriet said, "But how will you manage such a large house by yourself?"

"The service is sending others for me to interview. I don't have high hopes. With most girls, I spend more time pointing out what they missed or showing them how to do the job properly than they do cleaning! I wonder why I bother."

Harriet was aware of Pearl's exacting standards, but suspected she had set an unreasonably high bar based not only on the performance of her former maid, Agnes, but also on her affection for the young woman.

"So are you going to explain your wearing a dress or what?"

Over an enormous slice of pecan pie, Harriet explained her change in attire by catching Pearl up on her new investigation.

"But you're still wearing a man's hat and shoes," Pearl

observed. "Good for you, Harry. Never let anyone rob you of what makes you, you."

Mistaking Harriet for a man at their first-ever meeting, Pearl had called her Harry. After several corrections, Harriet had given up on making her real name stick. Truth be told, she found the older woman calling her Harry endearing. It spoke to their surrogate mother-daughter relationship. That they were both attracted to women added particular strength to their bond.

Pearl eventually asked, "How are you getting on with that new Polish friend of yours?"

Harriet readily shared her apprehensions and uncertainties—discussing the matter was, after all, the primary reason she'd come.

"You do realize, Harry, that Barbara is likely to be every bit as anxious as you are. Declaring one's affection takes courage. You're not a person who takes such things lightly. And nothing you've said about Barbara suggests she's any different. The interest you share in one another isn't understood by most people out there." Pearl spun a finger in the air as if it were a lasso. "But there's a lot of people who don't understand a lot of things. Never let the ignorance of others stifle your spirit. Do so, and you'll live a life of regret." She reached across the table and grasped Harriet's hands. "I know something about regret, Harry. Mind you, hardly did I suffer in this grand pile of bricks with a decent man as a companion. But neither did I experience the joy of being in love. At some point, you, and only you, must decide if love is worth the risk."

While Pearl spoke, Harriet's eyes teared at the corners. The woman's words touched her deeply, resonating wisdom that didn't sugarcoat romance like the lyrics of "Dear Midnight of Love," which played softly on the phonograph.

> *Dear Midnight of Love,*
> *Why did we meet?*

Dear Midnight of Love
Your face is so sweet.
Pure as the angels above,
Surely again we shall speak,
Loving only as doves,
Dear Midnight of Love.

Pearl tilted her head toward the music. "As you probably know, that's May de Sousa singing. But did you know that John Coughlin wrote that number?"

The reference to the notorious ward heeler and alderman yanked Harriet's thoughts back to her investigation. Pearl had lived in Chicago for decades. As a wealthy resident likely to have contributed to various politicians' campaigns over the years, her perspectives on the mayor and other city authorities could provide an interesting insight into Harriet's case.

Pearl confirmed the rampant corruption in City Hall. She explained that the Gray Wolves, especially the two First Ward aldermen, ruled a political machine based on graft and protection money from the numerous saloons, brothels, and gambling dens in the Levee District, just south of the Loop, the portion of elevated train that encircled the main downtown area. Their annual First Ward Ball reliably attracted thousands of guests and was notorious for outrageous costumes and immoral behavior, rumored to devolve into orgiastic pleasures. When Harriet shared the reporter Steven Bliss's guess that Eugene Eldridge had his sights set on Saloon Micky, Pearl replied, "If that muckraker had tried, he'd have been playing with fire while wearing a suit doused in kerosene. There can't be much wonder he didn't live long enough to succeed. Whether it's other aldermen, ward underbosses, police captains, county attorneys, city inspectors, or department commissioners, there's no shortage of men filling their pockets at the public's expense. The dollars at stake are enormous, Harry. I know this detecting business is your job, but be careful poking your nose into their business. If something were to happen to you, Toby and I would miss your visits. No one enjoys my cakes and pies as much as you do."

Harriet did indeed enjoy the seemingly endless parade of treats produced by Pearl's oven, just not in the over-abundant quantities Pearl served. How the woman stayed rail thin was a marvel. What accounted for it? Age? Heredity? Pearl being in perpetual motion? Harriet had never been bothered by her heft, yet her bicycling speed would undoubtedly improve if she were ten pounds lighter.

"Harry, I nearly plum forgot. I have something for you."

Harriet started to protest, claiming a full belly, when Pearl said, "Upstairs. Follow me."

Intrigued, she followed her friend up the grand staircase leading to the second floor. She had visited Pearl's ances-tral mansion several times—the first being her very first day as a detective—but never failed to be awed by the thick carpets, gilded frames holding oil paintings of ances-tors and landscapes, and finely carved banisters. Although Pearl's home was massive and opulent, she seemed only to inhabit the kitchen and adjacent orangery. On the few oc-casions Pearl led Harriet to other parts of the three-story mansion, it was like exploring a different home altogether, one that not even Pearl seemed all that familiar with.

Standing in Pearl's late husband's bedroom, Harriet watched Pearl rummage in a large wardrobe. "Here we go," she announced cheerfully, presenting a pristine caramel leather satchel, essentially a soft-sided briefcase. "Horace didn't cotton to this. It was his birthday present one year. Which? I've long since lost track. But here's why I thought of you, Harry." She dug inside the satchel and lifted out a thick strap. "This attaches so you can wear the bag over your shoulder instead of having to carry it by the handles. With all your racing about the city on that bicycle of yours, I thought it might come in handy. Now, if you don't like it or don't think you'd have a use for it, I'll just put it right back where it's been sitting for years. Won't matter to me one bit. However, if you want it, I'd be happy for you to have it."

Harriet connected the strap, slung the satchel over a shoulder, and positioned it to rest against her back. Imagining riding her Victoria, she nodded. "This will do nicely. Quite nicely, indeed. Thank you, Pearl. I should get many years of solid use from this."

"Good. I'm glad you like it. One more thing out of this wardrobe. And, you know, there's another reason I thought you should have that satchel."

Replying to Harriet's questioning look, Pearl said, "We can't have you buzzing about Chicago in trousers and carrying a dadgum handbag."

When Harriet arrived at the Prescott offices the following day, she found Charles Bonner's door locked and a scribbled note affixed to the glass reading "*Gone for the week.*" Chagrined, she confirmed his absence with his secretary, Judith Middleton.

"Not that it's any business of yours, but yes," Judith confirmed. "Mr. Bonner was called away to Missouri on an important case. He left an hour ago."

Fuming, Harriet marched to her office. Nearing her door, she saw a slip of paper matching the one on Bonner's door. Her anger dissipated as she pulled the page from the doorframe. Unable to wait, she read the note while standing in the hallway. There was no salutation nor signature. Scrawled in thick black ink, it read: "*Tonight. 7:00. Arbuckle Hall.*"

Chapter 9

With ten hours until the Socialist Labor Party meeting, Harriet followed an idea sparked by a conversation the night before with her brother. Aubrey had told her about schoolmates who had gotten into trouble by not keeping their eyes on their own math exams. Harriet's worry hadn't been that Aubrey, who excelled at figures, had cheated but that others had glimpsed his answers. Aubrey relished describing the teacher's anger. After catching the culprits red-handed, the teacher had lifted both boys from their chairs by their shirt collars before marching them off to the principal's office. Harriet's dismay was countered by Aubrey's surprisingly mature assessment: "Just because you tell a kid to do something doesn't mean he'll do it. Some kids just take it as a challenge to do the very thing they're not supposed to just to show they can."

Later that night, Harriet had tossed and turned. The conversation with Aubrey mixed with thoughts of her case. Before leaving for the police station, Lucy Fara had instructed her children to stay inside the apartment. Their mother must have been away for twenty or thirty minutes while fetching the authorities. But had the children obeyed and not opened the door that entire time? Lucy had said she'd been alarmed by the sounds of a violent altercation just outside her door. Surely, the children must have heard the same noises. Had they been able to resist peering into the hallway to see what they were *not* supposed to see? Of particular interest were the boys, ages ten and eleven, though Harriet didn't completely discount the two younger children, a four-year-old boy and a girl of three.

Harriet would begin at the sprawling Home for the Friendless, where the two older boys had reportedly been taken. The home was located north of downtown in the Washington Park area at Fifty-First Street and Vincennes Avenue. The journey by bicycle should take her less than an hour. And since she would not be presenting herself as a representative of the settlement, she could wear the clothing she preferred, making the journey in trousers far more expedient.

If the city's new jail, with its blunt use of stone, had been designed to intimidate visitors, what could be said of a building that made the jail look as welcoming as a doll's house by comparison? The Home for the Friendless was a massive, five-floor, steeply-pitched-roofed structure with a soaring center tower capped by a conical dome and flag, framed by two round columns ending in castle parapets. She couldn't imagine the boys' dread when laying eyes on their new home. What had the architects been thinking? Why create a building that is more fitting for Dracula than children? Harriet hadn't read the novel, which shared a title with its main character, published the year before, but Aubrey had. Given his enthralled recounting of the blood-thirsty Transylvanian count, she never would.

Reprising her role as Lucy's sister-in-law, Harriet presented her credentials to the matron on the other side of a high counter just inside the main entrance. The matron's curious gaze lingered on Harriet's attire. Harriet realized that her men's clothing provided a benefit. Too distracted by Harriet's unconventional wardrobe, the matron didn't challenge her identity. Recalling Mrs. Horak's mentioning the boys' names, Harriet asked to visit with Chester and Grover Fara.

The matron glanced at the wall clock and grimaced—a discouraging sign. "How old are they?"

"Ten and eleven," Harriet answered, realizing she didn't know which boy was which age.

"The eleven-year-old will be just starting his study hour. But the other boy should be enjoying the playground hour. What is the ten-year-old's name?"

Drat. "Chester," she guessed, squeezing her new satchel for reassurance. The matron raised a finger before disappearing into an adjacent room. Several minutes later, she returned wearing a frown.

"Chester Fara is eleven, not ten."

Harriet had used the time wisely to prepare a response to this fifty-fifty possibility. "Indeed, he is," she said smoothly. "Grover is the younger of the two. If your records have that reversed, you'll no doubt want to correct the error."

"But I asked you . . ." the matron *harrumphed*, then added, "Never mind. This way."

The settlement house, the tenement, the jail, and now the orphanage. Each building pulsed with a particular energy and enveloped visitors in an atmosphere of particular smells and sounds. Whereas the settlement house was spic-and-span and hopeful, the tenement exhausted and downtrodden, and the jail mean and untrustworthy, her present surroundings felt simply cold.

The matron led Harriet through a dizzying series of hallways until they arrived at the opposite end of the building. They exited into a fenced outdoor playground filled with dozens of shrieking children, dashing about the grounds chasing one another, kicking balls, or playing unrecognizable games they'd likely made up on the spot. The frenzy was a stark contrast to the building's whisper-quiet interior.

"I take it you know which one he is," the matron said

wearily. "I'll come back for you in a half hour. Don't try to find your way out alone. You'll only get lost. I don't want to have to come searching for you."

Another matron stood nearby, observing her charges with just enough interest to keep her eyes open. As Harriet was supposed to be the boy's relation, she couldn't very well ask the woman which one was her nephew. Nor could she ask another child without drawing unwanted attention. And so, despite the cacophony to overcome, she filled her lungs, cupped her hands around her mouth, and shouted, "Grover Fara! Where are you? Auntie Harriet has come to visit you!"

After three more shouts calling out for Grover, Harriet managed only to gain the attention of a girl who was exceptionally tall for her age. Apparently, her height allowed her to boss the others, including the boys. Harriet recognized the girl's tomboyishness and wondered if it were a phase to be outgrown or something more fundamental to her nature, as her own tendencies toward male pursuits and clothing turned out to be. After giving Harriet several sideway glances, the girl marched toward her, wearing a smirk.

"You get dressed in the dark?" the girl said.

Harriet didn't need to hear more to decide she didn't much like the girl. She was mean—the type of child who sought any excuse to bully.

"Hello," Harriet replied curtly, choosing to deny the girl the quarrel she sought to instigate.

"You're too young to be Grover's mama. You his sister? You don't look anything alike. Grover's skinny."

Harriet wouldn't allow the child to interrogate or intimidate her. If the girl were indeed the playground bully, she'd recognize when outmatched. In Harriet's experience, all it would take was a stern rebuke. "Who I am is none of your concern, young lady. Now, unless you prefer I report your ill manners to the matron, you'll point out which child is Grover Fara right this instant."

The girl's hard expression melted. "Grover ain't here. He's in the infirmary."

So unexpected was the news that Harriet at first thought the girl was continuing her antics. But her matter-of-fact expression seemed to indicate sincerity. It seemed inexcusable that the matron who'd greeted her hadn't known Grover's condition or whereabouts. But what did she know about running a large orphanage? Perhaps each child's daily condition wasn't immediately added to their file. Or possibly Grover had only recently taken ill.

"Which way is the infirmary?" Although Harriet couldn't help but ask the question, she doubted her ability to navigate the massive complex on her own.

"You want, I can show you," the girl offered.

Harriet looked toward the matron. Surely, she wouldn't allow one of her charges to go traipsing off with a stranger.

The girl seemed to sense Harriet's misgivings. "It's okay. I sneak off all the time."

"I wouldn't want to be the reason you get into trouble."

The girl shrugged and turned to walk away.

"Wait." Harriet didn't want to contribute to the girl's delinquency, but she was desperate to speak with one of Lucy's children. If she were to ask permission from a matron, wouldn't she be instructed to return when Grover's health improved? And what if, God forbid, he didn't recover from what ailed him? Having learned nothing, leaving the orphanage now would be a lamentable waste of time and opportunity.

"How far is it?" Harriet said. "To the infirmary from here?"

"Not far." The girl shrugged again.

The matron was now at the opposite end of the grounds, reprimanding two boys arguing the score of a game of marbles.

"Lead the way," Harriet said. "But please be quick about it."

The girl escorted her to a door different from where

she'd entered the playground. The temperature inside this part of the building was cooler. A smell of mildew hung in the air. The girl strode ahead, not looking back. Harriet found her pace reassuring—the girl knew where she was going. Still, the number of turns was disorienting. Harriet lost all sense of direction. Never would she have found the way on her own. The girl rounded yet another corner ten paces ahead. Harriet turned that same corner and stopped abruptly. The girl was nowhere in sight. Harriet spun in a circle, wishing for a door she'd missed. There was none. She'd let the child get too far ahead and lost her. Or she had been played the fool by allowing the girl to draw her into the building's depths, where she'd been abandoned on purpose.

Furious, Harriet realized too late she should have trusted her instincts about the girl. She imagined her giggling behind a nearby wall. Now, she had no choice but to blindly continue, finding the way on her own or running into someone who would show her the way.

No sooner had she chosen a direction that an older man appeared, pushing a bucket and mop. His bright eyes and smile were a mismatch with his scraggly beard, dingy coveralls, and boots. "You look lost as a priest in a whorehouse."

His bawdy remark disarmed her apprehension. "I'm in search of the infirmary. I fear I've taken a wrong turn." Registering his baffled expression, she added, "Or two."

"I should say so, miss. Infirmary is clear in the other wing."

Swallowing a groan, she closed her eyes and took a breath. "I don't suppose you could show me the way?"

Ten minutes and a dollar later, the custodian left Harriet at the entrance to the infirmary. The smell of bleach and lemon was overpowering. A nurse wearing a white dress with puffed sleeves and a brimless cap attended to a boy, much too old to be Grover, who was holding his stomach and whimpering in pain. The room's two other beds were unoccupied, covered by pressed white sheets. The nurse appeared to take in stride a stranger hovering in the doorway and looking uncertain. She told Harriet to take a seat; she'd not be five minutes. Harriet was happy to get off her feet. Despite three empty chairs, Harriet chose the one next to the other person in the infirmary—a red-headed boy about ten years old. Looking glum, he pressed the palm of his small hand to his cheek.

"Hello, Grover," Harriet said softly as if not to startle him.

The boy's eyes flashed recognition. There was no time to draw him slowly into conversation, and considering his toothache, he was prone to being untalkative.

"I am a friend of your mother's, Grover. I'm trying to help her. I'm trying to help your entire family. Your mother, your brothers, your sister, and you. But I need your help. I must ask you about the day something terrible happened in your building's hallway. A man was hurt right outside your door. Your mother hurried away to find him help. She told you not to open the door before leaving you and your brothers and sister alone in the apartment. That it wasn't safe. She said that, Grover, because she loves you and was worried for your safety. But I understand you must have been terribly worried about your mother just like she was worried about you. So it's perfectly understandable if you opened the door and peeked outside." She leaned closer to him, lowered her voice. "I know I would have done. But there's something you don't know, Grover. You did the right thing when you and your brother opened that door. Because whatever you saw might help me help your mother. But for me to do that, Grover, for me to help your mother and family, I need you to tell me exactly what you saw when you opened that door."

Of course, Harriet didn't know if any of Lucy's children had disobeyed her order. But dealing with her own brother for years, she had learned that eliciting his confession to eating the last brownie, breaking their grandmother's gravy boat, or borrowing her bicycle without asking was far easier when he thought she already knew he'd done it. She stared at Grover, holding her breath.

"Chethster opened the door." He winced in pain. "For a second." He pressed his cheek harder.

"For only a second?" She mocked disappointment. "Why, that would mean your brother closed the door so fast you'd have missed out on seeing anything," she clucked. "What a shame. You're quite sure that's what happened?"

Grover nodded, saving his words. She leaned in close again. "You can tell me. It will be our secret. Did Chester step into the hallway?"

The boy grimaced, but not from the pain; he was annoyed. "No! I told you. It was only a second."

The nurse glanced their way. "Is there a problem? I'll only be another minute."

"Quite all right, thank you," Harriet replied before returning her attention to Grover. "I have a guess why Chester closed the door so quickly. Do you want to hear my guess?"

Curious, he nodded, though wary.

"I think Chester saw something that frightened him. I think you did, too."

Another grimace. "We weren't scared," he declared. "We just didn't want her to tattle on us."

"I see." Crestfallen, Harriet thought she understood— the boys didn't trust their little sister not to tell their mother, and so their bold act of defiance had been short-lived.

Grover puffed his chest. "That old lady don't scare us."

Harriet jerked as a current of adrenaline shot through her. The nurse approached, her footsteps clacking on the shiny, hard floor.

"Who?" Harriet's voice was desperate. "What old lady? A neighbor?"

The nurse now stood before them. "You must be new to the Home for the Friendless. I've not seen you before. How may I help?" Her gaze bounced between Harriet and

Grover, making it unclear to whom the remark was intended.

Harriet stared beseechingly at Grover. A hand still pressed to his cheek, he mumbled something.

"Miss?" The nurse's brows lifted into a question. "Is this boy your charge?"

Ignoring the question, Harriet placed a hand gently on his shoulder. "Please, Grover, tell me so I can help you and your mother. You said an 'old lady.' Which old lady?"

The nurse took a half step forward. "Miss, I really must insist—"

"Please, madam," Harriet snapped, too close to the truth for politeness.

"The old lady that lives above us." Grover moaned. "She was in the hallway, standing over the dead man."

Chapter 10

Traveling Chicago streets by bicycle had its benefits. The freedom to pedal off at a whim and maneuver through road congestion was high on the list. Had Harriet ever been sedentary for a day in her life, aside from being bed-ridden during a bout of childhood measles, she might also add the merit of exercise. Still, there were drawbacks. Bicycling against a chilly headwind, dodging pedestrians, and steering clear of ruts in the cobblestone or timber roads could dampen her enjoyment considerably. Another disadvantage was riding after dark, which demanded she travel at a slower, more cautious speed. The realization vexed Harriet. There wasn't enough time to visit the tenement building before the start of the Socialist Labor Party meeting that evening. As eager as she was to find out who lived above the Faras' former apartment, it would have to wait until morning.

At home in her bedroom, she stood before the open wardrobe, flummoxed. What did one wear to a meeting of socialists? More to the point, could she get away with wearing men's clothing? Never would she compromise her investigation, but how could a pair of trousers thwart her success in mingling with everyday citizens or finding Jorinda Grimm? Besides, she was attending a meeting of progressive-minded socialists, not a chummy gathering of captains of industry at Mr. Prescott's Chicago Club. Although her intention wasn't to make a statement, given the crowd, who's to say her rejection of convention wouldn't be admired? Before changing her mind, she reached for Pearl's late husband's most casual suit.

In the living room, Aubrey appraised her from where he lay sprawled on the sofa. "Your tie is crooked."

She felt for the ends of the bow and made an adjustment. "Better?"

"I thought you went back to wearing dresses."

"Remember when Aunty and Uncle insisted we attend Sunday services with them?"

His pained expression told her he did.

"You had to wear that hand-me-down jacket that was too big and discount shoes that pinched your toes? That's what wearing dresses is like for me. I wear them when the occasion demands. Sometimes, being a detective requires that I wear traditional women's clothing. Otherwise, I can wear what *suits me*."

He groaned at the intended pun.

"I shouldn't be away for more than a few hours. I'll try not to wake you when I return." Her words were sincere but unnecessary. She'd have to ride her bicycle into his bedroom while ringing its bell to wake him. Besides, he didn't turn in before eleven o'clock.

Arbuckle Hall was a dance venue on weekends. Harriet had been there once on what she would admit only to herself had been a date—*with a boy*. The event resulted from her workmate's plea at the grain elevator to accompany her on a double date—the only arrangement the other girl's parents would allow. Harriet had steadfastly refused until she was told a dinner at a white-tableclothed restaurant would be included. As it turned out, even an entrée of boneless beef short rib à la bourguignon didn't make up for her escort's shortcomings. Nor did the dessert of chocolate and vanilla éclairs. Her date, a boy named Lionel Pluck, had smelled of tobacco, and his refusal to shave the scant wisps of blond hair above his lip appeared to be a battle of wills that his reluctant mustache was winning. Worse yet, he continually stepped on her toes when dancing. After that night, she'd vowed *never again*! And so, with memories of a never-to-be-repeated date with a boy, she climbed the steps to the entrance of Arbuckle Hall.

The tall, creaking door opened to darkness. Harriet didn't remember the dance floor as being so dark. The hall's only light emanated from four torchères on the raised stage at the room's far end and another half dozen along each wall. Had the building any windows, the evening moon's exceptional brightness would have helped considerably.

The number of moving shapes suggested modest attendance: perhaps thirty, no more than forty people. According to her watch, she'd arrived a quarter hour early. Whatever opportunity she might have to speak with party members would occur before and after the meeting. Spying a refreshments table, she crossed the floor and joined in line behind a man with shockingly long hair that spilled from beneath a dark-green Tyrolean hat with a red-tipped feather tucked into the band. His shoulders were narrow, and he smelled of honeysuckle.

Harriet shuffled forward with the others, eventually taking her turn to ladle punch into a cup and placing a cookie onto a small plate, hoping the dark bits were chocolate, not raisins. She observed the huddles of attendees, deciding which to approach. His back to her, the man with long hair was conversing with a short man wearing gold-rimmed spectacles. She thought, *Why not them?*

Stepping up to the men, Harriet extended a hand. "Allow me to introduce myself . . ." Her eyes widened as they fell on the face of the long-haired man.

She took Harriet's hand. "Hello and welcome. I am Brunhilda Struff."

Harriet knew she wasn't the only woman in Chicago to wear men's clothing. Every woman who'd attended the Black Rabbit's annual gala wore a man's suit, many choosing a tuxedo. But that had been in a private club that emphasized secrecy. Here was another woman who boldly wore men's clothing in public—or semipublic, as was the case. Harriet was intrigued. Moreover, the woman's long nose, sharp cheekbones, and strong, square jaw combined to create an improbably handsome countenance.

"The pleasure is mine. My name is Harriet Dunn." Adopting her mother's maiden name hadn't been planned. She just said it. No one would recognize her real name, let alone suspect she was an operative with the Prescott Agency, but in the moment, offering her true identity felt unwise.

After exchanging introductions with the man, Harriet explained she was attending the party meeting for the first time because of a long-simmering passion for social justice and a growing frustration with the progress made by the nation's two dominant parties. Her remark earned a solemn nod from the man. Brunhilda Struff, however, remained inscrutable. Did she question Harriet's interest in socialism? Doubt Harriet's identity? Or was she wondering if her clothing indicated something more than a preference for trousers?

Before arriving, Harriet had devised a story to raise the subject of the People's Cause unobtrusively. "When I was speaking with an acquaintance who shares my support for an eight-hour workday and safe working conditions, he suggested I attend a meeting of the Socialist Labor Party or perhaps the People's Cause. Not knowing which would better suit my interests, I came here when I could find nothing about the other organization." She let her last words hang in the air. Brunhilda Struff exchanged a brief, knowing glance with the other man.

"I don't suppose either of you have heard of them?" Harriet said. "The People's Cause?"

The slight shake of Brunhilda's head intended for the man was nearly imperceptible.

Pressing on, Harriet said, "I don't suppose any of their membership is in attendance this evening?"

"Good heavens, no," the man said, appalled by the notion.

"You looking for anyone in particular?" Brunhilda sniggered. "Or will any member do?"

"Jorinda Grimm," Harriet offered.

"Who?" The man looked as though she'd named Dumpsey Deazil from *The Wallypug of Why*.

"Where did you hear of that name?" Brunhilda asked.

Circumspect, Harriet avoided mentioning Eugene Eldridge, instead opting for ambiguity that stayed close enough to the truth so she wouldn't say something to conflict with what they might know. "From a friend. He is the colleague of the woman's fiancé."

The man sniffed. "We don't consort with such people."

"Oh? And why is that?" Harriet asked, sensing his eagerness to criticize the other organization.

"We're socialists. Not anarchists," he said defensively.

Brunhilda reached for his arm. "That's enough, Philip."

"Anarchists?" Harriet feigned incredulity. "Surely, that can't be. Perhaps they are overzealous. Caught up in the righteousness of their cause, their enthusiasm is misunderstood."

Philip raised his chin. "Young lady, you have no idea what you're talking about. The People's Cause espouses violence. We don't condone their methods. They are not welcome here. Such unbridled behavior set us back decades. I'll have you know—"

"Philip!" Brunhilda's expression lost all uncertainty. "I said, that's quite enough."

That Philip was adamant in renouncing violence was understandable. A dozen years ago, the Haymarket Affair had devolved into a riot after someone threw a bomb, killing many policemen and protestors and resulting in the unjust conviction of eight activists. The ordeal dealt a major setback to the labor movement. The Socialist Labor Party had struggled to maintain influence ever since.

Brunhilda stepped back and gestured toward the dance floor. "It's time we find our seats."

Uninvited to join them, Harriet returned to the refreshment table before finding an empty chair at the back of the hall, happy the cookies were indeed chocolate chip. The two-hour meeting was largely uneventful. A few energetic speeches drew murmurs of assent, keeping her from nodding off for too long. The meeting concluded unceremoniously, and the members shuffled out. Brunhilda Struff was among the first through the exit. She offered no farewell. Harriet would have liked to engage someone else in conversation before they all departed, but like a dam breaking, the flow was one-way, determined, and rapid.

Stepping into the cool night air, Harriet raised her jacket's collar. The moon appeared brighter than before. She took a long moment to admire the night sky, grateful for the light that would make her bicycle ride home less treacherous. She gave a start, feeling something bump against her. Dropping her gaze from the night sky, she saw that the last attendees had just passed and descended the steps. Brunhilda's companion, Philip, was among them. Harriet put a hand to her hip. Something was inside the jacket pocket that hadn't been there before—she was sure of that. The jacket had belonged to Pearl's late husband. She had emptied the pockets of his clothes when she'd removed them from his wardrobe and packed them into a suitcase. Harriet pulled out a folded piece of paper. Holding it so that the moonlight illuminated the page, she saw it was an advertisement for Vorwaerts Turner Hall. A photograph depicted dozens of male youths performing gymnastics in short pants, dark knee socks, and sleeveless shirts. Six boys lined up snuggly, one after the other, each performing a handstand on one set of parallel bars.

Despite the uncertainty of why someone had slipped

that particular advertisement into her pocket, she determined it was a clue. Moreover, she decided it must be related to her inquiry about the People's Cause.

Hands shaking, Harriet unlocked her bicycle chain. The case might crack open if she could find the People's Cause and Jorinda Grimm, Eugene Eldridge's former fiancée. Solving her second case—a murder involving a corrupt politician—might prove her doubters wrong once and for all. As much as she tried not to let the naysayers at the Prescott Agency erode her confidence, the sideways glances, the smirks, and the whispers took a toll. She told herself to ignore them and imagined the reassuring words her mother might offer: "The best way to silence your critics, Harriet, is to do precisely what they say you can't."

Mounting her Victoria, she turned toward the river and glimpsed a figure in shadow. Before she could discern more than a shape, the person ducked into an alleyway. Fear whipped through her. Was someone watching her? Was she being followed? Was it the same person who had slipped the advertisement for Vorwaerts Turner Hall into her pocket? Could it be Philip? Or someone else at the meeting she hadn't met? No. It was none of them. Everyone there had worn a bowler hat like her own or a derby— except one person. Brunhilda Struff had worn a distinctive Tyrolean hat. Just like the person in the shadows.

Chapter 11

Harriet arrived home just after ten o'clock to a note slipped beneath the door. Her first thought was disbelief that Susan hadn't first discovered it and chewed it to bits. Harriet unfolded the paper and recognized the handwriting at once. Barbara must have left it recently. Had she come earlier, she would have knocked and Aubrey would have answered and placed the note on the table. The contents were brief.

> *Dearest Harriet, you'd delight me to no end if you would kindly meet me tonight at the Black Rabbit.*
> *—Yours, Barbara*

Harriet peered beneath Aubrey's bedroom door for a fragment of light to indicate he was awake. There was none. *Odd,* she thought. He never turned in before eleven. Sister and brother had established cardinal rules to mitigate quarrels. One was the other's bedroom being strictly off-limits—unless invited to enter after knocking. Reasoning that she wouldn't violate their pact by quickly peeking inside his room and not crossing the threshold, she cracked open his door. Light from the living room spilled across the neatly made bed. Her stomach tightened. She raced to the bathroom—also empty. Just then, the front door opened behind her.

She whirled around. "Aubrey! Where on earth have you been? You gave me an awful fright!"

"You just got home yourself," he pointed out.

"How do you know that?"

"You're still wearing your coat and hat."

"Yes, well. That's beside the point. We agreed you're not to go out alone at night. Not unless we've discussed it beforehand."

He stamped past her toward his bedroom. "You're not my mother," he fumed.

How many times had they had this argument? Would she ever make him understand he wanted it both ways? Only too happy to have her perform certain parental duties—cooking, cleaning, and earning the money that kept the heat on and the cupboards stocked—he bristled whenever she attempted to exert any authority over him. Unwilling to let the matter go, she hardened her voice. "I want to know where you've been. You will tell me this instant."

He spun around in his doorway. "I was with my friends. Some people have friends, Harriet." And with that, he slammed his bedroom door behind him.

Fists clenched at her sides, she took deep, steadying breaths. Not only was she furious, but the noise would elicit a visit from the next-door neighbor the following morning. The man in 3C seemed to relish any reason to appear at their door, angry and unreasonable. His most recent complaints were Susan's meowing, which he claimed was so loud he couldn't think straight, and Aubrey's singing in the bathtub that sounded like "someone tortured in a well."

Aubrey's remark, insinuating she had no friends, stung. Just as he knew it would. Growing up, her tomboyishness had been off-putting to both girls and boys. Girls found her unrelatable. Boys found her threatening. In the three years she had worked at the Rock Island Grain Elevator offices after graduation, she'd kept to herself, avoiding awkward conversations among the girls about the handsome men in the office, the latest fashions, or popular dance halls. But recently, things had changed for the better. Matthew McCabe was a colleague, but she also considered him a friend. And Pearl Bartlett—she was undoubtedly a friend, too. Then there was Barbara. Lovely, lovely Barbara. Her mood suddenly brightened. As soon as she fed Susan, she was going out. Hopefully, Barbara would still be at the Black Rabbit when she arrived.

The Levee District was a hotbed of vice: gambling, prostitution, bawdy entertainment, and saloons by the dozens. Harriet was troubled that the Black Rabbit sat surrounded by such establishments, as if its queer clientele—mostly men—was enough to put it on equally nefarious footing. Still, she appreciated that the neighborhood's riffraff cared not a whit about those who came and went from the Black Rabbit—the same would not be said about a well-heeled or more reputable district whose more inquisitive residents would be inclined to ask questions about so many dandies secreting above a former shop in a little-traveled alleyway. Although men composed the majority of the Black Rabbit's membership, several dozen women had equal privileges. Barbara had introduced Harriet to the private club the week before on the occasion of its annual ball. This was Harriet's second visit and her first time arriving alone.

She wheeled her bicycle to the unmarked entrance. Her knock was met by the opening of a small, narrow window set high within the door. A set of eyes appeared. Remembering the man's name, Harriet said, "Good evening, Albert. I don't suppose—"

"Miss Morrow, isn't it?" he chirped brightly.

A wave of emotion washed over her. She hadn't appreciated how important it was that she be welcomed here.

More than remembering her name, Albert seemed genuinely pleased to see her. She couldn't recall a time in her life when she wasn't conscious of not being an ordinary *girl*. But at the Black Rabbit, no one batted an eye at her uniqueness. Here, her difference was accepted and even embraced. After twenty-one years of living, Harriet had found a place where she could be herself. More than enjoyable, it was as vital to her spirit as air to her lungs.

Inside, Albert hopped down from the stool he used to compensate for his diminutive stature. Had he been so immaculately attired during her first visit? Before, had apprehension distracted her from noticing his finely tailored, sky-blue silk suit with black velvet lapels?

"As captain of the Black Rabbit, I welcome you, Miss Morrow." Albert bowed. His formal tone and gesture tickled Harriet. She might have been calling on palace royalty instead of visiting a queer club off an alleyway in Chicago's seediest district. "Miss Wozniak mentioned your possible attendance this evening."

Harriet breathed relief. "So Barbara, Miss Wozniak, is still here?"

"Indeed, she is, assuming she didn't exit the premises out the back way. And that, you should know, is only to be done in an emergency. Thank God we haven't been raided yet."

Yet. The dangers of a visit to the Black Rabbit were understood to her. But she had compartmentalized them to being challenged when coming or going. She'd learned from prior experience that enforcing the club's rule that visitors—members and guests alike—never arrive or leave in their "party attire" was one of Albert's chief responsibilities. A police raid, a horror resulting in a ride in a police wagon, a fine, and a criminal record, would jeopardize her job at the Prescott Agency. She'd heard of queer men paying bribes to avoid punishment, but she hadn't the money to satisfy a dirty cop's greed.

As if reading her thoughts, Albert appraised her men's clothing disapprovingly.

"This is not a costume," she explained. "These are my everyday clothes. I understand the club's rules, and I intend no disrespect. But surely, you'd not have me change into a dress to gain admittance only so I may change into my regular clothes, which are perfectly acceptable upstairs?"

Albert's expression telegraphed his amazement. "You go out like that in public? All the time?"

"Whenever possible," she answered, then deciding the remark overstated her courage, added, "I've only just started."

Harriet understood Albert's amazement. Although her bold act paled in comparison to a man wearing a dress in public, it was still a risk. Had she been found out and arrested, the punishment dealt her could be a fine of as much as one hundred dollars—Chicago Ordinance 1297, as Prescott had cited. But Matthew McCabe had told her about men arrested for indecency and being brutalized by the police and other jail prisoners.

Albert looked as if he was figuring out a math problem in his head. Apparently reaching a conclusion, he wagged a finger; a large ruby and gold ring reflected the moonlight. "Take care that you're not seen when making your way to us. We can't draw unwanted attention." He tilted his head toward the staircase. "Go on then. You've kept Miss Wozniak waiting long enough. You may leave your bicycle there in the corner. You needn't worry that I'll make off with it. My feet won't reach the pedals." He added a self-deprecating wink.

Upstairs, Harriet bypassed one of the former apartment's bedrooms, which was used by women wishing to shed their usual apparel or effects in preference for something more festive, which in more than a few cases meant gentlemen's dress. She understood a room farther down the hallway was reserved for men for the same purpose. She hurried to join the revelry in the main hall—the former parlor and dining room—which could be heard through the corridor wall.

The door opened to a rush of music. Gloria, the performer Harriet had met during her previous investigation, stood on a small stage in the corner wearing an elaborate white feathered gown and matching headpiece with a brim shaped like a bird's bill. As the crowd joined in, his bright tenor voice filled the hall:

> *Oh she is the Belle of New York*
> *The subject of all the town talk!*
> *She makes the old Bowery fragrant and flowery*
> *When she goes out for a walk*
> *She's soft as a snowy white dove!*
> *She's simply created for love.*
> *The fellows all sigh for her.*
> *They would all die for her.*
> *She is the Belle of New York.*

Barbara must have been watching the entrance. She sidled alongside Harriet by the song's second verse and handed her a glass of champagne—in truth, a splash of white wine in seltzer, affectionately called Levee Bubbles by club members. Barbara had pulled her lustrous, black hair into a tight bun, painted her lips red, and wore a men's brown suit that Harriet knew was a cast-off from her uncle, saved from a donation bin.

"I had nearly lost hope," Barbara said, clinking her glass against Harriet's.

"I can't stay for long, I'm afraid," Harriet explained. "I must be at my best tomorrow. Most nights, I'd never have considered coming out at all. But I knew if I'd stayed home, I'd have tossed and turned in anger at my brother. I figured if I'm to be up, better to be here."

Barbara's expression tightened, signaling displeasure.

"Oh, dear. Have I made you wait too long?" Harriet asked.

"It's not that."

"Then what?"

"I hoped your presence was due to wanting to be here, as opposed to not wanting to stay home."

Realizing her unintended slight, she grasped Barbara's arm. "Forgive me, Barbara. Let me start again. There is simply no place I'd rather be. Brother or no brother. Truly."

Barbara's expression softened into a smile. "Then I suppose you really have no other choice than to dance with me."

Gloria appeared to have finished for the night, transferring musical duties to the phonograph near the small stage opposite the bar. "Sweet Blue-Eyed Maid" flowed from the contraption, amplified by its wide-mouthed horn. Harriet was entirely unaccustomed to dancing, let alone with a woman. Holding hands and standing close to Barbara was the most prolonged human contact she'd had since clinging to her brother at their mother's funeral. That had been four years ago. Overwhelmed by thoughts past and present, she choked back tears at once sad and joyous.

They turned a slow circle, allowing Harriet's gaze to sweep the small crowd. Matthew McCabe stood at the bar. He was alone, and Harriet thought, looking forlorn. The song lasted another two rotations. With each turn, Matthew took another long pull from his glass. She didn't know him well enough to know whether he was a strong drinker, but something was amiss. She could sense his unhappiness from across the room.

The audience applauded the tune's final flourish. Harriet asked Barbara if she wouldn't mind if they visited with Matthew. She knew her answer but felt it polite to ask nonetheless. Matthew had been instrumental in helping Harriet find Barbara's sister. Barbara would forever hold a soft spot in her heart for him. It didn't hurt that he was amiable and wore his handsomeness nonchalantly, as if he'd never looked in a mirror once in all his life.

Seeing them approach, he said, "If it isn't my two favorite ladies. Good evening, Harriet, Barbara." His smile
wasn't without effort.

After a moment of pleasantries, Barbara asked what
Harriet had been wondering. "How is it possible that a
fine gentleman like yourself appears unhappy at the Black
Rabbit?"

In an instant, the veil of good cheer slipped from his
face. Barbara traded a concerned look with Harriet before
saying, "Well, I for one am glad you're momentarily free.
That means you may do me the honor." She offered her
arm so he might escort her to the dance floor. The gesture
impressed Harriet. Others would ask further questions;
Barbara knew better.

Gloria slipped a new cylinder onto the phonograph.
The selection, a peppy, up-tempo number, stirred the half
dozen couples to a lively two-step driven by a syncopated
beat. Since Harriet had first heard the ragged-time music
at the World's Fair five years earlier, it had rapidly increased in popularity. Harriet watched Barbara and Matthew dance. The possibility that two people she admired
might become friends made the pleasant moment special—
perhaps she was witnessing a new type of family forming
around here.

"Shame. He's a fine fella."

Harriet turned back. The bartender pointed his chin in
Matthew's direction.

"Shame? How's that?" Harriet said.

"Whoever he was waiting on never showed up. He's
been here for two hours. Most fellas would have given up
hope a long time ago. Goes to show you how much he
must like the other gent, late or not."

Harriet couldn't contain her curiosity. "Do you know
this other man?"

"Can't say that I do. Which is a bit odd. We don't get
many newcomers. It doesn't go unnoticed when we do, especially if they're handsome. Whoever Matthew was wait-

ing on must really be something. He wouldn't stand around all night for just anyone."

"No, I don't suppose he would," Harriet said, glancing at Matthew and Barbara.

The bartender chuckled. "Not unlike yourself, come to think of it."

"Me? What have I got to do with it?"

"Barbara was waiting on you same as Matthew for his mystery man. Only difference is you are here."

Harriet hadn't questioned Barbara's desire that she join her, but the bartender made their meeting sound momentous. Was it? They'd known each other only a few weeks. Was she ready for more than flirtation? Is that what Barbara wanted? Suddenly, the delightful, carefree evening took on weight. Her friends' laughter interrupted her rumination. Barbara held Matthew's arm as they approached. The dance had improved his mood considerably. He appeared his usual jolly self. It quickly became apparent how the rest of the night would be spent—the three of them together. Harriet didn't mind. She found Matthew good company, and his presence prevented further thought about the meaning of her burgeoning relationship with Barbara.

"So tell me," Matthew asked Harriet, "how is your case progressing?"

Harriet gave Barbara an apologetic look, presuming she'd prefer they not discuss work.

"I was going to ask the same thing," Barbara said encouragingly.

"Well, then, as it happens . . ."

Despite her intention to keep the story brief, there seemed no end to Matthew's questions. When she finally concluded by stating her plans to return to the tenement building to speak with the upstairs neighbor and visit Vorwaerts Turner Hall, Matthew insisted on accompanying her to the gymnasium.

"Your intrepidness is commendable, Harriet, but your

marching into a German gymnasium alone will be met with the same shock as me showing up in a women's public bath. As detectives, we must blend into the scenery. We do ourselves no favors when our very presence calls attention." He raised a hand to stave off the objection he sensed was coming. "I understand the need to follow up on a lead. That's why I am going with you. Besides, you can't be certain who slipped the advertisement into your coat pocket or why. It could be related to your inquiry about the People's Cause, but that's only a guess, however reasonable. There's no telling what you might find there."

"He's right," Barbara agreed. "If it helps to convince you, I will feel much better if Matthew goes along."

I don't need a babysitter, Harriet wanted to argue. But knowing she would sound petulant, she swallowed her bother. Barbara squeezed her arm and said, "Perhaps proving yourself as a detective might occasionally require you to behave in ways that go against your natural inclination toward independence."

They were both right, of course. And Harriet knew that if Pearl Bartlett were present, she might say, "Don't let your pride fuss with your success, Harry!"

Harriet loosed a long sigh. "Fine. But don't think I won't hesitate to perform a handstand or swing on the rings if that's what it takes to solve this case."

Barbara and Matthew exchanged wide-eyed stares before Harriet betrayed her seriousness with a grin. "Though I'd prefer it not come to that."

Chapter 12

"*The old lady that lives above us.*" Those had been Grover Fara's words when describing the woman he'd seen standing over Eugene Eldridge's body in the hallway. Harriet knew the apartment he'd referred to. When she had visited the tenement three days earlier, four doors had gone unanswered. One of those had been the home directly above the Faras. When Harriet had asked the resident Edita about who lived there, she claimed to have never met the family but had heard they were quiet and reserved and had only recently arrived from Germany. Harriet hadn't jotted down a surname in her case notes and couldn't recall Edita mentioning one. No matter. She would discover firsthand what she needed to know about the building's newest residents.

Usually, Harriet wouldn't think of paying an uninvited visit to strangers at eight o'clock on a Saturday morning. But today her intention was precisely that. She hoped to arrive before the residents living above the Faras departed for the day.

Not even a half block into her ride, Harriet cursed under her breath. Although she had enjoyed her night at the Black Rabbit, she wished for more sleep, and the cold morning wind off the lake swirled miserably up her legs despite a flannel petticoat. She'd had the forethought to wear mittens—why not bloomers? At least her hair, tucked snugly into her bowler, provided good insulation and fast pedaling helped to mitigate the chill.

Harriet had learned long ago to be vigilantly observant when riding her bicycle. Oblivious children or distracted adults too often strayed into her path, buggies lurched out from side streets, and contents spilled from buckboards. However, the greatest nuisance by far was other bicyclists— *male bicyclists*. Harriet found most women courteous, law-abiding, and usually traveling at a pace that safeguarded against collisions. Men, however, rode the roads as if they owned them. On numerous occasions, when compelled to ring the bell affixed to her handlebars, alerting another bicyclist of her presence, nine times out of ten, it was for a man.

Despite the crowded streets, teaming with all manner of transportation, she noticed one particular person on horseback had been traveling the same route for the past quarter hour. Had it been longer? With her eyes necessarily fastened on the road ahead, she couldn't risk a long look back to be sure. The person in the saddle was about Barbara's size and wore a hat and a long dark coat. The horse was equally nondescript: brown.

However, at some point during her journey, the rider had taken a turn. Or so she hoped. Either way, she could no longer see them.

She entered the tenement, dark and dank as she remembered. Her newfound familiarity made navigating the narrow hallways less precarious, though she remained on guard. The building's eerie silence exaggerated her footsteps, and she feared someone bursting from their home to protest her presence. She passed Mrs. Horak's street-level apartment, then Edita's on the second floor, before winding her way to the third. At the top landing, she stood at the entrance to the apartment directly above the Faras, felt for the reassuring bulk of her derringer pistol in her coat pocket, and knocked.

Sounds of movement emanated from the door's other side. A moment later, the face of a middle-aged man filled a six-inch opening. His mussed hair and blinking eyes suggested he had just woken up.

"Yes?" he said, his voice raspy. His head's few remaining black strands stood at odd angles. Despite his near-baldness, he looked no older than forty.

"Might I have a word with the woman of the house?" Harriet would have liked to ask for the woman by name, but Grover hadn't told her what it was, had he known it.

"Who are you?" the man further narrowed his eyes. "What do you want?"

"I apologize for the early hour, sir. My name is Harriet Morrow. I have come as a representative of the University Settlement House to introduce our services, many of which are sure to benefit your household." Doubting that her impromptu performance was convincing, she feared the door might be slammed in her face.

"Wait there."

Apprehension wriggled up her spine. Had he gone to fetch his wife? Or a weapon to persuade her to leave at once and never return? Should she run while she still had the chance? Harriet squeezed her new satchel, listening to an exchange of low voices from inside the apartment, unable to discern the words. As abruptly as the man had departed, he reappeared, revealing the same six inches of his face.

"We need nothing," he said tersely. "Goodbye." He backed away, closing the door.

"But I don't understand," Harriet objected. "Why have me wait if—"

The door slammed shut. She raised her hand to knock again but thought better of it. She wouldn't talk her way inside. With no reasonable explanation for her insistence, she would only draw more suspicion. The situation brought to mind advice Mr. Prescott had dispensed during the previous week's detectives' meeting: *It is the door most forcefully shut that an operative must, at all costs, find a way to open.*

A moment later, Harriet stood at the threshold of Antonia's apartment. The woman she'd met while shoveling coal in the basement stared back at her.

"You," Antonia said, her greeting emotionless. "What do you want?"

It occurred to Harriet that she couldn't remember if she'd introduced herself before to Antonia as a new neighbor or an employee of the settlement house. Were she alone, she'd have berated herself for not capturing such a detail in her notebook so she might refresh her memory *before* putting herself in such an awkward position. Hoping bluntness would change the subject, she asked, "Can you tell me who lives above the Faras' former home?"

"The Decas?" Antonia blinked and leaned into the hallway, gazing toward her former neighbor's apartment. "Why are you asking?"

Harriet pressed on, "And Mrs. Deca, is she usually at home when her husband's at work? Is he gone most days?"

A man, presumably Antonia's husband, appeared at her side. "Who is this woman?" Giving Harriet an unwelcoming look, he said, "Why are you asking such questions?"

"She is a new neighbor," Antonia explained, reminding Harriet that she'd allowed the woman to think she had moved into the Faras' former apartment.

Most workers, like those at the nearby stockyards, had only one day off each week, if at all. She might have guessed that day would be Sunday, not Saturday. But there they all were. Now she had no choice but to muddle through and learn what she could before another door closed in her face. Using what Antonia had just told her, she said, "I'm worried about Mrs. Deca. I haven't seen her for days."

The husband took a step closer. "Why ask us when she lives upstairs?"

"I fear I have gotten off on the wrong foot with Mr. Deca. I can't imagine what I might have done to upset him, but I find his abruptness unsettling. I had hoped to ease my mind about Mrs. Deca's well-being without unnecessarily bothering him and the household." Playing on the couple's sympathies, she sighed. "But if checking on my friend must entail Mr. Deca's ire, then I shall endure it." Harriet turned toward the staircase leading up to the Decas' apartment.

"She's taken to her bed," Antonia announced. "Which, considering, is expected."

Harriet's mind raced. Had Mrs. Deca been injured when Eugene Eldridge was killed? Or had she been harmed afterward as a warning to keep what she had witnessed secret? Straining to mask her frantic thoughts, Harriet tried for a measured tone. "Yes, of course. I just thought . . ." The moment stretched uncomfortably, but she couldn't be the first to speak; she had no idea what Antonia was talking about.

Finally, Antonia broke the silence. "I'm sure we will hear cries any day now." Antonia glanced toward the ceiling. "The baby can't come soon enough."

Pregnant? Grover Fara hadn't mentioned the woman being pregnant. Indeed, her round belly would have been as noticeable as her age, if not more so. Presuming Mr. Deca's wife's age was near Lucy's, would Grover refer to a pregnant woman of his mother's generation as an *old lady*? Or did another woman live with the Decas? She could be a mother, an aunt, or no relation at all—perhaps a friend fallen on hard times. Harriet understood that all too well. She and Aubrey had been taken in by their aunt and uncle when they had nowhere else to go.

Playing her hunch, Harriet said, "The family is fortunate to have an extra set of hands to help once the baby arrives."

The remark drew curious looks from the couple. "Who would that be?" Antonia's husband said.

"You can't mean her mother?" Antonia scoffed. "The busybody is hardly any help. She's more work than any child. Always complaining. At least we don't have to listen to her."

"We listen," the husband interjected, "we just don't understand her."

"She speaks only German," Antonia explained.

Would detecting ever be easy? Notwithstanding a protective husband and a bedridden woman who could give birth at any moment, Harriet didn't doubt she would eventually find a way to interview Mrs. Deca's mother. But she'd never learn German in a matter of days. She must find someone to translate for her, compounding the task significantly.

After wishing Antonia and her husband a good day, she left the building and mounted her bicycle. She would have to deal with the grandmother later. Thankfully, she had another lead to pursue. And it promised to be eventful.

Chapter 13

Vorwaerts Turner Hall was on the city's north side on Twelfth Street. Harriet was neither German nor a neighborhood resident, so she had never been to the castle-like three-story limestone building. After leaving the tenement, she had stopped by the agency and asked those colleagues present if they knew anything about the place. A new secretary, Anna Heinz, who was of German descent, proved a fount of knowledge, explaining that "*Turnverein*" translated to "gymnastic union." Shortened to "Turner" or "Turners," the word referred to the movement's followers who believed physical fitness and discipline were essential to achieving a healthy society. Initially formed in resistance to Napoleon, the Turners had established a sizable presence in Chicago, forming more than thirty athletic clubs across the city. Their current political goals—workers' rights, tax relief, and freedom of speech—aligned with the progressive pursuits of the Socialist Labor Party. That an advertisement for Vorwaerts Turner Hall had been slipped into her pocket at a party meeting made ideological sense, if still unexplained.

Harriet dismounted her bicycle and gazed at the inscription above a third-floor window. *Gut Heil*. Not understanding German, she jotted the words down in her notebook.

She would ask Anna Heinz what they meant when she returned to the office. For now, she must wait for Matthew McCabe. She checked her wristwatch. He had four minutes. He'd not be late. She wondered if punctuality was his nature or on account of their boss's insistence that "An operative shall never be tardy if he wants to remain an operative." Like all of his sweeping pronouncements, Prescott's remark hadn't included *her*. She told herself, *One step at a time. One* case *at a time.*

"A pugilist might take your dour expression as an invitation to enter the ring," Matthew chuckled, approaching on the sidewalk.

"You have me wrong, Mr. McCabe. I'm not so proper a lady as to give notice before throwing a punch."

"I'll remember that," he said, suddenly looking uncertain.

Inside, sounds reminiscent of a playground surrounded them. The bare walls reverberated with shouts, clanging, and running footsteps, creating a cacophony. A dozen or more adolescents swarmed a surprising number of gymnastic apparatuses—parallel bars, rings suspended from the rafters, large mats on which several pairs of boys wrestled, and a boxing ring in which two gloved men traded blows. Despite there being no tennis court, a man with an extraordinary handlebar mustache held a racket and demonstrated a proper backhand stroke to a girl of about sixteen. Harriet's eyes grew larger as they fell upon four other girls tossing a basketball back and forth—they all wore bloomers. Having a pair herself, Harriet appreciated their comfort, offering more freedom of movement than a man's trousers. She had first seen the billowed-legged garment at the Woman's Congress of the World's Columbian Exposition. An energetic woman had spoken about the apparel's virtue as a health aid conducive to physical exercise. Yet even with the bicycling craze of the past decade, few women were bold enough to wear them as they were still considered scandalous by much of the population.

"It appears women and girls are welcome here," Matthew said.

"Is that your way of saying your insistence to serve as my chaperone was unwarranted?"

"One can never be too cautious, Harriet. But it appears you're quite right. Your presence presents no danger. But now that I'm here, I am curious to see all that a German gymnasium has to offer. If you don't mind?"

Harriet caught Matthew's gaze hanging on a handsome blond man swinging on the rings. "Not at all. Your keen observation might spot something of interest I might be inclined to overlook."

Cheeks turned slightly pink, he cleared his throat before saying, "I shall keep my eyes peeled."

She hadn't intended to embarrass him, but that she had pleased her. Only by trusting each other with their greatest secret was such a ribbing possible.

They strolled the facility undeterred. Everyone there appeared too absorbed in their exercise to pay them any mind. After their amazement at discovering a two-lane bowling alley, they entered a corridor leading to the rear of the building. Hearing what sounded like someone rapidly tapping a steel pot with a spoon, Harriet said, "I wouldn't have expected a kitchen."

"And you'd be right," Matthew said as they entered a room where two people were fencing. Dressed in identical snug white jackets and with faces hidden behind dark wire-mesh masks, they appeared like violent ghosts advancing and retreating in a dance to the death. One of the swordsmen lunged. His movement revealed a long pigtail as it swung from his back over his shoulder. Though impossible, Harriet felt a twinge of recognition. The combatants' next round ended with the pigtailed man thrusting his sword past the other's parrying defense to press the tip of his blade to his opponent's belly. The touch ended the match. The two men stepped back, stood at attention, and removed their masks after raising their weapons before them in salute.

Harriet's loud gasp startled Matthew. "What is it?" he said. "You couldn't think he'd actually been stabbed?"

"No, no. It's not that. The man . . . it's a woman—"

"Yes, I can see that. A formidable one at that."

"Matthew, that woman was at the Socialist Labor Party meeting. Her name is Brunhilda Struff."

It took a moment for him to make the connection. "Could she have slipped you the advertisement for this place?"

Harriet recalled departing the meeting. She'd thought it might have been the man named Philip. Had she been wrong? Was it possible that with more deftness Brunhilda had snuck the paper into her coat pocket earlier? Matthew touched Harriet's arm to gain her attention. "I'll wait for you by the entrance. Presuming it was her"—his gaze shifted to Brunhilda—"she'll be more likely to reveal her intentions for luring you here if you're alone."

Harriet nodded in agreement as Matthew disappeared back down the hallway. She had been slightly fearful of Brunhilda before—when the woman hadn't been armed. Reassured by the presence of others, Harriet approached her.

Brunhilda regarded Harriet as if she were a regular presence. "You fence?" she asked. Reaching for a white towel, she dabbed sweat from her forehead and neck.

"I wish I did," Harriet replied, realizing the answer was honest. "It looks most exhilarating."

Brunhilda walked over to a wall of equipment and returned with another jacket, mask, thickly padded glove, and sword. "Then it would seem you're long overdue for your first lesson."

Too shocked for words, Harriet stared at the equipment.

Brunhilda pressed the tip of the sword. "This weapon is called a foil. See. The tip is blunt. The worst that can happen is a clumsy opponent might bruise you. I am not clumsy. Here. I'll help you put this on properly."

As Harriet allowed Brunhilda to help her into the tight-fitting jacket, she wondered if it was possible the woman didn't recognize her from the Socialist Labor Party meeting. She must. And yet she gave no indication of it. Once Harriet was outfitted, Brunhilda said, "We'll start with the basics. First, how to properly hold your weapon." She stood behind Harriet, wrapping arms around her and manipulating her right hand into a precise grip. The woman's body pressed against hers was arousing. Harriet glanced at the entrance, half-expecting to see Matthew standing there with a wide grin. Then a more sobering thought: how long would he wait before concern pulled him back here? His return wouldn't be unwelcome. As strangely alluring as she found Brunhilda, she also sensed danger, whether or not the other woman were armed with a sword.

Harriet stood masked with her foil raised to Brunhilda's. She was told the exercise would be a simple parry. To the oncoming thrust, Harriet would intercept the opposing blade with the midpoint of her own. After a half dozen moves, Brunhilda said, "Are you serious?"

Competitive by nature, Harriet snapped, "I'm doing my best." Hearing Brunhilda chuckle behind her mask, she added, "A good teacher shouldn't ridicule her student."

"I am referring to your interest in the People's Cause, *Harriet*."

Harriet halted. Not only was she remembered, but so was the reason for her visit to the party meeting. "You doubt me?"

"We must be sure. *I* must be sure."

"I am here, aren't I?"

"We need to address your movement."

For a moment, Harriet thought Brunhilda's remark might be some sort of code. But Brunhilda's meaning was literal. She set down her foil and once again stepped behind Harriet, this time placing hands on Harriet's hips, shifting her weight, and repositioning her feet. "Achieving proper footwork in fencing is essential. You are more stable this way. When you attack and retreat, you shuffle forward and back. Like so." She pushed and pulled at Harriet, never loosening her grip on her hips. The sensation was confusing—while trying to concentrate on the correct performance, she couldn't deny titillation. Then she noticed Matthew in the doorway, wearing a look of serious worry. It took her a moment to understand why. Beneath the mask, she was unrecognizable. He didn't know where she'd gone.

"You asked if I were serious, and I said I was," Harriet said. "What proof do you require?"

Brunhilda stepped around to face her. "Monday night. Third floor." She pointed her gloved hand toward the ceiling. "Seven o'clock. Use the stairs off the alley. Bring no one." She reached out and patted the top of Harriet's mask as if she were an obedient dog. "You show promise. I'll take the foil. Leave the rest on the bench."

Removing her mask, Harriet avoided eye contact with Matthew, not wanting Brunhilda to know they'd come there together. She exchanged the borrowed items for her coat and hat and wordlessly passed by him on her way toward the exit, risking only a glance that implored him to say nothing. Once outside, she stopped and waited for him on the front steps.

A moment later, he sidled up to her. "That was the most awkward tango I've ever seen," he deadpanned. "I don't suppose you charmed her senseless?"

"I should think I did a good bit better." Mischief twinkled in her eyes. "I scored an invitation to the dance."

Chapter 14

Several miles south of downtown, Harriet, Matthew, and Aubrey arrived at a large undeveloped parcel of land on the lakeshore. The hired buggy's driver pulled the reins, slowing the horses to a stop at the entrance to Rowley's Gun Club. The weekend visit was the result of a series of negotiations. In return for Aubrey's promise not to touch Harriet's pistol, she had asked her colleague to instruct her brother on the derringer's proper use. Matthew had agreed in exchange for Harriet's pledge to carry her weapon at all times and ensure it was loaded before venturing into any potentially dangerous situation. Theodore Prescott had insisted on the same when assigning her current investigation. In truth, she would have done so regardless of either man's dictate. While working on her previous case, her gun had been all that stood between her and occupying a grave next to her parents. She needed no further convincing.

Harriet and Aubrey followed Matthew to a small clapboard building. Matthew presented his membership credentials to Mr. Rowley and introduced Aubrey as his younger brother. Mr. Rowley remembered Harriet from her previous visits as Matthew's cousin from Wisconsin.

The falsehood, conjured by Matthew, was to comply with club rules that a woman be accompanied by a member—all men—and because family members received a discounted admission. It had only been two weeks, but to Harriet's eye, the proprietor had added a few pounds, his red frayed suspenders strained over his big belly. He set down his whittling and rose from a stool.

Aubrey wasn't the only Morrow excited to be there. Harriet was eager to purchase a holster. The satchel Pearl had given her was a tremendous improvement over a traditional lady's handbag, but still, drawing her derringer with haste would prove difficult—no menacing person would wait patiently while she rummaged through either bag. Mr. Rowley surprised her with his eagerness to help select a model of appropriate size for her derringer. After strapping on three holsters that hung obtrusively from a belt and rested uncomfortably against her hip, Mr. Rowley snapped his fingers and dug inside a cabinet to retrieve an Ellery Arms Pocket Holster for a right draw. "Mind, this'n requires a pocket large enough to fit the holster. Otherwise, it'll keep the gun snug so that it don't jostle in your pocket. Another reason to like this'n is you don't gotta unbutton your coat to get to it. Just slip your hand into your pocket, pull 'er out, and *BANG!*" He fired a shot at Matthew using his finger as a pistol.

After nods from Matthew and Aubrey, she placed two dollars on the counter.

Mr. Rowley assigned them to a shooting lane at the range's farthest reaches, explaining, "You'll have plenty of space out yonder. Men get distracted when a girl is shooting." Dispelling any suggestion that Harriet's female form would be the reason, he added, "They worry about a girl's aim."

Unwilling to let the remark pass, Harriet quipped, "I'm sure Annie Oakley might beg to disagree."

Mr. Rowley guffawed and slapped a meaty hand on the counter. "I suspect you'd be right about that, miss!"

As the threesome trudged across the grounds, Aubrey said, "That pocket holster is a slick item. I'll grant you that, Harriet. But what'll you do when wearing a dress? You'll have no pocket."

She'd asked herself the same thing when handing over the payment. Half of the year, when the weather demanded an overcoat, she would have a ready external pocket. Otherwise, when she must wear a dress with no coat, she would have to return to keeping her pistol in her satchel—another reason she intended to wear women's clothing only when the job required it.

Having lost interest in Harriet's recent purchase, Aubrey turned to Matthew. "How old are you?"

Matthew slid him a sideways glance. "How old do you think I am?"

"Thirty?" Aubrey cocked his head as if a different angle would provide a hint.

"Not for two more years."

"If you're twenty-eight, shouldn't you be married?"

"Aubrey!" Harriet scolded, knowing the question, cheeky under the best of circumstances, was especially awkward for Matthew. "That is most certainly none of your concern. You'll mind your manners or we shall turn right around this instant. Mr. McCabe is doing you a great favor by allowing you to come here. You will show him proper respect."

Cowed and head-dropped, Aubrey didn't appreciate his sister's tongue-lashing. That it was administered in front of a man he clearly admired made it all the worse. As for Matthew, whether his look of unease was due to Aubrey's impudence or Harriet's reprimand—or both—was uncertain.

They walked in silence. Matthew eventually replied, "Love doesn't come easy for everyone, my young friend. When your time comes, may you be fortunate that it does."

Aubrey opened his mouth to speak, but Harriet's flared nostrils and hard stare made him think twice.

Matthew said brightly, "Harriet's pistol, the one we'll be shooting today, is a Remington Double Derringer. John Wilkes Booth used a not-so-dissimilar gun in the assassination of President Lincoln. The weapon's compact size makes for easy carrying and concealment."

When they arrived at their shooting lane, Harriet withdrew her pistol from her new holster. Matthew said, "This derringer double barrel fires two .41-caliber copper rimfire cartridges filled with black powder." He showed Aubrey how to load the pistol by breaking open the barrels at a hinge at the top and sliding a cartridge into each chamber before handing the gun back to Harriet. "I apologize, Harriet. It's your gun. You've proven yourself to be skilled in its use. You should be showing him."

With a nod, she took the pistol, closed the barrels, cocked the hammer, and raised the gun, her arms outstretched. Aiming toward the target, she pulled the trigger twice. Each shot emitted a loud pop and puff of black powder. She deftly extracted the spent cartridges and slipped two new ones into the barrel but hesitated before handing the weapon to Aubrey.

"This gun is not a toy. It was made for one reason alone. To cause serious harm to another person. As Matthew just reminded us, its intended use is often to kill. Bringing you here and teaching you to shoot is purely pragmatic. A gun is too great a fascination for a sixteen-year-old boy to resist. I'd rather you learn to shoot under supervision and gain the knowledge to prevent a horrible accident. Still, let there be no misunderstanding between us. You are not to touch my pistol in any circumstance other than this."

The eye roll that was her brother's common reply whenever he felt lectured was absent. But as much as she'd like to attribute his restraint to respect for her authority, she'd have bet the price of a packet of cartridges that it was because he wanted to appear mature in front of Matthew.

In between rounds, Harriet discussed her investigation

with Matthew. "I don't suppose you know anyone with an ability to speak German?" she asked.

"*Du bist ein sehr gutaussehender Mann.*"

"You! Why haven't I known this? All this time, including our recent outing to the gymnasium, and you said nothing?"

"That's the entirety of my foreign vocabulary, I'm afraid. And before you ask"—he glanced Aubrey's way and lowered his voice—"I'll tell you what that means later. Why do you ask?"

Unable to hide her disappointment, she explained that Mrs. Deca's mother lived with the family above the Faras' former apartment and that Grover Fara claimed that he and his brother, Chester, had seen her hovering over Eugene Eldridge's body in the hallway just outside their door. "So, you see, once I devise a plan to speak with the grandmother, I need someone alongside me to translate."

"Why not Pearl?"

Harriet's and Matthew's heads snapped in Aubrey's direction.

"Pearl? Pearl Bartlett?" Harriet was quite sure they knew no other Pearl, but she was too doubtful not to clarify.

"What other Pearl is there?" Aubrey said, with the return of his familiar eye roll.

"What makes you think Pearl can speak German?" Harriet replied.

"Last Sunday when we were eating dinner at her house, I asked her about the cake she made for dessert. Remember? She called it a Black Forest cake. She told me her mother and grandmother were German and they taught her how to make it."

Considering this information, Harriet realized she'd never had reason to ask Pearl about her heritage or maiden name. Having German parents—presuming her father was also German—didn't necessarily mean Pearl had learned the language or was still conversant. But if she were, Harriet might have finally caught a lucky break. The grandmother might be inclined to speak with a woman of her generation, and when it came to talking, few could match Pearl Bartlett.

Harriet would have left her brother and colleague and rushed to Pearl's mansion had it not been Saturday, the day Pearl spent without fail in Evanston with her sister. Fortunately, she and Aubrey would join Pearl for dinner the following evening. The tradition of Sunday supper at Pearl's was just two weeks old, but Harriet could tell Aubrey looked forward to it as much as she did, though for different reasons: the evenings filled her with warm memories of family gathered around a table. For Aubrey, she suspected he savored a break from her mediocre cooking.

As Aubrey took aim, he said, "Or why not ask Barbara? She speaks German, too."

"Barbara is Polish," Harriet said. "She speaks Polish."

Aubrey turned from the target. "Who put a bee in your bonnet?"

"I'm not cross. I'm simply correcting you."

"That's all you ever do! You're not my mother, Harriet."

Having to witness the siblings' quarrel, Matthew grimaced uncomfortably. Harriet immediately regretted her instinctive need to correct. This was a big day for Aubrey, and she had unintentionally embarrassed him in front of a man he looked up to. Aubrey fired two quick shots. She didn't doubt that he was imagining her as the target.

Striving to regain the day's jolly mood, Harriet said, "I was thinking we could all enjoy a spot of supper after we are finished here, but I'm afraid I've too much work to tend to." She looked suggestively at Matthew. "But you two should go on without me. I would be happy if you did. My treat."

Aubrey's eyes fixed on Matthew, eager to hear his reaction to the proposal.

"Well . . ." Matthew drew out the word, rubbing his chin. "I suppose my young friend and I could manage dining at Henrici's, feasting on their finest steaks and sampling every last dessert on their menu. Since it's your treat and all."

Aubrey managed to not drop the pistol but the same couldn't be said for his jaw. Harriet looked as if she'd stepped in fresh manure.

Seeing his jest had been taken seriously, Matthew said, "Though, on second thought, a maître d' and white tablecloths are too fussy for us young city gents." He ruffled Aubrey's hair. "How about we try the new place, Berghoff's? I hear they make an excellent hamburger steak sandwich."

"Let me fire two more shots!" Aubrey said excitedly.

"*Thank you,*" Harriet silently mouthed.

On the way out, they stopped by the shooting range office so Harriet could purchase a few items—a small canister of oil, a tiny bristle brush, and a soft cloth to clean the pistol, along with two packets of cartridges. Mr. Rowley appeared to relish performing a maintenance demonstration for Aubrey. Once it was shiny as new, she slipped the derringer into her holster. The snug fit pleased her intensely.

Leaving the range, Harriet tried handing Matthew a dollar, but he brushed it away. "That's entirely unnecessary, Harriet. It's my pleasure."

"No, no. I insist," she argued. "It was my idea, and I'm happy to do it."

Matthew shook his head. "You can buy me a beer one of these days." Then, with Aubrey practically skipping with glee beside him, he waved down a buggy.

Harriet watched them depart with a lump in her throat. Her gratitude for Matthew was immeasurable. Her colleague had offered crucial assistance in solving her first case and had become a trusted friend. Now, he was providing her brother time with an older male—a void left by their father's death four years ago. She could think of no finer role model.

Buy him a beer, she would. Presuming she would cross his path one night soon at the Black Rabbit, she'd repay him with a pint of the club's finest stout. Perhaps two.

Chapter 15

Despite her three-story mansion having a grand dining room, Pearl took all her meals at a simple round table in the airy but cluttered kitchen adjoining the orangery. When Aubrey and Harriet first joined Pearl for Sunday supper, Aubrey expressed disappointment at not dining at the twelve-foot-long mahogany table in the formal room. Pearl had rebuffed the notion, saying, "My mother insisted we have dinner in there every night. All of us children had to dress as if we were meeting the queen of Prussia. Which, if you knew my mother, wasn't far off the mark. To this day, I can't walk through that room without a shudder. Why on God's green earth would I want to spoil a good supper by eating in a room with all the warmth of a mausoleum?"

Harriet shuffled around Pearl's kitchen table, arranging the place settings according to their host's unorthodox preference of folded napkins above the plates and the cutlery below. Pearl had declared the configuration to be common sense, and Harriet and Aubrey had accepted the explanation, as they did with everything swirling around Pearl Bartlett, as part of her eccentricity.

"Becker!" Pearl answered when Harriet asked her maiden name. Pointing an enormous carving knife for emphasis, she added, "And would you believe that means 'baker' in German? I guess I have sugar in my veins and butter on my brain! Ha!"

Aubrey shot Harriet an I-told-you-so look.

"You never said," Harriet replied. "I suppose I assumed your people came from England."

"Dreadful place. Soggy. Snobby," Pearl quipped. "Not on your life. My parents came here from what was then the Kingdom of Hanover. Which, if you didn't know—and why would you?—is smack-dab in the middle of what's now Germany." Pearl paused her carving of the roast. "You look unconvinced, Harry. I should think it is obvious. Why else would I have named Toby, Toby?"

Harriet's and Aubrey's heads turned in unison toward Pearl's large white cat, who sat on a kitchen chair, fastidiously cleaning his face. Aubrey was the first to ask. "Toby is German?"

"You asking about the cat or the name?" Pearl said, her eyes still fastened on the roast.

"Are there German cats?" He glanced at Harriet for help.

"I suppose if a cat is born in Germany that would make it a German cat. I can't rightly say if Toby is a German name, but Tobias is. I know of one man, Tobias Mayer, a famous mathematician and astronomer. I suppose you could say he spent his career mooning over the moon. Ha! My great-grandfather was a colleague of Tobias Mayer's at the University of Göttingen. I've no reason to remember the man but for his portrait hanging in our parlor."

"Pearl doesn't sound like a German name, though," Aubrey said, impressing Harriet with his tenacity to unravel the mystery of Pearl's heritage.

"Put the potatoes on the table, would you?" Pearl replied, handing him a large serving bowl. "Not all things in life are worth the fight, son. The proper spelling of my name turned out to be one of them. *P-E-R-L-E* was an uphill battle, let me tell you. At some point during my adolescence, I just stopped correcting people." She paused for a chuckle. "I never did tell my mother. Lord have mercy. You should have seen the look on that woman's face when she saw my and Horace's wedding invitations. You could practically hear the whistle of steam pouring out her ears. She swore a blue streak—in German, of course—before marching off to the printer."

"Do you still speak the language?" Harriet asked.

"Why do you ask, Harry? What's gotten into you two? Why all these questions?"

Harriet told Pearl about the grandmother who lived above the Faras' former apartment. Pearl described her German as "proficient," thanks to her mother's demand that she and her siblings speak only German at home, a tradition Pearl's sister kept alive to that day. When Harriet described her scheme to have Pearl accompany her to the tenement building to cajole the grandmother living above the Faras into conversation and learn what she knew about the murder of Eugene Eldridge, Pearl readily agreed to go along but cautioned Harriet about raising her hopes, saying, "Just because we'll understand one another, doesn't mean she'll want to talk."

Once again, Theodore Prescott's words floated in her mind. *It is the door most forcefully shut, Miss Morrow, that you must find a way to open.*

"Yes, I know, Pearl. But we must try."

"The woman's name?" Pearl asked.

"I confess, I don't know. The daughter's surname is Deca—"

"Not German," Pearl interjected. "Not common anyway."

"The daughter is married, so Deca would be her husband's family name. I suppose we'll find out her mother's name tomorrow." Noticing Pearl's odd expression, Harriet said, "What is it? Something wrong?"

"I might be short on apples."

Unsure of the remark's meaning, Harriet shook her head.

"You'll understand tomorrow, Harry."

"Why not tell me now?"

"Do I strike you as the sort of person to spoil a surprise?"

For the morning's visit to the tenement, Harriet had offered to fetch Pearl by buggy, but Pearl had refused, saying, "Let's not spoil the surprise." Choosing to ignore the bewildering remark, Harriet agreed to meet her in front of the building at nine o'clock—an hour at which the men would surely be at work in the nearby stockyard. Per usual, Harriet traveled by bicycle.

While awaiting her friend's arrival, Harriet glimpsed a rider on a brown horse slip into an alleyway two blocks away. *Brown horse.* Could it be the same brown horse and rider she worried were following her the other day? How many brown horses must there be in Chicago? Thousands? Tens of thousands? Despite her misgivings, she shrugged it off. Countless people traveled the main roadways each hour, many on horseback. And brown was the most common color of horse.

Hearing a buggy approach from the opposite direction, Harriet turned.

"Good morning, Harry!" Pearl waved through the open window.

The buggy slowed. The horse stamped its hooves and whinnied. Harriet helped Pearl climb down while she held a large hat box.

"Is that a German tradition of some kind?" Harriet asked. "To bring a gift?"

"It works magic. Just you wait. Why are you in a skirt?" Raising a finger, she added, "Let me guess. Here at the tenement, you are to be a proper young lady."

"And a representative of the University Settlement."

Harriet led Pearl inside. If Pearl was disturbed by the dim, dank conditions, she didn't let on. Harriet moved slowly down the hallway to ensure Pearl kept up. Reaching the staircase, she turned back. "Mind your footing. The steps are uneven. I'm afraid our destination is on the third floor." They started up. The squeaking floorboards underfoot told Harriet her companion was right behind her. At the second-floor landing, Harriet halted. She pointed to a slightly darker spot on the floor, presuming that with greater illumination the discoloration would reveal itself to be a large bloodstain. "This is where it happened." Then pointing at the nearest door, she said, "That's where the Faras lived."

Pearl nodded her understanding. They continued up to the third floor. Standing before the Decas' apartment door, Harriet hesitated, nervous. Something told her there would be no middle ground in the pending encounter. It would be either a triumph or a spectacular failure. The outcome would be known in minutes. She knocked.

The sound of racing footsteps preceded the door's flying open. A woman approximately Pearl's age greeted them, out of breath and appearing frantic. "*Du bist der Arzt?*"

Pearl stepped forward. "*Nein, brauchst du eins?*"

"What is it?" Harriet looked from Pearl to the other woman and back. "What's going on?"

"I don't know," Pearl said, "but it seems they're expecting a doctor."

A woman's scream inside the apartment gave Harriet and Pearl a start.

The grandmother, presumably, turned and rushed back inside toward the outburst. Before Harriet could decide what to do, Pearl hurried after the grandmother. The apartment was as cramped and bleak as the others Harriet had seen during her first visit to the tenement. It took only a half dozen steps before she stood beside a small bed where Mrs. Deca lay, knees spread and drenched with sweat, in the throes of childbirth.

Harriet's eyes darted urgently around the room as Pearl and the grandmother spoke in German. Five other children, all younger than ten, sat silently huddled on another bed in the room's opposite corner, their knees tucked to their chins.

Pearl and the woman exchanged words in rapid-fire German.

"This is her daughter," Pearl explained to Harriet. "There's something wrong with the baby. The husband went for the doctor an hour ago and hasn't returned. I'm out of my depth here, Harry. Perhaps it's a miracle we're here. Boil some water and gather whatever clean towels you can find."

A quarter hour later, the mother's screams had drawn Antonia from her downstairs apartment into the Decas' home. Thankfully, Antonia, once a midwife, was familiar with the situation: the baby was positioned feetfirst instead of the correct orientation of headfirst. Antonia explained it was fortunate the baby wasn't coming out bottom first, which would further complicate the already precarious situation. "The danger is that the baby's head gets stuck when it doesn't come headfirst," she said. "Plus, there's a risk the umbilical cord becomes twisted and cuts off the baby's oxygen."

Harriet appreciated Antonia's knowledge, but it did little to quell her anxiety or the atmosphere of desperation. Despite Mrs. Deca's howls of pain, Harriet heard one of the Deca children whimpering on the other side of the room. With Antonia, the grandmother, and Pearl administering to Mrs. Deca, Harriet moved to console the children. The idea was short-lived. Her approach set them into fearful fits. Feeling useless however she tried to assist, she returned to Mrs. Deca's bedside.

Antonia's and Pearl's constantly shifting bodies blocked Harriet's view of Mrs. Deca, but she understood the situation had reached a critical point. The poor woman's screams reached a fevered pitch. Pearl turned abruptly. "Harry, help!"

Harriet didn't move, unsure what she was being asked to do.

"Hold her hand and keep telling her to push," Pearl instructed.

Glancing down between Mrs. Deca's legs, Harriet gasped. A tiny body protruded from the mother, its head still inside the birth canal. Antonia cupped the tiny body in her hands. "We need to keep his back to us. Help me hold him securely," she said to Pearl before slipping a hand inside the mother to support his head. "We must keep his chin tucked to his chest. This is important."

Pearl shot Harriet a worried look. Harriet squeezed the mother's hand tighter. "Push, Mrs. Deca. Push!"

The mother, strands of wet hair clinging to her red face, huffed and puffed between agonizing moans. The next instant, the baby's head emerged. Mrs. Deca collapsed back onto the bed, releasing Harriet's hand. And just like that, the five Deca children were now six.

"*Gott sei Dank,*" murmured the grandmother.

"Thank God," repeated Pearl.

Half an hour later, the husband arrived to a room full of family, neighbors, and Harriet and Pearl. There was no doctor with him. He was clearly soused. Harriet had been watchful for an opportunity for Pearl to engage the grandmother, but the commotion in the tiny apartment had never allowed it. With the man of the house returned, she knew her chances had all but vanished. Apparently, Pearl also sensed their rapidly dwindling opportunity. She said something to the grandmother in German in a lowered voice to not attract the husband's attention. In return, the grandmother shook her head strenuously. Harriet observed the exchange, and a knot formed in her stomach. Pearl nodded and gently touched the woman's arm. She shrugged it off and said something in her native tongue. Whatever the words, her tone was angry, defiant. Pearl stepped back, hands raised, signaling peace.

Despite Pearl's hushed voice, the husband must have overheard. He stepped between them. "*Du hast nichts gesehen!*" he roared into his mother-in-law's face. Then, turning to Pearl, he shouted, "*Aussteigen!*" spittle flying from his mouth.

Pearl, whom Harriet had never seen frightened, cowered before grabbing her coat and racing into the hallway. A moment later, Harriet stood beside her on the landing, holding her own coat and hat.

"The lout ordered me out," Pearl said. "I'm sorry, Harry. That wasn't what you'd hoped for."

Pearl's understatement was so overwhelming that Harriet blurted a brief laugh. "What did he say to his poor mother-in-law?"

"*Du hast nichts gesehen. You saw nothing.*"

"So you asked her? You asked if she'd seen Eugene Eldridge?"

"Do you mind if we get out of here first, Harry?"

Harriet led Pearl down the three flights of stairs and into the morning sunshine. Despite the stench wafting from the stockyards, the outdoor air was a relief. Both women held a hand to their forehead to shield their eyes.

"The grandmother's name is Marie Batchelder. She claims the Fara boys must be confused," Pearl said. "She says they were frightened and saw things they didn't. Marie Batchelder is lying, Harry. Sure as that man went straight to the bottle and the arms of another woman while his wife was giving birth, Marie Batchelder is a liar."

Like the rope in a tug-of-war, Harriet was pulled in opposite directions. She wanted desperately to know more about what Marie Batchelder had seen but was also curious to follow up on why Pearl believed the husband had been with another woman—that he was drunk was self-evident.

"How can you be sure the grandmother was lying about what the boys saw?"

"I asked if she heard about a man being killed in the building. I said *nothing* about the Fara boys. If she's telling the truth—"

"She couldn't know that Chester and Grover Fara opened

their door and saw her. Moreover, she had no way of hearing about their account afterward. All four children were taken away to children's homes before she'd have had a chance."

Harriet was at once excited and frustrated. She had confirmed the grandmother, Marie Batchelder, as a witness but still had no way to extract her account.

"Don't look so down in the dumps, Harry. Let's give the family a day or two to settle down, and we'll return. With the man at work, I'll get Marie Batchelder to talk. Mark my words. That woman has a secret and is dying to tell someone."

Harriet let the "dying" part of the remark pass in favor of asking, "Why do you believe the husband had been with a woman?"

"The scoundrel had a long strand of hair, much too long for any man and longer than his wife's, stuck to his coat collar."

"But his mother-in-law seemed sure he'd gone for a doctor. Taking to the bottle is despicable enough without adding a woman to the betrayal."

"Not all men are louts, Harry. But after seventy years of kicking, my order of preference for all God's creatures is Toby first, other animals, children, women, and then men—your dear brother being a notable exception."

"I am grateful for your help today, Pearl. Truly, I am. And your optimism is appreciated. But I very much doubt we'll get past the front door next time, even with the husband away."

"Harry!" Pearl looked as if she had been slapped. "That's the first unkind thing you've ever said to me."

The ground shifted below Harriet's feet. She held no one in higher esteem or affection. That she had insulted Pearl was utterly mortifying. "I'm sorry, Pearl, but I'm . . . I don't understand."

"I don't go around tooting my horn, but my *Apfelkuchen* has won prizes."

Harriet started to laugh before realizing her friend was deadly serious. "I'm sorry, I still—"

"The hat box, Harry!" Pearl exclaimed as if it were as obvious as the bowler on Harriet's head.

"Yes, yes. Of course." In all the hubbub, Harriet had forgotten that Pearl had arrived with a large hat box. "You've done more than your share, Pearl. Wait here. I shall go and fetch it. I won't be more than a minute."

Pearl grabbed her arm. "Why on earth would you want to go and do that? That's our invitation back inside."

Harriet pinched the bridge of her nose. "Pearl, please . . ."

"There's a German apple cake inside that box, Harry. And believe you me, once Marie Batchelder gets a taste of the homeland, I'll be her new *bester Freund*."

For once, Harriet needed no translation. She hugged Pearl tightly, committing the words to memory.

Chapter 16

The sixth-floor offices of the Prescott Detective Agency exuded the cold efficiency of a well-run restaurant kitchen. There were no personal effects, no frivolous comforts, no adornments. The stark exception was Theodore Prescott's corner office. The principal's inner sanctum reminded Harriet of the lobby of the Palmer House hotel, a space deserving of words like sumptuous and elegant—and expensive. A week had passed since Mr. Prescott assigned Harriet to the case of the murdered muckraker. Although she had provided Madelaine with daily reports to be passed on to Prescott, today, he had requested an in-person update. Harriet didn't fear Prescott as did most operatives, but he did frequently unnerve her. His lofty standards were reflected in his agency's peerless track record for solving cases, his demand for professionalism in all aspects of detecting, and his schoolmaster scowl. At the recent Friday detectives' meeting, she'd witnessed him silence the chattering room with a subtle pursing of his lips before reducing the blustering Charles Bonner to a groveling hulk for arriving three minutes and thirteen seconds late. The occasion had caused her to wonder, not for the first time, which he would sooner sacrifice: his Catholic faith, the love of his family, or punctuality.

Given the three o'clock hour, Harriet's pressing worry was Prescott's legendary temper, widely known to be easily triggered after a midday meal that commonly included a high scotch-to-beef steak ratio at his private gentlemen's club on Michigan Avenue.

Madelaine tilted her head toward Prescott's closed double doors, indicating the agency principal was in. After a knock, Harriet slipped inside. Her boss stood behind his desk chair, hands folded behind him, gazing out the window. Although he must have heard her enter, he didn't turn or speak. She approached uncertainly, her apprehension increasing with each step. After a minute that felt like an eternity, she risked interrupting his thoughts. "You wanted to see me, Mr. Prescott?"

He swept an arm before him, indicating the expanse beyond the window. "Do you know when this all started, Miss Morrow?" Even though she knew he would eventually speak, hearing his voice nonetheless startled her.

"I'm not sure what you're asking me, sir."

Still facing the window, he said, "Chicago was incorporated as a town in 1833. At the time, the population was just three hundred and fifty people. Of course, the land's rightful owners were the Indians. That same year, a treaty forced those remaining to move west of the Mississippi River by 1838. Now, sixty years later, well over one and a half million people are scurrying about out there. A million and a half, Miss Morrow. Where did they all come from? Have you ever thought of that?" He finally turned to face her.

"Most from across the ocean, I should think," she answered, adding, "though, not all at once or in one boat."

The ends of his fastidiously trimmed mustache lifted in the hint of a smile.

"Tens of thousands of Germans, English, Irish, and Scandinavians. More recently, waves of Jews, Czechs, Poles, and Italians. With the war's end, an increasing number of former slaves are finding their way up north. Different nationalities, cultures, traditions, and languages all united by one goal." He paused, landing his gaze squarely upon her.

Understanding he'd implied a question, she answered, "To make a better life for themselves."

"And they chose Chicago as the city to do it in. That's a lot of people competing for the same thing, Miss Morrow. There are only so many jobs and places to live. People resort to doing what they can, taking what they can get. Along with the many hardships facing them, there's no shortage of men eager to take advantage of their vulnerabilities. It's this condition of desire and desperation that enables our city's powerful ward-based political machines."

He gestured toward a chair before his desk. "Sit, Miss Morrow." He followed by lowering himself onto his throne-like chair. "This matter of the murdered journalist bothers me greatly. Murders happen, of course. Did you know, on average, two occur in the city each week? To take another's life manifests the darkest of human nature. But this particular killing has a particular stench about it. Presuming the letter Gerald Cole received is truthful and that this Eugene Eldridge fellow had the goods on a corrupt politician, his murder is no coincidence. It must be connected. That means a Chicago politician, a man in a position of civic authority, either killed him or is complicit in his killing. There's no shortage of suspects. You'll recall our previous conversation about the Gray Wolves?"

Drawing Harriet's nod, he continued. "Whoever murdered the journalist or ordered the deed done thinks he can execute a citizen of this city with impunity. That cannot stand. This isn't the Wild West. He must be stopped, brought to account!" Prescott slammed his fist to the desk, causing a silver pen in its stand to topple and Harriet to jump. "I'm relying on you, Miss Morrow, to find the killer, along with the missing evidence necessary to convict him." He paused again, his words settling over her with the weight of a heavy quilt. "So. Now that you fully appreciate the intensity of my interest, tell me, Miss Morrow: How close are you to finding Eldridge's killer?"

After taking a deep, steadying breath, Harriet recounted her past six days of investigation. Although she had described all but the weekend's activities in her daily reports, she didn't consider giving Prescott an in-person summary onerous. To the contrary, the retelling was invigorating, and her boss's occasional "Is that so?" and "Most interesting" offered much-needed encouragement. When she told him about the previous day's visit to the tenement, his expression turned dour. Her stomach twisted. In an instant, she understood why. She'd been stupid for not seeing it coming.

"I'm astounded you thought it a good idea to involve that busybody Pearl Bartlett in your investigation. I understand that while searching for her maid you formed a parental—or grandmotherly—affection. Much to my consternation, Mrs. Prescott feels the same. Though I'll never know what either of you sees in the woman besides her ability to churn out a seemingly endless supply of cakes and cookies."

Harriet opened her mouth to defend her friend, but seeing Prescott's narrowed eyes, she decided not to press an argument she could not win.

"Need I remind you, Miss Morrow, it is the door most forcefully shut that must be opened? From what you've said, that door is at the tenement. Get the grandmother to talk. And under no circumstance will you ever again involve Pearl Bartlett in your work. Do I make myself clear?"

Harriet fought the urge to rebut his every point. First, she recalled his words about opening doors quite well—she didn't need reminding. Second, Pearl Bartlett was *not* a busybody. At Harriet's request, she'd been doing the agency a tremendous favor. Third, she couldn't communicate with German-speaking Marie Batchelder without Pearl. Theodore Prescott was unquestionably a renowned detective and her superior, but in this instance, he was just plain wrong. Still, she wasn't so foolish to tell him that. Ultimately, she would be judged by whether she recovered the evidence to bring the Gray Wolf to justice if, indeed, one of them was behind the crime. Prescott might be vexed that she'd not done as told, but she'd be forgiven as long as she succeeded. However, if she failed, she'd be shown no mercy for her insubordination. Her second case as an operative at the Prescott Agency would surely be her last.

"As you wish, Mr. Prescott," she said, starting to rise.

"I'm not finished."

She lowered back down and prepared for another round of scolding, though she couldn't guess for what.

"It's fortunate timing that the People's Cause will be gathering later today. I certainly hope you find Eldridge's fiancée in attendance or at minimum ascertain information that leads to her whereabouts without further delay. Now, I am finished." He dropped his gaze to an open page of the *Chicago Tribune* spread out before him. "You may go."

Returned to her office, Harriet understood why the other operatives were seldom found in theirs. Little investigation was done from behind a desk. The recent exceptions were Matthew and another colleague, who were assigned a complex tax fraud case that had them combing through stacks of documents. She didn't want to interrupt Matthew but rationalized that a visit would give him a break from his tedious examination of ledgers while allowing her to thank him again for taking Aubrey to supper. She had known her brother would enjoy the time spent with the dashing detective but hadn't imagined how much. From the "Best meal of my life" to "Matthew is the smartest person I know," Aubrey had spoken of nothing else from the moment he arrived home from Saturday's outing.

Unlike most of the men with whom Harriet shared the corridor, Matthew didn't smoke cigars or cigarettes, making his the only office other than her own that, when occupied, wasn't filled with acrid smoke. But that didn't mean his office was comfortable. Whereas hers was often unbearably warm, his was unusually cold. Knowing this in advance, she wore her hat and coat.

"How are you able to hold a pencil and calculate figures with frozen fingers?" Harriet said, mocking a shiver.

"You'd best not wind me up," Matthew replied, peering over a mountain of binders. "I'm already tempted to strike a match to these pages. The added benefit of a warm fire might prove too much to resist."

They took turns catching each other up on their work. Matthew was fatigued and disinterested, combing through tax documents. Harriet was frustrated and impatient, running into one dead end after another. Talking with Matthew, she didn't feel so alone and overwhelmed by her task. He related to her struggles and had his own. The conversation didn't solve either of their problems, but Harriet found relief in commiserating about their work. When they'd exhausted the topic of their separate investigations, Harriet turned to a personal subject: Aubrey.

"I can't thank you enough for spending time with my brother. To say he had a grand day wouldn't be the half of it."

"Truly, it was no trouble. Though I had no helpful advice regarding his living situation, that's best resolved between you and him, as I'm sure you will agree." Registering Harriet's baffled expression, he continued. "Has he not mentioned any of this to you?"

"I haven't the foggiest idea what you're talking about."

"Oh, dear." Matthew's expression turned sheepish. "I assumed . . ."

"You've no choice now but to tell me. Don't think I won't hound you relentlessly until you do."

"I've no doubt Aubrey loves you, Harriet. You must know that, surely."

"Now you're frightening me, Matthew. Better to just come out with it."

"Yes, I suppose now I must. Aubrey has it in his head that he is going to live with Pearl Bartlett."

Harriet's jaw dropped.

"Understand," Matthew said, "the boy's at an age when his brain is telling him to exert independence. He feels bossed by his sister while his friends boast of adventures, though as Aubrey describes them, they are ridiculously embellished. More than anything, it's obvious that he has not gotten over the loss of your parents. My sense is he's searching for a way to escape his unhappiness. Unfair as it is, Harriet, and it is terribly unfair, you are the easiest person for him to blame. As a surrogate parent, you are a constant reminder that his real parents are dead. He looks to Pearl as a permissive and indulgent grandmother *with a mansion*. He has conjured a fantasy of living there with her, thinking he would be free to do as he pleases, have Pearl cook him wonderful meals, and impress his friends by showing off his opulent home."

"I had no idea." Learning something so momentous about her brother from someone he barely knew stung. She understood a sixteen-year-old boy would be disinclined to confide in his sister, especially when he held her responsible for his unhappiness, but the magnitude of Aubrey's self-centeredness was a shock. Still, she was grateful he had Matthew to talk to, knowing his counsel would be sensible and wise. Swallowing her pride, she said as much.

"I know you find this upsetting, Harriet. I'm sorry, but I had to tell you. What chance do you have of resolving a problem you don't know exists?"

So jumbled were Harriet's emotions that she couldn't settle on a single feeling. Furious that Aubrey wasn't grateful for her efforts to protect and provide for him, she was also sympathetic to his lingering grief. She was disappointed by his selfishness, but he was sixteen. Wasn't expecting him to exhibit greater maturity unreasonable? She was offended that he considered their family home not good enough, yet she couldn't deny the appeal of having a bathroom to herself, having plentiful hot water, and not constantly cleaning up after him.

"Thank you for telling me, Matthew."

"Again, I'm sorry, Harriet. Are you all right?" Matthew leaned over his paperwork. "You realize, of course, that if Aubrey learns I told you how he's feeling, he'll be angry at both of us—me for betraying his confidence and you for being in alliance with me."

"Good grief, Matthew. If you can't talk sense into him, who will? He can't continue to entertain such a ridiculous illusion. And yet, if he's truly so miserable living with me, I fear it's only a matter of time until he runs away."

"I've been giving this thought," Matthew stood and raked a hand through his hair. "You trust Pearl, yes?"

Harriet's eyes flashed with alarm. "Yes, of course. Completely. Why?"

"I suggest you raise the issue with her in Aubrey's presence. Not directly, but subtly. Perhaps as a joke or a silly idea. Something like 'Pearl, your home is so big. Have you ever considered taking in lodgers? Would you ever consider inviting anyone to live with you?' If Pearl is truly averse to the possibility, let her be the one to disabuse Aubrey of the notion. That should put the matter to rest. As for the primary problem of his discontent, I've been thinking about introducing him to a new and exciting activity. I haven't been his age for more than a decade, but still, I recall how a fresh outlet can prove a marvelous distraction from a daily routine that feels restrictive and ho-hum."

"What have you in mind?"

"Boxing."

"Boxing!"

"You must know he's a fan of the sport. When I finally persuaded him to talk about something other than living in a mansion, it was boxing. Primarily, Bob Fitzsimmons."

"I've never understood the fascination." Harriet's grimace reflected her distaste. "Aubrey has always been gentle, more comfortable with his nose in a book than aiming a fist at one. Ever since he read about Wyatt Earp refereeing the bout between Fitzsimmons and Sharkey, he's been obsessed—who's fighting who and for what title."

"It's not a bad skill for a young man to have. I promise I won't allow him to fight anyone. Not at first. We'll work a bag with gloves and cover the basics. Let's see how it goes. Regardless, you can be confident he'll be with me. And it will give him something else to focus on."

"Where will you take him? Not Vorwaerts Turner Hall?"

He shook his head, dismissing the notion. "My people are Scottish, not German. I'm not presuming I'd be unwelcome at the Turner Hall, but as you already know, I don't speak the language. Several of the operatives and I belong to a nearby gymnasium. I'll take Aubrey there."

Harriet let out an audible sigh of resignation. Although she didn't like any of this, Matthew offered a reasonable suggestion, and although he was under no obligation to do so, she appreciated his intervention.

"Thank you, Matthew. That's now two pints I owe you. At this rate, you'll be drinking on my tab for the next month."

He glanced beyond her as if to ensure the door was securely closed. "Will you be going to the Black Rabbit this weekend?"

She chuckled. "Looking to collect so soon?"

"If you must know, that was my subtle way of asking about Miss Wozniak."

Barbara was a topic of mind-spinning confusion. There was no question Harriet had feelings for her. However, acknowledging those feelings complicated her life immeasurably. Before Barbara, there was a teasing desire for other women. But with Barbara in her world, she was forced to confront the reality that she was profoundly different. She was terrified. She was exhilarated. Barbara made her happy. Barbara made her miserable. One moment she was determined to kiss Barbara square on the mouth in the middle of Michigan Avenue, consequences be damned. The next, she wanted to run away with Barnum & Bailey, never to be heard from again. Head swimming, she muttered, "I confess the situation is confounding."

The look Matthew returned was unreadable. Until it wasn't. Plain as a trolley schedule, she read his face. He understood—completely. They remained in that knowing silence for the longest time, just looking at each other. Harriet decided Matthew's lightly freckled nose was beautiful and his eyes were the kindest shade of blue. And despite her insecurities of being heavy in her frame with a nose and broad jaw more suitable for Bob Fitzsimmons than any Harriet, she didn't mind him staring back at her, for she knew he liked her just as she was. And in that moment, two words came to mind. *Bester Freund.*

Chapter 17

At precisely 6:55 P.M., Harriet dismounted her bicycle. Unlike when attending the Socialist Labor Party meeting, where she allowed for time to mingle before the meeting got underway, this night she wanted to observe those gathered at the People's Cause meeting without drawing attention, so she timed her arrival for just minutes before the meeting's scheduled start. The group's secretive nature might invite scrutiny of a newcomer. "*As a detective, you want to be the one asking questions,*" Matthew had told her. Her mission to find Jorinda Grimm, Eugene Eldridge's former fiancée, could begin in earnest once she understood the atmosphere inside the room. Having never attended a radicals' meeting, it was better to keep a low profile. When she did present herself, as she had at the socialists' gathering, she would borrow her mother's maiden name, Dunn.

Harriet took a modicum of comfort by knowing Theodore Prescott and Matthew McCabe knew her whereabouts. As a precaution, she'd asked Aubrey to alert Matthew if she wasn't home by the time he turned in for the night—usually around eleven. Entrusting her brother with that responsibility would have been questionable before he became enamored with Matthew. Now that he had, he seemed to relish having a reason to visit Matthew at his home in the dark of night. Harriet understood the possibility, which she hoped was remote, played into her brother's adolescent fantasy of spies, shadows, and villainous intrigue. Still, that he was properly motivated was reassuring. And whatever misgivings she might have about him venturing out at night alone were outweighed by the risk to her safety if he must.

She followed a young couple about her age up the stairs that clung to the rear of Vorwaerts Turner Hall. Although the moonlight had lit the streets for her ride, it didn't reach the back side of the three-story building and the narrow staircase. She was grateful to have someone lead the way and stayed close behind the couple. When another person began to climb after her, shaking the steps, she gripped the railing tighter and looked down. The angle and darkness obscured his face. A derby hat topped a figure so massive that, for a moment, she wondered if she wasn't seeing two people ascending side by side. The groaning of the staircase made her quicken her pace, nearly bumping into the couple ahead.

Her relief in reaching the top floor gave way to a fresh wave of apprehension. The steeply pitched roof made for a claustrophobic room packed with people and no better lighted than outdoors. She stood on her tiptoes and shifted from side to side to see past the dozens of heads between her and the room's opposite end, where a single unshaded bulb hung from the rafters. The stink of perspiration and mold stung her nostrils. More people entered behind her, further cramming the tight space and pushing her forward against another body. Finding the closest source of the odor, she winced and covered her nose.

A man appeared beneath the light bulb. Given his elevation, he must have been standing on a rostrum. His countenance and build were so ordinary that Harriet imagined his description would match half the men in Chicago. "Welcome!" he bellowed, his piercing tenor voice hushing the room. "Citizens, friends, and fellow workers!" The crowd shuffled and settled themselves. "I stand before you not as

a leader but as a friend and neighbor." Murmurs of satisfaction rippled across the room. He put a hand to his
chest. "My heart swells at seeing so many patriots. We are
assembled here together, as always, united by a belief that
the worker is the one true and honest heartbeat of this
nation. We stand united knowing that for far too long,
industrialist robber barons, propped up by corrupt ward
machine politicians—bloodstained bills spilling from their
pockets—have exploited the laborer to enrich themselves
with no regard for his ill-treatment, meager wages, and
daily suffering! Well, my friends, tonight, join me in proclaiming that the exploitation of workers must end once
and for all! Our oppressors must be defeated!" The room
erupted in applause and shouts of agreement. The man
smiled widely, basking in the crowd's enthused response.
After a long moment, he raised his hands to coax their silence and continued. "You have joined your fellow citizens
tonight because of your strong and courageous commitment to our cause—the People's Cause. Our cause is just.
Our cause is noble. And as God is my witness, our cause
will be victorious!" Several men in the audience offered a
loud "Whoop!" or "Here here!"

"Together, we shall achieve what others have failed to
do. Why? Look around you. Yes, that's it. Look around
you. The answer is found in the face of each citizen to your
right and left, before you and behind." Heads swiveled in
every direction. More curious than obedient, Harriet
turned each way to observe the looks of serious resolve on
the members' faces on either side of her.

"We, here in this room, refuse to accept morally bank-
rupt rules designed by those in power to strengthen their
white-knuckled grip on power while crushing the honest
worker beneath their bootheels!" Another eruption of cheers
and applause. "We, you and I, will earn our fair share because we are unafraid to spill the blood of those who
drain life from *us* in order to stock their mansions with
silver, dress their wives in silk and satin, and ensure their

lineage continues as a new generation of our oppressors. Meanwhile, the noble worker is squeezed into vile, rotting tenements. The noble worker labors until he drops from exhaustion. The noble worker is rewarded with sneering contempt for wishing himself better treatment than a starving dog. I say, fellow citizens, our time is nigh! The pomp and pageantry of the coming anniversary will be our time! If the blood of politicians and industrialists must flow, let us be unafraid to open the vein!"

The crowd went wild, stamping their feet and loudly proclaiming their allegiance to the cause.

"Nearly thirty-three years ago, this nation ended one civil war. Will you join me for the next?" The crowd cheered its assent. "I said, will you join me!"

A bolt of terror shot through Harriet as the bellicose response shook the floor and hurt her ears. She was thankful there was no outlet for the crowd's furor. Otherwise, she had no doubt violence would erupt.

Harriet had come in search of Jorinda Grimm. Was she a believer in revolution? And what about Eugene Eldridge? He'd supposedly met Jorinda at one of these meetings. Had he been there as part of his investigation? Or had he become radicalized? Whatever the answers, Harriet found it was impossible to search for Jorinda. The space was too crowded, and the fiery speech made conversation impossible.

The ordinary-looking man was replaced on the rostrum by the huge man who had followed her up the rear staircase, making her think the raised platform must be made of steel to support his weight. A drummer she couldn't see produced a *rat-a-tat*, and the man started singing in German. By the second line, the entire crowd had joined in. They swayed from side to side, voices raised in an anthem she'd never heard. Given that everyone was standing cheek by jowl, Harriet had no choice but to move with them. The song ended with thunderous applause.

The man to her left jostled her roughly. Annoyed, she

turned to give him a stern look, but the man was no longer there. Instead, Brunhilda Struff stared back at her. She leaned close, a strand of her long hair grazing Harriet's hot cheek. "Enjoying yourself?"

The truthful answer—that she was aghast by the call for violence—wouldn't have served her mission. Instead, she told Brunhilda what she thought she'd want to hear. "Most inspiring."

Standing beside the mysterious woman, Harriet endured two more speeches—neither as fervent as the first—and three more songs, all in German. She couldn't check her watch without Brunhilda noticing, and she didn't want to appear impatient, although she was. The possibility that the night would end without discovering anything to progress her investigation was distressing. Sensing the meeting would soon conclude, she took a gamble and asked Brunhilda, "I don't suppose you've seen Jorinda Grimm?"

Harriet fought the instinct to say more. Prescott had coached her to offer the bare minimum in such circumstances. Liars embellished their fiction, exposing themselves unnecessarily.

Brunhilda must have heard the question, but she didn't reply. She kept her eyes fixed on the woman who now occupied the riser and was read an arcane declaration that sounded as if it had been written by a committee of verbose lawyers. "You'll excuse me," Brunhilda said curtly before pushing her way toward the back of the room. Minutes later, the meeting ended with the crowd reciting—again in German—an oath in unison. The attendees began to file out. To Harriet's surprise, most exited through an interior door, not the exterior staircase. If most people had also entered that way, why had she been instructed to approach from the rear of the building?

Harriet spun in a frantic circle, looking for Brunhilda. Once again, the woman had departed abruptly without saying goodbye. Harriet couldn't abide wasting the opportunity. Although it was rash, she hurried to the nearest woman and asked if she knew Jorinda Grimm. The woman appeared sincere in saying she'd never heard of her. Heart thumping in her chest, she repeated the question to five more people as they awaited their turn through the narrow door to the interior staircase. They all uttered variations of the same thing: they had never heard of Jorinda Grimm.

Harriet shuffled out among the last attendees. Everyone chatted excitedly in German, denying her any overheard comments of interest. On the front side of Turner Hall, the moon shone brightly, illuminating the spot where she'd left her bicycle. Drawing closer, she saw something affixed to her handlebars and quickened her pace. It was another advertisement for the hall. This time, someone had scrawled a message across the front.

I have what you are looking for. Meet me on the roof of the tenement. Come at once. Come alone.

Chapter 18

Be brave, Harriet told herself.

As many times as she had ridden her bicycle in the dark, never had her destination been a tenement in a rough part of the city. Before setting out, she'd noted the time: 9:35 P.M. That gave her nearly ninety minutes to visit the tenement and return home before Aubrey alerted Matthew McCabe that she was late. While that provided some reassurance, it was hardly satisfying—Matthew would look for her at the Turner Hall, not the tenement. Still, she convinced herself she had no choice. Someone claiming to have what she was desperate to find had summoned her. The lead was too promising to ignore, and, besides, she had no other.

At the *Progressive Age*, Steven Bliss had been confident that Eugene Eldridge's fiancée was named Jorinda Grimm and that the two had met at a meeting of the People's Cause. But of those asked, no one had heard of her. Was she new to the organization? Or just unknown? When Brunhilda had heard the name Jorinda Grimm, she'd gone quiet and abruptly left. Harriet's instinct told her the mention of Jorinda's name and Brunhilda's sudden departure were related. Adding to Harriet's apprehension were the provocative speeches, singing, and oath taking at the gathering. When given a chance, should she warn someone? Alert the authorities? To what end? She would consult with Mr. Prescott, but she knew he'd say that inflamed speeches were lawful and that she was allowing herself to be distracted from her primary task. More distressing, he would ask if she had done as ordered and returned posthaste to the tenement to interview the grandmother—*without Pearl*. For a different reason entirely, she was indeed returning. But not, she presumed, to see Marie Batchelder.

Harriet was grateful for the moonlight, although it didn't fully compensate for the lack of streetlamps in the blocks surrounding the stockyard. She slowed her pedaling, scrutinizing the road ahead for bumps and holes. Hearing a shout, she instinctively turned her head. A man staggered out of a saloon and shouted another profanity, then gestured obscenely as if his remark weren't offensive enough. Glad to ride quickly away, she returned her eyes to the road just as her front tire caught in a rut. Her bicycle twisted, pitching her over the handlebars. Her body slammed onto the road, knocking the breath out of her.

She lay on her back, looking up at the moon, as a sharp sting of pain shot through her knee, and her right hand throbbed miserably. She rolled onto her side and began gently climbing to her feet.

"That's a hell of a way to get my attention."

Harriet didn't acknowledge the man. The proximity of his voice told her he was fast approaching. Despite the pain, she hurried to stand and hobbled to where her bicycle lay a few feet away. Thankfully, the tires were intact and the frame hadn't bent. She set the bicycle upright, arched a leg over the lower bar, and, with a wince, lowered herself onto the seat.

"Hey! Where do you think you're going?" The man stumbled toward her.

Provided the bicycle was ridable, she wouldn't get up to speed before he was upon her. She pulled her derringer from her pocket holster and pointed it straight at him.

"That's far enough." Her command came across coolly—
he needn't know it was because she had bitten her tongue
during the tumble.

The man's bloodshot eyes bulged. The pistol's silver barrel glinted in the moonlight.

He raised his hands but didn't stop his approach. She
pulled back the hammer. *Click.*

That stopped him.

"Turn and walk away. Now."

For a long moment, neither of them moved. The man
opened his mouth to speak but apparently rethought the
wisdom of any remark. Reluctantly, he sniffed and turned,
muttering another profanity under his breath. Harriet
couldn't deny the strong urge to pull the trigger. Not to
shoot at him, but near him—close enough to make him
jump. To frighten him and make him feel as vulnerable as
she did. But she wouldn't waste the bullet. Besides, the
sound would drag more men from the saloon, which was
the last thing she wanted.

Ten minutes later, she opened the front door of the tenement building. The dimly lit conditions never changed.
Given the late hour, it was quiet. She suspected most families would have turned in for the night as it was well after
supper and anyone who could work would be up at dawn.
She made her way to the staircase, grateful for her familiarity with the layout. Reaching the third-floor landing,
she hesitated. Never having a reason to go to the roof, she
had no idea how to get there. After roaming the front half
of the hallway and finding no door other than those into
apartments, she searched the back half. A narrow door she
might have presumed opened to a janitor's closet revealed
an even narrower, steeply pitched set of stairs. Three steps
up, the door swung shut behind her, giving her a start.
Now in the pitch black, she raised a foot, feeling for the
next stair, and proceeded slowly up. Two tight turns later,
she arrived at a door that someone had left cracked open,

allowing a sliver of moonlight to spill onto the staircase. She pushed open the door and stepped onto the tenement's roof.

In an instant, she smelled it. Smoke.

She spun around, looking for the source, and gasped. A wood pile had been set ablaze. Flames rapidly spread across the timber roof. She could never stop it herself. She must alert the residents and send for help. Stumbling down the staircase to the third floor, she wasn't sure whether the sound filling her ears was coming from her footsteps or the roof's groaning as it succumbed to flames. She fell against the door and twisted the knob. It spun freely in a complete circle. The door didn't budge. She pushed. Nothing. With her shoulder, she threw her weight against the door. Still nothing. Had someone blocked it from the other side? Was this why she had been summoned there? To be burned alive? But that couldn't be! If someone wanted her dead, they had plenty of chances to kill her without threatening the lives of residents and burning down their homes. Desperate, she screamed for help and pounded on the door. *Pop!* She looked up but couldn't see in the dark. There wasn't much time before the fire sprinted downward, collapsing the roof and consuming the walls. *Pop!* She continued to pound the door. She screamed for help. Smoke rapidly slithered down the enclosed staircase and filled her lungs. She coughed violently.

Voices! Then scraping. Frantic shouts of alarm erupted on the other side of the door. Awareness of the fire was spreading, but could anyone hear her cries for help? Coughing hard, eyes stinging, she kept pounding. Was this to be her fate? To die in a tenement fire? Would there be anything left of her remains that Aubrey could identify? Her bicycle! That might tell people the body burned beyond recognition was hers. She couldn't shout any longer. The smoke was too thick. Her fists were raw. The noise in the hallway and other parts of the building was so loud she lost all hope that anyone could hear her. A thought struck. She fumbled for her pistol. Aiming as best she could toward the doorknob a foot away, she fired. The sound reverberated in the small, enclosed space, hurting her ears. She reached for the doorknob. It was intact. A hole an inch away confirmed she'd missed her target. *Damnation!* One more bullet. She fired again, closer. The sharp *clang* told her she'd hit metal. Elated, she reached again for the knob—it was blasted to bits. Still, the door wouldn't budge. Something must be blocking it from the other side. She slumped down onto the lowest step. A moment later, she lost consciousness.

With eyes closed, Harriet coughed. Pain squeezed her chest. A nurse sat her up, patted her back, and dabbed a moistened cloth at the corners of her eyes and mouth. Harriet's lids fluttered and slowly opened. Her body ached, and she felt lightheaded. She didn't know the time, but daylight streamed through the hospital ward's window.

Oh, Aubrey! He would be beside himself with worry. As would Matthew. Had anyone notified Theodore Prescott about her brush with death? She'd been foolish to be so quickly drawn to the tenement alone at night. What had she been thinking? That Eldridge's killer would be waiting on the roof to hand over the incriminating evidence?

Harriet lay back on her pillow and wept. The nurse gently squeezed her hand, saying she was lucky to have survived. One of the residents, in his panic to flee, had tripped over a board that someone had wedged against the door to the roof. As the man scrambled to his feet, the door swung open, revealing Harriet's collapsed body. He'd carried her out of the building, and an ambulance had brought her to the hospital. As if the nurse could read the thought behind Harriet's furrowed brow, she said, "I'm told no one died in the blaze."

An hour passed before Harriet was able to speak without coughing. The nurse assured her she would get word to her brother. With the clock striking the noon hour, Theodore Prescott burst into the ward with a doctor and two nurses in tow. He rushed to her bedside, wearing a frown.

"Good heavens, Miss Morrow. This won't do at all." He turned to the doctor, who had followed in his wake. "Jasper, why in Hades was I not immediately informed that one of my operatives was admitted and under your care? Do we not have a well-established understanding of such matters?"

Harriet knew only a handful of doctors, and all had displayed unquestioned authority. To see one wither under Mr. Prescott's admonishment was unsettling to Harriet and an obvious shock to the nurses who accompanied him.

"Come now, Theodore," the doctor said, finding his voice, "this patient was brought to us in a most serious condition. To my knowledge, you have no girl detective. Why would I think she'd be one of yours?"

Harriet's voice was too damaged for her to speak up, and she wouldn't have if she could. The men's argument about Prescott's *girl* detective was too intriguing.

"Well, I do, now," Prescott bellowed. "This is Miss Harriet Morrow. Give me your full report." Harriet's interest turned to annoyance as the men discussed her condition while completely ignoring her. She exhibited each symptom the doctor listed: cough, shortness of breath, hoarseness, drowsiness, eye irritation, and swollen nasal passages. She was glad she seemed to have passed the stages of confusion, nausea, and vomiting.

When Prescott had heard enough to convince him that his operative would fully recover, he finally turned back to Harriet.

"What in blazes were you doing in the tenement at that hour, Miss Morrow?"

Her attempt to answer erupted in a coughing spell that caused Prescott to wince and back away from her bed.

"Yes, well . . . I suppose our discussion can wait."

"She is otherwise well enough to take home, Theodore."

"Me?" Prescott looked galled at the notion that he would accompany Harriet home.

Harriet was no more pleased with the idea than was her boss. Theodore Prescott filled a particular place in her world, one that didn't extend to the modest apartment she shared with her brother. It wasn't that she would be embarrassed by his thinking her home was shabby. Instead, his physical presence would feel like an intrusion into the one place that was hers, where the outside world and all of its elements—including her boss—remained safely outside the walls.

"Harriet!"

All heads turned toward the entrance to the ward and the tall, slender boy running toward them.

"Aubrey," Harriet croaked, suppressing a cough. "Just in time. I'm ready to go home."

Chapter 19

Just after dawn the following day, Harriet climbed out of bed and slipped into her housecoat. She made a cup of coffee while Susan rubbed against her ankles. Today, she would resume her investigation. Despite everyone's opinion that she do nothing but recuperate for several more days, she refused to stay cooped up for another minute. She was sufficiently recovered, restless, and desperate to know the extent of the damage done to the tenement and the condition of its residents. Presuming the Decas still had a home, Harriet would need Pearl to interpret a conversation between her and Marie Batchelder—despite Prescott's dictate that she not involve his neighbor. While there, she might also talk with Edita and Mrs. Horak, the two other women she had spoken to during her first visit. They had all refused to discuss the murder, but Harriet hadn't known to ask about Jorinda Grimm. Could Eugene Eldridge's presence that day have anything to do with Jorinda? It may be a long shot, but Harriet had to find out.

First things first. She needed to wash her hair and take a long soak in the bath to ensure she didn't smell like a campfire. Pearl must eventually be told about her near escape from the blaze. If she didn't tell her, Aubrey would. But that could wait. Her friend's worried questioning would be too taxing, and whatever horrid sight might await them at the tenement would be enough distraction.

Although Pearl was an early riser, arriving at her home before eight would be impolite. Harriet turned her attention to breakfast. She hadn't made waffles, her brother's favorite, for months and decided to surprise him. Cracking eggs and stirring batter were minuscule achievements, but they were ones she could control. Despite feeling discouraged, she was comforted by the morning's stillness and the familiar feel of her mother's wooden spoon in her hand.

Harriet had been so preoccupied with her investigation that she hadn't given much concern to her brother's fantasy of moving in with Pearl. She was grateful that Matthew would take Aubrey boxing on Thursday, hoping the new activity would redirect her brother's focus. As if her thoughts had woken him, he lumbered out of his room at seven.

"What are you doing?" He yawned, rubbing a fist in his eye.

"Ensuring we both start the day off with a triumph."

He dropped his hand from his face, revealing his eye roll. "You made bacon?"

"I know that's not a question because the smell pulled you from bed fifteen minutes early. But what you don't yet know is that I also made waffles."

The speed at which her brother ate rivaled only Susan's. With plates cleared, they readied themselves for the day. Later, when she returned to the kitchen, Aubrey did something he never did—he offered to wash the dishes. She suspected it was a kindness on account of her recent hospitalization. Watching him at the sink, she noticed his neatly combed hair, tucked shirt, and shined shoes. Little clues that would have escaped her notice had she not been looking for them. Was there a schoolmate he was trying to impress? A teacher? Someone else? Unable to compartmentalize her thoughts, her mind drifted back to her investigation. How many clues entered her field of view without her recognizing them? Reflecting on her previous case, she realized how much she had missed seeing when all had ultimately been revealed. Perhaps that was a quality separating a good detective from a great one: the ability to see what others don't—*before it's too late.*

With her brother out the door to school, she returned to her bedroom and reluctantly reached for a dress. The women at the tenement remained under the impression she was a representative of the settlement house. The morning's travel would not be by bicycle. She'd left her Victoria two nights ago at the tenement. She checked her coin purse for the nickel streetcar fare. Usually loathe to ride the slow and herky-jerky trolley, for once, she didn't mind. The past twenty-four hours had taken a toll on her. Sitting for the several-mile-long journey to within a few blocks of Pearl's Prairie Avenue mansion was preferable to putting forth physical effort.

Pearl would have commented on Harriet's arrival on foot had she seen her stroll up the sidewalk, but, like most days, she was busy in the kitchen at the back of the massive house.

Hearing Harriet's request that she accompany her again to the tenement, Pearl protested. "Harry, I have my principles. And one is to never drop in on a person without something from my oven."

Harriet glanced around the kitchen, grimacing at Toby, who was trolling the counter for crumbs. "What about those?" Her eyes fell upon a plate of brownies beneath a glass cover.

"*Pfft.* I made those yesterday."

"They're perfect," Harriet declared, "unless you don't want to share them."

Pearl huffed, "The day I take day-old brownies to anyone outside this house is the day I hang up my apron for good. And that day is long off, Harry."

Pearl was adamant about baking something fresh, but Harriet refused to wait hours just so Marie Batchelder could be presented with just-from-the-oven cookies. Sweets would be nearly beside the point to Marie and the Deca family when they'd barely escaped the building's fire.

Given the ultimatum of going along—with or without the brownies—or being left behind, Pearl acquiesced and wrapped the brownies in a red-checkered dish towel. In the foyer, Pearl tugged on suede leather gloves dyed a creamy lavender and a long, heavy coat the color of caramel icing. Instead of a hat, she draped a robin's-egg-blue silk scarf over her head, knotting it beneath her pointed chin. Harriet couldn't decide if her friend looked more like an incognito vaudeville star, a chic Bohemian, or simply Pearl Bartlett. Harriet realized she had never traveled with Pearl and was taken aback by the extravagance of the carriage that Pearl summoned for the few-mile journey.

"Life's too short to suffer cobblestone streets in an inferior buggy, Harry. The last time I decided to save a dime, the jostling nearly rattled my dadgum teeth clean out of my head. On top of that, you may have noticed that at my august age, I'm practically skin and bones. All that sits between me and a buggy's hard bench is a prayer I don't fracture my tailbone. You, on the other hand, are generously padded. Meaning no disrespect, Harry. Just stating a fact anyone can see."

Had anyone else said such a thing, she'd have rightly taken offense. But Pearl hadn't said anything intentionally unkind—or untrue. And Harriet wasn't about to complain about riding to the tenement in a luxurious hansom cab, especially after nearly an hour's jarring ride on the open-air streetcar.

The carriage made quick work of the journey. With loud whinnies, the horses halted, ceasing their hooves' *clop, clop, clop* on the cobblestones. The driver dismounted to open the door.

Pearl peered out. "He's taken us to the wrong address."

"I made no mistake, madam," the driver said sharply, opening the door.

Harriet leaned into the open doorway to see what had drawn Pearl's remark. As her eyes made sense of what she saw, a chill seized her, rendering her speechless. The driver took her shaking hand and helped her down from the carriage. Noticing Harriet's horrified expression, a look of alarm stretched across his face. "Are you quite all right, miss?"

"Good God, Harry!' Pearl exclaimed, climbing down. "The place is half-burned to the ground!"

Standing side by side on the sidewalk, they stared up at the charred remains of the tenement building. The fire had consumed the entirety of the third floor before decimating half of the second. From what could be ascertained from the outside, the flames hadn't reached the ground level.

"Those poor people," Harriet groaned, placing a hand on her heart. "The Decas, Antonia, and all the other residents. Their homes are destroyed." She'd anticipated damage but never such extensive devastation.

"It must have been recent by the look of things," Pearl observed. "When were you here last?"

"Two days ago," she said, deciding on a lie. She would beg for Pearl's understanding and forgiveness later. "With you on Sunday."

A man emerged from the building. Judging by his worn dungarees, he was on his way to work at the stockyard.

"Excuse me, sir," Harriet called, rushing to his side. "Can you tell us what happened here? We know people inside."

"Happened night before last," he said. "You can't tell from the look of things, but most got off lucky. Bunch of fellas were coming home from a late night and saw flames leaping from the roof." His gaze strayed to the few charred timbers on the third floor that jutted like tombstones into the open sky. "The fire marshal seemed sure that's where it started."

"On the roof?" Pearl stepped forward, never one to be shy. "They say how?"

The man removed the toothpick tucked at the side of his mouth and used it to emphasize his next point: "That's just it. Seems there ain't no way it could've started on its own. No way, no how. Somebody set fire to the building on purpose."

Harriet and Pearl traded fearful looks. There were many unanswered questions, yet Harriet was certain that the arson must be connected to Eugene Eldridge's murder—and her investigation. That she was lured to the roof to discover it ablaze seemed an impossible coincidence.

"Did anyone come to harm?" Pearl asked. "Harry and I were here the day before last. We helped Mrs. Deca give birth. Did anyone . . ." She trailed off, unable to say it out loud.

The question would have been worrisome had the nurse not told Harriet that no one had been lost to the flames.

"Like I say," the man said, "luck was on our side. Those men caught sight of the fire not long after it started. They got everyone out. But that didn't save their homes." He gestured broadly toward the building. "Seven apartments are nothing but ashes. Not a teapot or stitch of clothing left. Shouldn't have to tell you that no one who lives around here has much to their name to start with." He chuckled ruefully. "You're living high on the hog if you've got one decent pair of shoes and second pair of socks."

"Thank the Lord they got out in one piece," Pearl said.

Harriet asked, "Where did they go? The families who lost their homes, where are they now?" She had been told that only one apartment—the Faras' former home—was vacant. Given the size and cramped conditions of the apartments she'd been in, no neighbor would have room to take anyone in—let alone a family of nine!

The man shook his head, heavy with sorrow. "That's the ache in it, ladies—no place *to* go. I arrived after everyone was already out of the building. I hear one woman got taken to the hospital, but word was she'd probably recover. We all stood right where we are now and stared up in disbelief as the fire ate up the entire top floor. When it was over, those of us who had a home to return to did. Those who didn't . . . well, all I can say is they've gone somewhere. I best be getting on. I'll be late for work." He turned and walked away.

"What do we do now, Harry?" Pearl said, holding the bundle of brownies before her.

It was fortunate that Pearl had come with Harriet. She didn't doubt she'd have wailed like a lunatic were she alone.

"Say!" The man hollered from halfway down the block. "I do recall a bossy woman with spectacles showed up as the firemen called it quits. She was talking up a storm with those of them who'd been living on the top floor. Came across like a lady who's used to being in charge. Maybe she was with the city or something." With that, he continued on his way.

Cradling the brownies in one arm, Pearl used her other to squeeze Harriet's arm. "See there, Harry. Not all is lost. You got yourself a bona fide lead right there. We could go to City Hall and ask around. Maybe someone there can tell us if they know anything."

A spark of hope, albeit tiny, ignited within Harriet's chest. She knew someone who matched the description of the woman who'd arrived at the scene. Moreover, that same woman excelled at giving orders, lived nearby, and happened to be in the business of assisting immigrants.

Chapter 20

Though they would travel separately—Pearl in the hired carriage and Harriet putting her stamina to the test on her reclaimed bicycle—Pearl insisted on meeting Harriet at the University of Chicago Settlement House. A long-time admirer of Jane Addams and Ellen Gates Starr's work at Hull House, Pearl was curious to tour a settlement and eager to meet the University Settlement's founder, Mary McDowell.

"Besides," Pearl shouted through the window of the rocking carriage, "Somebody's got to eat these dadgum brownies, Harry! I didn't bring them all this way for nothing. There ain't no way they're making a round trip."

Envisioning the faces of the children to whom she'd read the story about the Wallypug's adventures, Harriet knew Pearl's brownies would be devoured in minutes, if they even lasted that long. Then again, given her assessment of Mary McDowell, the head resident would allow dessert—for either children or adults—only once a satisfactory meal had been eaten, and then with strict moderation.

Having arrived at the settlement, Pearl asked, "What's she like?" referring to Mary McDowell as they passed through the entrance gate.

Not wanting to bias Pearl's opinion one way or the

other but also wanting to prepare her for the woman's abruptness, she answered, "Mrs. McDowell is a serious woman who seems in all ways up to the task of leading the settlement's important work. I found her to be exceedingly competent and purposeful."

"Hmm . . ." Pearl bunched her lips. "Sounds like my sister, a no-fun Nellie. The only way to coax a smile from her is to pay the bill when dining at *her* invitation."

The curt remark took Harriet aback. She'd assumed Pearl and her sister got along well. Why else spend every Saturday in her company? Perhaps, like Harriet's relationship with her brother, the bond between siblings was stronger than their disagreements.

Harriet led the way to the main building, which housed the residents in upstairs flats. She wished to find Mary McDowell straightaway, but surely, anyone on staff or another resident could tell her whether the settlement had just taken in families whose nearby apartments had been destroyed by fire.

As Harriet and Pearl entered the foyer, the head resident appeared, descending the staircase. Mary McDowell appeared to recognize Harriet, whom she knew as Theodore Prescott's visiting niece. "I didn't expect to see you again, but I'm glad you've returned. I am in desperate need of help." Peering down her nose, she examined Pearl, saying, "And who is this? I don't suppose she is your grandmother?"

The comment was odd but logical. They bore no family resemblance. Whereas Pearl was uncommonly tall and spindly with sharp features, Harriet, standing five feet seven inches, was stout as a Greco-Roman wrestler and shared a square jaw, thin lips, and big ears with the nation's first lady, Ida Saxon McKinley.

"Please. Come with me," said Mary McDowell, speeding down the hallway.

Harriet whispered to Pearl, "She thinks I'm Mr. Prescott's niece. I'll explain later."

Entering a room at the back of the building, Mary Mc-Dowell handed each of them a stack of clothing and said, "I had no choice but to accommodate several families with nowhere else to go. I'm working to find them permanent lodgings, but for now, I've got them set up as best I can in the gymnasium." Addressing Harriet, she added, "You remember which building that is?" Too rushed to await confirmation, she hurried from the room.

Harriet and Pearl exchanged shrugs and crossed the grounds to the gymnasium. Having no time to consider how many refugees the settlement received, Harriet was shocked to see several dozen people, more than half of them children, clustered by family in makeshift camps on the gymnasium floor. Some slept on the small rugs the children in the kindergarten used for nap time. Others munched apples or sipped steaming liquid from tin cups. The adult's sorrowful expressions pained Harriet's heart. These people had begun the day before last with the meagerest possessions and prospects. Now they had lost even that.

"Oh, Harry," Pearl sighed. "This is horrendous and then some."

Harriet didn't doubt her friend's sincerity. And yet Pearl's presence suggested the opulence of her mansion. Could a society be considered just when one person could live with such abundance while countless others struggled to climb out of poverty and destitution? What justified one having so much when so many had nothing? The night before, Harriet had been upset by the speeches at the People's Cause meeting that advocated violence. Surely, there were better ways to achieve the goals of safer working conditions, fair wages, nonderelict housing, and politics free of corruption. Weren't there? Harriet's parents had believed in peaceful means to convince those with power and wealth to share it. And yet women were still denied the right to vote, millionaires became richer on the backs of workers, and political graft remained rampant among ward bosses. Harriet spied Mrs. Deca cradling a bundle that must be her newborn son. What could the mother of six, Antonia's family, or the other residents from the tenement possibly do to achieve even marginally better lives for themselves? Things had to change. Otherwise, what could Mrs. Deca possibly wish for her children? Why bring them into a world that promised only hardship and misery?

After Harriet explained to Pearl that these women believed her to be a representative of the settlement house, they approached the Decas apprehensively. Considering what they'd been through, they would surely be distraught.

Harriet halted. "Pearl, do you see Marie Batchelder anywhere?"

"I was about to ask you the same thing, Harry."

Out for a stroll? Using the privy? Lending a hand in the kindergarten? The grandmother could be anywhere. And yet Harriet sensed something amiss. Given the recent tragedy, wouldn't the family stay close?

Mrs. Deca glanced up, her eyes pools of despair. She clearly hadn't slept or had a chance to wash. Harriet felt a hand grip her arm. With a start, she realized it wasn't Pearl, who stood on her opposite side—it was Antonia.

"You're alive!" Antonia exclaimed. "When I didn't see you earlier, I thought the worst. I thought . . ."

"Alive? But . . ." Harriet was unsure. Had Antonia witnessed her being carried unconscious from the building?"

Antonia continued. "When we first met in the basement, you said you had moved into the Faras' apartment. As it mostly survived the fire, I hoped you were all right. But when I asked after you, no one had seen you."

That Antonia had been concerned about her was touching. But Harriet was furious with herself for not keeping clearer track of which residents knew her as a resident opposed to a settlement house representative. She vowed to adopt only one false identity for a particular place or group of people in the future, lest she confuse herself into making a catastrophic flub.

Antonia's gaze drifted to Mrs. Deca. "I wouldn't try to speak with her. Not now. The family has been through too much. She has taken it particularly hard. She hasn't spoken a word since it happened."

Harriet felt a surge of emotion. The family's anguish must be immeasurable. "I'm so very sorry for their loss. And for yours, Antonia. For your family and everyone here. It's an unimaginable calamity. I'm just glad you are alive, safe and sound. That everyone survived."

"A miracle," Pearl offered, finding her voice.

"Yes," Harriet agreed, "a miracle indeed."

Confusion crossed Antonia's face. "You do not know?"

"Know what? Has something else happened?" Harriet sputtered the words in time with her galloping heart.

Antonia frowned. "How could you not know?"

"My granddaughter has been staying with me the past few days," Pearl interjected smoothly. "I've not felt well. She is not to blame."

Accepting the explanation, Antonia said, "We didn't all make it out of the building."

"I don't understand." Though in that instant, Harriet sensed what was coming.

Antonia explained, "It was dark, and the smoke made it nearly impossible to see. With everyone rushing to get out, she must have stumbled."

Pearl gasped, also guessing Antonia's next words.

"The grandmother took a bad fall down the stairs. I'm sorry to say she is dead."

Chapter 21

Not wanting to overburden Matthew McCabe—who'd been exceedingly generous with his professional counsel, not to mention the time he spent with Aubrey—and knowing Theodore Prescott wanted to hear about her progress, not frustrations, Harriet rode to Polish Downtown. Harriet had visited the Wozniak family home several times while searching for Agnes, Barbara's younger sister and Pearl Bartlett's missing maid. Now Harriet was returning for a different but no less disturbing reason: a man had been murdered, families had been left homeless, and Harriet hadn't a clue about what to do next. Barbara was reliable in lending a sympathetic ear, and Harriet missed her terribly. She hoped an unscheduled visit would be welcome and other family members would be away, avoiding an awkward encounter requiring Barbara to explain the reason for the Prescott operative's reappearance.

Harriet needn't have worried about other Wozniaks; only Barbara was home. The two women sat in the family's tiny, cluttered kitchen next to a window wet with condensation from the boiling pot on the stove. The smell of cabbage and onion hung in the air. Over a pot of tea, Harriet recounted her discoveries since she'd seen Barbara several nights back at the Black Rabbit—from events at the Turner

Hall, where no one had heard of Jorinda Grimm, to the tenement and barely escaping with her life. So intense was Barbara's interest in the speeches given at the People's Cause meeting that she expressed only passing concern about Harriet's brush with death.

"You do realize," Barbara said, becoming unusually animated, "history has proven that violence is often required to advance society. Revolutions are bloody, it is true. And destructive. And deadly. There can be no denying these facts. But they are also necessary. No cause, however noble, gets anywhere by asking nicely for those with power and wealth to share it. Doing so is folly! Our nature as human beings is to look out for ourselves and our families. Have you noticed, Harriet, that the people who share the most are those with the least? Do you know why that is? I will tell you. It's because the poor understand how much it means to receive a gift of kindness. A loaf of warm bread. A pint of fresh milk. A well-made coat with all the buttons. A good pair of shoes with soles to last another season. A rich person gives away only enough to satisfy their conscience or to stand in front of a building with their name etched in stone above the entrance, wave to the crowd from the front steps, and declare, 'See? Look at me! Admire and applaud my benevolence.' Such gestures keep the workers at bay but do nothing to improve the lives of millions who live in poverty—not in any meaningful and long-lasting way. No, Harriet. Revolution is the tool of the people. It may not be pretty, but it alone is effective. It is the only way."

When Barbara had finished, Harriet struggled to find words. She agreed with some of what Barbara had said, but to support violence—revolution!—was beyond the pale. She hadn't come to quarrel but couldn't stay silent; otherwise, Barbara might think she agreed with her on all counts. She took a breath to calm her emotions so her tone wouldn't be strident.

"As much as I believe women should have the vote, that

stockyard workers should be paid a wage that allows them to feed, clothe, and house their families properly, that a work week should have reasonable limits, that the tax we pay should be commensurate to one's income and then used properly for schools, roads, and clean water—and not to line the pockets of the Gray Wolves and other corrupt politicians—I cannot condone bloodshed or mayhem to achieve those ends." She looked beseechingly at Barbara. "Surely, you can't be serious in arguing for violence? How can one support a means that promises more societal harm than the ills it seeks to remedy?"

It seemed it was now Barbara's turn to struggle for a rebuttal. She stared at Harriet as if the words had hit her as hard as a slap. Aside from the sound of boiling water, the room was silent. Harriet could hear herself swallow. She wanted to blurt out a string of words to prove their agreement and close the distance that had just opened wide between them. But she couldn't. She wouldn't. Barbara was wrong. And yet she was resolute. Perhaps the topic of social progress was one they shouldn't discuss. After all, she could no more expect to change Barbara's mind than Barbara to change hers.

"You are naïve," Barbara said sharply, breaking the silence. "And young. You were born in America. You own a home. You have a good-paying job." She placed her hands on the table, pushing herself to her feet. "How could you understand?"

Like the striking of a match, Harriet's anger flared. Breathing hard, she raced through possible retorts, rejecting each for another more powerfully charged. When she was about to give voice to a remark sure to raise the room's temperature, wisdom grabbed hold of her tongue. Barbara stood at the stove, her back to Harriet, stirring whatever was cooking in the pot. Searching her brain for something mollifying to say, Harriet moved toward Barbara. Drawing near, she abruptly halted. Barbara was humming—as if nothing had happened, as if she had not just insulted Harriet, dismissing her life's challenges and making her out to be a person of privilege and somehow the enemy.

Harriet closed the apartment door gently behind her. She didn't want the sound to give away her anger and hurt. It was better to slip away and not dwell on what had happened. Whether she and Barbara might reconcile was a thought she couldn't consider—not now. There could be no distractions. She had been wrong to come there. She must concentrate her energies on one thing: solving her bloody case.

Her breathing still labored from inhaling so much smoke the other day, Harriet rode slowly to her favorite spot on the lakeshore, where Fullerton Avenue met Lincoln Park. She had visited there countless times as a child with her parents and brother to picnic and swim each summer. A place of fond memories and natural beauty, the expanse never failed to provide solace. Now, it was too early in the season for the site to attract much activity, and Harriet shared the area with only a young couple strolling the dirt path that traced the lake's shoreline. Observing the man and woman, she noted their comfort with each other—the way the woman leaned into her beau's shoulder, the way he wrapped his arm around her waist as if he were more complete with her nestled beside him. Not even half an hour had passed since she'd resolved to ban Barbara from her mind, yet seeing the two lovers, she couldn't help but envision Barbara's face, the crook of her nose, her roomy hips, and her lustrous black hair. Meeting Barbara and finding community at the Black Rabbit had stirred previously unthinkable thoughts of what a romance with a woman might entail—both the thrill and the fright of it. She had been so overwhelmed by the fraught aspects of a relationship between two women that she hadn't considered the challenges of being emotionally vulnerable with another person—male or female.

The death of Mayre and James Morrow had crippled Harriet in despair. Her recent quarrel with Barbara pricked that very spot of her heart that she'd worked hard for years to callous. Again, she resolved to push everything but her investigation from her mind.

With fists balled tightly and held to her sides, she gazed across the lake. She took a long, steady breath—then another. Closing her eyes, she listened to the gentle slapping of the water against the bank. And thought.

Jorinda Grimm—just because a few people didn't recognize the name didn't mean she was a phantom. As far as Harriet knew, Steven Bliss gained nothing by lying about her being Eugene Eldridge's fiancée. She was out there, somewhere; Harriet felt certain.

Marie Batchelder—whatever she witnessed would now never be known. *Unless.* Could she have told someone what she saw? Grover and Chester Fara hadn't volunteered what they'd seen. Who's to say there weren't others?

Brunhilda Struff—what was her story? She appeared in peculiar places—none more so than behind a fencing mask—only to disappear without a word. Moreover, Harriet was nearly certain she'd been watched by a figure in shadows wearing a Tyrolean hat and riding a brown horse.

Mike "Saloon Micky" Powers and "Irish Dan" Walsh—had one of the notorious Gray Wolves been the subject of Eugene Eldridge's investigation and had him killed? Had one of them followed that dastardly deed by burning down half of the tenement building? If so, why? Did they suspect a resident might know of their guilt? Or did they think the evidence incriminating them was hidden somewhere in the building and needed to be destroyed if it couldn't be recovered?

Sensing something nearby, Harriet opened her eyes. A seagull flew by so unnaturally close that she reflexively ducked. As if satisfied by gaining her attention, the bird turned and flew south toward downtown. Her gaze followed its path. She would never admit to anyone her belief that she'd just been given a sign—a sign leading down-town to City Hall.

Of all the curious subjects and suspects on her list, the aldermen were the only persons she had not interviewed. How did one arrange a meeting with an alderman? She was no one of importance or influence. She was hardly worth their time. If either man was concerned with the is-sues of a voter, as a woman, she was irrelevant. For a brief moment, she considered presenting herself as an operative with the Prescott Agency, but she'd likely not be believed, and either way, the Gray Wolves were on the side of vice. Moreover, Prescott would not want to gain their attention. And even if he were unopposed, why would an alderman agree to a meeting with anyone other than the agency principal?

Suddenly, a thought struck. The audacity of it! She closed her eyes again, envisioning how it might play out. If she failed, the punishment would be sure and swift. But if she succeeded, she would invigorate her case, sending it speed-ing like a runaway locomotive on an unstoppable path—with her standing in the middle of the tracks.

Chapter 22

The idea of disguising herself as a man had been planted in Harriet's mind when, as a young girl, she read S. Emma E. Edmonds's memoir titled *Nurse and Spy in the Union Army*, which chronicled the woman's harrowing adventures after joining the Union Army as Franklin Thompson. This would be the second time Harriet borrowed whiskers from her brother's kit of disguises, initially purchased for a school play. The first occasion was during her previous investigation when, like now, she pasted on a beard and bound her breasts in order to do something a woman wasn't allowed.

The case of the murdered muckraker hinged on the belief that Eugene Eldridge had been killed because he had the goods on a powerful politician. Steven Bliss had guessed the evidence incriminated one of City Hall's Gray Wolves. The *Progressive Age*'s editor, Alexi Scholtz, had mentioned the recent murder of one of Saloon Micky's henchmen, a man who had gone by the name Bat. Theodore Prescott and agency client Gerald Cole of the Municipal Voters' League were adamant that accusing a city official of misdeeds—let alone murder—without evidence to prove it would be disastrous. But Harriet's investigation had stalled—the only path left to follow led to City Hall.

THE CASE OF THE MURDERED MUCKRAKER   181

Harriet had briefly met Alderman Mike Powers when he arrived at the University Settlement to meet Mary McDowell. She believed she knew something about men like him—they valued money and power above all else. As Harriet Morrow, she had neither. But Harry Dunn, a private detective from Philadelphia, Eldridge's hometown, *could* approach the aldermen. Bearded, breasts bound, attired in Pearl's late husband's finest suit and shoes and carrying his handsome satchel—by the traditional handles—Harry Dunn would visit City Hall and request separate meetings with Dan Walsh and Mike Powers. Presuming the aldermen would be too intrigued to refuse an appointment with a notable visitor from the East—distant enough to slow any attempt to verify his identity—he would then reveal himself to be employed by Eugene Eldridge's grieving parents, desperate for answers about their son's death.

Harriet dared not think about the repercussions were she exposed. For a moment, she considered informing Matthew McCabe of her plan, seeking the reassurance of someone knowing the danger she was inviting. But he'd not endorse her plan. Instead, he would tell her the idea was crazy and try to dissuade her. Prescott would forbid it outright. She might have entrusted Barbara with the information, but they were not on speaking terms. That left her brother and Pearl, neither of whom could be involved. Putting them in harm's way was unthinkable. She determined that being a detective entailed risk—and it was hers alone to bear.

Staring into the mirror and muttering curses under her breath, she tugged gently on the right side of the false beard, but the paste had set. Were her mission less perilous, she might convince herself that lopsided whiskers wouldn't be noticed, but the high stakes demanded better. She would peel off the beard, scrub her face, and start anew.

A half hour later, satisfied with her voluminous black beard and matching bushy sideburns and eyebrows, she contemplated her shape. Since her last foray masquerading as a man, she had rethought her approach to concealing her bosom. Once in the Black Rabbit's dressing room, she'd observed a woman squeezing her breasts beneath an extremely slim-fitting gentlemen's vest. Later that evening on the dance floor, the same woman, wearing a men's snug suit, appeared nearly as flat-chested as Aubrey.

Harriet had never worn the finest suit from Horace Bartlett's wardrobe. Admiring the quality fabric and immaculate stitching and appreciating the Mandel Brothers label sewn into the jacket's silk lining, she had saved it for a special occasion, presuming that would be the next ball at the Black Rabbit. Still, she was grateful for it, along with the hand-me-down mahogany-hued leather lace-ups with FOSTER & SONS, LONDON stamped into the soles.

With her unruly mop of wiry brown hair stuffed into the crown of her bowler, she appraised herself in the mirror a final time. Satisfied, she confirmed that two copper rimfire cartridges were loaded into her derringer, slipped the pistol into her pocket holster, and pushed her bicycle out the door.

City Hall, near the Prescott Agency offices and also on LaSalle Street, stretched the entire block's length between Washington and Randolph Streets. The massive five-story French Renaissance building projected might with a façade primarily of sandstone and brick, a double story above the second featuring soaring columns and pillars of granite, and an attic floor decorated with allegorical representations of arts and science, commerce, and agriculture.

Not since visiting the World's Columbian Exposition had Harriet marveled at a space's grandeur. The stairs and balustrades were constructed of iron with colored marble wainscoting. The soaring interior walls were covered in white oak and ornately decorated. And the coffered ceiling featured enormous chandeliers of eight lanterns encircling an iron frame like a carousel. Examining the directory, she was amazed that the building's exterior belied yet another floor—a basement, which housed the fire, police, and health departments—making six levels in all.

After a stop on each lower floor, Harriet, as Harry Dunn, pushed his way free from the back of a crowded elevator compartment onto the fourth floor, where the offices for the City Council were located. Like a down-on-his-luck card shark, she—*he*—was going all in on his last hand.

Harry followed signs to a door with a bronze plaque emblazoned with the name DANIEL C. WALSH. He was greeted inside by a woman whose secretarial skills, whatever they might be, were likely overshadowed by her youthful beauty and waist the size of Harry's shirt collar. The secretary sat behind a desk and before a window oddly small for the ceiling's soaring height. To Harry's amazement, the secretary showed him into Alderman Walsh's private office with dispatch. Striving for a baritone register—his voice already hoarse from the recent smoke inhalation—Harry Dunn introduced himself to the alderman and explained the reason for his visit.

"Irish Dan" Walsh appeared more of a curmudgeonly grandfather than an infamous political operative. Clean-shaven and of pasty complexion, he wore a scowl that suggested indigestion from an overly spicy lunch. His chubby fingers, laced together and resting on his prodigious belly, might have been enlisted to help ensure the buttons on his pin-striped vest didn't pop. From behind a large oak desk, he met Harry Dunn's claim of being a visiting detective with as much interest as he might a guttersnipe begging for a spare coin. It was only when Harry repeated the name Eugene Eldridge that Walsh's eyes flickered recognition.

"Wait a second"—he snapped his fingers, leaning forward in his chair and producing a harsh squeak—"he's the fella got himself shot in a tenement over by the stockyards." After a pause, he added not a respectful "Sorry for your loss" but rather "So there's your answer. You'll find him in a cemetery six feet under. Knowing he was a muckraker, can't say I'm sorry."

Walsh hadn't recognized the name Eugene Eldridge at first and appeared unfazed by hearing that Eldridge's parents had enlisted the services of a professional detective. More curious still, Walsh believed Eldridge had been shot, not stabbed. Was it possible for an alderman to give no attention to the murder of an upstanding citizen in his own ward? Undoubtedly, the public's safety must be paramount among his obligations. Even if he were as corrupt as his reputation suggested, he couldn't completely ignore his civic duties—or could he?

"As I have stated," Harry repeated the victim's name, careful to annunciate as if to convey some respect for his passing, "Eugene Eldridge's parents have charged me with looking into the matter. Is there nothing you can tell me about the crime?"

"Balderdash," Irish Dan rocked back, producing another startling squeak. "Crime? As I already said, a muckraker goes sneaking about a tenement, looking to stir up trouble . . . if trouble should find him first, some may rightly say he had it coming. Besides, the City of Chicago has the finest police department in this entire country. As for the muckraker's parents sending some detective all the way from Philadelphia, they're wasting their money. No disrespect, but we have the world's best detectives, too. Pinkerton, Prescott"—another shift of his weight, squeak of his chair—"something needs finding, they're the ones to do it. Again, no disrespect."

Harry harrumphed, annoyed by the alderman's disregard for the matter's importance. "Is that so?"

Irish Dan winked. "I put my money on it. Now, if you don't mind"—his small eyes shifted toward the door—"I got a meeting with his Honor."

Harry expressed his gratitude for the alderman's time before returning to the dark, narrow corridor to stroll the hallway in search of a door with Mike Powers' name

on it. Hopefully, the next encounter would be more en-
lightening.

The first indication that Harry's visit with Mike Powers
would be decidedly different from the meeting with Irish
Dan was the secretary who greeted him as he stepped into
the area outside his private office.

"Good day, sir. Welcome to Alderman Michael Powers'
office. How might I help you?" The young man spoke
with the rehearsed efficiency of a streetcar operator. Had
Harry not met the alderman at the University Settlement,
he wouldn't have reason to think the secretary with his
distinctive combination of neatly parted blue-black hair,
eyes the color of a July sky, and lips as plump and red as a
Jonathan apple was so entirely out of place. Whereas Mike
Powers was odious and his clothes ill-fitted, his secretary
was devastatingly handsome and crisply attired.

Again, employing a deeper-than-usual voice, Harry
Dunn explained he was a private detective from Philadelphia and requested to see the alderman.

"I'm terribly sorry, Mr. Dunn, but I'm afraid Alderman
Powers is luncheoning at present. On other days, I might
suggest you wait, but his afternoon schedule has no time
available. The same is true for tomorrow and the day after,
as it happens."

Reluctant to wait for what could be days to get an audience with Powers, Harry patted his belly. "It is that time,
isn't it? Say, I don't suppose you'd share the name of the
alderman's favorite restaurant with a famished visitor? A
man like Mr. Powers will surely have a refined palate, requiring the finest fare. I'd appreciate a recommendation."

The secretary didn't hesitate to oblige, answering, "Henrici's. The alderman has a standing reservation."

Eager to not prolong the encounter, Harry thanked the
secretary and departed the office, mindful to stiffen his
gait and restrain the sway of his hips—a result, he realized,
that wasn't altogether different from Harriet's usual stride.

The secretary had given no indication that he had suspected Harry Dunn's authenticity—Harriet had, after all, worn a beard and lowered her voice's register. But was Harriet Morrow otherwise so different? Before, at the Black Rabbit, Harriet had been so captivated by the characters surrounding her that she'd never wondered how she might appear to them. That she was not typically feminine was no revelation. She had understood that by age fourteen. But was she naturally *manly*? It was one thing to prefer pursuits commonly associated with boys and men, but wanting to be a man was an entirely different thing. Harriet didn't. Nor did she believe Matthew McCabe harbored any desire to be a woman. Why were gender expectations so rigid, and why did one's defying them cause such consternation among the public? Like thoughts of Barbara, such ruminations frayed her wits. As soon as she pushed them from her mind, a remark, a look, or a gesture would remind her she wasn't like most other women and must constantly manage herself not to invite suspicion. No sooner would that thought enter her head than she'd question her decision to wear men's clothing. *You're doing yourself no favor, Harriet!* Still, she was who she was. She wouldn't live by senseless rules she had never agreed to. And so she resigned herself to the fact that she would forever be different. Society may never accept her, but she could accept herself.

Henrici's was nearby, just around the corner on Randolph Street. The restaurant was another place she'd never been. She didn't need to see a menu to know the price of a meal would exceed her weekly wage. That a public official could afford to dine there regularly suggested a secondary source of income that dwarfed his pay as an alderman.

Reinhabiting the persona of Harry, she entered the restaurant, noting the soft scraping of silver against china and the genteel chatter of several dozen patrons. The maître d' greeted the unfamiliar guest obsequiously. In return, Harry Dunn announced himself as the luncheon companion of

Alderman Mike Powers. The claim earned a purse-lipped nod as the host examined his reservation book before glancing across the dining room adorned with gold-framed paintings and crystal chandeliers to a table for two near the window, where Mike Powers sat alone with a champagne bucket beside his table.

"I'm sorry, sir," the maître d' cooed, "but I'm afraid Alderman Powers made no mention of anyone joining him today."

"Quite all right," Harry declared. "There's nothing ol' Mike likes better than a good surprise."

Chapter 23

To the sputtering objections of the maître d' in tow, Harry strode confidently toward the alderman's table, zigzagging his way around white-linen-covered tables occupied by Chicago's gentlemen and ladies of wealth and privilege. The frazzled maître d' practically leaped in front of the uninvited guest as he reached Saloon Micky's table.

"I'm terribly sorry, Alderman Powers. I told this gentleman—"

Harry thrust out a hand, "Harry Dunn, sir. Private investigator from Philadelphia. I won't take more than a few minutes of your time."

Mike Powers' cologne was pungent, and from Harry's angle of observation, the few oiled hairs clinging to his head looked like someone had drawn pencil lines from front to back on his scalp. The abundance of food he'd ordered was remarkable given his slender frame. As he set down his wine, the many rings on his fingers clinked against the crystal glass.

While the maître d' continued his apologies, Harry sat in the chair opposite Mike Powers, calm as you please. "I'll have water with lemon, thank you."

Powers seemed amused by the maître d''s consternation and too intrigued by the curious guest to have him removed. Instead, he said, "It's quite all right, Reginald. Mr. Dunn may stay." Powers returned his attention to Harry, asking, "Now then. What's all this about?"

Knowing that the audience with Powers could end at his whim, Harry came straight out with it. "I was hired by the family of the late Eugene Eldridge to look into his most unfortunate death. He was murdered, in case you are unaware of the crime and its circumstances. Although Eugene had become estranged from his parents, they are parents nonetheless. As you might imagine, the death of a child is an unfathomable loss. Mr. and Mrs. Eldridge are bereft, naturally. Their sorrow is understandable, as is their anger. You see, whoever murdered their son remains at large. I have been charged with finding Eugene's killer so the culprit is brought to justice and his family may receive some peace of mind."

Harry scrutinized Powers' face for any indication of emotion. If inscrutability was an asset to a politician, the alderman was blessed with an impressive ability to give nothing away.

"That's unfortunate, Mr. Dunn." Powers cocked his head like a spaniel sensing a rustling in the reeds. "But I fail to see why you feel compelled to share that sad story and interrupt my otherwise fine lunch." He hoisted a bottle from the bucket and poured pink wine into his glass.

Harry had hoped to elicit a telling reaction from Powers but, having failed, decided to test him further. "Before his death, Eugene told his parents he was working on an investigation sure to make a name for himself. Of course, his parents—"

"You said they were estranged. And yet they're talking?" Powers' gaze intensified.

Gratefully, a waiter appeared with Harry's water. He took a long sip, then hatching an idea, said, "My impression is that Eugene contacted them out of the blue because he was finally onto something that might make up for his history of disappointments. You see, Eugene comes from a long line of successful businessmen. The family's wealth is significant. His father and mother disapproved of him becoming a journalist—*a muckraker*. Regrettably, just when the parents had reason to hope Eugene might achieve a degree of success, his life was taken."

Harry took another sip, hoping that the story he'd developed didn't sound too far-fetched.

"Fascinating . . ." Powers drew out the word; the tone made it uncertain whether he intended sincerity or sarcasm. "But none of that answers my question. Why are *you* here?"

"According to Mr. and Mrs. Eldridge, Eugene claimed to have had evidence to prove the corruption of a Chicago public official. He also mentioned your name, Mr. Powers, during their final telephone conversation."

Brief as it was, a flash of alarm crossed the alderman's face.

"Let me explain," Harry continued. "Mr. and Mrs. Eldridge believe their son might have been working with you to root out corruption among your colleagues. If that is true, I'm hoping we might work together, sharing information with the goal of discovering the target of Eugene's investigation and, ostensibly, his killer." After pausing to take yet another sip of water, Harry added, "Presuming you don't already know."

Staring at the alderman three feet away, Harry imagined his thoughts. With no way of knowing he was being told an elaborate fiction, he must be unsettled to learn Eugene had influential parents. Furthermore, he would be unnerved to learn they had hired a private detective to investigate their son's murder. However, the alderman should be relieved hearing that the parents presumed Powers was an ally and not a suspect. Harry didn't know whether Powers, if indeed guilty, had recovered the evidence purported to have been in Eldridge's possession. If he had, the arrival of a Philadelphia detective might be a nuisance but hardly a threat—unless the detective discovered proof he was implicated in Eldridge's murder or some other crime. However, were the evidence still missing, might Powers not view Harry Dunn as someone who might serve a helpful purpose? After all, what harm could come by having a professional detective search for what he was desperate to recover? As long as Powers believed he could get hold of the evidence before Harry Dunn could do anything with it, why not let him conduct his investigation?

After an uncomfortable silence, Powers spread his hands wide and grinned. The light catching his numerous rings created a momentary kaleidoscope of color against the window. "I'm afraid I have no recollection of meeting your muckraker . . . name again?"

"Eugene Eldridge," Harry supplied.

"Right, right," Powers nodded at each word. "He was with which newspaper, did you say?"

"I didn't."

"That's right." He snapped his fingers. "You mentioned the *Progressive Age*."

A test? Harry didn't hesitate. "I most certainly did not. Eugene worked independently, apparently. His parents don't have much in the way of details, I'm afraid."

"Is that a fact? The *Progressive Age*. You never heard of them?"

"I've only just arrived in Chicago. But rest assured, I shall begin my inquires in earnest forthwith."

"Well, Mr. Dunn. I'm afraid you have your work cut out for you." Powers dabbed the corners of his mouth with a starched white napkin before folding it carefully and laying it beside his empty plate. "Chicago's a might bigger than your quaint Philadelphia." He flicked a finger toward the window and stood. "I do wish you luck." Then, as if a fresh thought struck, he said, "Of course, I'd not be a very good ambassador of our fine city if I offered no assistance. Should you hear anything that might pique your interest related to the Elridge man—"

"El-*dridge*," Harry Dunn corrected.

"Right, of course, Eldridge. I insist you keep me apprised. Anything at all, you let me know. Agreed? I can't help if I'm kept in the dark. My office is just around the corner—fourth floor, City Hall. Where are you staying, if I may ask?"

Another test? "As I said, I've only just arrived and have yet to secure lodgings."

"Ah, well then. The Palmer House is where you must stay. Tell them you are visiting our city as a guest of Alderman Powers. You'll be sure to get good treatment as a result. And should you stay for lunch, I recommend the pork loin"—he raised a finger—"*with* the applesauce. Good day, Mr. Dunn."

Harriet watched Mike Powers depart the dining room, greeting diners with smiles and backslaps on his way out. He was nothing if not confident. He was also guilty. And not as clever as he thought. He might have gotten away with pretending not to recall Eldridge's name once, but twice was, as they say, gilding the lily.

Chapter 24

Now that Harriet had baited Saloon Micky, she had created several problems for herself. The first was that he believed she was Harry Dunn, a private investigator from Philadelphia, a fiction she must maintain whenever in his presence. If he sought to verify her story, he might start by looking for Mr. Dunn at the Palmer House—a hotel she couldn't begin to afford. She could ask Mr. Prescott if the agency or the client, Gerald Cole, might cover the expense, but that would require she tell him what she'd done, and she feared he'd be angry that she had taken such a risk by directly engaging two of the notorious Gray Wolves. But she wouldn't remain in her boss's good graces by keeping secrets from him either. She would have to hope her success in luring the aldermen into a dialogue about Eugene Eldridge would be enough to escape his wrath, if not gain his approval.

After receiving encouragement from Matthew McCabe, which, by his expression, was forced, she resolved to inform her superior. When she presented herself as Harry Dunn, Madelaine didn't recognize her and was put out that a visitor had gotten as far as Prescott's office door without her being advised. Only when Harriet spoke, causing Madelaine's jaw to drop, did she understand the gentleman standing before her was Prescott's junior-most and only female operative.

"The gall!" Madelaine challenged. "What are you playing at? Think you'll have some fun at my expense, do you?"

Confused, Harriet stood tongue-tied before realizing the secretary thought the disguise was solely intended to fool her. As she opened her mouth to explain, Prescott opened his door, grabbing the attention of both women. For a split second, he looked merely annoyed to see a visitor not on his calendar. Then he blinked and reared back. "Morrow?"

"Sir," Harriet replied, "might I have a word?"

As Madelaine grumbled indiscernible objections, Harriet followed Prescott into his office. The moment she closed the door, she knew the encounter would carry a different tone. Prescott hadn't continued around his desk to sit as he had at all their previous meetings. Instead, he stood in the middle of the room and stared at her. She struggled not to wilt under his penetrating gaze. Worst of all, he still hadn't said anything. Unsettled, she shifted her weight but stood tall. If this was the first test, she must pass it. Finally, he removed his spectacles, pulled a handkerchief from a breast pocket, and wiped the lenses before putting them back on.

"Are you fully recovered?" he asked. "Do you feel quite well?"

It took her a moment to understand he referred to her recent brush with death at the enflamed tenement and not her disguise.

"I've been short of breath, which I notice most when riding my bicycle. My throat is also still quite sore. All things counted, I should consider myself lucky."

Prescott *harrumphed*. "Luck is the mistress of gamblers and daredevils. A Prescott operative trades on sound judgment."

Having no good reply, she let the remark hang between them.

"You will, of course, explain *this*"—he drew a finger in the air from the tips of her shoes to her hat—"but first, a few observations."

Harriet expelled a long breath, causing her mustache to tickle the end of her nose. Would his "few observations" be a recounting of the reasons she was being fired? How long would he prolong what she feared was the inevitable?

"I presume you know how many operatives I employ?" Prescott asked.

"Twelve, sir."

"Twelve. And of those twelve, how many are women?"

"One, sir."

"One. So, why, Miss Morrow, do you think I would want the one woman I have employed as a detective to galivant as a man?"

For the second time in a matter of minutes she was speechless. Prescott thought she was disguised as a man because of personal preference.

He continued. "It's one thing to wear a man's shoes, which, if I'm not mistaken, and I'm not, are Foster and Sons. I'd like to know how you came about such astonishingly extravagant footwear, but that can wait for later. You wore men's shoes when I hired you, so I shouldn't be surprised that you do so now. But last week, you chose to escalate matters by wearing an entire suit of men's clothing. I advised you of the legal penalties should the authorities wish to pursue the matter. But this"—this time he gestured toward her false whiskers—"is a good step too far. You resemble a squashed Abe Lincoln."

Deciding succinctness would best correct his misunderstanding—and wanting to expedite his reprimand—she explained, "Mr. Prescott, sir, I am *disguised* as Harry Dunn, a private detective from Philadelphia, hired by Eugene Eldridge's parents to find his killer. As Harry Dunn, I have approached Aldermen Daniel Walsh and Mike Powers and, based on a conversation earlier today at Henrici's with Alderman Powers, have confidently concluded that he knew Eugene Eldridge and was aware of his association with the *Progressive Age* newspaper. Moreover, I believe Powers knowledge of the journalist is because he was the subject of Eldridge's investigation and is responsible for his murder."

"You what?"

Harriet had anticipated a lambasting, not a gasp, and was suddenly more apprehensive than ever. She also knew the wise reply was none.

"Tell me everything," he said, moving briskly to his desk and pointing to an empty chair. "Sit. And spare nothing. If either man burped, I want to hear about it."

An hour later, she had recounted every detail down to the alderman's suggestion that she order the pork loin *and* applesauce. Remarkably, Prescott expressed only curious excitement.

"So it's reasonable to think Saloon Micky is our man. Reasonable, but not certain. I tend to agree that if he had recovered the incriminating evidence, he wouldn't bother with you. But after exhausting all means and still not finding it, why not allow a professional to help? The only threat to him is if you succeed and turn the evidence over to someone else. The situation you've created may give you access to Mike Powers, but that proximity puts you in grave danger. Still, this is a detective agency, not an ice cream parlor. This is dangerous work, and your assignment is to recover the evidence. As long as the matter is brought to a successful conclusion and this agency—*my agency*—is kept clear of the Gray Wolves' attention, I suppose I don't care if the job is performed by Harriet Morrow or Harry Dunn or Pudd'nhead Wilson."

Harriet's shoulders dropped. She had been on tenterhooks for the better part of the hour, but realized that this wasn't to be her last day as Prescott's sole lady detective. Moreover, Prescott's reference to Twain's fictional detective conveyed a playfulness he'd not express if he were only furious.

He continued. "Book a room at the Palmer House, and as the dishonorable alderman suggested, mention his name and don't be subtle about it. You want to ensure word of your reservation gets back to Powers. You don't have to stay there, I shouldn't think. I don't need to tell you you won't be there on holiday. There'll be no long soaks in the bath or nibbling Belgian chocolates in bed. You must only make daily appearances so whoever at the hotel serves as his eyes and ears doesn't get suspicious. Start with that. Let's see if Powers' curiosity compels him to contact you in the next day or two. If not, we'll consider how to motivate the cur's engagement. Is that understood?"

"Yes, sir," Harriet said. "And payment for the room? Such luxurious lodgings are well beyond—"

He brushed aside her concern with a flick of the wrist. "The bill will eventually be passed on to Gerald Cole at the Municipal Voters' League. But that's for another day. For now, put it on account. You need not outlay your personal funds."

"And in the meantime? Regarding the alderman, what would you have me do?"

"You might have heard the expression 'a game of cat and mouse?'"

"Indeed I have."

"Detective work with stakes this high is more a game of panther and snake, Miss Morrow. Neither opponent has a distinct advantage. Victory will go to the more wily competitor."

Harriet nodded but failed to glean relevant instruction from the analogy if any were intended.

"Be vigilant. Take whatever precautions are necessary to ensure you're not followed, especially when traveling home or here to the office. Again, I suspect Powers will make contact first. He'll be too anxious to learn about your progress. Keep me posted daily, without fail."

"Thank you, sir."

Harriet's hand was on the door handle when Prescott said from across the room, "Much is riding on your success, *Mr. Dunn*. Do not disappoint me."

Chapter 25

Disguised as Harry Dunn, Harriet walked the short distance to the Palmer House, arguably Chicago's grandest hotel. The seven-story behemoth on Monroe at State Street was a source of city pride and the lodging choice of dignitaries and other important visitors. Harriet recalled reading in the newspapers that the likes of Ulysses S. Grant, Mark Twain, Charles Dickens, and Oscar Wilde had all been guests. Although a lifelong Chicagoan, Harriet had only ever been as far as the lobby on a dare from her brother. The experience had been short-lived. Already feeling out of place, she had fought back tears of embarrassment when a bell captain sternly declared she had no business being there before promptly escorting her out by the ear. Now, she'd return as a paid guest and be on the lookout for that bell captain.

Harry accepted a key to a room "sure to be pleasing" as it was among the select few of the hotel's 850 rooms that had been set aside for "guests of the city's most esteemed leaders." Harry doubted Alderman Powers merited the accolade but was excited to see the room nonetheless. Before the desk clerk concluded Harry's registration, he regaled him with laudable hotel facts, including its having the most extensive collection of Impressionist art outside of

France, featuring works by Claude Monet, masterpieces by Louis Comfort Tiffany, and a magnificent ceiling fresco by the painter Louis Pierre Rigal. His final boast was a Chicago legend, so extravagant it seemed a gross exaggeration: the barbershop floor was inlaid with silver dollars.

The desk clerk appeared insulted when the gentleman from Philadelphia refused the assistance of a bellhop, turned incredulous when informed the guest had no luggage, and then became effusively sympathetic when hearing the reason: Mr. Dunn's suitcase had been ripped from his clutches by a street tough. Harry added, "Alas, there is a strong possibility you'll see me wearing the same attire throughout my stay."

Passing through the lobby en route to the elevator, Harry observed garnet-draped chandeliers, Italian marble, and marvelous mosaics everywhere he turned. On the sixth floor, he slipped a heavy gold key into the lock. Once safely inside, Harry loosed a long sigh of relief and returned to Harriet.

Her first impression was the room's quiet. How thick must the walls, floor, ceilings, and windows be to create a cocoon of silence in the heart of the city? She took in the surroundings—luxurious bedclothes, sumptuous carpeting that cushioned her steps, gorgeous wallpaper of cream and muted golds, and white gleaming wainscoting she couldn't imagine keeping free of scuffs in her own home. She was sorely tempted to shed her clothes, draw a hot bath, and slip beneath the four-poster bed's silk duvet. Perhaps before her investigation was resolved, she might allow herself the indulgence. However, as much as she might like to, she couldn't possibly. The steam of the bath might melt the glue holding her false whiskers.

Having established the name Mr. Harry Dunn in the hotel registry, she was free to leave, though she'd do so reluctantly. Her life was empty of hours that demanded nothing from her. Work was her choice but exhausting. Aubrey was family but exasperating. And her current case had her doubting her abilities. Her thoughts drifted to the homeless immigrant families huddled on the gymnasium floor of the University Settlement House. Their circumstances were a world apart despite being only a few miles away. She belonged neither here nor there, yet her heart was with those who struggled. As a woman, she was unequal. As a queer woman, she was an aberration.

Minutes later, Harry strode through the lobby toward the exit, mindful that he must not be followed. Although he was a detective, the subterfuge seemed overly cloak-and-dagger. Would Saloon Micky be so concerned about Harry Dunn that he would dispatch a henchman to trail after him? Although doubtful, Harry must err on the side of caution. If Theodore Prescott thought it necessary, he would be wise to trust his judgment.

Two blocks from the hotel, a tingle of alarm began at Harry's nape and wriggled down his spine. He slowed his gait and paused before a pet shop's window display. As much as the tumbling kittens drew his attention, his true purpose was to use the glass's reflection to observe his surroundings surreptitiously. A figure across the street dashed into the entrance of a milliner's shop, the movement too quick to discern more than the person's dark-hued clothing. Had the person not worn a Tyrolean hat, Harry might not have given it a second thought. Spooked, he hurried down the sidewalk at a pace just short of a run. After passing two storefronts, he ducked into a sandwich shop where he'd once ordered lunch, knowing there was a door to the alley near the public toilet. From there, he raced to the corner and immersed himself in a crowd of pedestrians before turning sharply onto a side street and jumping into a hired buggy. After disembarking at the public library and walking briskly among the shelves, he exited through a side door and hurried to where Harriet had left her bicycle, confident he hadn't been followed.

The evasive movement had been nerve-racking. The next time Harriet arrived at the Palmer House as Harry

Dunn, she would carry a suitcase with a change of women's clothing, complete with a frilly bonnet, and depart the hotel as a conventional Harriet after packing Harry's clothes and whiskers into the suitcase. Although the identity change should confuse whoever might be following her, she would continue to take a circuitous route as an added precaution.

Home safely, Harriet peeled the beard from her face, removed the too-tight vest, and sank into the tub. The water, which never quite reached a temperature as hot as she desired, became lukewarm sooner than she liked. Susan, however, was excited by her emergence from the bathroom. Harriet delighted in the kitten's affection, though she understood it was because of spending most of the day alone. She also knew it wasn't personal. Were Aubrey there, Susan would be on his lap or, if feeling frisky, attacking his toes as if they were tiny mice. *Where was Aubrey anyway? He should be home at this hour.* With Susan underfoot, she padded across the floor to the kitchen to peruse the ice box and make a decision on dinner, a task requiring more creativity as the week neared an end and, with it, the grocery provisions.

A sheet of paper sat next to the breadbox. In her brother's neat lettering, it read: *Gone boxing with Matthew. Then going to Pearls.* Harriet had forgotten about Matthew's offer to take her brother to the boxing gym. But why was Aubrey going to see Pearl afterward? Matthew had told her about Aubrey's desire to move in with Pearl. Had he gone there to press his plan? That would not do. Pearl shouldn't be put in the awkward situation of denying the sixteen-year-old his foolish aspiration.

She marched into her bedroom and, grumbling, tugged on her bloomers. If she must ride to Pearl's mansion, she would do so in her most comfortable attire. She fed Susan, donned her bowler and coat, and, with another groan, pushed her Victoria out the door.

* * *

Harriet entered Pearl's through the orangery door at the back of the house. She immediately heard singing. Nearing the kitchen, her ears confirmed the voices belonged to Pearl and her brother.

> *Late last night when we were all in bed,*
> *Mrs. O'Leary left her lantern in the shed.*
> *Well, the cow kicked it over, and this is*
>   *what they said:*
> *There'll be a hot time in the old town tonight!*

Harriet's arrival was met with the abruptness of a bucket of water dumped over a candle. The room fell silent. Aubrey glowered. Pearl appeared befuddled.

"I didn't intend to interrupt your merriment," Harriet said, feeling like an uninvited party guest.

Pearl waved a bony arm through the air. "Don't be silly, Harry. Grab that ladle, would you? You're just in time to serve the soup. It's ham and pea." She gave Aubrey a sideways glance and winked. "It'll put hair on your chest."

Harriet shed her coat, shooed Toby from the counter, and grabbed three bowls from the cupboard. Aubrey remained uncharacteristically silent.

"How was your day, Harry?" Pearl chirped. "Your brother, here, tells me he has a powerful right hook, got an A on his math exam, and that his history teacher complimented his writing."

Harriet couldn't decide which of two emotions she felt more strongly: jealousy that her brother—never forthcoming when she asked—had no reservations telling Pearl about his day or annoyance that he was so obviously manipulating Pearl, buttering her up before he suggested he move in upstairs.

"This fine young man also offered to help me move some boxes down from the third floor."

It was all Harriet could do to bite her tongue. Were she to unmask Aubrey's purpose, she would infuriate him, betray Matthew's confidence, and sour the mood for Pearl. She would have to wait for him to divulge his plan. However, she doubted he would broach the topic now that she was there.

Over dinner, Harriet answered Pearl's questions about the investigation. Pearl was usually curious, but her interest was tenfold since she had become involved with visits to the tenement and the settlement house. Between mouthfuls of meatloaf, Harriet recounted her several frustrations and setbacks. In addition to Marie Batchelder's unfortunate death, which Pearl had learned about alongside her, she had found nothing of intrigue at Eugene Eldridge's apartment, and despite visits to meetings of the Socialist Labor Party and the People's Cause, she was not an inch closer to finding Eldridge's fiancée. Only when she described her encounters with "Irish Dan" Walsh and then Mike "Saloon Micky" Powers while posing as Harry Dunn did her brother's mood shift from aloof to engaged.

"They're real aldermen?" Aubrey asked. "And you fooled them by wearing a disguise? What if you were found out? Would they put you in prison?"

Before Harriet could answer, Pearl waved her fork. "It's those Gray Wolves that should be locked up! They're all crooked. Those men were elected to serve the city, not line their own pockets."

"What do gray wolves have to do with the aldermen?" Aubrey asked.

Harriet and Pearl spent the next half hour educating Aubrey about the corruption in the Levee District and the public officeholders who enriched themselves. Not mentioning that she borrowed the beard from his disguise kit, Harriet explained how her fabrication precipitated a guest room at the Palmer House.

"How long are you going to stay in the hotel?" Aubrey asked, excited by the chance to experience the Palmer

House's luxurious surroundings. That, or to have the apartment to himself.

"I'm not overnighting there, merely coming and going. If Alderman Powers is to believe I am who I say I am, Harry Dunn must establish a presence."

Pearl refilled their water glasses. "Sounds like a frightful business, if you ask me—so much deception in the world. Saloon Micky swaggers about town as if he's an upstanding citizen. And now you are pretending to be a detective from Philadelphia—a male detective, at that!"

"Making people believe you're someone else is fun, Pearl," Aubrey said. "That's what actors in plays do. And people enjoy them. If they're good, people will pay money. I bet Richard Bennett is a rich man."

Harriet was impressed her brother remembered the name of the famous stage actor who starred in *The Limited Mail*, a play the siblings attended with their aunt and uncle several years back. That he did helped explain his enthusiastic participation in each year's school play.

As if reading her thoughts, Aubrey said, "This spring, my school is performing *The Little Glass Slipper*. You should come, Pearl. I'm going to audition for the prince. You can sit with Harriet. It doesn't cost any money. Tickets are free."

"I have a history with that story!" Pearl declared proudly. "Many folks these days know the tale as *Cinderella*. But I bet you didn't know it was originally called *Aschenputtel*? That's a German word, if you couldn't guess. You might recall me telling you that my great-grandfather was a professor at the University of Göttingen. Among his many esteemed colleagues were two brothers—Jacob, a professor and head librarian, and Wilhelm, a professor of German studies."

Harriet and Aubrey traded perplexed looks.

"What?" Pearl said, registering their bafflement. "Don't tell me you don't know who I'm talking about."

Aubrey lowered his soup spoon from his mouth. "Who?"

"Who?" Pearl reared back, aghast. "Why, the Brothers Grimm! That's who."

The second before, Harriet had taken a drink of water. Half choking, half coughing, she tried not to spray it across the table.

Now it was Pearl and Aubrey's turn to exchange baffled looks.

Swallowing awkwardly, Harriet cleared her throat and shouted, "Grimm! That's the surname of Eugene Eldridge's fiancée—the woman I've been searching for and unable to find. Jorinda Grimm."

"Harry!" Pearl exclaimed, jumping from her chair and rattling the dinnerware. The sudden movement startled Harriet and Aubrey. Toby, who'd been sitting in Pearl's lap, made a dash for the orangery. "It's a fairy tale! Don't you see?"

Aubrey shook his head and shot his sister a worried look. Harriet wondered if Pearl might be having an episode.

Pearl explained. "Jorinda is the young woman in the fairy tale 'Jorinde and Joringel.' I've not heard that name since I was a child and was told the story by my mother—in German, of course. I'm not sure it's at all familiar here in America. The story is about a shape-shifting witch who lives in a castle. She lures animals and birds to her castle and kills them for food. The lovers, Jorinde and Joringel, are engaged to be married. One night, on a walk in the forest, they stumble upon the witch's lair. She turns Jorinde into a nightingale and petrifies poor Joringel. Being a fairy tale, the story ends happily enough. Joringel dreams of a magical flower, which he finds and breaks the spell, returning Jorinde to a woman and putting an end to the witch's evil."

"Jorinda Grimm," Harriet muttered, stunned by the revelation. "Eldridge's fiancée must be a contrivance. All this time I've been searching for a woman who doesn't exist."

"She could be a real person," Aubrey countered. "Maybe

she made up the name Jorinda Grimm just like you made up Harry Dunn."

"But why hide her true identity?" Harriet wondered aloud. "Surely, Eldridge would eventually find out? Whatever the woman's reasons, they can't be admirable."

"This calls for a toast," Pearl announced, pulling champagne flutes from a tall glass-fronted cabinet. After setting one before each table setting, she returned with a white ceramic jug and poured.

"Pearl," Harriet said with a grimace, "you must know Aubrey is not old enough—"

"Don't get your undies in a twist. It's grape juice," Pearl replied. "Still, it will serve our purpose."

"What exactly are we celebrating?" Harriet asked.

"We figured out that Jorinda isn't really Jorinda," Aubrey answered.

Pearl pointed a bent finger at Aubrey. "Precisely."

Harriet was about to argue that they were confusing a setback with an accomplishment when Pearl lifted a glass. "To progress!"

"To progress," Aubrey repeated.

Although unconvinced, Harriet didn't want to spoil the moment. She raised hers as well and clinked glasses before setting down her grape juice without a sip. Her mind raced. According to Steven Bliss, Eugene Eldridge had met Jorinda at a meeting of the People's Cause. It made no sense for Eugene to share a fabricated name with his friend. What could be the benefit of lying? The same went for Steven Bliss—he gained nothing by being untruthful about what Eugene had told him.

"Tarnation, Harry," Pearl scolded, pulling Harriet from her ruminations. "Always so quick to see the half-eaten cookie. Don't you see what's happened here? We three turned a simple supper into an event of astonishing discovery. You now have a new lead in your investigation." When Pearl didn't get the desired reaction, she continued. "*Hmm.* I can see you're not of the same mind. All right, then. Tell me this. What *did* you know about this Jorinda Grimm character before tonight?"

"She is purportedly a radical socialist," Harriet offered.

"I see . . ." Pearl drew out the words as if she were a lawyer cross-examining a witness. "And that is all you knew of the woman?"

"Yes," Harriet replied, unsure where Pearl was headed.

"And what can you now add to your body of knowledge because of this fascinating dinner discussion?"

A momentary silence fell over the dining table. Toby returned, hopping up onto Pearl's lap. Harriet shrugged.

"She's German!" Aubrey declared.

"Exactly," Pearl confirmed. " 'Jorinde and Joringel' is German. And so is your radical socialist."

Chapter 26

Aubrey helped Harriet lift her bicycle into the back of a buggy as Pearl waved goodbye from the front porch, holding Toby in the crook of her arm. Harriet was exhausted and relieved not to ride the several miles home. The rocking of the seat, usually jarring, was oddly soothing. She settled back and was about to nod off when Aubrey said, "I think I'll live with Pearl."

Harriet was glad her eyes were closed. Otherwise, she knew they would give away her irritation. Although too tired to discuss the complicated subject, she couldn't avoid it forever. Perhaps it was best to tackle it headfirst before he had time to convince himself further of the ridiculous notion. After a long sigh and a silent promise to stay calm, she opened her eyes.

"And why would you want to do that?"

"She's got that giant house. And with me not around, you would have the entire apartment to yourself?"

His opening salvo nearly made her smile. "That's terribly considerate of you."

Unsure of her sincerity, he said, "And you're always complaining about how you have to clean up after me. You wouldn't have to."

"I see. So Pearl would do that for you? Is that it?"

"No." He flashed annoyance. "I'll clean up after myself."

"So you would do for Pearl what you don't bother to do for your sister?"

"I'd be living in her house. It's different."

Harriet took a breath. She wanted desperately to point out that he was living in *her* apartment—her name was on the deed—but that wasn't how he saw things. It was, after all, his childhood home as much as hers. Hardly was he a guest or tenant. But neither was she his cook and maid.

"Have you raised this idea with Pearl?"

How long had her brother been at Pearl's before she'd arrived? Had he broached the subject? If he had, what would Pearl have said? Knowing her, she'd not have sugarcoated her position. But was Harriet right in presuming it would be a no? Pearl was fond of Aubrey. There was no question about that. But Pearl would never assent to such a momentous request without first speaking with Harriet. Would she?

"Not yet. I was going to tonight. But then you showed up, and all we could talk about was your investigation."

Letting that pass, she asked, "Have you given any thought to how your living with Pearl would affect her? She seems quite content with her life at present."

"I'd keep her company."

"She has Toby, and she doesn't strike me as lonely."

"I'm not a cat."

Harriet blurted a laugh.

"This isn't a joke, Harriet."

"No, Aubrey. It is not. But have you considered that by asking Pearl, you will be putting her in an awkward position? She will find no pleasure in telling you no. However, I'm sure you are welcome to visit as often as you like." After a moment's consideration, she thought it wise to add, "Within reason, of course."

"What makes you so sure she'll say no?" Aubrey was teetering between desperate and distraught.

She hadn't wanted this conversation, but this far in, there was no way out. Still, she must be careful. Despite his boyish adolescent bluster, he was emotionally fragile when it came to the possibility of rejection.

"I can't be certain, Aubrey. No more than you can be sure she will agree." She took another breath. "How about this? Why don't you sleep on the matter? Better yet, give it another week. Then, if you still think it's the right thing to do—for both of you—don't ask her outright. Instead, why don't you offer to stay overnight with her on the weekend to keep her company? If she accepts your offer, see how it goes. If she prefers to remain alone, it will be much easier for her to decline a kind gesture than a proposition that might make her feel like she's rejecting you, which she would never intentionally do. Surely, you know how fond she is of you."

What remained unspoken was Harriet's hurt in knowing her brother didn't want to live with her any longer. Who had changed? Him? Or her? Aubrey had pleaded with their aunt and uncle to allow him to move into the apartment with her, and she'd been elated. Not only did she not want to live alone, but she also would have missed him terribly. They had their quarrels. What siblings didn't? Despite the extra responsibility and his orneriness and messiness, she had never contemplated him leaving before reaching his majority. And even then, the notion was discomforting.

To her amazement, Aubrey agreed with her suggestion. She couldn't be sure, but she suspected he had been nervous about Pearl's reaction and appreciated the more measured approach. Returning home, they exchanged wishes for a good sleep before closing their bedroom doors. It was all she could do to kick off her shoes, remove her bloomers, and crawl into the bed. Susan jumped up and turned three circles before deciding on the best spot among the blankets. The room was dark but not pitch black. She gazed up at the painting she had taken from Eugene Eldridge's apartment. It was sometimes easy to forget the victim at the center of an investigation. By all accounts, Eugene had been a decent man. An excellent reporter. And a fine artist.

Before that night, she'd never have questioned his being a fiancé. He might have thought he was going to marry, but who exactly? Is an engagement legitimate if the bride is not? She stared up at the portrait of the nude female figure—her modest sideways pose, her long, dark hair draped across her body, her wry smile. Was she Eugene's Jorinda?

Harriet's breath caught. Susan gave a start, jostled by Harriet's shudder beneath the bed sheet. It couldn't be true.

It was.

For more than a week, the portrait had rested on her bedroom's bureau. Eugene's life had been taken before he had completed the painting. But now that Harriet knew she wasn't looking for Jorinda, the person in the painting—finished or not—was unmistakable. It was Brunhilda Struff.

Chapter 27

A fitful sleep would suggest *some* amount of sleep, which Harriet figured she'd barely achieved. The realization that Brunhilda Struff was Jorinda Grimm had her tossing and turning all night. Why had Brunhilda lied to Eugene? What was her game? More importantly, whose side was she on?

This was a morning for extra-strong coffee—and two cups. Adding to her fatigue, she felt torn in several directions. She must report to Theodore Prescott at the agency, stop by the hotel's front desk—as Harry Dunn—to see if Saloon Micky had left a message for him, and return to the *Progressive Age* to ask Steven Bliss if he had recalled anything else since their initial meeting. Still, another uncertain task demanded action. Presuming Brunhilda Struff could even be found, she needed to figure out a good way of approaching her.

Bowing to logistics, Harriet decided to begin the day at the Palmer House. Readying herself, she realized several problems at once. The beard borrowed from her brother may have sufficed for his starring role as Sir Francis Chesney in the school's one-night run of the farce *Charley's Aunt*, but it was not made for multiple wearings—Harry Dunn was losing his hair. With a bit of paste and stealing clumps of whiskers from the pair of excessively bushy sideburns, she patched together a serviceable beard. She also had to skimp on the amount of paste used to affix the facial hair as the tin was nearly empty. If that weren't bother enough, her jaw, chin, and the area below her nose had developed a slight rash. She was glad Aubrey or one of the play's other cast members had peeled the label from the tin. She shuddered to think what odious ingredients she was smearing onto her face. At some point during the day, she would visit a costume shop and replace her whiskers and paste with items of higher quality.

She packed her least favorite shirtwaist and skirt—a low bar among slim pickings—and a hideous sunbonnet, a hand-me-down from her aunt, into a suitcase. She wouldn't ride her Victoria. A detective from out of town would not travel by a lady's bicycle, and her comings and goings from the Palmer House required evasive routing better done on foot. With one last appraisal of her men's suit clothes, polished oxfords, and bow tie, Harry Dunn set out.

Would entering the Palmer House ever cease to elicit a thrill? The lobby's opulence was unparalleled, and the sophisticated manner and dress of the guests created a rarified atmosphere that Harriet imagined at places such as Buckingham Palace and the Vanderbilt's Biltmore Estate. Once again, she was grateful that Horace Bartlett had a penchant for fine men's clothing. She may feel out of place in such grandiose surroundings, but as Harry she wouldn't look it.

Harry approached the registration desk and inquired whether he had received any correspondence. The clerk gave a sharp nod, saying, "As it happens, Mr. Dunn, I do have something for you." He handed Harry a white linen envelope. Receiving it, Harry hoped his trembling hand wasn't noticeable. Only one person would leave Harry Dunn a note. Alderman Powers had apparently believed the ruse. The

THE CASE OF THE MURDERED MUCKRAKER 215

question remained: If Harry was successful in reeling him in, then what? A confession, albeit inconceivable, would be meaningless without witnesses. As with his alleged involvement in Eugene Eldridge's murder, nothing short of unassailable evidence of his guilt was needed—and nothing about the alderman suggested damning proof would come easily. Saloon Micky wore ill-fitted clothing, gem-studded rings, and preposterous hair, but sloppy he wasn't.

Despite growing impatience with the elevator's stops at each floor on the way up to the sixth floor, Harry waited until he was inside the room. Returned to Harriet, she plucked a silver letter opener from a stationery tray on the desk and released the envelope's contents.

> *Dear Mr. Dunn,*
> *I trust you have settled in nicely at the Palmer House and that you find the accommodations to your liking. In my position as a city official, I have a keen interest in your investigation of the most unfortunate passing of a Chicago newspaperman. A free press is a hallmark of a healthy society, as you will doubtless agree. Knowing that you and Mr. Eldridge's family believe his death suspicious and unresolved is indeed cause for great concern. As I conveyed at our first meeting the other day, the matter has my fullest attention. I must say, it is mightily reassuring to know you are making inquiries. While I hold the professionalism and capabilities of the fine men of this city's police department in the highest esteem, it is conceivable that you might discover valuable information that they have not. At a minimum, a fresh set of eyes to examine the details of the case will surely do no harm. In the great and sincere hope that you have made progress, I would appreciate your attendance at my office this afternoon at three o'clock so we might discuss all that you have learned. Considering your*

reputation, I am sure whatever it is you can share will not disappoint.
   Most kind regards,
   The Honorable Michael Powers   -

Harriet reread the letter, wincing each time her eyes fell on the word "Honorable." In city government, the honorific was reserved for the mayor, and besides, Saloon Micky was undeserving of such respect.

She wondered how to make the most of the forthcoming meeting. As Harriet Morrow, a detective with the Prescott Agency, she would share nothing with Saloon Micky. However, as Harry Dunn, a visiting detective, perhaps *he* might induce the overconfident alderman to reveal an incriminating fact unintentionally.

As she refolded the stationery and returned it to the envelope, a clump of beard fell onto the desk. She felt the whisker-less, sticky spot on her chin and realized that any notion of leaving the hotel as Harry was impossible. A reordering of activities was required.

Six hours before she was due at City Hall, she exited the hotel as Harriet, with Harry's clothing in the suitcase. She would have liked to avoid changing yet again, but her brother's borrowed whiskers were in too sorry a state to wear any longer. She would return to her disguise of Harry Dunn once she'd purchased a decent replacement beard.

Entering several shops, she zigzagged through the aisles before abruptly dashing out a side door. Once confident she had evaded any followers, she plucked a nickel from her satchel and boarded a streetcar to the *Progressive Age* newspaper offices.

Harriet hadn't anticipated interrupting Alexi Scholtz's work, but Steven Bliss was not at his desk. The editor watched Harriet approach, suitcase in hand, his face inscrutable. In response to her amiable greeting, he stared at her in silence. Presuming the reason for his chilly welcome, she said, "I'm terribly sorry to bother you, Mr. Scholtz. I came to speak with Mr. Bliss, but he appears to be away. Can you tell me when he will return?"

"Who knows you came here?" Alexi Scholtz demanded, his tone more frightened than angry.

This was nothing like the reception she had received on her first visit. The man was having a bad day, confusing her for someone else, or was displeased to see her again for a reason she couldn't fathom.

"If you must know, my employer, Mr. Prescott, is aware of my visit here last week. Operatives detail their activities in daily reports for the principal. Why do you ask?"

"You told no one else?" Alexi Scholtz said gruffly, stepping closer to Harriet as if proximity would draw a truthful answer.

Taken aback, Harriet said, "Mr. Scholtz, I'm getting a distinct sense that something is awry."

"Shortly after your first visit here, three days to be precise, Steven left the office for his lunch break."

"Surely, one's taking lunch away from the office is not so unusual that—"

"He has never returned."

The four words overwhelmed Harriet's ability to speak. Or think. *He has never returned.*

Alexi Scholtz continued, "I can't help but think it has something to do with you."

"Me?" Harriet looked over her shoulder at the young journalist's empty desk. "But that makes no sense. I barely know the man. Besides, there are any number of reasons that might account for his absence: a sudden illness, an urgent summons from a loved one, more favorable employment."

Now, it was Alexi Scholtz who looked dismayed. "Miss Morrow! Steven was quite content with his position at this newspaper. Were he not, he would have brought the matter to my attention. It is completely at odds with his character to just up and leave without notice. Also, that particular day was special to Steven. A story months in the making was nearly finished and scheduled to run in the following day's edition. It is inconceivable that he would have abandoned it. As for the other reasons you suggest, they can all be dismissed. Steven lives with his parents. I have been to the family's home and spoken with his mother and father. I can assure you that they are beside themselves with worry. The last time they saw their son was on the morning of the day he went missing. As much as I don't want to think it, I must conclude he is the victim of foul play."

"Have you notified the authorities?"

"Of course. Though, you'll understand my skepticism of both their interest and capabilities. At the *Progressive Age*, we see our duty as more than simply being the mouthpiece of government. Here, we print the truth—a concept this city's authorities, including the police department, often take issue with."

"Perhaps then . . ." Flustered by the situation and the accusation that she was somehow responsible, she threw up her hands. "Was he assigned to another story that might have put him in harm's way? Could he have angered the wrong person? What about the man called Bat? During my previous visit, you mentioned the grisly business of his body pulled from the river. Might Steven have been looking into his murder? With Eugene Eldridge no longer around to investigate the Gray Wolves, perhaps—"

"We all know who was behind that!" Scholtz roared. "Saloon Micky. As to the fate of young Steven, I stand by my assertion that it has to do with you. And I very much fear for his fate."

Harriet felt a jolt of panic. Saloon Micky had gone out of his way to mention the *Progressive Age*. Did he suspect someone at the newspaper might be in possession of the missing evidence? With Eldridge out of the picture, might Powers have set his sights on his friend Steven Bliss? Harriet shared her worry with the editor.

"Aha!" Alexi Scholtz exclaimed. "There you have it! You came here, Miss Morrow, as part of your investiga-

tion into the murder of Eugene Eldridge, a freelance journalist with whom this newspaper had a relationship. You
then stirred up the malevolence of that no-good criminal
Powers. I think the question of your responsibility in Steven's
disappearance has been answered."

Harriet suppressed her urge to argue further. What Alexi
Scholtz asserted was far-fetched. As she'd already pointed
out, she hadn't known Steven Bliss before that day. Their
meeting was brief, and she hadn't seen him since. Moreover, she'd not mentioned the newspaper's name to Powers;
it had been the other way around. There was absolutely
nothing linking her to . . .

Seeing Harriet turn pale, Alexi Scholtz motioned toward a nearby chair and poured her a glass of water. With
trembling hands, she gripped the chair's arms and slowly
lowered herself, unable to mask her shock at the realization. She examined the connections that had formed in her
mind from various angles, desperate to see the chain of
events any other way. She could not.

When visiting the Socialist Labor Party meeting, she
had offered a reason for looking for a woman named Jorinda Grimm: "She is the fiancée of my friend's colleague."
At the time, she'd been almost proud of conjuring an association that so deftly straddled detail and vagueness. Could
that error in judgment have cost Steven Bliss his life? To
anyone uninvolved in Eugene Eldridge's murder, the remark would have been harmless. But to someone who *did*
have a hand in his death, valuable information had been
conveyed: *a colleague of Eldridge's knew about Jorinda
Grimm*. It wouldn't have taken much detecting for Brunhilda Struff to discover who that colleague was. But if she
were behind Steven's disappearance, why? What did she
have to gain by silencing the young man? What threat did
he pose? It made more sense that Saloon Micky was responsible. Presuming he had ordered the killing of Eldridge,
why not follow up by eliminating other journalists whom
he perceived as potential threats?

Leaving the newspaper offices, she wished she could have reassured Alexi Scholtz that Steven Bliss would eventually appear and that it was not as dire as it appeared. Instead, she shared the editor's grave concern. Only time would reveal what had happened to the man. Harriet suspected that would only occur when his dead body was discovered.

Chapter 28

Six months before, Aubrey had selected the false beard he wore for the school play from a shelf where it sat next to a pair of clown shoes and a magician's wand at the far back of a variety shop near their apartment. It took Harriet less than a second inside the two-floor downtown location of McGillicutty's Costume Emporium to appreciate the store was a world apart. Had she not been in a rush, she imagined spending hours perusing the merchandise. From there, she could reenter the world as a Roman gladiator, an Egyptian pharaoh, a Western sheriff, or what appeared to be hundreds of other personas. Her wish to disguise herself as a run-of-the-mill gentleman from the East should be as easy as ordering toast at a diner. The trick, however, would be matching her former beard, mustache, and sideburns.

After a quarter hour of searching, she employed the assistance of a clerk and found a set of similarly colored whiskers that would suffice, though not perfect. When the clerk offered to trim each piece to Harriet's desired length as a complimentary service, Harriet eagerly agreed. To her purchase, she added a jar of glue and a brush the clerk claimed to be "the choice of New York's finest stage professionals." She had come seeking good quality items but was now worried about the price tag. Still, Harry Dunn must be convincing, and having a reliable disguise for future cases helped to justify the one dollar and twenty cents expense. She used the changing room to complete her transition to the Philadelphia detective.

Appraising herself in the mirror, Harriet's thoughts drifted to Barbara. She suspected that if anyone would see through her deception, it would be her. They had not spoken for days, not since their quarrel. How many times had Harriet replayed the words they had spoken? Despite searching for a soothing interpretation or less contentious outcome, there was only one conclusion: they disagreed on a topic Harriet considered fundamental. When next in Barbara's presence, she wouldn't be able to avoid thinking of her approving violence to right societal wrongs. Harriet wholeheartedly agreed with Barbara that those wrongs must be addressed but would never condone bloodshed as a remedy. Could she ever see past their disagreement? Could Barbara? Had their romance ended before having a chance to begin? Shoving the troublesome topic from her mind, she departed the changing room and settled her bill.

For practical reasons, Harry Dunn returned to his room at the Palmer House and deposited his satchel before walking to City Hall, briefcase in hand and derringer at the ready in his pocket holster. He took his time, thinking about what to say to Mike Powers. He respected the alderman's perceptivity—and the threat he posed. Every discovery in the investigation pointed to his guilt. Although he may not have been present in the tenement and plunged the knife into Eugene Eldridge's belly, it seemed most likely that Powers had ordered it done, just as he was responsible for Bat's murder. What remained a mystery was the possible connection between the alderman and Brunhilda Struff. Was Saloon Micky pulling Brunhilda's strings from behind a curtain? If that were true, two seemingly distinct threads of the investigation would intertwine neatly.

But what was their connection? Brunhilda was a radical socialist, and Saloon Micky was a corrupt politician—everything a person like Brunhilda despised. That they were in cahoots was as likely as Harriet teaming up with "Irish Dan" Walsh.

Upon entering Alderman Powers' office, Harry Dunn was met by the winsome secretary. Whether Harry was remembered because of his previous visit or because his name had been entered in the appointment calendar situated prominently on the secretary's desk, he was greeted by name.

"What say you, young man?" Harry replied. "I trust you're enjoying a good day."

The secretary replied with a tight smile and stood. "The alderman is expecting you. This way, Mr. Dunn, sir."

Harry placed his suitcase in the small lobby and followed the secretary the short distance into Mike Powers' office. The alderman sat behind an extraordinarily cluttered desk. Seeing both the secretary and Powers together in the same room, Harriet was struck by the men's stark physical differences. Even the lone trait they shared—slenderness—complimented the secretary but made the alderman appear sickly. Although it wasn't uncommon for a gentleman to employ a male secretary, the young man's beauty raised the question: Did Powers happen upon such a good-looking employee, or had he sought one out?

Harry kindly accepted an offer of tea, saving him from having to ask. However, concerned that a sip from a steaming beverage might loosen his whiskers, he had no intention of raising the cup when provided. Powers ordered coffee with two lumps of sugar. With a knowing nod, the secretary backed out of the room. When the door closed, Powers began the conversation amiably by asking whether Mr. Dunn was happy with the level of comfort and service at the Palmer House and his general opinions of the city and how it differed from Philadelphia. Playing along,

Harry was midsentence in sharing an observation about Chicago's elevated rail when Powers interrupted, suddenly impatient with the topic he had just initiated.

"So tell me, how is your investigation progressing? What have you discovered? And please, Mr. Dunn, leave nothing out. I am a man who revels in details, believing them essential to knowledge. I'm sure you agree."

"I suppose there are occasions where the details can prove instrumental." Harry shrugged theatrically. "Alas, this is not one of them. Open-and-shut case. A tale as old as time. I'll be departing for Philadelphia soon, I should think."

Harry hoped the remark would unsettle the seemingly unflappable alderman. It appeared to have worked. He twisted a ruby ring on his pinky finger, taking a moment to respond. "Oh?" He looked up, feigning an overdone nonchalance. "So you have solved it, have you? And who is the guilty party?"

"Best that I should first notify the police. Protocol. I'm sure you understand. As a visiting detective, I must follow procedure. No reason to ruffle feathers. Of course, given your position, the police will surely relay the particulars of my findings to you posthaste."

Powers continued to spin the ring on his finger as if in time with the gears in his head. "You are correct that the police won't hesitate to inform me of whatever information you might provide them. Given that, I fail to see how you might 'ruffle feathers' by telling me now yourself. Much more efficient, I should think. As a busy man, time is precious. So then. Who do you believe killed the muckraker?"

A man like Powers wasn't used to someone refusing his request. But Harry Dunn would not back down—not yet. Confidence in the plan demanded he see it through. "It's not a matter of who I believe stuck the journalist, but who I *know* did the dastardly deed. However, given the circumstances, I can tell you that the killer is quite typical. In my line of work, you see this all the time. As I said, open-and-shut."

A light knock at the door was followed by the secretary's entrance, balancing a tray with cups and saucers. Harry imagined the secretary had performed this afternoon ritual for his boss countless times. He waited for the secretary to set the tray onto the corner of Powers' desk to say, "Still. It's a shame about the muckraker, Eugene Eldridge. Ghastly business."

The secretary's hand, steady just moments before, now trembled. Liquid sloshed over the cups' rims and onto the saucers and tray. Harry was relieved for the secretary's sake that none spilled onto the desk, suspecting the alderman hid a temper beneath his implacable façade. The secretary's glance at Powers wasn't returned. The alderman ignored both his secretary and the spilled beverages, staring coldly at Harry Dunn.

"A shame?" Powers considered. "I don't think so. That would be the case only if the muckraker hadn't deserved it."

While Harry struggled to maintain his composure, Harriet fought the urge to punch the smug scoundrel in the nose. His remark seemed tantamount to a murder confession, and his involvement seemed unquestioned. The mention of Eldridge also rattled the secretary, as hoped. Although it was hardly an unequivocal confirmation that Powers was responsible for Eldridge's murder, his secretary must see and hear enough to suspect the nefarious deeds of his boss, even if he didn't witness them firsthand.

Powers waved away his secretary's apologies and determination to clean up the spills and dismissed him from the office. "Now. Where were we? I believe you were about to reveal the name of the person responsible for your clients' son's death." He folded his hands on the desk, calling attention to a delicate sapphire ring she hadn't noticed before. He leaned forward, waiting.

"Lovers' quarrel," Harry Dunn said, adding an ambivalent shrug. "But that's all, and I do mean all, you're getting out of me, Alderman."

A genuine smile stretched across Powers' face. *What a fool,* Harry imagined him thinking. *The supposed professional detective from Philadelphia had gotten it so utterly wrong.* He knew Powers was delighted to learn that he would soon leave town and take with him a story to ensure Eldridge's parents didn't consider him a suspect.

Harry stood, pinched the brim of his hat, and bid farewell to Alderman Powers. Turning back from the doorway, he said, "I suppose you're right. There's no harm in telling you. The murderess's name is Jorinda Grimm."

Upon hearing the woman's name, Powers' expression was blank. For a moment, both Harry and Harriet believed he had never before heard the name.

Chapter 29

Matthew pulled a hand through his hair, leaving red strands on end to catch the sunlight streaming through his office window. "I don't know, Harriet—or should I address you as Harry? It sounds unnecessarily risky."

Postponing the effort of shedding her whiskers and changing back to her usual clothing, she had returned to the agency as the Detective Harry Dunn. "There's no point in pretending you don't know full well who I am, so, please, call me Harriet. It would be silly otherwise."

With a nod, Matthew continued, asking, "How can you even be sure you'll find Brunhilda there?"

His concern about Harriet's intention to visit the Vorwaerts Turner Hall in search of Brunhilda Struff was understandable, but she felt she had no choice. "I have seen Brunhilda only two places. The first was at the Socialist Labor Party meeting, where I would gladly return. But with Charles Bonner away working on another investigation, I have no way of knowing when they will next meet. That leaves the Turner Hall, where I encountered Brunhilda twice: first fencing, then the next night at the People's Cause meeting on the building's third floor."

"Perhaps another operative might have information on the SLP," Matthew tried.

Harriet shook her head. "They meet in Arbuckle Hall, and it's not in the story. The Turner Hall is."

"I confess, Harriet, you've completely lost me."

Harriet recounted Pearl's story of Jorinde and Joringel, the Brothers Grimm fairy tale. "Jorinde and Joringel are lovers tormented by a witch who lives in *a castle*. We've been to Turner Hall. How would you describe its appearance?"

"Surely, that's a coincidence."

Harriet huffed. "I'm not suggesting Brunhilda designed the building, Matthew. I am simply saying that particular detail of the story couldn't have escaped Brunhilda's notice. Moreover, the witch's lair is high in the castle."

"The hall's top floor?"

"Still think it's a coincidence?"

"Yes, I do."

Harriet neglected to mention the part of the story where the witch lures animals to her castle lair and kills them for food, instead focusing on the happy ending when Joringel breaks the witch's spell and ends her evil once and for all.

"And Mr. Prescott? What does he say about your plan?"

"Madelaine says he is not due back to the office for another hour. That will give me time to sharpen my argument."

"Only an hour? I'm not sure any amount of time will be sufficient to solve your dilemma. Finding Brunhilda will get you only as far as hearing Saloon Micky practically confess to having a hand in Eldridge's murder, which is not far enough. Without Eldridge's evidence, all you have are suspicions, however reasonable they may be."

Too frustrated to stay seated, Harriet began pacing her small office. "What would you have me do then? Surely, not sit on my hands! I stupidly told Brunhilda about Steven Bliss and his knowledge of Jorinda Grimm without meaning to. The next thing you know, poor Steven goes missing. I must pursue both of them—Powers and Brunhilda—

until I discover their roles in all this. Only then will I find my way to the evidence—if it can even be found."

Nearly an hour later, Harriet still hadn't convinced Matthew, but she had worn him down with her insistence that progress demanded that she confront Brunhilda. Before leaving her office, he wished her luck with Prescott. She accepted his well-wishes but knew he was counting on Prescott to disapprove of her plan. She would soon find out.

Adding to her anxiety, Prescott returned to the agency forty-five minutes late and appeared tired and unhappy to see Harry Dunn standing by his office door. Harriet had used the time to hone her remarks to the most salient, knowing her boss appreciated brevity and succinctness second only to a case's speedy resolution. And so, with dispatch, she recounted what had transpired in the past twenty-four hours.

Ignoring her disguise—had he become used to it?—he said, "You sound better, Miss Morrow," confusing her with the abrupt change of topic. "Your breathing . . . you commented before that you weren't feeling one hundred percent when pedaling your Victoria. A handsome bicycle, I might add. Mrs. Prescott has gotten it into her head that she must have one." He sniffed. "Ladies on bicycles. What's next?"

"The vote," she muttered.

"What's that?"

Grateful for her last-second circumspection, she averted an unhelpful quarrel by saying, "How do you know I own an Overman Victoria?"

"I am, above all else, a detective, Miss Morrow."

"Yes, of course, sir."

"So?" Seeing she'd forgotten his question, he repeated, "Your lungs?"

"I'm hopeful progress will be made."

He pursed his lips, a sign she recognized as displeasure. "I can't have my operatives working at less than their best.

I'll make arrangements for you to see a specialist. Madelaine will inform you of the particulars once I do so." He raised a hand, preempting her rebuttal that an appointment was unnecessary. Her next thought was Charles Bonner's weight and the various and obvious physical challenges of several of Prescott's other male operatives: Mr. Clemens' missing hand, rumored to have been lost to an ax-wielding embezzler, and Mr. Shoemaker's noticeable limp, the result of a fall from a speeding train. Still, that her boss was concerned about her health was touching. Plus, he wouldn't bother if he wasn't keeping her on as an operative.

The conversation returned to the investigation. Had Matthew been there, she would have had to conceal her gloating. Prescott enthusiastically supported her plan. Reiterating his belief that "cases aren't solved behind a desk," he encouraged her visit to Vorwaerts Turner Hall but cautioned her from "traipsing off on another perilous excursion," citing her ill-fated journey to the tenement building following the People's Cause meeting. He also asked for confirmation that she carried her pistol—loaded. Unsatisfied with her reassurance, he demanded to see it with his own eyes. More interested in her new pocket holster than the derringer, he asked, "May I?" and removed the pistol, holding the holster close. Peering down his spectacles, he admired the quality of the leather and fine stitching. "It would seem you have made a commitment, Miss Morrow."

"I find it practical, sir. But you're correct that it should serve its purpose for years to come.'"

Returning the pistol and holster to her, he said, "Provide Madelaine with the receipts, including the cartridges. She'll see that the expenses are added to your wages. Now. Back to brass tacks. Regarding Saloon Micky, I can see no fault in your logic in concluding that the Gray Wolf could be in cahoots with the German woman. Still, there is nothing ironclad to prove any affiliation. Still, between them, it appears they are responsible for the murders of no less than three persons: Bat, one of Saloon Micky's henchmen turned disloyal, Eugene Eldridge, and now the muckraker's friend and *Progressive Age* journalist . . ."

"Steven Bliss."

Another pursing of his lips. "It's imperative that Harriet Morrow not be added to the list."

"I couldn't agree more. Though Alderman Powers knows me as Harry Dunn."

Prescott smiled. "Indeed. I would prefer he keeps safe, as well."

After shedding her disguise, Harriet rode to the Turner Hall emboldened by the story Prescott had regaled her with before she left his office. Decades before, when starting out as a detective, he had been frustrated by a case involving a masterful cat burglar. Early into his investigation, Prescott identified the thief: a wealthy owner of a Gold Coast mansion similar to those that had been burgled. Despite Prescott's certainty of the gentleman's guilt, he lacked the hard evidence to convince a judge. After examining dozens of pilfered jewelry boxes and emptied safes, trailing the suspect for weeks and desperately searching his home for stolen goods, the young Prescott decided his only recourse was to confront the man and "rattle his cage." According to her boss, "Most criminals live in constant fear of being found out, going to any length to prevent getting caught. However, others take such pride in their deceit that they perversely relish being found out. Otherwise, their criminal brilliance goes unapplauded."

By all indications, Mike Powers appeared determined to remain safely beyond the reach of the law in order to continue his criminal enterprise. But what about Brunhilda Struff? What type of criminal was she?

The conclusion of Prescott's story hadn't been the tidy resolution she might expect from such a narrative. After confronting the suspect, there had been no gushing confession, no gleeful reveal of the absconded rubies and diamonds—certainly no plea to end his torment with an arrest. Instead, the man had challenged Prescott to thwart his next heist, which he promised would make his previous thefts look like "snatching a lollipop from a toddler." What followed was an exhausting game of cat and mouse that ended with the burglar falling off the roof of a State Street mansion; a burlap bag filled with exquisite silver lay beside his contorted body.

Harriet thought she understood the message of Prescott's tale. Still, his final words removed all doubt: "The unbothered crook is unlikely to slip up."

How would Brunhilda react to being questioned about the murders of Eugene Eldridge and Steven Bliss? Would she, like Prescott's cat burglar, allow pride to push her beyond her limit? Would hubris cause her to falter? To slip up? The young Prescott had indeed rattled the thief's cage. Harriet intended to do the same to Brunhilda Struff.

Chapter 30

Stepping inside Vorwaerts Turner Hall, Harriet was reassured by the dozens of people tumbling, swinging, and performing all manner of athletic feats. A public attack would seem uncharacteristically cloddish for Brunhilda, who apparently took pleasure in games of intellect and sleight of hand. A quick visual sweep of the hall's main gymnasium showed no sign of her. Eyes peeled, Harriet made her way to the back of the building and the unmistakable sound of clashing steel blades. She took a deep breath and turned the corner.

Two figures—both men, judging by their physiques—clad in tight white jackets, their faces obscured behind protective masks, lurched forward and back in a battle of swordsmanship. They appeared evenly matched, taking turns attacking and retreating. Artfully aggressive, the contest was mesmerizing, and she had to remind herself that, although it's a sport, were the sword tips real, the contest would result in bloodshed. The bout triggered thoughts of Matthew having taken her brother to the boxing gymnasium. She'd had concerns about him fighting, but was fencing so different? Was her interest in one sport so different from her brother's in another?

After several minutes of combat, one fencer lunged, nearly dropping to one knee, his arm outstretched. The foil's blade flexed as the blunted tip pressed against his opponent's chest. The touch ended the match. They stood tall, removed their masks—confirming they were indeed both men—and saluted each other with a downward swipe of their swords.

With no other fencers present, her thoughts drifted to the other part of the building where she had encountered Brunhilda: the witch's lair at the top of the castle. Retracing her route when leaving the People's Cause meeting, Harriet felt disappointment strike when she found the door leading to the third floor locked. Fortunately or not, she knew another way up.

The metal stairs clinging to the building's rear façade were no less rickety than the first time she'd climbed them. Still, they seemed less precarious in the light of day. Reaching the top, her frustration peaked. The door wouldn't open. Muttering curses, she jiggled the handle roughly. It twisted with a *click*, having merely been stuck.

Yes, well, that's more like it.

The room was unoccupied—the silence an unsettling contrast to the tumult filling the space during her last visit. There was no interior illumination. Scant sunlight filtered through the grimy windows at the side and front, making visibility possible through a veil of floating dust motes. Curious, she crossed the room toward the makeshift metal rostrum that had elevated the speakers above the crowd. Several wooden tables were positioned against a wall. On one table, sitting beside a large tin of black powder, was a box filled with electrical wires, metal casings, iron pellets, and a bundle of long cotton strands. Stepping closer, she observed various tools: screwdrivers, plyers, and tin snips, among others. *Odd*, she thought. Every activity in the hall was dedicated to exercise and athletic pursuits. *What was all this?* Moving closer still, her shoe toe bumped a small crate beneath the table she hadn't noticed in the scant light. Curious, she crouched down. Someone had nestled several new leather saddlebags inside. Slowly, she lifted a flap.

Oh! She jumped back, falling hard on her rump.

Any explanation was preferable, but there could only be one. The dynamite stuffed into the saddlebags had a singular purpose: an explosion.

Nearly stumbling down the back staircase, she skipped the last step, jumped to the ground, and started running toward her bicycle. Turning the corner, she skidded to a stop. Fifty feet ahead, a brown horse stood tied to a post. She spun in a circle, seeing no one. Again, she considered there must be hundreds, if not thousands, of brown horses in the city. What were the chances this was *the* same brown horse she'd seen before? More importantly, was the rider the same? Did they wear a Tyrolean hat? Were the circumstances any different, she might have lurked in shadows, waiting to see who returned to the saddle. But given what she'd just observed in the hall, she had no time to waste.

Pedaling fast to the agency, she considered her possible actions. With no actual bomb to report, she could only argue her belief of a threat. What would Prescott do with her information? What *could* he do? She didn't imagine her word would be sufficient to precipitate a storming of the Turner Hall by police, along with an interrogation of everyone present. She was thankful her responsibility went only as far as informing her boss. The decision wasn't hers. Whatever happened next would be up to him.

"Mr. Prescott has left for the day," Madelaine told an anxious Harriet. "He and Mrs. Prescott are attending a gala for the Art Institute this evening." Had Madelaine delivered the message just last week, she would have taken delight in relaying discouraging news to Harriet. But the principal's secretary, like several other women in the agency, appeared to be warming to the young woman detective—

at least, they were no longer openly hostile. Harriet allowed herself a moment to appreciate that some progress was being made with her colleagues, however slight.

Harriet's dejection swelled when she rushed down the corridor and arrived at Matthew McCabe's office. He was also absent. Given the nearly five o'clock hour, he must have concluded his work for the day.

She spun in a circle, exasperated and indecisive. *Think, Harriet. Think. What would Matthew advise you to do? What would Prescott* instruct *you to do?*

Behind her desk, door closed, she closed her eyes and took slow, steadying breaths. This wasn't the time for panic. She wasn't as lost as her emotions would have her believe. Was she closer to the truth than when assigned the investigation? Yes. Did she have suspects? Yes. Did she believe she could solve her case?

She mulled the last question repeatedly. Doubts were her enemy as much as Brunhilda Struff and Saloon Micky. Her late mother's words found their way to the front of her unsettled mind: *The surest way to defeat, Harriet, is to give up. You may try your darndest and not succeed, but you—and only you—can decide when to quit.*

Harriet opened her eyes with a decisive nod and rolled a sheet of paper into the typewriter. Her parents didn't raise a quitter.

The routine of summarizing her activities and observations further soothed her frazzled nerves. Once captured on paper, events lost much of their urgency. She considered that nothing she'd seen at the Turner Hall was now less critical, but she had muted her alarm. After leaving her report with Madelaine, she would return first thing in the morning to speak with Prescott. Although it would be Saturday, he treated the day no differently than any other besides Sunday, when he attended services with his family and spent the remainder of the day at home.

* * *

Wheeling her bicycle into the apartment, Harriet sniffed. Garlic? Too curious to properly hang her coat, she draped it over her Victoria, hung her hat on the handlebars, and entered the kitchen.

"Barbara?"

"Welcome home, Harriet. You're just in time."

"Hope you're hungry," Aubrey said, standing beside Barbara and stirring garlic and butter in a skillet. A carton of opened spaghetti sat on the counter next to three plump tomatoes. Susan lay on the floor in wait for any scraps that might fall.

Harriet briefly explained the reason for her later than usual arrival. In exchange, Barbara explained her presence. "I thought you could use a nice supper to end your week," she said. "Lucky for me, I have a very eager helper."

"We're making spaghetti," Aubrey declared. "With meatballs!"

"So I see," Harriet noted brightly. "I hope you don't think me rude, but if you don't mind, I will go and quickly wash up. I won't be more than a few minutes."

In the bathroom, Harriet splashed warm water on her face and tried to settle her thoughts. She considered Barbara's appearance equally delightful and consternating. While she was happy to see her and relieved the ice had broken since their recent argument, she was also bothered that Barbara had apparently brushed it off. However, realizing she had a choice between fixating on the quarrel or enjoying what promised to be a tasty dinner, she chose the latter. The difficult conversation she must have with Barbara could wait. She moved to her bedroom to change into more comfortable clothing.

Moments later, a light rap on the door was followed by Barbara slipping inside. Taken aback, Harriet shrieked and covered her bare chest with crossed arms.

"I'm terribly sorry to intrude, Harriet, but what I must say can't be put off for a moment longer. I wanted to prepare a nice dinner for you, that's true. But the primary reason I came here tonight is to apologize for our previous argument. I'm sorry that my words were strident. But please understand that for generations my ancestors have struggled to survive while rulers who cared only about protecting their power and wealth did nothing but ensure their continued riches at the expense of the poor's suffering. The subject ignites my passion. For that, I am not ashamed, but never would I condone the killing of innocents, especially the young. I know that I upset you the other day. And for that, I do apologize."

Harriet nodded. She wanted to rush the few feet between them and embrace Barbara but couldn't. That would require her to lower her arms, exposing her breasts. She was entirely unprepared for that amount of intimacy. Instead, she walked over to Barbara and kissed her firmly on the mouth. It wasn't a long kiss, but it was emphatic. Harriet was determined the gesture not be misconstrued as sisterly affection.

Barbara's eyes bugged. "I take it all is forgiven," she said, smiling. "I do hate to cut our *talk* short"—she raised a brow mischievously—"but I must get back to the kitchen. Your brother shouldn't be left alone for long in the kitchen. He nearly confused the sugar for salt."

With Barbara out of the room, Harriet finished changing. How long had it been since she had truly looked forward to something? Tonight had just become that time. Wearing a comfortable shirt and trousers, she returned to the kitchen. "What a feast you two are preparing."

"The pork for the meatballs came from Damian," Barbara said, referring to her neighbor Damian Swiatek, whose family owned a sausage factory in Polish Downtown and whom Harriet had met during her previous investigation.

"It all looks and smells divine," Harriet cooed.

"You sit. Rest," Barbara suggested. Cocking her head, she

added, "You look tired. And am I wrong, or do you appear to have a rash on your face? Is everything quite all right?"

Preferring to avoid talk of her case that mention of wearing a false beard would evoke, Harriet replied, "Nothing that time won't remedy. Now, I don't suppose I can be of any help?"

"You can clean up after supper," Aubrey replied, drawing Harriet's frown. Her brother was nothing if not predictable. Forget that she usually did the shopping, prepared the meals, *and* washed up afterward. Given an opportunity to contribute modest effort, enjoy a delicious meal, and assign his sister the chore of putting things in order afterward, he hadn't hesitated. Still, she was happy to oblige and stay off her feet for at least the next hour.

That Aubrey eagerly accepted Barbara's instruction showed promise. He would never have listened as intently or responded unquestioningly had Harriet been giving the orders. While the parameters of the siblings' relationship had been established long ago, how well Aubrey and Barbara would get along was yet to be determined. Harriet didn't know if she was destined to be with Barbara or for how long, but she was reassured by seeing them work together amicably.

The dinner conversation was pleasant. Aubrey was uncommonly talkative, which Harriet attributed to having an audience in Barbara.

". . . and then Tubs hit a ball to left field, and Sherman scored, and we won."

"You really shouldn't call him Tubs, Aubrey. I doubt he appreciates that." Harriet knew her brother would recoil at the admonishment but felt the need to issue it. Moreover, she couldn't have Barbara thinking she condoned such disparaging talk.

"Geez, Harriet. Tubs isn't fat, if that's what you're worried about. He's skinny like me."

"Then why do you call him that?" Barbara asked, relieving Harriet of the question.

"Tubs's real name is Harry Tubberfield."

"A nickname then," Harriet sighed, her worries allayed.

"Lots of guys have them," Aubrey explained.

"Did you ever have a nickname?" Barbara asked Harriet with a mischievous grin.

"No, I never—"

"You did too!" Aubrey argued. "Harry!"

As Barbara chuckled, Harriet protested. "I hardly think that qualifies as a nickname."

"And you?" Barbara turned the question to Aubrey.

He looked at Harriet for help. If he had had one growing up, he couldn't remember it. She replied with a slight shake of her head.

"I guess not," he said forlornly, as if he had missed out on something important.

"Well, then. We must rectify that wrong immediately," Barbara declared. Playing on his long and detailed earlier recounting of his time spent at the boxing gym with Matthew, she offered, "How about Mitts?"

He groaned. "They're gloves. Not mitts. Besides, nicknames are supposed to be short for your real name."

Harriet imagined she and Barbara were working through the same exercise in their heads and failing to conceive a worthy suggestion.

"Well, not all nicknames." Harriet thought of Bat, Saloon Micky's henchman. However, not wanting that name to be her example, she said, "What about Buffalo Bill or Billy the Kid?"

Barbara clapped. "I've got it! Aubrey 'the Kid' Morrow."

The next instant, Harriet jerked. Her chest tightened. She fought to breathe—even more so than after the fire. Barbara's and Aubrey's heads snapped in her direction, sensing something amiss.

"Harriet?" Barbara gently touched her arm. "Are you quite all right? It's just a silly suggestion. If I've said something—"

"No, no. It's not that," she said, her voice trembling.

Aubrey looked on with concern, unsure what to say or how alarmed he ought to be. Harriet glanced at her wristwatch. It was nearly eight o'clock—too late for visitors, but this could not wait. She jumped up from the kitchen table and raced from the room. As she pulled on her coat and hat, Barbara and Aubrey looked on dumbfoundedly from the kitchen doorway.

"Harriet!" Aubrey found his voice. "What's the matter?"

Wheeling her bicycle out the door, she turned back. "Forgive me. It was a wonderful meal. Don't worry. Everything should be sorted out soon enough, but I must go out."

"Where?" Aubrey demanded.

"The University Settlement House," she replied, as if it were obvious.

"Surely, whatever it is can wait till morning," Barbara pleaded, looking desperate.

"If only that were so, Barbara." Closing the door, she said, "Alas, I fear it may already be too late."

Chapter 31

Harriet was painfully reminded of her reduced lung capacity as she pedaled at less than her usual pace toward the University of Chicago Settlement House. As frustrating as her strained breathing was, given the darkness and the poor road conditions, she couldn't have ridden at top speed anyway. She quieted her desperation to get there with haste. A few minutes wouldn't make a difference at this point.

She was new to detective work and believed she would improve with experience. Still, she berated herself for overlooking such a glaringly obvious clue. Moreover, she'd had several opportunities to follow up on it. If only she had recognized it for what it was, she might have solved her case a week ago—provided her hunch proved correct. Now all she could wish was that her chance to recover Eldridge's missing evidence hadn't been lost forever.

After thirty-five minutes of skirting potholes and debris, she coasted to a stop before the settlement gates. Unlike at her previous visits, which had been during the day, this time the main entrance was locked. She saw no way to alert anyone inside the property of her presence. Looking up at the iron gate that interrupted the fence, she was grateful she wore trousers. She would have to climb. The problem was the gate's height. *You're a detective, Harriet. Be creative.*

Finding no trash bin or discarded crate to stand on, her eyes fell upon her Victoria. She chained it close to the gate and wedged the front tire at an angle between two slats to prevent its wheels from rolling. Grabbing hold of the gate, she climbed onto her bicycle seat, first by knee, followed by foot, and unfolded to a standing position. The top of the gate pressed against her belly. Glad that no one was there to witness her next inelegant move, she gripped the top of the gate, jumped, and threw a leg over the top. Grimacing, the cold iron bars poked her painfully. Eager to get the climb over with, she shifted her weight toward the opposite side, lifted her other leg over, and dropped to the ground with a thud.

Inside the property, she had a decision: alert Mary McDowell or proceed to the gymnasium. The head resident knew her as Theodore Prescott's visiting niece. How might she take the news of Harriet's true identity and purpose? Given sufficient explanation, Mary McDowell was likely to understand, but Harriet couldn't take the chance of a prolonged argument. Enough time had already been wasted.

She hurried to the gymnasium. Thankfully, the door was unlocked. It had been two days since she was last there. Roughly half of the families remained. Harriet rushed from group to group, searching for the Decas. It took only a few minutes to see they were not there. However, Antonia was. Harriet ran to where she and her family had set up their makeshift camp.

"You!" Antonia's tone was unclear.

Choosing to disregard the remark, Harriet leaped to the matter at hand. "The Decas? I don't see them. Please, Antonia. I must find them. It's quite urgent."

Harriet's last remarks reset Antonia's mood; she traded

her annoyance for alarm. "You've done nothing but lie. Who are you really? Does Mrs. McDowell know you are here?"

"Please, Antonia. I will return and explain everything to your satisfaction, but not now. I must hurry. If you know where—"

"Tell this woman nothing." Antonia's husband stepped up, holding a toothbrush and sneering. "You should leave. Does Mrs. McDowell know you're asking these questions?"

Harriet suppressed her desire to shout. She understood these people had reason to distrust others, but to begin explaining everything that was in her head would only invite endless questions she couldn't abide. She decided to double down on her lie. "Not only is Mrs. McDowell aware of me being here, it was she who sent me. So. Unless you want me to go and fetch her, which I can promise will vex her mightily, I'll appreciate you simply answering my question. Please."

Hearing the possibility of a visit from Mary McDowell, the husband answered for the couple. "They moved back to the tenement. Just this afternoon."

Harriet's gaze bounced from husband to wife and back again. Were they serious? Seeing that they were, she argued, "But that's not possible. Their apartment was destroyed, along with the entire top floor and half of the second."

"They moved into the Faras' old place," Antonia said. "Yes, you heard right. The Faras' old place. The apartment you said *you* had moved into. But you don't live at the tenement. In fact, no one here or there has any idea who you are. The only thing we *do* know about you is that you've got a mighty strange interest in the murder."

"I understand your suspicions," Harriet said. "Truly, I do. I am in fact . . ." Harriet revealed her real identity and purpose, concluding with, "And so, it's a matter of life and death. I must find the Decas. You're quite certain they have returned to the tenement?"

Antonia spoke, despite her husband's opposition. "Although damaged, the Faras' apartment mostly survived. Whatever the condition, the family will have privacy. With their newborn, it seemed only right that they should have it. We took a vote and all agreed."

Beneath Harriet's bowler, her thoughts were a mad scramble. The past two weeks, she had raced from the office to the settlement, from home to the tenement, from the *Progressive Age* to the Palmer House. Adding to that were numerous identity changes from Harriet to Harry and back again. She raised a hand and gently touched the rash on her face, a result of the glue and abrasion from peeling off the beard. She chuckled ruefully. She was like a dog chasing its tail around and around, getting nowhere.

Harriet considered her next move. Traveling to the settlement house in the late evening hour was one thing; arriving at the tenement well after dark was another. Memories of the fire and being trapped in the stairwell added to her trepidation. She envisioned her welcome when confronting the Decas. Her knock would be met by a surly and quite possibly inebriated Mr. Deca, a crying baby, upset mother, and unsettled children. Would it matter? Her purpose didn't require their warm reception—or did it? She did, in fact, need their cooperation, which stood better odds if the husband were absent. However, tomorrow was Saturday, and despite Sunday being the customary day off for a man working at the Union Stockyard, the husband had been home last Saturday when Pearl and she visited. Had that been an exception or his regular schedule?

She recalled a bit of advice Matthew had shared during her first case: *Investigations have a rhythm of their own. Sometimes, a case beats faster, sometimes slower than a detective would like. But forcing things rarely produces a positive result. You must work the case as it unfolds. Be vigilant, be aggressive. But never rush. It is the chief mistake made by new operatives who put impatience before prudence.*

Resigned to following her colleague's counsel and feeling utterly dejected, she tramped across the grounds. It struck her as fitting that she must climb over the gate again—another repeated exercise to put her back where she started.

"Wait!"

The shout gave Harriet a start. She whirled around. Antonia hurried toward her, waving something.

The woman spoke as she approached. "If you're going to the tenement, please, will you take this to the Decas? The mother has been reading this to the children. She believes it's good for their English. In their hurry to leave earlier, it was left behind. It's a small comfort, I recognize, but I'm sure the children will enjoy hearing the rest of the story."

Antonia handed Harriet a book: *The Wallypug of Why* by G. E. Farrow.

In that instant, Harriet's plan changed. Whether she saw the book as a sign from above or an excuse to justify her impulse to race to the tenement at that moment, it didn't matter. Her mind was made up. Damn prudence! Prescott often lectured that *cases aren't solved behind a desk*. To that, she would add *or at home with your tail tucked between your legs.*

As soon as Harriet forgot about her breathing troubles, an activity rudely reminded her. Scaling the gate had just delivered that message. Still, she was hardly an invalid, and shortness of breath couldn't stop her from doing what needed to be done. The streets became increasingly treacherous as she neared the tenement. Not eager to repeat her painful spill from the other day, she balanced urgency with caution, noting the objective had broad application to the business of detecting. Arriving at the building, she chained her Victoria to the same post under the same streetlamp she had used when coming there after the People's Cause meeting. It had proven safe before.

The main entrance was unlocked—was it ever not? Now familiar with the layout, she trudged up the stairs, another reminder of the toll the fire's smoke had taken on her lungs. She'd never visited the Faras'—now Decas'—home as it had been unoccupied during previous visits. Still, she knew which one it was. She listened, ear to the door, hoping to hear voices or movement inside, an indication that she wouldn't be waking the household and compounding her intrusion. There was only silence.

Her light rapping on the door was eventually met with a muttered voice, footsteps, and the appearance of Mrs. Deca. Hardly did she look refreshed, yet she appeared to have gotten some rest since Harriet had seen her last. The dark circles beneath her eyes had muted to a faint gray, and she'd combed her hair and tied it back with a pink ribbon, a cheerful color at odds with everything else in her life. As Harriet was ushered inside, it became evident that Mrs. Deca believed Mary McDowell had sent Harriet to check on them. Harriet made a mental note of the brilliance of Theodore Prescott's idea for her false persona. It repeatedly had served her purposes.

Also apparent was Mr. Deca's absence. He had been soused the last time Harriet saw him, and Pearl had spotted a long strand of hair on his coat collar. That he wasn't at home now with his wife, infant son, and five other children on Friday night was despicable but unsurprising.

The baby and three other children were asleep, leaving the two oldest sitting upright in the room's smallest bed. Regardless of whether they recognized Harriet from before, they watched her warily.

The events of the past several hours had not allowed Harriet time to devise a sound strategy for dealing with Mrs. Deca. But given the reason she was there, there was likely no way to soften the bluntness of the truth. She might as well cut to the chase.

"Mrs. Deca, I believe your brother was a former associate of Alderman Mike Powers, widely known by the nickname Saloon Micky. Your brother had a nickname of his own: Bat, short for Batchelder."

Harriet paused to gauge Mrs. Deca's reaction. Her stoic reaction told Harriet what she needed to know: she wasn't wrong.

"Furthermore, I believe the loss of your brother and your mother, for whom you have my sincere condolences, is because your brother, Bat, had proof of Saloon Micky's corruption. Having worked for the alderman explains how he came to possess what he did. Make no mistake, Saloon Micky would have demanded the return of whatever Bat took—at any cost. Was your brother blackmailing the alderman? Attempting to take over some of his nefarious businesses? Or just turning the tables on him, however briefly, to show he too could be the boss? Bat knew Saloon Micky probably better than most. He couldn't have underestimated the threat. If I'm correct, Bat gave the incriminating evidence to your mother for safekeeping. I imagine he thought it would be the last place anyone would look—a tenement building apartment inhabited by an immigrant family with the last name of Deca. The precaution wasn't for nothing. He was killed sometime thereafter, presumably by other men working under Powers' direction. That the evidence was hidden here in the tenement explains the muckraker Eugene Eldridge's presence that day. He had come looking for it. I believe he discovered your mother's name through correspondence with the immigration records department at one of the country's ports of entry. The appointment ledger I found noted a date of a letter received just days before his murder. As you all recently arrived in Chicago, your address would have been recorded as well."

Harriet paused again. Mrs. Deca had yet to refute or question anything she had said. And so, she continued. "As long as the evidence remains missing, Saloon Micky will not stop looking for it. We need no further convincing of his determination to retrieve it. My intention is not to

frighten you, Mrs. Deca. Though your brother's murder
has surely already done that. But I must know, and you
must tell me truthfully, what did Bat give your mother, and
where is it now?"

Mrs. Deca crossed the small room, shifted the contents
in a worn burlap bag, and lifted something out. Returning
to where Harriet stood just inside the doorway, she said,
"I am not religious. But my mother . . . she was raised to
believe such things. Still, such a gift from Louie was strange.
I kept it because it reminded me of her. It was among her
few things not lost in the fire."

She handed Harriet a Bible. "Louie is my brother's real
name. We never called him Bat. My mother hated the
nickname and forbid anyone in the family from using it."

Noticing Mrs. Deca's sudden look of distress, Harriet
said, "Please, don't worry, Mrs. Deca. I will put this right.
You can trust me. But to do so, I must borrow this. I intend to return it to you as soon as possible. Please. Let me
take it. Your brother and another two men were killed because of this. When returned to you, it will be safe. You
can keep it as a remembrance of your mother without fear.
I know it seems the most unlikely of books to present a
threat, but that is very much the case."

Harriet shifted her satchel from against her back to her
front, opened it, and, after Mrs. Deca reluctantly nodded,
tucked the Bible safely at the bottom.

"Oh, one more thing." Harriet started to lift the children's book from her satchel.

"You should not make promises you cannot keep."

Recognizing the voice, Harriet froze. She now understood the reason for Mrs. Deca's pained expression. Brunhilda Struff stood behind her in the open doorway.

The next instant, Harriet felt a sharp blow to the back
of her head—and her world went black.

Chapter 32

Thick with dust, the air was hard to breathe. Harriet's head throbbed. She winced, opening her eyes. It was dark. She was grateful for the dim conditions, fearing that were she subjected to bright light, her head might explode. She sought to reach around for some indication of where she was but couldn't; her hands were tied behind her back. With fingers spread, she touched the wall behind her. It was gritty, uneven. The floor was dirt. A basement? She sniffed. Coal. Yes, it was a tenement basement. How long had she been there? Minutes or hours?

Still strapped over her shoulder, Harriet's satchel rested against her chest. Its lighter weight and reduced bulk confirmed her fear: Brunhilda had taken the Bible. She hadn't, as Mr. Prescott would say, "Dillydallied." Harriet shifted her position and felt the derringer in her coat pocket. Apparently, Brunhilda had only been interested in the evidence. Otherwise, why not take the pistol? Or her wristwatch, which pressed painfully into her flesh beneath the rope binding her wrists. Neither was of much value, but would Brunhilda know that?

After weeks of work, Harriet had led Brunhilda straight to the Decas' door. The notion that the German woman would prevail was maddening. Harriet didn't know how to stop her, but until she was thoroughly defeated, she must try.

Stretching her legs, she realized they were also tied together by rope. Why hadn't she been gagged? Had Brunhilda appreciated that with the filthy air she might not be able to breathe? Or had she presumed Harriet's calls for help would be unheard in the depths of the building? More fascinating, if she had set the tenement fire and blocked Harriet's escape, why allow her to live now?

Harriet rolled onto her side, shooting a spike of pain down her neck. For a moment, she remained still, waiting for the ache to subside. With her knees beneath her, she raised her head and torso. From that position, she could move slowly by scooting, inch by inch, one knee before the other. As her eyes adjusted to the scant light, she spied a destination: the shovel she had used to fill Mrs. Horak's coal bucket.

In what seemed an hour later, she wriggled her way to the shovel. She knocked it onto its side with her head—an effort nearly splitting her brain in two—and shimmied her way to where she could touch the shovel's blade. Positioning the rope binding her wrists against the blade, she began to saw. With no means to assess her progress, she kept at it. However long it might take—five minutes or five hours—it was her only option.

In about half the time it had taken her to reach the shovel, she felt an abrupt release. Bringing her hands around, she uncoiled the rough rope from her wrists. She winced, crying out in pain. The sawing motion had rubbed her skin raw. She reached down to untie her feet, but Brunhilda had tied the knot too tight to be undone by hand. Gripping the shovel's handle, she placed the blade against the rope binding her ankles and vigorously drew it up and down. Able to improve her technique from this position, it took her only ten minutes to free her legs.

Excited, she stood too fast. The blood rushed from her head, making her dizzy. She raised the shovel and used it to steady herself. When she'd been hired, Prescott remarked that her stout ankles would serve her well, given the physical rigors of detective work. *Rigors, indeed.*

She emerged from the basement's side door and, observing the pinkish-orange sky of sunrise, pulled back her shirt cuff to expose the face of her watch. It was 5:00 a.m. Harriet's heart sank. Brunhilda had a head start of about eight hours. Hope of thwarting the woman's plan dwindled.

She reentered the building from the back The two flights of stairs separating her from Mrs. Deca and her family felt like an ocean away, but she couldn't leave without first checking on them.

Her knock went unanswered. "Mrs. Deca, it's me. Harriet. I'm alone. You don't even have to open the door. But I must know if you're all right. Mrs. Deca?"

Harriet listened hard and was rewarded with the faintest sound of footsteps.

"Mrs. Deca?"

"Has she gone?" The woman whispered from the door's other side.

"She is gone. I'm sure. Tell me, please. You and your family, are you unharmed?"

The door cracked open, revealing a sliver of Mrs. Deca's face. The dark circles had returned beneath her eyes. The baby started to cry in the background. The door opened further, and Mrs. Deca handed Harriet her hat. "It fell off when she bashed you."

Harriet took the hat with a nod, not realizing it had been lost in the fracas.

"The way you fell to the ground, I thought you were dead. Before I could think of what to do, the woman carried you away. I locked the door. What else could I do?" She looked over her shoulder. "I have six little ones to look after. They must be my only concern. Whatever that woman's business with the Bible or with my brother or the man who was killed just there"—she pointed her chin toward the landing outside her door—"is not my concern. It can't be. Please understand. People like me, we must not, as you say, 'rock the boat.' You saw what happened to Mrs. Fara, yes? One mistake and your life is as good as over."

Harriet did understand. It broke her heart to hear the woman express her powerlessness. She couldn't risk inciting another visit from Brunhilda or placing herself and her family in Saloon Micky's sights. With no reason to linger and her head throbbing, Harriet wished Mrs. Deca well and left.

Descending the stairs was much easier than climbing them, but her bicycle required exertion she feared she couldn't withstand. She would gladly pay for a buggy or hansom cab, but neither was possible to come by given the neighborhood and the early hour. Reluctantly, she mounted her Victoria. She wouldn't try to pedal all the way home— she couldn't. Fortunately, Pearl's mansion was less than half the distance, and she was an earlier riser. Still, there was another reason Pearl's house was her decided destination: Theodore Prescott lived next door.

Harriet hadn't reached the end of the block before a thought struck, forcing her to the side of the road. Breathless—but not because of her lungs—she grappled for her satchel. She couldn't believe it had taken her so long to check. Fingers fumbling, she unclasped the snaps and peered inside.

"Well, I'll be switched!" she shouted, thrusting a fist into the air. Shaking with excitement, she cast off, pedaling with gusto. Despite the odds and the considerable damage done to her body, Harriet Morrow had just gotten a second wind.

Chapter 33

"Oh my stars!" Pearl exclaimed. "What happened to you?"

Harriet's head pounded, her lungs ached, her wrists were raw, and she was exhausted. But Pearl couldn't be told all that. First things first. She needed to have her head looked at.

Taking Harriet by the arm, Pearl led her gently into the kitchen. "You're not wearing a hat, and there's blood on your shirt collar—" Pearl gasped, examining the back of Harriet's head. "Oh, Harry! You have a nasty gash on your scalp."

Harriet was told to "Sit. And stay put" while Pearl raced upstairs for ointment and bandages. While Harriet waited, Toby jumped into her lap. He had never done that before, always remaining aloof, as is typical for many cats. He turned in a clumsy circle, laid down, and began to purr. She chuckled softly. "And I didn't think you liked me." The animal's warmth and stillness calmed her. If she allowed herself to lower her head, she had no doubt she'd fall dead asleep in seconds.

Pearl's fast-approaching footsteps preceded her bursting into the kitchen, arms laden with medical supplies. She spread everything she'd brought out on the table.

Harriet quipped, "I hope you don't plan on performing surgery."

"Jest if you must, but this is no laughing matter. You can't see what I can." She shook her head and grimaced. "I patch you up as well as I'm able, but you really ought to get to a doctor to have this looked at properly. I suspect he'll put in several stitches."

Pearl cleaned the wound. Harriet squealed in pain when Pearl switched from hot water to alcohol. "I know, I know. But it can't be helped. Better a sting than an infection."

Harriet cursed under her breath. "Bees sting. That is *not* a sting."

"This will be tricky with your hair, but I'll do my best. You won't be winning any beauty prize, but I'll need to wrap some gauze around your head to keep the bandage in place. If you're concerned about its appearance, I can find you a scarf to wear over it."

With her wound bandaged, Harriet was led into the parlor, a room she had only ever passed through, and was instructed to lie back on a sofa that appeared never to have been sat on. Only then was Harriet allowed to tell Pearl what had happened since they'd last seen each other. Her recounting ended with, "Now I must get over to Mr. Prescott's and inform him of all I have discovered. He's sure to be put out by my early morning appearance on his doorstep, but once I relay my news, I should think all will be forgiven."

The two women briefly squabbled about Harriet's condition and what she could and could not do. Ultimately, they agreed that Pearl would escort her to "Teddy's doorstep." Afterward, Pearl would visit Aubrey to explain his sister's abrupt departure and inform him that she was injured but would recover.

Pearl loaned Harriet the robin's-egg blue scarf she had worn for their last outing, and as the monumental grandfather clock in Pearl's parlor struck seven o'clock, each loud *bong* rattling her brain, they walked next door to the Prescotts'.

The symmetrical two-story Italianate mansion fitted the

man's personality. Both were immaculate, well-appointed, and showy. As they stood before the black-lacquered entrance, the door chime bellowed inside, alerting the family to visitors. Harriet knew Prescott thought his neighbor was a busybody—an impression that wouldn't make their reception any warmer. Regardless, Pearl had insisted.

The door swung open, revealing a boy about twelve years old. He shared his father's compact frame, narrow nose, pointed chin, and penetrating gaze. Despite the early hour, he was dressed.

"Hello, Mrs. Bartlett," the boy said politely, adding a "Hello, miss" for Harriet. "I'll go get Mother. Come in."

Before Pearl or Harriet could redirect him, he scampered off inside the home. Obviously not a first-time visitor, Pearl didn't hesitate to enter the foyer. Like the mansion's exterior, the interior was meticulous, every surface clean and without a scratch. A mirrored coat stand and an intricately patterned rug appeared to be of high quality and to receive little use.

"Pearl?" Mrs. Prescott appeared from an adjoining room. "Is everything quite all right? It's quite early, as you must know." Seeing Harriet, her eyes widened. "Who is this?"

Harriet introduced herself and explained she was an employee of Mrs. Prescott's husband, for whom she had urgent information to convey. Duly alarmed, Mrs. Prescott promised to return with him shortly and left them to wait again in the foyer. At this point, Pearl should have gone. Harriet was eager to avoid an encounter between Pearl and the man of the house.

"Pearl," Harriet said, "we agreed you would accompany me here. It's best that I speak with Mr. Prescott—"

"Did you see the way she looked at you?"

Taken aback, Harriet touched the scarf cloaking her head bandage. "Is it a terrible fright?"

"Not that, Harry. She couldn't help but notice you resemble their Jennie."

It took Harriet a moment to remember that at the conclusion of her previous investigation, Pearl had confided that Harriet shared a physical likeness with the Prescotts' only daughter, Jennie, who had died from accidental drowning. That Jennie had been the apple of her father's eye provided a plausible explanation for Prescott's taking a chance in hiring a young, untested woman for the role of operative: Harriet reminded Theodore of his daughter.

"What in tarnation!" Prescott barked, striding into the foyer. "Have you any idea of the hour? And on a Saturday?" Focusing on the scarf Pearl had tied to Harriet's head, his tone changed to curiosity. "What on earth are you wearing?"

Any worries Harriet might have had about waking her boss were unwarranted. He was very much awake, smartly attired, and, considering the white napkin stuffed into his shirt collar, had just come from the breakfast table.

"Now, Teddy," Pearl scolded. "Harry has momentous news, so you can stop your fussing. But before any of that, you should know a crazy woman bashed her in the head. I need you to promise you'll be mindful of that before you go racing off to right the world's wrongs."

Harriet was shocked. Pearl spoke to Theodore Prescott as if he were the twelve-year-old boy who'd answered the door. Moreover, she didn't need anyone to speak for her. Showing Prescott that she could handle the job on her own was crucial. Pearl was acting like an overprotective mother. That wouldn't do, no matter the sincerity of her concern.

"Pearl, please. You need to go. I will come around later when my business is concluded." When Pearl didn't budge, she lowered her voice. "We had an agreement."

"What's this about your head being bashed?" Mr. Prescott said.

"Whose head has been bashed?" chimed Mrs. Prescott, who had reappeared in the doorway, looking alarmed.

"Oh, for heaven's sake," Harriet protested.

"A crazy German woman at the tenement—"

"Pearl, please! I appreciate your help, but that's enough. Go. Home."

Pearl pointed a bent finger at Theodore Prescott. "Teddy, she's your responsibility now." Turning to Mrs. Prescott, she smiled warmly. "Winnifred, I'll be back later with a cake. I haven't decided on what yet, but you can tell the boys it'll have the chocolate frosting they like."

With Pearl finally out of the house, Harriet was ushered into the dining room, where Mr. and Mrs. Prescott examined the turban-like bandage on her head. While Harriet informed her boss about her discoveries, Winnifred *clucked* and *tsk-tsked* her opposition to Harriet doing anything other than going straight to the hospital. Both Prescotts, however, froze when Harriet arrived at the part of her story where she said, ". . . and so I have obtained it. I have Eugene Eldridge's evidence."

"What? Where?" Prescott gasped the words.

Still wearing her satchel, Harriet snapped open the clasps and removed the worn black Bible. As if it were fragile, she gently placed it on the dining room table. Prescott, having no such caution, snatched it up. While he thumbed through the pages, she explained that Brunhilda Struff had snatched a children's book, mistaking it for the item Mrs. Deca had given her.

"Do you know what this is?" he asked, practically breathless.

"It's a Bible, Teddy," Mrs. Prescott said matter-of-factly.

"Please, Winny. I can see that, but that can't be all it is." He looked up at Harriet. "Miss Morrow?"

"I've not had a chance to examine it," she answered.

A single sheet of twice-folded paper fell out of the book. Prescott picked it up and growled. "Tarnation, where are my damn spectacles!"

Winnifred frowned and pointed to her husband's eyeglasses, which were resting on the morning *Tribune* spread out at the head of the table. Prescott scrutinized the paper from the Bible for several minutes. The silence was occasionally broken by his sharp inhalation. Harriet looked on, watching his facial expressions for any indication of what the page revealed.

When finished, he dropped onto his chair. His hand holding the paper flopped onto the table. "Unbelievable," he announced. "You're lucky to be alive, Miss Morrow. The alderman has every reason to eliminate whoever stands in his way of reclaiming this information."

"Sir?"

"It's a page from a ledger. It shows payments to Saloon Micky from numerous businesses in the Levee District— protection payments, Miss Morrow, otherwise known as extortion. It includes names, dates, and amounts. Bully for you, Miss Morrow, for I do believe this will ensure Powers' undoing." The room turned so quiet that the second hand's ticking could be heard on the mantle clock. Suddenly, Prescott sprang to his feet with the abruptness of a jack-in-the-box.

"These next few hours are the most crucial yet. Saloon Micky must know we have recovered what will amount to a long prison sentence. Moreover, if it can be proved that he had a role in the journalists' deaths, he'll likely hang. We must act with dispatch. I understand that you are injured and feel unwell. Mrs. Prescott is probably right. It's best you go straightaway to the hospital to have your head wound properly examined."

Horrified that he would suggest such a thing, Harriet insisted she was fit enough to accompany him. This was her investigation, after all. As long as she could stand, there was no way she would not see it through to the end.

The sparkle in his eye told her he was pleased with her decision. "Very well then, we must be off," Mr. Prescott proclaimed triumphantly. Mrs. Prescott's scowl showed her displeasure with the decision.

Climbing to her feet, Harriet refused to acknowledge her dizziness. Straightening her shoulders, she stood tall. "Where are we off to, sir?"

"The offices of the Municipal Voters' League to consult with our client, Gerald Cole. I'll telephone ahead and have him meet us there. The accounting on that ledger page will set off a firestorm. It's vital that the information is turned over to someone in government who can be trusted to bring Powers to justice. Presumably, that person is the young prosecutor John Scanlon. Still, utmost care must be taken. The Gray Wolves' reach is long and wields great influence. Should this evidence fall into the wrong hands, not only will justice be denied, but I shall fear for our very lives."

Chapter 34

"At full chisel!" Prescott commanded the driver as he and Harriet climbed aboard a hansom cab for the Municipal Voters' League offices. With a lurch, they set off.

In the weeks Harriet had known her boss, she had witnessed his expressions, ranging from incredulous to delighted, from furious to stoic, but never before had she observed acute worry. He bunched his lips, fiddled with his shirt cuffs, constantly shifted his weight, and peered out the window twice every minute to monitor their progress. "Can't this infernal contraption go any faster," he muttered angrily. Then, leaning out the window, he shouted at the driver. "I said with all speed! Good God, man, I could walk faster!"

Harriet nervously squeezed her satchel. The cab was already hurtling down the street at a pace that caused her jaw to clench and her back to stiffen.

"This is why I have steadfastly refused cases involving the Gray Wolves or those otherwise appearing overtly political," Prescott lectured. "Every investigation presents unique threats and challenges, but I avoid like the plague those that combine the three age-old corruptors of mankind. Do you know of what I speak, Miss Morrow?"

Guessing, Harriet answered, "Political power is one, I presume?"

"Quite right." He slapped a knee to emphasize the point. "Along with wealth and fame, even if that fame is notoriety. It all amounts to the same. A person winds up believing they are extraordinary. That the laws and rules governing a civil society are for others—certainly not for them. What's worse is that a toxic combination of power, wealth, and fame allows those consumed with their importance to get away with their egregious behavior, even when that behavior turns criminal. It's a vicious cycle. Immunity encourages them to commit more outrageous acts, believing their lofty status will protect them—which it often does. Still, when one leg is kicked from beneath their perch, the balance is upset. They will do anything—*anything*—to avoid a fall. Saloon Micky and the other Gray Wolves are such men. They are a festering wound on our city, but the cure cannot be one of half measures. It must be overwhelming. Conclusive. The beast must be cut off at the head."

Although she did not doubt Prescott, she didn't like hearing how perilous their undertaking was or the thoroughness of the remedy required. She quieted her jangled nerves by knowing she was in the company of the renowned Theodore Prescott, soon to be joined by Gerald Cole. These were men who wielded significant authority—and were on the side of good. She must hope it would prove enough.

Given the high social status of the Municipal Voters' League membership, it was unsurprising to find its offices housed in a stately Gold Coast mansion. Prescott started climbing down from the cab before it came to a complete stop. Harriet raced to keep up. Despite the man having shorter legs, he strode to the building's entrance with alacrity.

Taking the red-carpeted steps inside the building two at a time, Prescott appeared to know where he was going. Turning right at the landing, Harriet followed him into a high-ceilinged library cloaked in a light haze of cigar smoke. She recognized Gerald Cole from their meeting two weeks before in Prescott's office. He sat in a wingback chair near the window, reading the morning's *Tribune*.

Hearing them approach, Cole glanced up. Seeing Theodore Prescott determinedly striding toward him, he quickly climbed to his feet.

"Theodore? What's so urgent—"

Prescott waved the Bible before him. "By Jove, we've got it!"

Cole's gape-mouthed expression preceded his words. "The Eldridge evidence?"

"Precisely," Prescott declared proudly. "I told you I'd get it. And I did!"

Harriet grimaced at receiving no credit or acknowledgment of her presence.

"What is it?" Cole asked, reaching out.

Prescott handed him the book. "I refolded the page in question. It's tucked in the front. As you'll see, it is a ledger showing various payments from First Ward businesses to Mike Powers. It unequivocally proves the rascal is guilty of massive extortion. It's long been common knowledge that the man has been awarding utility contracts for personal financial gain, but his graft is shockingly widespread. There are dozens of businesses listed, each paying monthly protection money. It would amount to tens of thousands of dollars if multiplied over years."

Harriet knew Cole to be wealthy, but even he gasped at the princely sum. "Powers would kill to get this back."

"I fear he has," Harriet said, stepping forward. "More than once." She explained her belief that Alderman Powers, after ordering the murders of Louie 'Bat' Batcheler and Eugene Eldridge, had sought to tie up loose ends by having the young *Progressive Age* journalist, Steven Bliss, killed. She furthermore believed the grandmother, Marie Batchelder, was another casualty, although indirectly, of Powers' plotting.

"We must get this into safe hands with haste," Cole declared.

Prescott took the Bible from Cole and, to Harriet's astonishment, handed it to her. "I couldn't agree more, Gerald. When you first brought this matter to my attention, you said the letter's anonymous sender instructed you to turn whatever was found over to a young prosecutor named John Scanlon. Is this still the case? Have you any reason to distrust him? Have you or your colleagues here at the league learned anything about him? I'm sure I don't need to tell you that him being new to the department could be taken one of two ways."

Cole nodded, indicating he took Prescott's point. "He hasn't had time to fall prey to corruption, but he may be naïve or impressionable to those for whom nefarious dealings are their stock in trade."

"Precisely," affirmed Prescott.

"We know little about Scanlon, I'm afraid," Cole continued. "A graduate of the University of Michigan. Raised somewhere outside Detroit. He has been at the job for less than a year. Previously, he was in private practice in Peoria for a few years. A week back, I put in a call to a partner of the firm where he'd been employed. He said he didn't know much about Scanlon personally but vouched for his legal acumen. Given that the letter's sender believes him to be a man of integrity and that we know most men in the office are not, I say we trust him."

Prescott appeared unconvinced but relented. Harriet guessed he had no better option for which to argue. "Miss Morrow?" He turned to her. "I don't suppose you have learned anything in the course of your investigation to shed light on the prosecutor? Has his name ever come up? Any mention of him at all?"

"No, sir. None."

Prescott surprised her for the second time in a few minutes by asking, "And what would you do, Miss Morrow? You've got us this far. Trust Scanlon? Or not?"

Could they see her squirming beneath her coat? Usually, she bristled at standing by while the men made the decisions. Now she was exposed to the other side of it: the responsibility that came with the privilege of making important decisions.

The weight of the men's penetrating gazes nearly buckled her knees. She resolved to stand tall, firm. "I would say we choose to trust." Her answer appeared to meet with their satisfaction. "However," she quickly added, drawing raised brows, "we shouldn't just hand over the ledger. Instead, we should prolong the meeting and probe his defenses. Ask questions to test his allegiances. The conversation won't result in a guarantee of his intentions, but if he is indeed honorable, he should gain our confidence. And if not— our doubts."

As it was a Saturday morning, before they set off, Cole made several telephone calls to arrange a special meeting at Prosecutor Scanlon's office in the courthouse on the corner of Clark and Randolph Streets, next door to City Hall.

Thirty minutes later, Harriet found herself seated between Theodore Prescott and Gerald Cole in a hansom cab en route to an encounter of vital importance to the city. And to think, just one month ago, she was a bookkeeper at the grain elevator. Her heart swelled with pride. She would allow herself the moment to appreciate what she'd accomplished, but the case wasn't finished. She wouldn't let down her guard until the matter had been satisfactorily concluded—in other words, when Prescott said it was.

Still, with only a mile to go and Prescott and Cole by her side, she couldn't imagine anything going too far wrong.

Chapter 35

"What the blazes is taking so long!" Prescott fumed.

Whereas Harriet thought his complaints about the previous cab's speed were unwarranted, now she agreed. The slow *clop, clop, clop* of the horses' hooves matched the cadence of a ticking clock.

"Have you forgotten the day, Theodore?" Cole asked.

Prescott bristled. "You think I've gone batty, Gerald? Of course, I know what day it is! It's April nineteenth . . . Oh."

"The parade!" Harriet blurted. That she had forgotten about the annual parade commemorating the Civil War's end, now thirty-three years passed, was excusable given the demands of her investigation. But what accounted for Aubrey not mentioning it? In previous years, they had looked forward to the event with high anticipation, always attending together. It was inconceivable he would choose to miss the festivities. She shoved the worrisome thought from her mind, hoping that instead of another sign of his growing displeasure with his older sibling and dissatisfaction with living under the same roof, he was at an age where he preferred to go with his friends.

"Of all days!" Prescott protested. "If only people knew what menace grips this city while soldiers march in formation and drums and trumpets play."

As they approached the courthouse, the cab halted abruptly.

Prescott stuck his head out the window to shout at the driver. "We've still a block and a half to travel. Why have you stopped? Get on with it!"

"Streets blocked off, sir," the driver explained. "Dignitaries have set up a stage for viewing the parade on the steps of City Hall."

"Oh, for crying out loud," Prescott huffed, climbing down from the cab.

Harriet followed Cole, both of them nearly running to keep pace with the fast-striding Prescott. The crowd was thick and growing. Thousands of residents jockeyed for a prime spot to view what was usually a half-mile-long procession of celebratory floats festooned with spring flowers, marching brass bands, military regiments on foot and horseback, and government officials.

Prescott turned back to ensure he hadn't lost Cole or Harriet in the crowd and ordered, "Keep up! I want to conclude our business and get out of here before the parade begins."

Arriving inside the courthouse was like stepping from the path of an oncoming tornado into a storm shelter—immediately, the surroundings turned silent and still.

"Third floor," Cole said, reviewing the directory on the lobby wall.

As if in reverence for the building's quiet, they made their way wordlessly up in the elevator. The door opened to a dimly lit, long and narrow corridor. Cole led the way. John Scanlon was waiting for them at the entrance to the prosecutors' wing. Harriet's first impression of the junior lawyer was his ordinariness. Nothing about him stood out, from his brown hair to his brown suit to his brown shoes. Then he spoke, and Harriet's assessment of him instantly changed. His voice was deep, warm, and rich. She imagined him standing at the top of the courthouse steps giving a rousing speech or behind a pulpit, bringing the faithful to shivers and tears.

Scanlon escorted them into his private office, which was strangely shaped like a letter T, at the end of a corridor. Two chairs for guests sat before his desk. Cole took one without hesitation. Prescott took the other after Harriet refused it with a determined head shake. With them all situated, the meeting commenced.

During the earlier telephone conversation between Cole and Scanlon, the prosecutor had apparently been apprised of the prevailing facts. Not skipping a beat, he took charge, commanding the conversation despite being junior to both Cole and Prescott in age and prominence. To Harriet, he paid no more attention than if she were a hat someone had left on the stand. Her opinion that the meeting should proceed cautiously to ascertain Scanlon's veracity was disregarded. Only minutes after arriving, Prescott presented Scanlon with the Bible.

"King James," Scanlon observed before opening the cover.

"The Bible is inconsequential," Prescott noted. "If there was intention in choosing it, it is contempt."

Discovering the folded page from the ledger, Scanlon read for so long that Harriet figured he must have examined every ledger entry three times before raising his gaze. "Well, gentlemen. This is indeed interesting."

Did Scanlon's understatement convey admirable steadiness or a profound underappreciation for the information's gravity? Prescott appeared to view his remark as the former and Cole as the latter.

The next quarter hour was spent discussing what to do with the evidence, who would be notified, and what safeguards would be taken to protect it. Ultimately, it was agreed the ledger would be placed in Scanlon's office safe and taken first thing Monday morning to Edward C. Akin, the Illinois state attorney general and Scanlon's fellow alumnus of the University of Michigan. Fortunately,

Scanlon also claimed a personal relationship with Akin, having met him several times—once dining at his residence. Moreover, Akin's wife, Louise, had taken a shine to Scanlon's young wife, also named Louise.

Harriet was unsure of the plan, but was certainty even possible given the pervasive skullduggery in City Hall? By all accounts, Scanlon seemed on the up-and-up, and she took reassurance that Prescott and Cole believed him to be honorable.

As they moved to leave, Scanlon held them back by saying, "If you don't mind me asking, there's one thing I still don't understand . . ." Once everyone settled back down, he continued. "The sender of the letter who got this entire business started, who is he? We still don't know. I appreciate one's desire to stay clear of politics, but Alderman Powers is a criminal. He will be prosecuted and held to account. I fail to see why the letter's sender would continue to feel the need to remain in the shadows. On the contrary, I should think he'd be proud of what he set into motion and its outcome. He has done the city of Chicago a great service." Addressing Cole, he pressed, "And you've no idea, none at all, who might have sent the letter and the payment for Prescott's services?"

"Untraceable" was Cole's one-word reply, which Scanlon accepted as a conclusive answer.

"Then, gentlemen, I believe our business here is finished."

For a second time, everyone started for the door. Cole, Prescott, and Harriet departed after a round of firm handshakes. She wished for the feeling of resolution, but like a bolt of lightning in the night sky, she couldn't help but feel a thunderclap was imminent.

They emerged into the noon-hour sun, with the crowd surrounding City Hall now counting in the thousands. Cole, eager to avoid the full brunt of the crowd and wishing to return to the peace of the league's environs and his newspaper, told Prescott he would see him at their club on

Monday and bid them farewell. The bright sunshine hurt Harriet's eyes and caused her head to throb more acutely. Prescott noticed her discomfort.

"Miss Morrow? How are you faring? Perhaps it's time to get that head wound tended to." Prescott suggested they take a hansom cab forthwith to a physician he knew who practiced at St. Luke's Hospital on the Near South Side. Harriet again demurred, but Prescott insisted. "Follow me. And so there's no question between us, yes, that is an order." With that, he began pushing his way through the crowd.

The density of the multitude challenged her ability to stay close to Prescott. But she must. Given his height, if she lost sight of him, it might be for good.

A body bumped her from the side, sending her stumbling. Startled, she snapped, "Hey, there! Mind yourself—" *Who was that?* Her mind raced to place the man who'd just knocked into her. She had only caught a glimpse of him before he pushed deeper into the crowd. It was the large man. The large man who had followed her up the rear staircase of Vorwaerts Turner Hall. The large man who had given a fiery speech. Scanning the immediate crowd, she noticed other people who looked vaguely familiar. Had they also been at the People's Cause meeting? Harriet's eyes darted from face to face, searching for an answer. The speeches that had upset her, what had they said? She thought hard, trying to remember. "*We are unafraid to spill blood . . . our time is nigh! The pomp and pageantry of the anniversary . . . thirty-three years ago, this nation ended one civil war. Will you join me, citizens, for the next?*"

The next instant, it hit her—the saddlebag filled with sticks of dynamite. The large man had the bag and four others like it draped over his shoulder.

Chapter 36

Harriet reached out and grabbed Prescott forcefully by the shoulder to stop him.

"Say, now!" he bellowed, turning back. "Oh, Miss Morrow, what's gotten—"

The words tumbled from Harriet's mouth. "The People's Cause . . . Vorwaerts Turner Hall . . . large man . . . speeches . . . dynamite . . . bomb." Had she made any sense at all? Did Prescott understand the urgency? Or did he think she was mad?

"Where? Where is this man?" Prescott demanded.

Pointing into the throng, she answered, "He went that way." As soon as the words left her lips, she knew they would only frustrate. She might as well point to the sky and say, "Right there! That blue spot, there."

Prescott declared, "We shouldn't be the only two people searching for him. Keep on the lookout for him, but our first action must be to alert the police. We must increase our chances of finding him. Fast. Besides, once found, I doubt the two of us alone could safely apprehend him, given his size as you describe it. Also, odds have it that other radicals are present, making us sorely outnumbered." He paused abruptly. "Are you quite sure you're well enough for this?"

Harriet was unsure but knew only one answer would satisfy either of them: "I can do this. I must. I fear we have little time as it is."

She had barely issued her last word when Prescott started elbowing his way toward City Hall's elevated entrance and the viewing stage erected for the dignitaries. With each step ascended, Harriet gained a greater appreciation for the number of Chicagoans who had come out to celebrate the anniversary of the Civil War's end. She estimated there must be ten thousand people gathered around the steps and lining the street to enjoy the parade. Prescott was wise to have made a beeline for the stage; where senior political officials gathered there were also police officers to protect and control access to them.

Prescott marched up to a blue-uniformed, mustached man who, judging by his distinctive homburg hat and double-breasted jacket with two gold stars on each lapel, was the officer in charge. He introduced himself as Lieutenant Kerr. As the two men spoke, they became increasingly animated—their voices raised, their movements more emphatic.

"You're quite sure?" the lieutenant said.

Prescott gestured to Harriet. "This is my operative, Miss Harriet Morrow. She is certain about what she claims. And before you question her veracity because she is a woman, let me assure you, there is no reason for doubt. On the contrary, Miss Morrow has proven reliable in her observations and judgments. Now. Time is wasting. We must find the man in question before he blows up half this crowd—and every senior official with them!"

Had the lieutenant any lingering reservations, they vanished once he understood the threat to the city's executives. He summoned several nearby officers and instructed them to fan out into the crowd, working in pairs. "The fellow we're looking for is a large man carrying several saddlebags, who we must assume is physically powerful. Your primary objective is to separate him from the saddlebags. Surprise is likely to be your ally in that undertaking. We can't have him spooked and then rush to detonate his explosive. Our mission is to prevent this calamity, not be the cause of it. If at all possible, before you confront him, call for the assistance of other officers. But don't set upon him in a pack. You'll only call attention to yourselves. Act with dispatch, but be smart. Now. Go get him."

Lieutenant Kerr's professionalism and decisiveness impressed Harriet. Prescott, however, didn't share her confidence in the police's abilities.

"The police aren't total incompetents, but I trust us to find your big man more than I do them. Moreover, despite the good lieutenant's instructions, finesse is not a hallmark of the police department. Those men have a singular modus operandi: act with force. Mind you, many officers are very fine men, Kerr appearing to be one of them, but too many others, Miss Morrow, are nothing but nincompoops with nightsticks."

They used the vantage point from the top of the steps to survey the crowd. As most people had claimed their place to view the parade, movement among the crowd had settled. Discerning the shape of individual bodies was difficult with so many people pressed against each other. Harriet found it easier to focus on persons still on the move and determine if they were someone of unusually large size.

"If this man intends to recreate the deadly mayhem of the Haymarket affair, he'll likely want to inflict maximum damage."

Harriet said, "Given the speeches at the People's Cause, current politicians are their primary enemy."

"Making this stage"—Prescott's gaze swept the four rows of nearby officials, among them Mayor Harrison, Governor Tanner, and Illinois' two United States senators, Cullom and Mason—"a radical's honey hole."

Her stomach twisted. Soon after first seeing the dynamite hidden in the saddlebag, she had convinced herself there was no urgent action to take. Had she made a disastrous mistake? What should she have done? Bang on Prescott's door? Race to the authorities? And say what? Admit that she had trespassed into Turner Hall and found highly suspicious materials? Possessing dynamite wasn't against the law. Or was it? Should she have kept vigil, watching the building for nefarious activities? Had it come to this because of inexperience that prevented her from appreciating the magnitude of the threat?

"See anything?" Prescott's question pulled her from her ruminations.

"No. Perhaps he has found himself an out-of-the-way place where he'll not be noticed."

Prescott nodded and focused on the area below them. Harriet leaned out over the edge of the viewing stage, following his gaze. The platform jutted out from the top step toward the street, supported beneath by crisscrossed wooden beams. The sides and front of the underlying structure were cloaked in red-white-and-blue bunting. As soon as she thought it, Prescott exclaimed, "Under the stage!"

Harriet imagined that in other circumstances, Prescott would have encouraged caution. But spurred on by the high stakes, he didn't hesitate. He raced down the steps and yanked back the nearest swath of bunting and dashed beneath the stage. Fortunately, the many gaps in the covering allowed for visibility. It took only a second for them to spot the man. His back to them, he was bent low at the other end of the structure. He didn't turn his head. He either hadn't heard them because of the surrounding noise or was too committed to his task to acknowledge them.

Prescott reached inside his jacket and pulled out a gun, larger than her derringer but not too unwieldy to conceal.

Seeing his, she realized she should do the same, letting out a faint grunt of frustration with herself for not having thought of it on her own.

Guns drawn, they moved forward—not at a creep, but at a cautious pace sensitive to alerting the man to their presence. That the stage had been erected on cement helped considerably; there were no snapping twigs or gravel scraping underfoot. Prescott paused and motioned for Harriet to approach the subject from the right. He would do so from the left. He cocked his weapon and gestured for her to follow suit. She did, swallowing hard. If there was any shooting, she wished Prescott would fire first and that his initial shot would be the only one needed.

Once the distance between them and the man had closed to about twenty feet, Prescott halted and raised a hand, signaling Harriet to also stop her advance.

"Hands up!" Prescott ordered.

With her derringer aimed at the crouched man, she fought to keep her hands steady. The man must have heard Prescott but gave no indication that he had.

"I said, hands up!" Prescott shouted louder, more insistent.

Again, the man kept at his task. As much as Harriet knew she must keep her eyes fixed on the man, she couldn't help but glance at Prescott. What would he do? His options were few: issue additional commands—which appeared likely to go unheeded—continue to advance or fire his pistol. She was grateful the decision wasn't hers to make.

"I'll say it only once more," Prescott threatened. "Hands up, or I'll shoot."

The man turned and began unfolding himself from his crouched position. In that instant, she realized that although he was large, he was not *the* large man.

"Mr. Prescott!" she shouted. "It's not him."

Prescott threw her a harsh look. "Not him? Are you quite sure?"

"Yes, sir. I'm sure. It's not him."

Turning his attention back to the man, Prescott rushed toward him, furious. "What in blazes are you doing skulking around under here?"

Now standing tall, the man revealed the task that had engrossed his attention: using a large wrench, he'd been tightening bolts of one of the support beams for the platform above.

"Tarnation!" Prescott bellowed before wheeling around and hurrying out from beneath the stage.

Returned to daylight, they stood again to survey the crowd. Feeling her boss's ire, she started to apologize for the mishap when a bolt of adrenaline flashed through her.

"There!" She pointed, arm outstretched, to a pushcart laden with bouquets. Having regularly attended the parade since she was a child, Harriet knew the flowers were offered to women in the parade as they passed by. The large man stood beside the cart.

"Are. You. Sure," Prescott challenged.

"One hundred percent."

"Alert as many police officers as fast as you can. Take no more than two minutes. Your aim is to surround the man. Don't let him get away with the saddlebags. While you do that—"

"He's moving!"

"Damnation," Prescott cursed.

She grabbed Prescott's arm without thinking. "Sir! The saddlebags! He's left them beneath the flower cart. If they explode . . ." Her gaze lingered over the dozens of women and men standing close to the cart. Then she saw a group of children and a woman vaguely familiar to her. *Oh! No, no, no, no!* She was Miss La Croix, the childminder, and with her were the children from the settlement house's kindergarten. Again, Harriet didn't think. She dashed down the remaining steps and into the throng toward the saddle-bags.

"Miss Morrow!" Prescott shouted. "Stop! You'll get yourself blown to smithereens!"

Not slowing, she yelled over her shoulder, "There's no time! We must save the children!"

Chapter 37

Running toward the flower cart, Harriet considered what to do once she reached it—provided the dynamite didn't explode beforehand. She dared not avert her eyes to check her wristwatch, but she estimated it must be nearing twelve o'clock, the hour of the parade's traditional start. She didn't know anything about bombs other than their purpose to inflict death and destruction. How was it designed to go off? Removing the saddlebags from the vicinity didn't seem possible. Movement might cause them to go off. And where could she take them that there weren't people? The middle of Lake Michigan was hardly an option.

Approaching the children and the cart, she realized the first thing to do was clear the area. And fast. She grabbed Miss La Croix by the arm and spun her around.

"Oh!" the woman shrieked.

"I've no time to explain," Harriet rushed her words. "There is a bomb nearby. You must get the children to safety. Now. Run. Take them as fast and far away as you can."

Miss La Croix started sputtering objections and questions. Harriet gripped her firmly by the shoulders and gave her a rough shake. "Please. There's no time. You and the children are in grave danger. You must go. Now!"

"What's this?" Mary McDowell appeared, wearing a

stern look. "What's your business here." She blinked rapidly. "Wait. Aren't you—?"

"Mrs. McDowell, I'm not Theodore Prescott's niece. I'm one of his operatives."

"Is that true, Theodore? What on earth is going on?"

Harriet spun around. Prescott had caught up to her. He had collected six police officers along the way. Seconds later, Mary McDowell and Miss La Croix begin hurrying the confused children away from the viewing area. It was agreed they would have a two-minute head start to hopefully ensure they would not be trampled once the threat was announced to the broader crowd. Other police officers had been notified of the danger and began escorting the dignitaries from the stage and into the relative safety of City Hall. The six officers who'd arrived alongside Prescott cleared the crowd from the area immediately surrounding the flower cart and held them back by maintaining a perimeter.

When two minutes had passed, Prescott gave Harriet a nod. She drew her pistol and fired into the air. Something most unexpected happened: nothing. No alarm. No panic. No mad dash to safety. The crowd misconstrued the *Pop!* as a ceremonial gunshot related to the festivities. Lieutenant Kerr, understanding that the situation required an unambiguous warning, sprinted up the steps and spoke into the megaphone that had been set up on the stage to announce the parade's participants as they passed.

"Ladies and gentlemen, you must immediately disperse. Make your way, now, as far and as fast from this area as possible. Go any direction. But move away from here. Fast as you can."

As with Harriet's warning to Miss La Croix, the crowd didn't immediately disperse. Instead, they objected and shouted toward the stage, "We'll not miss the parade!" and "We're not going anywhere!" and—getting a hearty laugh from the crowd—"Get off with you, you killjoy mutton shunter!"

Flabbergasted by the unconcerned response and ignoring the insult, the lieutenant took a moment, then apparently deciding nothing short of the terrifying truth would compel the crowd, shouted into the megaphone. "There is a bomb! You must run! Now!"

There was a split second of silence, followed by a massive movement of bodies comparable to a dam breaking. The surging crowd buffeted the officers protecting the flower cart. As the crowd rapidly receded, Prescott examined the area surrounding the saddlebags, then slowly circumnavigated the cart, looking high and low. He stood abruptly.

"Good God," he said loudly so the officers could hear. "There's a makeshift blasting machine affixed to the underside of the flower cart. As the flowers are handed out, the weight will shift, eventually causing the cart to tilt, not unlike a children's seesaw, and work like a plunger, detonating the dynamite." His voice lowered, he added, "Quite ingenious, really. The devil could have roughly estimated when it would go off, ensuring himself and his murderous comrades adequate time to achieve a safe distance from the explosion."

The crowd that had taken hours to assemble had disappeared in minutes. Now, standing far from the cart, Prescott and Harriet watched, alongside Lieutenant Kerr, as two of his "explosives experts" deactivated the bomb. Even at a distance, Harriet could sense the men's relief when they backed away from the cart and waved, signaling there was no longer a threat.

In the ensuing minutes, Harriet learned that the quantity of dynamite would have resulted in the deaths of hundreds, given the tightly packed crowd. She also received word that the large man had been apprehended, along with six accomplices who were nabbed while trying to escape by buckboard. Harriet was eager to know if Brunhilda Struff had been among them. After she provided a description of the woman to one of the officers involved in the radicals' arrest, he disappointed her with his certainty that she had not.

"I'm afraid I must accompany Lieutenant Kerr to the police station," Prescott informed Harriet. "I had intended to escort you to St. Luke's, but you'll understand the police have immediate questions that must be answered. They also want to interview you, but I have informed Kerr of your injury, and he's agreed that it can wait until after you have been examined at the hospital. Although I should be no more than an hour, you should go ahead. I'll come as soon as I'm able. When you arrive, ask for a Dr. Gordon. Tell him you work for me. And don't fail to mention the issue with your lungs. Gordon is not the specialist I had mentioned for your breathing difficulties, but he is a physician nonetheless. He may have something useful to say about it. And Miss Morrow"—he delivered his most serious look—"that is an order."

Harriet didn't like hospitals. Not since both of her parents had died in one. The places had an off-putting antiseptic smell about them, a somber air. She mollified her misgivings with the fact that although they were places of dying, they were also places of healing. She would do as Prescott asked and go to St. Luke's. The truth was, her head hurt, and she would feel better having it looked at by a professional.

Flagging down a buggy proved difficult. The police had blocked off the area surrounding City Hall. Harriet walked around the block to the courthouse entrance. As a buggy slowed in response to her wave, she froze. Her skin tingled in fright. She knew the odds, and yet . . .

In her bones, she knew it to be true. The brown horse hitched to a nearby post belonged to Brunhilda Struff.

Chapter 38

Harriet retraced the route through the courthouse to John Scanlon's office. Sure that Brunhilda's horse was hitched out front, she needed to settle her mind by confirming that nothing was amiss upstairs with the prosecutor. The junior lawyer had been vouched for, but that wasn't foolproof. Could he be in cahoots with Brunhilda and Saloon Micky after all?

The floor of the building was quiet. The sunlight no longer illuminated the corridor, making the passageway more eerie. Reaching Scanlon's office door, she abruptly slowed, seeing it was ajar. No other office door in the hallway had been open, even slightly. There was no sound. She pushed the door open. Scanlon had gone, but nothing appeared out of order. She expelled the breath she'd been holding. Most importantly, there was no sign of Brunhilda Struff. Relieved, she turned to leave.

With a hand on the door handle, she stopped. *What was that?* Had she heard something? Alarmed, she glanced down the corridor. Was someone coming? *M'mph.* She turned back toward the sound and rushed inside the office. Behind the desk! Scanlon! The blood drained from her head. She dropped to her knees. The prosecutor lay on the floor, gagged, his feet and hands tied. Horrifying as the discovery was, a particular observation made it much, *much* worse: she recognized the knots.

Harriet worked quickly to undo the bandana pulled tight across his open mouth and tied behind his head. He gasped for air, spittle flying from his lips.

"Did you see her?" He croaked, his eyes wild.

Taken aback, Harriet said, "See her? Was she only just here?"

He nodded frantically. "I can't believe you didn't run into her in the hallway."

While he spoke, Harriet fumbled with the knots. Like those Brunhilda had used to restrain her in the tenement's basement, they were too tight to undo by hand.

"There's a pocketknife in my drawer," Scanlon said.

She found the knife and cut through the rope, freeing his hands and legs.

"The Bible?" Harriet asked, her voice trembling. "Please tell me it's in your safe."

He shook his head. "She took it. She threatened to kill me if I didn't hand it over."

Harriet jumped to her feet. "If she's only just left, I might still catch her."

Running down the corridor, she heard Scanlon shout after her, "You mustn't confront her. She's much too dangerous!"

Harriet didn't reply. There was no time. Besides, action was the only possible solution. The elevator would be too slow. She bounded down the stairs. Less than a minute later, she burst out of the courthouse. Her eyes fell on the brown horse a half block away. Brunhilda was tucking something into the saddlebag. She then mounted the horse. Harriet's gaze darted in every direction, desperately searching for some way to follow her. *Damnation, if only I had my bicycle!*

With dread, she watched Brunhilda turn the horse and

depart. Several thoughts competed for primacy: she hated the German woman, her head hurt, she was out of breath, and horses frightened her. The last thought was relevant because three police horses were hitched nearby and she intended to borrow one of them. Having never ridden a horse, she must decide instantly which animal would be most gentle and take direction. Choosing the mare, she untied the reins. The horse shuffled sideways a few steps. "There, there," she said soothingly. "We're going to be great friends. But I need you to help me. *Please.*" She stroked the bridge of the animal's nose before repeating the movements she'd watched Brunhilda perform—she placed one foot in a stirrup, gripped the saddle's horn, and hoisted herself up, throwing her free leg over the horse. While getting the animal turned in the right direction, she frequently glanced in Brunhilda's direction to avoid losing sight of her. Harriet pulled the right rein and turned the animal. With a little kick of her heels, the horse began to move. By the time Harriet was in pursuit, Brunhilda was a block and a half ahead of her. Although the bomb scare had cleared the vicinity around City Hall, the parade route ran for a mile. Thousands of people were still milling about, making travel slow going. Had Brunhilda wanted to make a fast escape, she couldn't. Harriet was grateful; she couldn't imagine pushing the horse to a trot, let alone a gallop.

Might a policeman notice she was absconding with a police horse? She was ambivalent as to whether that would be a good thing or not. She would appreciate an officer's help in apprehending the woman, but he might arrest her instead for stealing police property. As they continued north of downtown, Harriet's guess about where they were going became more confident. When they turned onto Twelfth Street, there was no doubt. She was going to Vorwaerts Turner Hall.

Still a block and a half ahead, Brunhilda halted the

brown horse in front of the hall, removed something from the saddleback, and disappeared inside the building. Minutes later, Harriet tied the police horse next to the brown horse. She dismounted and took a brief moment to rub the horse's nose. "You have been most helpful, friend. I promise you the finest apple in all the city. But first I must ascend the castle to put an end a most consternating witch's evil."

Drawing her derringer, she raced into the hall. As it was a Saturday afternoon, the main gymnasium was crowded with youth exercising in short pants. She didn't see Brunhilda. Whatever the woman's purpose, it didn't involve balancing on a beam or swinging by rings. She reholstered her pistol so as not to alarm anyone unnecessarily. Making her way around dozens of athletes, she headed toward the interior staircase leading to the upper floor. Entering the fencing area, which was oddly empty and quiet, her determination grew. She'd had enough of Brunhilda Struff's deception and violence. The woman had lied from the moment Harriet had met her. She had lured her to the tenement, destroyed many families' homes, inadvertently caused Marie Batchelder's fatal fall, nearly burned Harriet alive, and then bashed her head. Now she had stolen the vital evidence that Harriet had nearly died trying to obtain. It was high time Brunhilda Struff got her comeuppance.

Harriet reached into her pocket for her pistol.

No sooner had she drawn her derringer than someone lunged from around a corner and whacked it from her hand. Harriet watched in horror as Brunhilda picked it up. Shaking her head, she *tsk-tsked*. "Harriet, Harriet, Harriet. You are persistent, but you cannot win. Hard as you may try. The revolution will not be stopped. Not by you. Not by anyone. It is human destiny. Over time, too few acquire too much. That imbalance must be corrected. Our cause—the People's Cause—is just. For that, it will not fail. It cannot fail."

"You're nothing but a criminal. You are all criminals. You would have killed dozens, perhaps hundreds, at the parade." Harriet shook with anger. "You'd have killed the children! That is not justice. That is murder. That is not a revolution. That is a massacre!"

Had Harriet ever seen Brunhilda smile? Certainly not sincerely as she was now.

"The explosion was the others' idea. I disagreed. I don't believe in taking the lives of the innocent if it can be helped. That's why you and the prosecutor are still alive. Still, if the majority of my comrades in the movement wish for certain . . . actions, who am I to stop them?"

Furious, Harriet continued. "Why do you even want the Bible? If your sworn enemies are corrupt politicians, why get in the way of Saloon Micky receiving justice? Scanlon would have seen to it. Unless . . ." Did Gerald Cole and Prescott have it wrong? Could Scanlon be trusted?

"I know nothing about Scanlon other than that he is part of the government and has a courthouse office. That alone makes him an oppressor."

Harriet threw her hands up in exasperation. "But *he* is in a position to do something with Eldridge's evidence. Don't you see what you've done? Scanlon was going to take the evidence to the attorney general. Saloon Micky would have been prosecuted for his extortion and other crimes. Why steal the evidence that would result in his conviction? What good can you possibly do with it that's better than putting Powers behind bars and showing the entire city that justice can prevail even for those in power? You're fighting against what you claim is your most important principle. It's madness!"

Brunhilda scoffed. "The difference between us is that you naïvely trust those in governmental authority to act justly. I do not."

"You haven't answered my question. What will you do with the evidence?"

"Have you ever seen an animal caught in a trap, Harriet?" She paused, slowly raising a brow. "No? Well, it's a horrible thing, let me assure you. The animal will do anything to get free. Even gnawing its own flesh."

Harriet gasped. "You're going to use him!"

"The alderman will soon be working for us. He can do much for the People's Cause. And he will. Otherwise, he will be exposed and ruined. Self-preservation is a powerful motivator."

"That doesn't make any sense. One hour ago, your so-called comrades were perfectly willing to blow up hundreds of innocent people to agitate for government overthrow, and now you plan to coerce a dirty alderman to expose the other Gray Wolves?"

Brunhilda reared back as if she'd been slapped. "Who said it was one or the other? We will achieve our goals by all means necessary. From outside the palace walls—and from within."

"Did you kill Eugene Eldridge? Are you Jorinda Grimm?" Harriet's fury intensified, causing her head to throb miserably. "And poor Steven Bliss? Did you kill him just because he knew you existed? Good God, woman! Steven didn't even know your real name. How could you?"

"That was not my doing. I've no doubt Aderman Powers is responsible. But, as I say, by all means necessary."

"I'll take that as your approval."

"Take it however you like. Again, I don't condone the killing of innocents. And yet"—her expression turned cold—"for some, they prove to be too much of an irritant to deal with any other way."

"You caused Marie Batchelder's death and destroyed seven families' homes. You tried to kill me in the fire!"

"I was in a mood, what can I say?"

"Did you have anything to do with Louie Batchelder's murder?"

"Yes and no."

When Brunhilda seemed satisfied that Harriet was baffled by her vague reply, she repeated, "From outside the palace wall and *from within*."

Suddenly, Harriet understood her perfectly. "You were Bat's Jorinda Grimm before you became Jorinda Grimm to poor, unsuspecting Eugene. Bat didn't come up with the idea to betray Saloon Micky. That was all you. But before you could get ahold of what Bat had on his boss, Powers had him killed. But no matter. You were still determined to see your plan through, so you set your sights on Eldridge. You just won't stop. Now you intend to blackmail the alderman—using his corruption against him, working your way up the halls of government. Who's next, the mayor? The governor?"

"We're going upstairs." Brunhilda pointed the barrel of Harriet's pistol toward the staircase.

Harriet knew that if she went upstairs—to the witch's lair—she would never make it out alive. Her only chance was to remain on the main floor of Turner Hall and hope that someone would come along. Surely, Brunhilda wasn't so brazen as to shoot her in front of witnesses. Having shot into the air to the alert the crowd, Harriet knew the gun now had only one bullet, but with good aim and at close range, that would be all it took. Harriet had to buy herself time. Appreciating that Brunhilda had tired of talking, Harriet decided on action. Although her own gun was pointed at her, she walked over to the wall of fencing equipment, lifted a foil from the wall, and positioned herself at one end of the fencing lane. And waited.

For the second time, Brunhilda produced a genuine smile. After dropping the derringer into her pocket, she unlocked a long wooden crate, retrieved a sword, and took a position opposite Harriet. How many times had the German woman fenced in her lifetime? Hundreds? Thousands? Harriet had no illusion that she could win the bout. That was not her objective. She needed only to embroil the woman in a competition she couldn't refuse until they were no longer alone. At that point, Harriet would make a run for it, seeking safety among the dozens of people in the hall's gymnasium.

The women raised their foils in salute. Brunhilda extended her arm fully, pointing the tip of her weapon at Harriet—she hadn't done that before. Harriet swatted it away with her sword's blade. Again, Brunhilda extended her arm, pointing her blade menacingly. Again, Harriet moved to parry the woman's blade, but as she did so, Brunhilda lunged with speed and ferocity.

Oww! Harriet cried out. The tip of Brunhilda's foil jabbed her side, hurting more than any touch during their previous fight. Harriet glanced down. The blade that should be blunted had pierced her jacket, leaving a small hole. She felt a trickle of blood beneath her clothing.

The sword was real.

Harriet realized her grave error. She had inadvertently given her opponent a far quieter way to kill her. *Think, Harriet! Think!* She couldn't possibly outfence the woman. If she tried to escape, she would be shot or stabbed. There would be no talking her way out of the peril. There was only one option.

With her arm fully extended, Harriet pointed her sword at Brunhilda. She gave it a slight flicker as if to taunt her opponent. Next, Harriet waved her blade wildly before holding it still, again pointing the tip at Brunhilda. Not getting the desired reaction, Harriet repeated what she hoped would be viewed as highly amateurish moves. Although Harriet couldn't see Brunhilda's expression behind her mask, she imagined it teetered between baffled and amused, thinking her competition was an imbecile. For a second, Brunhilda lowered the tip of her blade and chuckled. *That* was the reaction Harriet wanted.

Harriet leaped.

The two bodies crashed onto the mat. Brunhilda lost control of her foil; it clattered onto the floor beyond the mat and came to rest several feet away alongside Harriet's.

The women grappled for an advantage. Harriet's head screamed in pain. Her compromised lungs fought for breath. The puncture wound on her side stung painfully. Although she was strong, so was Brunhilda, and Harriet was hardly at her best. She wouldn't withstand a prolonged fight. With a surge of fury, she slammed Brunhilda's head against the floor. With her foe momentarily stunned, Harriet scrambled to her feet. The next instant, Brunhilda rolled over, reclaimed her sword, jumped up—and froze.

Harriet had retrieved her derringer while they'd wrestled. She pointed the gun at Brunhilda.

"You wouldn't," Brunhilda mocked, wielding her foil. "You don't have it in you."

"You're wrong."

Brunhilda didn't hesitate. She attacked, her sword's deadly tip aimed at Harriet's heart.

Harriet had a split second to decide which of them was right.

Chapter 39

Harriet hadn't intended to kill Brunhilda when she fired her pistol. So she was relieved when, hours later, the surgeon reported that the woman would survive. Harriet had followed the horse-drawn ambulance in a police wagon alongside Lieutenant Kerr and several of his officers. Theodore Prescott arrived at the hospital shortly after that. Rather than being pleased about her success in apprehending Brunhilda Struff and recovering—again—Eldridge's evidence, he was furious that she had not gone straight to the hospital after being told to do so. Moreover, he was dismayed to learn that his only female operative had still not undergone an examination of her head wound and injured lungs and was instead sitting in the waiting room for visitors. When he then saw her bloody shirt and the makeshift bandage applied to her side by one of Kerr's men, he had a conniption. Moments later, at his insistence, Harriet was rushed into an examination room.

At five o'clock that evening, dizzy and drowsy from morphine and with both her head and stab wounds stitched and bandaged and having received a determination that her lung function would steadily return over the course of months, she listened as Prosecutor Scanlon informed her and Prescott that once Brunhilda was discharged from the hospital, her trial would result in multiple convictions, including for conspiracy, robbery, kidnapping, and attempted murder. Scanlon was also confident that Saloon Micky would be brought to justice and was sure to hang for ordering the murder of Eldridge and the abduction of Bliss— a murder charge withheld until the younger muckraker's body was found, presuming it would be. Harriet was gratified knowing that the guilty would be punished but was concerned about winning the release of Lucy Fara and reuniting her with her children. On that subject, Scanlon also proved helpful. He promised to speak with his colleague responsible for Lucy's case first thing Monday morning. Although Lucy's release could take days or even weeks, he assured her that with Powers' arrest, it was only a matter of time.

Harriet asked if she could return the Bible to Mrs. Deca, but that request was denied. Although the book's only purpose had been to conceal the incriminating page from the ledger, it was evidence nonetheless. However, Scanlon reassured her that once the trial was over, he saw no reason that it couldn't be returned to the family.

Prescott helped Harriet into a buggy and ordered her to rest for the next week, adding, "Should I see you sneak into the office, Miss Morrow, I shall ask Madelaine to be your supervisor." His threat that she would be demoted to a secretary won her promise to oblige, though she doubted he really meant it.

Harriet arrived home to find Aubrey and Barbara playing cards at the kitchen table. The previous evening's pots and pans had been cleaned, the dishes put away, and the pleasing scent of lemon hung in the air. She realized it was the first time in years she had returned home to anyone other than just her brother. Far from intrusive, Barbara's presence felt natural—a finding both comforting and worrisome; it was much too soon to contemplate such an arrangement.

Speaking for Aubrey, Barbara told Harriet their many questions could wait. "All that is important is that you're here, safe and sound. Would you like anything to eat? Or drink?"

Another effect of the morphine was an upset stomach. Harriet waved away the suggestion of food. "Perhaps just a glass of water."

Barbara nodded and ran the tap.

"Now, let's get you to bed."

Exhausted, Harriet didn't quarrel. Despite the siblings' rule about entering each other's bedroom, Aubrey rushed ahead and laid out an extra quilt. Harriet crawled beneath the covers under the watchful eyes of Barbara and Aubrey, who perched at the foot of the bed. With her head on the pillow and Susan snuggled beside her, Harriet closed her eyes and fell fast asleep.

Chapter 40

In the two weeks since Harriet had solved the case of the murdered muckraker, she had received a string of good news.

Although it had taken six days for the lawyers and judge involved in Lucy Fara's prosecution to drop the charges, she had been freed. Proving more difficult had been winning the release of her two boys from the Home for the Friendless. It had taken a visit from Harriet, a forceful Theodore Prescott, and a badge-wearing Lieutenant Kerr to finally convince the orphanage's stubborn matrons to release Grover and Chester. In the past hour, the last two of her four children had arrived at the University Settlement House, where, thanks to Mary McDowell, Harriet had arranged for the family to live.

Pearl Bartlett had started frequenting the settlement after striking up a friendship with the head resident. Harriet wasn't surprised the two women hit it off. Pearl offered practical wisdom, free labor, and a significant bank account to help support the settlement's noble works. In return, Mary McDowell offered Pearl a sense of purpose beyond Toby and her cake pans.

Scanlon had proved trustworthy, after all. Alderman Powers had been arrested and awaited trial on several felony counts, including conspiracy to commit murder, extortion, and bribery. Harriet didn't deny her glee when reading a recent *Chicago Tribune* headline: LADY DETECTIVE OUT-WITS SALOON MICKY!

The First Ward alderman's downfall resulted in another favorable outcome—one wholly unimaginable. Harriet wouldn't have considered the lost employment of Powers' handsome male secretary if Matthew McCabe hadn't brought him up in conversation. Improbably, the secretary, a man named Boyd Cleveland, had been the fellow Matthew had been pining for the last time Harriet had visited the Black Rabbit. Although a relationship between two men was still very much forbidden, Boyd revealed the name of his former boss to Matthew and explained that he now felt safe to explore a relationship. Harriet guessed the secretary's reason was that he no longer had to worry about Saloon Micky's spies discovering his secret life. She was astonished to learn the real reason from Matthew: Boyd had indeed feared Saloon Micky, not because he wouldn't abide a queer on his staff, but because he was violently jealous.

Flabbergasted, Harriet had sputtered, "But surely . . . the two of them—"

"Not on your life," Matthew assured her. "Still, men like Saloon Micky get so drunk on power that they start thinking they can do whatever they want. Can have *whoever* they want."

The revelation stirred Harriet's emotions. The injustice surrounding her was shocking. Were she to dwell on its pervasiveness, she feared it might overwhelm her. Instead, she resolved to do as her brother suggested. "Do what good you can as a detective, Harriet, and don't let anyone make you wear a dress if you don't want to."

Gratefully, Aubrey's plan to live with Pearl had been short-lived. He claimed a change of mind, but Harriet knew the truth: he'd been disabused of the notion after spending the previous Saturday at Pearl's mansion. When he'd arrived that morning at nine o'clock, Pearl, who had rejected each maid the service had sent her, greeted him with a pair of work gloves and a long list of chores. Whether Pearl had suspected his desire to move in with her and knew action over words would convince him otherwise, Harriet might never know. But Pearl being Pearl, she likely had.

Mary McDowell gave Miss La Croix Sundays off, and the childminder chose this one to visit her brother in Peoria. Harriet wasn't sure if the head resident considered her filling in at the settlement house kindergarten a temporary or permanent arrangement. Harriet just knew she would gladly do so for as long as her detective work allowed it. Plus, it was only a short bicycle ride from the settlement house to Pearl's, where she and Aubrey continued their tradition of sharing Sunday suppers.

With two dozen children gathered around her ankles, Harriet sat on a tiny stool. She read from the book recovered from Brunhilda and slipped into her satchel before the police arrived at Vorwaerts Turner Hall that fateful day.

Why, in her own little play-room at home. The door by which she had entered had entirely disappeared and Ellen was just entering by the usual door with a teatray.

"Why, Miss Girlie," she said when she came in, "how quiet you have been all the afternoon. You must have been fast asleep."

"I'm sure I haven't!" cried Girlie indignantly, rubbing her eyes, though, and staring about her rather confusedly.

"I've been having the most lovely adventure!"

Epilogue

Two months after Harriet had solved her second case, she passed by Henrici's during the lunch hour and, through the window, caught sight of Alderman Daniel Walsh sitting at what had been Saloon Micky's regular table.

Well, aren't you quick to swoop in, she thought.

Three steps later, she whirled around and entered the restaurant. Not bothering with a perfunctory stop at the maître d' podium, she strode past a stupefied Reginald and entered the dining room, making a beeline for Irish Dan. The Gray Wolf sat enjoying a veal chop and a glass of heavy-looking red wine. Reginald, coming to his senses, scurried after her, shouting objections to her intrusion. She paid him no mind, stopping before the alderman's table.

"It was you," Harriet accused, staring him in the eye.

Irish Dan raised his gaze. After a long pause, he produced a maddening smirk and applauded slowly.

"So you admit it?" She stood defiantly, quivering with anger.

"When you visited my office, I confess I had my doubts. You were not at all who I envisioned when conceiving my scheme. You might be interested to know that your disguise did indeed fool me. It was my secretary who saw through it.

Her beauty belies her discernment." He grinned. "Surprised? You wouldn't be the first."

"You as much as told me it was you."

He feigned shock. "Did I?"

"Yes. Though I realized only a minute ago that you meant your words literally. You said, 'Chicago has the world's best detectives' and mentioned Pinkerton and Prescott by name, adding that if anyone were to find the muckraker's killer, it would be one of them. When I challenged you on the point, you said, and I quote, 'I put my money on it.' "

Casually, he poured a second glass of wine and set it before the place setting opposite him. "Sit." He extended a hand toward the chair. "Please. Do me the honor."

Too intrigued to refuse, Harriet sat. Spine straight, she had no intention of joining the man in a drink. She wouldn't give him the satisfaction—he appeared to have an overabundance as it was.

He said, "I will also admit you proved me wrong. Perhaps it is more accurate to say that Theodore Prescott proved me wrong when assigning you to the case. News that Prescott had a woman detective, let alone one so young, was a shock, to say the least. Considering who you were up against, I doubted you had it in you to 'get your man,' as it were. It would seem Prescott's confidence in you is not as misplaced as your unorthodox appearance suggests. I suppose only time will tell whether a person of your unique . . . *comportment* has what it takes to be a professional detective." Irish Dan took a long sip of wine, making her wait for his next remark. "Were the circumstances different, I might be compelled to wish you luck." He shrugged. "Alas, it would seem you and I are destined to forever be opponents. Should our paths cross again, be advised that my present civility will not extend to those future encounters. Business is, as they say, business."

Harriet asked, "Did you know Gerald Cole would enlist the services of the Prescott Agency?"

Irish Dan tilted his head from side to side, trying to decide his answer. "Oh, I suppose, knowing Cole, I thought he would choose either Pinkerton or Prescott. To be frank, I am somewhat surprised by his decision. Although a fine firm by reputation, the Prescott Agency has yet to achieve the same level of acclaim or notoriety, depending upon which side of the fence you sit, as its crosstown rival. I have often wondered if Cole didn't take my letter to Theodore only after Robert and William Pinkerton refused the assignment." Another shrug. "Regardless, seldom has an investment delivered such a lucrative return. Do pass along my most sincere thanks to your superior. He has proven himself to be every bit Allan's equal; may he rest in peace. I might be tempted to go as far as 'his better,' but we can't have old Theodore getting a swelled head, now can we?"

"How certain were you of Powers' guilt?"

"Had I placed a bet on who killed that muckraker in the tenement"—he winked—"and I'm not saying I didn't, I would have put my money on Micky. The man has no scruples. But considering the situation he'd allowed, he really had no choice but to make an example of Bat. But the journalists?" He sniffed. "The act smelled of desperation. And when one's enemy shows desperation, the shrewd competitor senses opportunity."

Irish Dan raised his glass. "To you, Miss Morrow. Thanks to your diligent and unconventional efforts, Alderman Michael Powers' corruption has been revealed, and justice will be done. The dumb lout will likely swing for his numerous crimes. Moreover, and central to my purpose, his significant business in the Levee District has now smoothly transferred to me. You may rest assured, I manage my affairs with far greater circumspection than the other First Ward alderman."

Sitting at her desk at the Prescott Detective Agency, Harriet considered Irish Dan's revelation with Prescott's words in mind: "Most criminals live in constant fear of being found out, going to any length to prevent getting caught.

However, others take such pride in their deceit that they perversely relish being found out. Otherwise, their criminal brilliance goes unapplauded."

No sooner had one Gray Wolf been caught than another took his place. Justice, it seemed, was a long game. *I best settle in for an extended battle,* she thought.

Harriet was young. She intended to have a long career as a detective. She couldn't right every wrong in the world but could do her part. She stood and opened the window, letting in a cool, refreshing breeze. Turning back, she was startled to see Madelaine in her doorway.

"He wants to see you," the secretary said.

"A new case?" Harriet blurted excitedly.

"I wouldn't be surprised, Harriet. It is what we do around here."

For the first time, Madelaine had addressed Harriet by her first name. Far from considering that disrespectful, Harriet took the familiarity as progress toward camaraderie. She rushed around her desk and shocked Madelaine with a friendly squeeze on the arm. "Quite right, Madelaine. It is indeed what we do."

Rushing ahead of the secretary and down the hallway toward her boss's office, she turned back and declared, "It is what I do!"

Author's Note

America's Progressive Era, 1890 to 1920, defined a period in which swelling immigration, urbanization, and industrialization fueled optimism that the country was moving in the right direction. However, that progress left much of the population behind. Social and economic justice issues—suffrage, child labor, poverty and gross wage disparity, dangerous working conditions, tenement housing, and political corruption—energized many Americans. To better understand this era, I relied heavily on the slim but information-packed *The Progressive Era: A History from Beginning to End* by Hourly History. Also highly informative was the voluminous *Chicago: An Intimate Portrait of People, Pleasures, and Power: 1860–1919* by Stephen Longstreet, and *Charter Reform in Chicago, 1890–1915: Community and Government in the Progressive Era* by Maureen A. Flanagan, Loyola University Chicago. I am indebted to these and all other cited scholars and authors.

To understand what Harriet's detective work might be like, I was informed by *Pinkerton's First Lady—Kate Warne: United States First Female Detective* by John Derrig, *Girl in Disguise* (a novel) by Greer Macallister, *Pinkerton's Great Detective: The Amazing Life and Times of James McParland* by Beau Riffenburgh, and *Pistols and Petti-*

coats: 175 Years of Lady Detectives in Fact and Fiction by Erika Janik.

To capture queer life at the end of the nineteenth century, I benefitted greatly from several books: *Gay American History: Lesbians and Gay Men in the U.S.A* by Jonathan Katz, *Gay New York: Gender, Urban Culture, and the Making of the Gay Male World, 1890–1940* by George Chauncey, *Chicago Whispers: A History of LGBT Chicago before Stonewall* by St. Sukie de la Croix, *Odd Girls and Twilight Lovers: A History of Lesbian Life in 20th-Century America* by Lillian Faderman, *The Boys of Fairy Town: Sodomites, Female Impersonators, Third-Sexers, Pansies, Queers, and Sex Morons in Chicago's First Century* by Jim Elledge, and *Out and Proud in Chicago: An Overview of the City's Gay Community*, edited by Tracy Baim. Any disagreement between these books' well-researched content and my story is either my exercising creative license or my mistake.

To understand indecency laws that could have been used to punish Harriet for cross-dressing, I'm indebted to Catherine Grandgeorge at Chicago's Newberry Library for pointing me to the 1897 Revised Code of Chicago Laws and Ordinances: https://archive.org/details/revisedcode ofchi00chic/page/276/mode/2up. Ms. Grandgeorge also called my attention to the 1897 Illinois Supreme Court case *Honselman v. People* that decided fellatio was an act of sodomy, a crime punishable by up to ten years in prison. While this law wasn't mentioned in the story, Matthew McCabe and his friends were doubtlessly aware of this legal finding, which would have haunted their search for intimacy.

Descriptions of tenement housing conditions were informed by reading *Tenement Conditions in Chicago* (1901) by The Investigating Committee of the City Homes Association, text by Robert Hunter, and by visiting New York City's terrific Tenement Museum, which I recommend highly. I was extremely fortunate to find *Health, Morality, and Housing: The "Tenement Problem" in Chicago,* a lengthy, in-depth government-commissioned report on tenement conditions in Chicago, ncbi.nlm.nih.gov/pmc/articles/PMC1447986/.

I learned about the University of Chicago Settlement House and its head resident, Mary McDowell, thanks to the "Mary McDowell and Chicago Settlement Houses" entry in the Encyclopedia of Chicago, encyclopedia.chicago history.org/pages/2410.html; *Mary McDowell and the Fight for Environmental Justice for Back of the Yards* inter active.wttw.com/chicago-stories/union-stockyards/mary mcdowell-and-the-fight-for-environmental-justice-for-the-back-of-the-yards; and the "University of Chicago Settlement" entry on Wikipedia en.wikipedia.org/wiki/ University _of_Chicago_Settlement.

Also helpful about settlements in general was *Hull-House Maps and Papers* published by Chicago Hull House.

The Gray Wolves and their nefarious activities are well cataloged in *Crime and the Civic Cancer-Graft* (1922), homicide.northwestern.edu/pubs/graft/; and summarized in the "Gray Wolves" entry in the Encyclopedia of Chicago, encyclopedia.chicagohistory.org/pages/540.html. Two actual Gray Wolves, both Levee District aldermen, Michael "Hinky Dink" Kenna and "Bathhouse" John Coughlin, inspired this book's fictional "Irish Dan" Walsh and Michael "Saloon Micky" Powers.

My learning about radical activities at the time was largely informed by *The Infernal Machine: A History of Terrorism* by Matthew Carr and *The History of The Haymarket Affair: A Study of The American Social-Revolutionary and Labor Movements* by Henry David.

Chicago's fascinating Turner Halls were brought to life thanks to "Chicago's Forgotten Turner Halls: Turnverein Vorwaerts" by John Morris on the Chicago Patterns website, chicagopatterns.com/chicagos-forgotten-turner-halls-vorwaerts-turnverein/; the City of Chicago's landmark website, webapps1.chicago.gov/landmarksweb/web/land

markdetails.htm?lanId=12982; and the Chicagology website, chicagology.com/prefire/prefire218/.

Another excellent source was "The German Turnverein
'Gymnastics' Movement in Chicago Began in 1852" from
the *Digital Research Library of Illinois History Journal,*
drloihjournal.blogspot.com/2019/06/the-german-turn
verein-gymnastics-movement-in-chicago.html.

The Palmer House stands today, although the Hilton
Corporation now owns it, palmerhousehiltonhotel.com/
about-our-hotel/.

Other real locations visited or referenced in the book
were described thanks to the following relevant links:

The Chicago Home for the Friendless, drloihjournal.
blogspot.com/2018/05/chicago-home-for-friendless.html;

Chicago City Hall, interactive.wttw.com/timemachine/
chicago%E2%80%99s-seven-city-halls.

Chicago Courthouse, illinoiscourthistory.org/resources/
858a0c70-b542-438b-88d3-087d86e131dd/Cookcounty-
history.pdf.

The Union Stockyard, "Backstory: Chicago's Union
Stock Yards and Turn of the Century Red Meat Wars" by
John L. Puckett, collaborativehistory.gse. upenn.edu/stories/
backstory-chicago%E2%80%99s-union-stock-yards-and-
turn-century-red-meat-wars; and WWTW/PBS's Chicago
Stories, *The Union Stockyards,* interactive.wttw.com/
a/chicago-stories-union-stockyards. https://www.wttw.com/
chicago-stories/union-stockyards/the-union-stockyards-a-
story-of-american-capitalism.

It's interesting to consider Harriet's rights as a woman
and lesbian in 1898 compared with those she would enjoy
today. While she could live as an out lesbian without fear
of complete societal ostracization, hardly would she enjoy
universal acceptance or equal treatment—and those rights
gained by a contemporary Harriet are under constant
threat of rollback. Also, consider that progressives in Harriet's time worked for the formation and bargaining power
of unions, better working conditions, fairer wages, the

elimination of child labor, a criminal justice system that didn't punish people of color and the poor more harshly than others, humane treatment of immigrants, and voting rights for all citizens. Still, more than one hundred and twenty-five years later, it's impossible not to recognize a current example of each of those societal ills tormenting today's America. Incremental progress may have been achieved on some issues, but hardly can we claim to have completed the job.

And yet, most Americans haven't given up trying. It's been the case from day one—literally. In George Washington's letter to Catharine Sawbridge Macaulay Graham, January 9, 1790, he wrote:

> *The establishment of our new Government seemed to be the last great experiment, for promoting human happiness, by reasonable compact, in civil Society. It was to be, in the first instance, in a considerable degree, a government of accommodation as well as a government of Laws.*

Fast-forward to July 17, 2020, forty-three presidents later, and consider Barack Obama's words:

> *America is a constant work in progress. What gives each new generation purpose is to take up the unfinished work of the last and carry it further—to speak out for what's right, to challenge an unjust status quo, and to imagine a better world.*

Like Harriet imagined a better world for herself, her brother, and her friends, so do we today. Onward we go.

Acknowledgments

Ability and perseverance will only get you so far. I'm grateful to my agent, Stephany Evans, at Ayesha Pande Literary, who identified and then deftly guided me to this opportunity to bring Harriet Morrow Investigates to readers. More than a smart publishing mind, Stephany is a superb editor and wise counselor.

I owe enormous thanks to my Kensington editor, John Scognamiglio, for seeing something in Harriet Morrow. His intelligent, insightful direction in resetting the series' time and place made this project possible, and his expert oversight of each book is invaluable. I owe special thanks to Kensington's Larissa Ackerman for promoting Harriet and to art director Louis Malcangi and illustrator Tom Haugomat for the stunning cover design of each book. Thanks to Jeff Lindholm for his meticulous copy edits. I also thank Jackie Dinas, Matt Johnson, Robin Cook, Carolyn Pouncy, and the entire Kensington Books team.

Paul Bradley Carr and Sarah Lacy at the Best Bookstore in Palm Springs exemplify the art of bookselling as strong author advocates and vibrant civic partners. Thank you to all independent booksellers—especially in smaller towns—for doing what you do.

My thanks to librarians for fighting the noble fight for knowledge, enlightenment, and inclusivity. When we read broadly and intelligently, society is improved in every way. My research efforts were assisted considerably by Catherine Grandgeorge at Chicago's Newberry Library, Maggie Cusick at the Chicago History Museum's Abakanowicz Research Center, and Johanna Russ at the Chicago Public Library Special Collections Division.

Thanks to Brett Goldston for his early reads and to Lori Rader-Day, Catriona McPherson, Alan Gordon (a.k.a. Alison Montclair), Karen Odden, Mariah Fredericks, and Lev A. C. Rosen for providing lovely endorsements of Harriet's first case. Thank you to Nina Simon, Lori Rader-Day, D. M. Rowell, C. J. Connor, and Sharon Nagel for joining me in conversation at various bookstore events. Thank you to Paul and Linda Somers for your Chicago-sized hospitality. And thanks to Mystery Writers of America, Queer Crime Writers, and Sisters in Crime for creating communities that celebrate and support mystery authors of all stripes.

Thanks to Cathy Powell at the Missoula Women's Health Clinic for her review of the birth scene and the description of Harriet's condition following her smoke inhalation.

Thanks to Jennifer Bartlett and Stephanie Krimmel for their partnership in creating and keeping my author branding looking sharp.

Finally, to my husband Brian Custer, thanks for all you do across all categories. You are the behind-the-scenes producer of this little enterprise. Harriet rides because of you.